LIVING ON THE EDGE
fiction by
Peace Corps Writers

edited by John Coyne

CURBSTONE PRESS

First printing, May 1999
Second printing, August 1999
Introduction copyright © 1999 by John Coyne. All stories are
copyrighted by the authors, as noted in the acknowledgements.
All Rights Reserved

Printed in Canada on acid-free paper by Best Book/Transcon Printing
Cover design and photograph: Susan Shapiro

This book was published with the support of the
Connecticut Commission on the Art and donations from
many individuals. We are very grateful for this support.

Library of Congress Cataloging-in-Publication Data

Living on the edge : a collection of short stories by Peace Corps
  writers / edited by John Coyne. — 1st ed.
      p.   cm.
  ISBN 1-880684-57-8
      1. Developing countries—Social life and customs —Fiction.
  2. Culture conflict —Developing countries—Fiction. 3.
  Americans—Developing countries—Fiction. 4. Peace Corps
  (U.S.)—Fiction. 5. Short stories, American. I. Coyne, John.
  PS648.D43L58   1999
  813'.0108321724—dc21   98-17464

published by
CURBSTONE PRESS   321 Jackson Street   Willimantic, CT 06226
      phone: (860) 423-5110   e-mail: books@curbstone.org
                    http://www.curbstone.org

Acknowledgments:

"White Lies," by Paul Theroux. Copyright © 1979. First published in *Playboy* in 1979. Copyright © 1979 by Paul Theroux. It also appeared in *World's End and Other Stories*, Washington Square Press, 1980 and in Paul Theroux's *The Collected Stories*, Viking, 1997. Reprinted by permission of the author.

"Exile," by Marnie Mueller. First published in *The Laurel Review* in 1989. Copyright © 1989 by Marnie Mueller. Reprinted by permission of the author.

"The Heroes of Our Stories," by Mark Brazaitis. Copyright © 1999 by Mark Brazaitis.

"Sun," by Kathleen Coskran. Copyright © 1999 by Kathleen Coskran.

"Easy in the Islands," by Bob Shacochis. Copyright © 1985 by Bob Shacochis. Originally published by *Playboy* in 1985.Reprinted by permission of Crown Publishers, Inc.

"The Water-Girl," by George Packer. First published in *The Virginia Quarterly Review*, 1989. Copyright © 1989 by George Packer. Reprinted by permission of the author.

"The Guide," by Melanie Sumner. "The Guide" from *Polite Society*. © 1995 by Melanie Sumner. Reprinted by permission of Houghton Mifflin Company. All rights reserved.

"On the Wheel of Wandering-on," by John Givens. Copyright © 1999 by John Givens.

"On Sunday There Might Be Americans," by Leslie Simmonds Ekstrom. Copyright © 1999 by Leslie Simmonds Ekstrom.

"The Egg Queen Rises," by Mark Jacobs. Copyright © 1999 by Mark Jacobs.

"Mad Dogs," by Eileen Drew. Copyright © 1999 by Eileen Drew.

"The Ones Left Behind," by Joan Richter. Copyright © 1999 by Joan Richter.

"A Virgin Twice," by Karl Luntta. Copyright © 1999 by Karl Luntta.

"Ma Kamanda's Latrine," by Marla Kay Houghteling. Copyright © 1999 by Marla Kay Houghteling.

"American Model," by Terry Marshall. Copyright © 1999 by Terry Marshall.

"Snow Man," by John Coyne. First published in *Monsters in Our Midst*, edited by Robert Bloch, a Tor Book. Copyright © 1993 by John Coyne. Reprinted by permission of the author.

"Alone in Africa," by Norman Rush. © 1984 by Norman Rush. Included in *Whites*, published by Knopf, 1986. Reprinted by permission of The Wylie Agency, Inc.

For Marian Haley Beil (Ethiopia 1962-64)

*An RPCV and artist who has done so much to advance
Peace Corps writers*

CONTENTS

WRITERS FROM THE PEACE CORPS

by John Coyne

For nearly four decades, Peace Corps writers have been going back, at least on paper, to the countries of their volunteer assignments. In novels, short stories, poetry and essays, Volunteers have written about their expatriate experiences in the developing countries of the world. Their Peace Corps experience has been a source of material, a creative impulse. For many it has become their literary territory.

Bob Shacochis, who was a Peace Corps Volunteer in the eastern Caribbean islands where his award winning collection of stories, *Easy in the Islands*, is set, makes the point that Peace Corps writers, "are descendants of Joseph Conrad, Mark Twain, George Orwell, Graham Greene, Somerset Maugham, Ernest Hemingway, and scores of other men and women, expatriates and travel writers and wanderers, who have enriched our domestic literature with the spices of Cathay, who have tried to communicate the 'exotic' as a relative, rather than an absolute quality of humanity."

Shacochis is not alone in this view. Short story writer Eileen Drew, winner of the 1989 Milkweed Prize and a Peace Corps Volunteer in West Africa, adds "I think we belong to a large bunch of authors writing across cultures, who grow out of a real tradition of expatriate or colonial writing that includes Conrad, E.M. Forster, as well as Paul Bowles and V.S. Naipaul, and the voices of minority backgrounds from Toni Morrison and Alice Walker, to newer writers like Gish Jen, Amy Tan, Faye Ng, Susan Straight."

Drew goes on to make the point that writers with a Peace Corps experience "bring the outsider's perspective, which we've learned overseas, to bear on the U.S. We are not the only writers to have done this, but because of the nature of our material, it's something we can't not do."

Since 1961, over 150,000 Americans have served as Peace Corps Volunteers. Unlike those who choose the expatriate life, Volunteers don't go to the ends of the earth to escape American civilization or, for that matter, to make money from the labor of others. They go to jobs that take them away from embassies, first-class hotels, and the privilege of being rich foreigners in poor countries. They live far from the capital, in villages that would never be tourist sites. And they don't just pass through foreign countries. They unpack their belongings, they settle down, they set about to do a job. And they write.

They begin by writing letters home, as Paul Theroux did in 1964 from Malawi where he taught secondary school. "My schoolroom is on the Great Rift, and in this schoolroom there is a line of children, heads shaved like prisoners, muscles showing through their rags. These children appear in the morning out of the slowly drifting hoops of fog-wisp. It is chilly, almost cold. There is no visibility at six in the morning; only a fierce white-out where earth is the patch of dirt under their bare feet, a platform, and the sky is everything else."

In over thirty years of writing, Theroux has produced some of the most wicked, funny, sad, bitter, readable, knowledgeable, rude, acerbic, ruthless, arrogant, moving, brilliant and quotable books ever written. And he began by writing about the life he knew in Africa as a Peace Corps Volunteer.

Theroux, perhaps the most famous writer among former Peace Corps Volunteers, used his African experience in his first three novels, and later in *My Secret History* and *My Other Life*. His short story, "White Lies" comes from an incident that also occurred to him in Africa.

"I took a trip to the shores of Lake Malawi, with some other volunteers. We were all fending for ourselves, cooking, washing, and so forth. One day I developed a skin condition—red bumps, pimple-like; and soon they were large and painful, erupting all over my back and shoulders. Each one held a maggot, which began as eggs laid on my shirt from *putzi* flies. For years I wondered how I could use this unexpected malady, and then I came up with this story."

Three hundred and fifty returned Peace Corps Volunteers have published books, many of which have been based on their experiences overseas. Norm Rush, who was on the Peace Corps staff in Botswana for five years, placed his National Book Award-winning novel, *Mating*, as well as his first collection of short stories, *Whites*, in Africa.

Not only did the African experience provide a literary landscape, it also provided subject matter. In his story, "Alone in Africa" he attempted to "capture part of the spectacular disparity in North American and Southern African sexual cultures."

Kathleen Coskran, winner of the 1988 Minnesota Book Award for her collection of stories, *The High Price of Everything*, set several of these stories in the Horn of Africa, where she was a volunteer. She says she has attempted to use her experience in these stories, "not to write about Ethiopia as if it is a strange, exotic, quaint place," but as a setting "to probe the character of the Americans, the expatriates who find themselves living in a place where they don't know what all the rules are."

John Givens, a Volunteer in Korea, says that the Peace Corps "suggested that experience was not limited to the mores and expectations of central California where I grew up. The 'wideness' of the world came home to me vividly in Korea, and I've been exploring the world ever since."

Novelist Marnie Mueller, author of *Green Fires*, a novel about Ecuador which won a 1995 American Book Award from the Before Columbus Foundation, says of her experiences in Ecuador, "it made me embrace other cultures, and has given me some of my richest material as a writer."

Eileen Drew lived in Africa as a child but didn't come to understand the land until she became a volunteer. "My father was an economist in the Foreign Service; as a result of his work, my family lived in several African countries. As an Embassy Kid I was insulated from African communities. For example, our homes were always in the midst of African cities, with African neighbors going about their daily business right beyond our walls, but I went to American schools and played with American and European kids; we ate only food flown in to our commissaries, we had air conditioning and good medical attention and never learned any local languages, only French. In the Peace Corps I had the chance to live and work among villages, and so it rounded out my experience in Africa."

The Peace Corps experience allowed these writers to live within the country, and not be isolated from it, as so many foreigners are when they live in the developing world. However, many of these short story writers and novelists could not begin to write until they physically left their country of service.

Melanie Sumner wrote her first novel, *Polite Society*, about Senegal, where she served as a Volunteer. This novel won a Whiting Writers' Award for 1995, but her novel in which the story, "The Guide," appeared was not written until she came home.

"In Africa I was writing maudlin letters and weird stories about co-wives who cut off each other's noses to spite their polygamous husbands. Then I visited a *marabout* who gave me a *gris-gris*, an African talisman, for writing a book. He said that I would write a book about Senegal, and the people would like it very much. I wore the *gris-gris* for a year before I began *Polite Society*."

Mark Brazaitis, winner of the Iowa Short Fiction Award in 1998 for *The River of Lost Voices*, did write his stories in Latin America. "I wrote crazily, thinking that I wouldn't remember or would not be inspired when I got back to the States." During the next year while studying for a Master of Fine Arts degree in creative writing at Bowling Green State University, Brazaitis discovered that he had not left the town behind. "I realized that I could close my eyes and be back in Guatemala." It was also in the Pokomchi-speaking villages of Santa Cruz Verapaz that he found his eyes for fiction. Here he had to "learn a new language with which to describe my life, find new words to describe things, and fit the words to what it was that I saw. I took so much for granted about the way we live in the United States, and about things I could not see. In Guatemala, I was forced to wake up."

Karl Luntta, a volunteer in Botswana, makes the opposite point about his experience of living in a strange land. "I've always been intrigued," he writes, "by what appears to be the inverse proportion of my time spent in a place to my understanding of its people and culture—the longer I spend in a place, the less I truly know about it." His story in this collection, "A Virgin Twice," is about an American in Africa who feels the same alienation. "The more he learns, the less he understands."

While the Peace Corps experience has given all these writers a lens on how Americans view others, many Peace Corps writers also wondered, and wrote about, how the host country nationals might look back at them. In her short story, "On Sunday There Might Be Americans," Leslie Simmonds Ekstrom writes about encountering Nigerians in the market place of Ayarou, near the Mali border. "One Sunday at Ayarou a small boy followed me all through the market.

He was shy and hesitant and I thought I could ditch him, but then he'd reappear in my shadow again. I finally paid him to go away. But I kept thinking about him—what his life might be like, how he perceived Westerners, and how easily Westerners become oblivious to the lives of ordinary people like him. Trying to imagine his life, I wrote "On Sunday There Might Be Americans."

Half way around the world, on the Solomon Islands, Terry Marshall, in his story, "American Model," approaches cross-cultural understanding (or misunderstanding) through the eyes of a beautiful young island woman who meets up with the fictional Robert Kincaid, hero of *Bridges of Madison County*.

Regardless of the approach, in story after story these writers depict the struggle that occurs when one crosses cultures, sometimes amusingly, as in "American Model," and at other times with tragic results. Eileen Drew was drawn to such an occurrence. "I began writing "Mad Dogs" with the doctor character in mind, to explore the expatriate as eccentric—as even somewhat mad." In "Snow Man" a young Peace Corps teacher tries to come to terms with his involvement with another volunteer, and the violent student strikes in Africa. Eileen Drew points out "how crazy all we Americans" were, at certain times, living in this strange culture.

The experience never leaves these Peace Corps workers. "For a long time after we returned from our time with the Peace Corps in Kenya," writes Joan Richter, "I was still sorting through the meaning of my experience there....I began to think, and still do, about the Kenyans I'd left behind, whose lives had also changed because of the crossing of our paths....My great fear was, and is, that good intentions might have unexpected and damaging consequences. 'The Ones Left Behind,' is a fantasized expression of that fear."

And as George Packer points out, "no matter how one leaves, everyone who lives and works in such a place leaves with regret— for the hopes raised and then disappointed, the expectations unmet, the inequality of options, the finality of departure."

Although the Peace Corps was launched at virtually the same time that Americans began fighting in Vietnam, the experience has, curiously, not had a comparable impact upon American literature. The war in Vietnam has yielded dozens of novels, movies, and television series—a seemingly endless national self-examination.

In contrast, the work and the world of the Peace Corps has until recently gone unwritten, or at least unpublished.

Recently an independent film producer asked if the Peace Corps still existed. And then she asked, "Is Sargent Shriver still the Director?"

It is as if the Peace Corps has been frozen in time, locked forever in a 1960 time capsule. There is a difference between making war and making peace. Everyone remembers when the shooting stopped in Vietnam, when our defeated troops were lifted by helicopter off the roof of the U.S. Embassy in Saigon.

The battles against hunger, poverty, disease, and illiteracy continue in their silence, and Peace Corps Volunteers continue to work, largely unnoticed, in the developing world.

The problem, perhaps, is that volunteers see themselves serving the country of their assignment and not any "corps," or, for that matter, even America.

To be a volunteer is to travel lightly in the developing world, without the heavy machinery, cultural and otherwise, of the U.S. The PCV isn't an Ugly American; she's a Silent One. Volunteer work overseas is private, personal, and often goes unheralded even by themselves. And even now, like soldiers coming home from battle, volunteers tend to find only in other PCVs a sympathetic and understanding listener.

Paul Theroux says it best in an essay summing up his tour in Malawi: "When I think about those years, I don't think much about the Peace Corps, though Malawi is always on my mind. That is surely a tribute to the Peace Corps. I do not believe that Africa is a very different place for having played host to the Peace Corps—in fact, Africa is in a much worse state....But America is quite a different place for having had so many returned Peace Corps volunteers....The experience was an enlightening one for most volunteers....We were the ones who were enriched."

Peace Corps writers are now enriching America through their writings. When one looks at the books being written by returned Peace Corps writers, it is striking how many of them are winning major book awards and claiming space on literary bookshelves. Volunteers are coming of age as literary persons. They are telling the stories of the Peace Corps, and more importantly, of life in the developing world. A world that Americans know so little about, or care to consider.

Most of these Peace Corps writers were born too late to be writers in Paris during the Twenties, and were too young to write the great World War II novel, but at last, four decades after it all began, there is emerging a genre which might best be called Peace Corps Writings.

Perhaps this is a small claim in the world of literature, but it is theirs alone to make. It will be through these writings that they will create a place for the Peace Corps experience in the minds of American readers.

LIVING ON THE EDGE

How I Came To Write This Story

In Malawi, in 1964, as a Peace Corps teacher, I took a trip to the shore of Lake Malawi with some other volunteers. We were all fending for ourselves, cooking, washing, and so forth. One day I developed a strange skin condition—red bumps, pimple-like—and soon they were large and painful, erupting all over my back and shoulders. Each one held a maggot, which began as eggs laid on my shirt from putzi flies. Using matches and tweezers my peace Corps buddy, Bob Maccani, dug them out—Zikomo kwambiri, Bambo Bob. For years I wondered how I could use this unexpected malady, and then I came up with this story, which is still one of my favorites, and full of detail from my experience in Africa.

—Paul Theroux

PAUL THEROUX (Malawi, 1963-65) was a Peace Corps Volunteer in Malawi, and after being forced to resign because of alleged political activities against the government, he taught at Makerere University in Uganda, then the leading university in East Africa. Later he taught at the University of Singapore for three years. His first novels were *Waldo, Fong and the Indians, Girls at Play* and *Jungle Lovers*. After his years in Africa and Asia, he lived in England for seventeen years. In this time he wrote a dozen volumes of highly praised fiction and a number of successful travel books. His most recent work is *Sir Vidia's Shadow: A Friendship Across Five Continents*. Theroux now lives in Hawaii and on Cape Cod.

WHITE LIES

by Paul Theroux

Normally, in describing the life cycle of ectoparasites for my notebook, I went into great detail, since I hoped to publish an article about the strangest ones when I returned home from Africa. The one exception was *Dermatobia bendiense*. I could not give it my name; I was not its victim. And the description? One word: Jerry. I needed nothing more to remind me of the discovery, and though I fully intended to test my findings in the pages of an entomological journal, the memory is still too horrifying for me to reduce it to science.

Jerry Benda and I shared a house on the compound of a bush school. Every Friday and Saturday night he met an African girl named Ameena at the Rainbow Bar and brought her home in a taxi. There was no scandal: no one knew. In the morning, after breakfast, Ameena did Jerry's ironing (I did my own) and the black cook carried her back to town on the crossbar of his old bike. That was a hilarious sight. Returning from my own particular passion, which was collecting insects in the fields near our house, I often met them on the road: Jika in his cook's khakis and skullcap pedaling the long-legged Ameena—I must say, she reminded me of a highly desirable insect. They yelped as they clattered down the road, the deep ruts making the bicycle bell hiccup like an alarm clock. A stranger would have assumed these Africans were man and wife, making an early morning foray to the market. The local people paid no attention.

Only I knew that these were the cook and mistress of a young American who was regarded at the school as very charming in his manner and serious in his work. The cook's laughter was a nervous giggle—he was afraid of Ameena. But he was devoted to Jerry and far too loyal to refuse to do what Jerry asked of him.

Jerry was deceitful, but at the same time I did not think he was imaginative enough to do any damage. And yet his was not the conventional double life that most white people led in Africa. Jerry had certain ambitions: ambition makes more liars than egotism does. But Jerry was so careful, his lies such modest calculations, he was always believed. He said he was from Boston. "Belmont actually," he told me, when I said I was from Medford. His passport—Bearer's address—said Watertown. He felt he had to conceal it. That explained a lot: the insecurity of living on the lower slopes of the long hill, between the smoldering steeples of Boston and the clean, high-priced air of Belmont. We are probably no more class conscious than the British, but we make class an issue it seems more than snobbery. It becomes a bizarre spectacle, a kind of attention seeking, and I cannot hear an American speaking of his social position without thinking of a human fly, one of those tiny men in grubby capes whom one sometimes sees clinging to the brickwork of a tall building.

What had begun as fantasy had, after six months of his repeating it in our insignificant place, made it seem like fact. Jerry didn't know Africa: his one girl friend stood for the whole continent. And of course he lied to her. I had the impression that it was one of the reasons Jerry wanted to stay in Africa. If you tell enough lies about yourself, they take hold. It becomes impossible ever to go back, since that means facing the truth. In Africa, no one could dispute what Jerry said he was: a wealthy Bostonian, from a family of some distinction, adventuring in Third World philanthropy before inheriting his father's business.

Rereading the above, I think I may be misrepresenting him. Although he was undeniably a fraud in some ways, his fraudulence was the last thing you noticed about him. What you saw first was a tall, good-natured person in his early twenties, confidently casual, with easy charm and a gift for ingenious flattery. When I told him I had majored in entomology he called me "Doctor." This later became "Doc." He showed exaggerated respect to the gardeners and washerwomen at the school, using the politest phrases when he spoke to them. He always said "sir" to the students ("You, sir, are a lazy little creep"), which baffled them and won them over. The cook adored him, and even the cook's cook—who was lame and fourteen and ragged—liked Jerry to the point where the poor boy would go through the compound stealing flowers from the Inkpens' garden to decorate our table. While I was merely tolerated as an unattractive and near-sighted bug collector, Jerry was courted by the British wives in the compound. The wife of the new headmaster, Lady Alice (Sir Godfrey Inkpen had been knighted for his work in the Civil Service) usually stopped in to see Jerry when her husband was away. Jerry was gracious with her and anxious to make a good impression. Privately, he said, "She's all tits and teeth."

"Why is it," he said to me one day, "that the white women have all the money and the black women have all the looks?"

"I didn't realize you were interested in money."

"Not for itself, Doc," he said. "I'm interested in what it can buy."

No matter how hard I tried, I could not get used to hearing Ameena's squawks of pleasure from the next room, or Jerry's elbows banging against the wall. At any moment, I expected their humping and slapping to bring down the boxes of mounted butterflies I had hung there. At breakfast, Jerry was his urbane self, sitting at the head of the table while Ameena cackled.

He held a teapot in each hand. "What will it be, my dear? Chinese or Indian tea? Marmalade or jam? Poached or scrambled? And may I suggest a kipper?"

"Wopusa!" Ameena would say. "Idiot!"

She was lean, angular, and wore a scarf in a handsome turban on her head. "I'd marry that girl tomorrow," Jerry said, "if she had fifty grand." Her breasts were full and her skin was like velvet; she looked majestic, even when doing the ironing. And when I saw her ironing, it struck me how Jerry inspired devotion in people.

But not any from me. I think I resented him most because he was new. I had been in Africa for two years and had replaced any ideas of sexual conquest with the possibility of a great entomological discovery. But he was not interested in my experience. There was a great deal I could have told him. In the meantime, I watched Jika taking Ameena into town on his bicycle, and I added specimens to my collection.

Then, one day, the Inkpens' daughter arrived from Rhodesia to spend her school holidays with her parents.

We had seen her the day after she arrived, admiring the roses in her mother's garden, which adjoined ours. She was about seventeen, and breathless and damp; and so small I at once imagined this pink butterfly struggling in my net. Her name was Petra (her parents called her "Pet"), and her pretty bloom was recklessness and innocence. Jerry said, "I'm going to marry her."

"I've been thinking about it," he said the next day. "If I just invite her I'll look like a wolf. If I invite the three of them it'll seem as if I'm stage-managing it. So I'll invite the parents—for some inconvenient time—and they'll have no choice but to ask me if they can bring the daughter along, too. They'll ask me if they can bring her. Good thinking? It'll have to be after dark—they'll be afraid of someone raping her. Sunday's always family day, so how about Sunday at seven? High tea. They will deliver her into my hands."

The invitation was accepted. And Sir Godfrey said, "I hope you don't mind if we bring our daughter—"

More than anything, I wished to see whether Jerry would bring Ameena home that Saturday night. He did—I suppose he did not want to arouse Ameena's suspicions—and on Sunday morning it was breakfast as usual and "What will it be, my dear?"

But everything was not as usual. In the kitchen, Jika was making a cake and scones. The powerful fragrance of baking, so early on a Sunday morning, made Ameena curious. She sniffed and smiled and picked up her cup. Then she asked: What was the cook making?

"Cakes," said Jerry. He smiled back at her.

Jika entered timidly with some toast.

"You're a better cook than I am," Ameena said in Chinyanja. "I don't know how to make cakes."

Jika looked terribly worried. He glanced at Jerry.

"Have a cake," said Jerry to Ameena.

Ameena tipped the cup to her lips and said slyly, "Africans don't eat cakes for breakfast."

"We do," said Jerry, with guilty rapidity. "It's an old American custom."

Ameena was staring at Jika. When she stood up he winced. Ameena said, "I have to make water." It was one of the few English sentences she knew.

Jerry said, "I think she suspects something."

As I started to leave with my net and my chloroform bottle I heard a great fuss in the kitchen, Jerry telling Ameena not to do the ironing, Ameena protesting, Jika groaning. But Jerry was angry, and soon the bicycle was bumping away from the house: Jika pedaling, Ameena on the crossbar.

"She just wanted to hang around," said Jerry. "Guess what the bitch was doing? She was ironing a drip-dry shirt!"

It was early evening when the Inkpens arrived, but night fell before tea was poured. Petra sat between her proud parents, saying what a super house we had, what a super school it was, how super it was to have a holiday here. Her monotonous ignorance made her even more desirable.

Perhaps for our benefit—to show her off—Sir Godfrey asked her leading questions. "Mother tells me you've taken up knitting" and "Mother says you've become a whiz at math." Now he said, "I hear you've been doing some riding."

"Heaps, actually," said Petra. "There are some stables near the school."

Dances, exams, picnics, house parties: Petra gushed about her Rhodesian school. And in doing so she made it seem like a distant place—not an African country at all, but a special preserve of superior English recreations.

"That's funny," I said. "Aren't there Africans there?"

Jerry looked sharply at me.

"Not at the school," said Petra. "There are some in town. The girls call them nig-nogs." She smiled. "But they're quite sweet, actually."

"The Africans, dear?" asked Lady Alice.

"The girls," said Petra.

Her father frowned.

Jerry said, "What do you think of this place?"

"Honestly, I think it's super."

"Too bad it's so dark at the moment," said Jerry. "I'd like to show you my frangipani."

"Jerry's famous for that frangipani," said Lady Alice.

Jerry had gone to the French windows to indicate the general direction of the bush. He gestured toward the darkness and said, "It's somewhere over there."

"I see it," said Petra.

The white flowers and the twisted limbs of the frangipani were clearly visible in the headlights of the approaching car.

Sir Godfrey said, "I think you have a visitor."

The Inkpens were staring at the taxi. I watched Jerry. He had turned pale, but kept his composure. "Ah yes," he said, "it's the sister of one of our pupils." He stepped aside to intercept her, but Ameena was too quick for him. She hurried past him, into the parlor where the Inkpens sat dumbfounded. Then Sir Godfrey, who had been surprised into silence, stood up and offered Ameena his chair.

Ameena gave a nervous grunt and faced Jerry. She wore the black satin cloak and sandals of a village Muslim. I had never seen her in anything but a tight dress and high heels; in that long cloak she looked like a very dangerous fly which had buzzed into the room on stiff wings.

"How nice to see you," said Jerry. Every word was right, but his voice had become shrill. "I'd like you to meet—"

Ameena flapped the wings of her cloak in embarrassment and said, "I cannot stay. And I am sorry for this visit." She spoke in her own language. Her voice was calm and even apologetic.

"Perhaps she'd like to sit down," said Sir Godfrey, who was still standing.

"I think she's fine," said Jerry, backing away slightly.

Now I saw the look of horror on Petra's face. She glanced up and down, from the dark shawled head to the cracked feet, then gaped in bewilderment and fear.

At the kitchen door, Jika stood with his hands over his ears.

"Let's go outside," said Jerry in Chinyanja.

"It is not necessary," said Ameena. "I have something for you. I can give it to you here."

Jika ducked into the kitchen and shut the door.

"Here," said Ameena. She fumbled with her cloak.

Jerry said quickly, "No," and turned as if to avert the thrust of a dagger.

But Ameena had taken a soft gift-wrapped parcel from the folds of her cloak. She handed it to Jerry and, without turning to us, flapped out of the room. She became invisible as soon as she stepped into the darkness. Before anyone could speak, the taxi was speeding away from the house.

Lady Alice said, "How very odd."

"Just a courtesy call," said Jerry, and amazed me with a succession of plausible lies. "Her brother's in Form Four—a very bright boy, as a matter of fact. She was rather pleased by how well he'd done in his exams. She stopped in to say thanks."

"That's very African," said Sir Godfrey.

"It's lovely when people drop in," said Petra. "It's really quite a compliment."

Jerry was smiling weakly and eyeing the window, as if he expected Ameena to thunder in once again and split his head open. Or perhaps not. Perhaps he was congratulating himself that it had all gone so smoothly.

Lady Alice said, "Well, aren't you going to open it?"

"Open what?" said Jerry, and then he realized that he was holding the parcel. "You mean this?"

"I wonder what it could be," said Petra.

I prayed that it was nothing frightening. I had heard of stories of jilted lovers sending aborted fetuses to the men who wronged them.

"I adore opening parcels," said Petra.

Jerry tore off the wrapping paper, but satisfied himself that it was nothing incriminating before he showed it to the Inkpens.

"Is it a shirt?" said Lady Alice.

"It's a beauty," said Sir Godfrey.

It was red and yellow and green, with embroidery at the collar and cuffs; an African design. Jerry said, "I should give it back. It's a sort of bribe, isn't it?"

"Absolutely not," said Sir Godfrey. "I insist you keep it."

"Put it on!" said Petra.

Jerry shook his head. Lady Alice said, "Oh, do!"

"Some other time," said Jerry. He tossed the shirt aside and told a long, humorous story of his sister's wedding reception on the family yacht. And before the Inkpens left he asked Sir Godfrey with old-fashioned formality if he might be allowed to take Petra on a day trip to the local tea estate.

"You're welcome to use my car if you like," said Sir Godfrey.

It was only after the Inkpens had gone that Jerry began to tremble. He tottered to a chair, lit a cigarette, and said, "That was the worst hour of my life. Did you see her? Jesus! I thought that was the end. But what did I tell you? She suspected something!"

"Not necessarily," I said.

He kicked the shirt—I noticed he was hesitant to touch it—and said, "What's this all about then?"

"As you told Inky—it's a present."

"She's a witch," said Jerry. "She's up to something."

"You're crazy," I said. "What's more, you're unfair. You kicked her out of the house. She came back to ingratiate herself by giving you a present—a new shirt for all the ones she didn't have a chance to iron. But she saw our neighbors. I don't think she'll be back."

"What amazes me," said Jerry, "is your presumption. I've been sleeping with Ameena for six months, while you've been playing with yourself. And here you are telling me about her! You're incredible."

Jerry had the worst weakness of the liar: he never believed anything you told him.

I said, "What are you going to do with the shirt?"

Clearly this had been worrying him. But he said nothing.

Late that night, working with my specimens, I smelled acrid smoke. I went to the windows. The incinerator was alight; Jika was coughing and stirring up flames with a stick.

The next Saturday Jerry took Petra to the tea estate in Sir Godfrey's gray Humber. I spent the day with my net, rather resenting the thought that Jerry had all the luck. First Ameena, now Petra. And he had ditched Ameena. There seemed no end to his arrogance or—what was more annoying—his luck. He came back to the house alone. I vowed that I would not give him a chance to do any sexual boasting. I stayed in my room, but less than ten minutes after he arrived home he was knocking on my door.

"I'm busy," I yelled.

"Doc, this is serious."

He entered rather breathless, fever-white and apologetic. This was not someone who had just made a sexual conquest—I knew as soon as I saw him that it had all gone wrong. So I said, "How does she bump?"

He shook his head. He looked very pale. He said, "I couldn't."

"So she turned you down." I could not hide my satisfaction.

"She was screaming for it," he said, rather primly. "She's seventeen, Doc. She's locked in a girls' school half the year. She even found a convenient haystack. But I had to say no. In fact, I couldn't get away from her fast enough."

"Something is wrong," I said. "Do you feel all right?"

He ignored the question. "Doc," he said, "remember when Ameena barged in. Just think hard. Did she touch me? Listen, this is important."

I told him I could not honestly remember whether she had touched him. The incident was so pathetic and embarrassing I had tried to block it out.

"I knew something like this was going to happen. But I don't understand it." He was talking quickly and unbuttoning his shirt. Then he took it off. "Look at this. Have you ever seen anything like it?"

At first I thought his body was covered by welts. But what I had taken to be welts were a mass of tiny reddened patches, like fly bites, some already swollen into bumps. Most of them—and by far the worst—were on his back and shoulders. They were as ugly as acne and had given his skin that same shine of infection.

"It's interesting," I said.

"Interesting!" he screamed. "It looks like syphilis and all you can say is it's interesting. Thanks a lot."

"Does it hurt?"

"Not too much," he said. "I noticed it this morning before I went out. But I think they've gotten worse. That's why nothing happened with Petra. I was afraid to take my shirt off."

"I'm sure she wouldn't have minded it if you'd kept it on."

"I couldn't risk it," he said. "What if it's contagious?"

He put calamine lotion on it and covered it carefully with gauze, and the next day it was worse. Each small bite had swelled to a pimple, and some of them seemed on the point of erupting; a mass of small warty boils. That was on a Sunday. On Monday I told Sir Godfrey that Jerry had a bad cold and could not teach. When I got back to the house that afternoon, Jerry said it was so painful he couldn't lie down. He had spent the afternoon sitting bolt upright in a chair.

"It was that shirt," he said. "Ameena's shirt. She did something to it."

"You're lying. Jika burned that shirt—remember?"

"She touched me," he said. "Doc, maybe it's not a curse—I'm not superstitious anyway. Maybe she gave me syph."

"Let's hope so."

"What do you mean by that!"

"I mean, there's a cure for syphilis."

"Suppose it's not that?"

"We're in Africa," I said.

This terrified him, as I knew it would.

He said, "Look at my back and tell me if it looks as bad as it feels."

He crouched under the lamp. His back was grotesquely inflamed. The eruptions had become like nipples, much bigger and with a bruised discoloration. I pressed one. He cried out. Watery liquid leaked out from a pustule.

"That hurt!" he said.

"Wait." I saw more infection inside the burst boil—a white clotted mass. I told him to grit his teeth. "I'm going to squeeze this one."

I pressed it between my thumbs and as I did a small white knob protruded. It was not pus—not liquid. I kept on pressing and Jerry yelled with shrill ferocity until I was done. Then I showed him what I had squeezed from his back; it was on the tip of my tweezers—a live maggot.

"It's a worm!"

"A larva."

"You know about these things. You've seen this before, haven't you?"

I told him the truth. I had never seen one like it before in my life. It was not in any textbook I had ever seen. And I told him more: there were, I said, perhaps two hundred of them, just like the one wriggling on my tweezers, in those boils on his body.

Jerry began to cry.

That night I heard him writhing in his bed, and groaning, and if I had not known better I would have thought Ameena was with him. He turned and jerked and thumped like a lover maddened by desire; and he whimpered, too, seeming to savor that kind of pain that is indistinguishable from sexual pleasure. But it was no more passion than the movement of those maggots in his flesh. In the morning, gray with sleeplessness, he said he felt like a corpse. Truly, he looked as if he was being eaten alive.

An illness you read about is never as bad as the real thing. Boy Scouts are told to suck the poison out of snakebites. But a snakebite—swollen and black and running like a leper's sore—is so horrible I can't imagine anyone capable of staring at it, much less putting his mouth on it. It was that way with Jerry's boils. All the textbooks on earth could not have prepared me for their ugliness, and what made them even more repellent was the fact that his face and hands were free of them. He was infected from his neck to his waist, and down his arms; his face was haggard, and in marked contrast to his sores.

I said, "We'll have to get you to a doctor."

"A witch doctor."

"You're serious!"

He gasped and said, "I'm dying, Doc. You have to help me."

"We can borrow Sir Godfrey's car. We could be in Blantyre by midnight."

Jerry said, "I can't last until midnight."

"Take it easy," I said. "I have to go over to the school. I'll say you're still sick. I don't have any classes this afternoon, so when I get back I'll see if I can do anything for you."

"There are witch doctors around here," he said. "You can find one—they know what to do. It's a curse."

I watched his expression change as I said, "Maybe it's the curse of the white worm." He deserved to suffer, after what he had done, but his face was so twisted in fear, I added, "There's only one thing to do. Get those maggots out. It might work."

"Why did I come to this fucking place!"

But he shut his eyes and was silent: he knew why he had left home.

When I returned from the school ("And how is our ailing friend?" Sir Godfrey had asked at morning assembly), the house seemed empty. I had a moment of panic, thinking that Jerry— unable to stand the pain—had taken an overdose. I ran into the bedroom. He lay asleep at his side, but woke when I shook him.

"Where's Jika?" I said.

"I gave him the week off," said Jerry. "I didn't want him to see me. What are you doing?"

I had set out a spirit lamp and my surgical tools: tweezers, a scalpel, cotton, alcohol, bandages. He grew afraid when I shut the door and shone the lamp on him.

"I don't want you to do it," he said. "You don't know anything about this. You said you'd never seen this thing before."

I said, "Do you want to die?"

He sobbed and lay flat on the bed. I bent over him to begin. The maggots had grown larger, some had broken the skin, and their ugly heads stuck out like beads. I lanced the worst boil, between his shoulder blades. Jerry cried out and arched his back, but I kept digging and prodding, and I found that heat made it simple. If I held my cigarette lighter near the wound the maggot wriggled, and by degrees, I eased it out. The danger lay in the breaking; if I pulled too hard some would be left in the boil to decay, and that I said would kill him.

By the end of the afternoon I had removed only twenty or so, and Jerry had fainted from the pain. He woke at nightfall. He looked at the saucer beside the bed and saw the maggots jerking in it—they had worked themselves into a white knot—and he screamed. I had to hold him until he calmed down. And then I continued.

I kept at it until very late. And I must admit that it gave me a certain pleasure. It was not only that Jerry deserved to suffer for his deceit—and his suffering was that of a condemned man; but also what I told him had been true: this was a startling discovery for me, as an entomologist. I had never seen such creatures before.

It was after midnight when I stopped. My hand ached, my eyes hurt from the glare, and I was sick to my stomach. Jerry had gone to sleep. I switched off the light and left him to his nightmares.

He was slightly better by morning. He was still pale, and the opened boils were crusted with blood, but he had more life in him than I had seen for days. And he was brutally scarred. I think he knew this: he looked as if he had been whipped.

"You saved my life," he said.

"Give it a few days," I said.

He smiled. I knew what he was thinking. Like all liars—those people who behave like human flies on our towering credulity—he was preparing his explanation. But this would be a final reply: he was preparing his escape.

"I'm leaving," he said. "I've got some money—and there's a night bus—" He stopped speaking and looked at my desk. "What's that?"

It was the dish of maggots, now as full as a rice pudding.

"Get rid of them!"

"I want to study them," I said. "I think I've earned the right to do that. But I'm off to morning assembly—what shall I tell Inky?"

"Tell him I might have this cold for a long time."

He was gone when I got back to the house; his room had been emptied, and he'd left me his books and his tennis racket with a note. I made what explanations I could. I told the truth: I had no idea where he had gone. A week later, Petra went back to Rhodesia, but she told me she would be back. As we chatted over the fence I heard Jerry's voice: She's screaming for it. I said, "We'll go horseback riding."

"Super!"

The curse of the white worm: Jerry had believed me. But it was the curse of impatience—he had been impatient to get rid of Ameena, impatient for Petra, impatient to put on a shirt that had not been ironed. What a pity it was that he was not around when the maggots hatched, to see them become flies I had never seen. He might have admired the way I expertly pickled some and sealed others in plastic and mounted twenty of them on a tray.

And what flies they were! It was a species that was not in any book, and yet the surprising thing was that in spite of their differently shaped wings (like a Muslim woman's cloak) and the shape of their bodies (a slight pinch above the thorax, giving them rather attractive waists), their life cycle was the same as many others of their kind: they laid their eggs on laundry and these larvae hatched at body heat and burrowed into the skin to mature. Of course, laundry was always ironed—even drip-dry shirts—to kill them. Everyone who knew Africa knew that.

How I Came To Write This Story

In 1984, shortly after democracy was reinstated in Argentina, I traveled to Buenos Aires. While there I delivered a package to an Argentine writer who had lived in exile for seven years in Mexico with a close woman friend of mine. He had just returned to his country. She had gone back to live in New York City. I was moved by their love, particularly its cross-cultural aspects, and the pain involved in exile. A few years later, I learned that he was sick with cancer. I immediately began to write a story of his death, imagining my friend's trip to Buenos Aires for his funeral. I worked on it for six months and then put it away. The writer lived. My friend stayed in New York. In 1988, I went to an artists' colony in Massachusetts. I brought "Exile" along. With renewed passion I entered the story again. But as I wrote, the plot began to change. It was no longer a trip back for a funeral, but now the story of my character's difficult love in a foreign land and his return with her to his city when the "dirty little war" was over. I finished "Exile", in an intense state of writing euphoria on my last day at the colony. My hero had lived and my heroine might remain with him in his land! I took the train to New York City on Sunday night. On Monday morning I read in the New York Times that the model for my character, Taxo, had succumbed to cancer in Buenos Aires on Saturday.

—Marnie Mueller

MARNIE MUELLER (Ecuador, 1963-1965) was born in Tule Lake Japanese American Segregation Camp in California. She has been the Program Director of Pacifica Radio in New York City, the Director of Summer Programming for the City of New York, and a freelance events producer. Since 1986, her short stories and poetry have been widely published and anthologized. In 1990 she won the River Styx Prize for Fiction. Her novel *Green Fires* was published by Curbstone Press in 1994. It won a 1995 American Book Award and the 1995 Maria Thomas Award for Fiction, and has been optioned for a feature film. Goldmann/Bertelsmann of Germany published a translation of *Green Fires* in 1996. Her second novel is *The Climate of the Country*, published by Curbstone Press in 1999.

EXILE

by Marnie Mueller

What she remembered most about the evening they met was how lonely he looked. She'd walked into Isadora Sanchez's house for the party honoring him, and through the crowd she'd noticed Taxo. He was standing in a group, but seemed not to be a part of it. He looked smaller than she'd imagined from the photo on his latest book. Older. He looked his full fifty years. Handsome, in a dark homely way, smooth yellow brown skin, eyes set a fraction too close, but startling in their blackness. She'd been singularly brazen—something she later attributed to being suddenly out of her mother's grasp—though still in her soft way, and had gone directly to his side.

"Beware the winds of Patagonia," she quoted from her favorite poem of his.

He put his arm, without hesitation, over her shoulder. "I'm flattered, Señorita," and led her into the patio.

She loved his touch immediately. There was a comfort in it as well as a sexual excitement. They sat on a mahogany bench in the shadow of the overhang and he stroked her fingers as they spoke. Their own voices sounded muted to her. The music coming from the room had more clarity. Beyond the impression of his loneliness, her memory of that evening was a confusion of feelings. Of wanting and not wanting. Of comfort and an awkwardness with each other that could almost be dislike, almost contempt. And certainly misunderstanding.

Martha Cohen had come to Mexico City to be free of her mother for a few weeks. Her father had died a half year earlier and she'd spent the time since helping her mother through the mourning period. She did this even though she had recently become sure her mother had never done anything to comfort her, except perhaps the time Martha had wet her pants in second grade and her mother had said she could stay home that afternoon. Otherwise, the care had always gone from daughter to mother, though Martha didn't know it until it was pointed out to her by her analyst. After a long recitation by Martha of how proud she was of her maturity in guiding her mother through this troubling period, her analyst had said, "That's all very good of you, Martha, very kind, but may I say, you've always tended to your mother's emotional needs, probably from when you were two years old. I think the pattern was established forty years ago."

On their first evening, Martha slept with Taxo. She moved into his tiny room off the patio they had been sitting in. Isadora provided this room and bath and food, she had said, for nothing for Taxo.

"It's the least I can do for him," Isadora confided to Martha, "after all he's been through."

"What has he been through?" Martha asked. She and Isadora were in the large Sanchez kitchen when she asked. Martha was waiting for the maid to finish folding their laundry. Isadora had insisted that Martha not do her and Taxo's laundry herself.

"No, no." Isadora pointed to where the maid worked with her back to them. She moved her finger with its long red-painted nail in a circular motion to indicate that they would finish their talk later, in private.

But Taxo told her himself. He told her three things in their first week together. That he was divorced with two teenage daughters, that he was Jewish, and that he had been tortured. This last had happened just before he escaped from Buenos Aires. It had decided his own conflict about leaving. They had taken him in one sunny afternoon and he hadn't seen daylight for weeks after that. He didn't tell her more. She had to learn from friends that they had stuck prods and stun guns on his testicles and over his heart. She knew that though he had no repercussions from the prods to his genitals—"To the contrary," he once laughed—he did have recurrent problems with his heart.

One night early in their time together, she was wakened to his stiffened body beside her. Afterward, she wondered if he'd made a sound that had brought her to consciousness, or if she'd simply sensed that something was wrong.

"Taxo, what is it?"

He was breathing in short, audible breaths.

She turned the light on. He held his chest. He wore nothing and it was as though the stun gun marks over his heart had grown larger, darker, almost black. His face was pale and he was sweating.

"Should I call a doctor?"

He shook his head. "It's passing."

"What is passing, for god's sake?"

She sat up and got her T-shirt from the bottom of the bed and pulled it over her head.

"No, no, no," he shook his head and smiled. "It is passing, my darling. This has happened before. It's the valve, nothing more. The doctors say the bastards harmed one of the valves with their fucking torture games. All the doctors say I can live this way to one hundred years." He took his hand from his heart and put it on her cheek. "It is nothing, they say, I promise you. Just a little malfunction in an otherwise perfect man."

"But what is it? What are the symptoms? What happens to your heart?"

"It fills up if I get too excited, or too tired. The broken valve works less well with fatigue. It's nothing. I only need rest and less excitement." He laughed. "Some would say that's all a poet does. Is relax, no?"

Martha knew about torture. She laughed sometimes that she had learned about torture from her mother, who herself had been tortured by the Nazis and who continued their legacy, practicing on her. In truth, she would say, seeing the shocked face of her listener, she had learned about torture from working for the past ten years at Amnesty USA. As the New York office coordinator of volunteer programs, she was in charge of letter writing campaigns to the Prisoners of Conscience. She'd read so many horror stories that she'd grown inured to them. She had met torture victims. She had never had one as a lover. On the night of the heart episode, she decided to stay in Mexico City.

"I have money," she told Taxo that night, lying beside him when neither of them could go back to sleep. "My father left me money when he died. I don't have to work. I can stay here and even support you."

When he didn't respond, she went on. "The truth is, I'd like to stay away from New York. From my mother. It's as simple as that. And now a perfect opportunity has been handed to me."

He turned toward her. He smiled a soft but dark smile. He ran a finger along the outline of her face. "I'd like you to stay. I can tell we'd get on well. But I refuse to be your very own political exile. Do you hear?"

"I hear you."

He slipped her T-shirt over her head and covered her breasts with his hands.

"This isn't too strenuous?" she asked.

"Love-making? Never," he murmured.

Back in New York she gave notice at the office and spent two weeks finishing projects. They hadn't found anyone to replace her at the end of the two weeks and tried to persuade her to stay for at least another month. She refused.

"For once I'm going to do something for myself," she told Frank Gilbert, the public affairs director.

"You call living with an exiled writer doing for yourself, Marty? They're hell to be with. You know that."

"You're mean, Frank. You're not wishing me the best."

"I'll always wish you the best, Mart. You of anybody in the world deserve the best."

When she went to visit her mother, she went steeled. She made a special point of telling her that Taxo was a Jew.

"He doesn't sound Jewish to me with the name Maldonado."

"He's a displaced Italian Jew, Mother. His family emigrated in the early thirties."

"How fortuitous," her mother said.

Usually that would have closed the subject between the two of them and Martha would have gone on to something lighter, less emotional. Or she would have suggested that since it was getting close to noon perhaps she could make her mother something nice to eat, "something special, Mother, that you don't make for yourself." But this time Martha didn't change the subject, didn't offer to make lunch.

"Mother, he's a very nice man," she said in a quiet but firm voice. "And I think you'll like him when you get to know him."

After a minute of complete silence during which Mrs. Cohen's face froze with cold fury, she rose from her chair. She walked toward Martha and stopped a foot away. "Young lady, don't you slash at me with your forked tongue. Don't you ever, ever dare speak to me that way again if you know what is good for you." And she turned and walked out of the room.

Martha sat trembling. Where earlier she had felt comforted by the sunshine spilling in through the large windows, now she was freezing and saw the light as gray. I must get out of here, she repeated to herself, but she couldn't move. Then she remembered her ticket back to Mexico City. Once on the plane she would be safe. The room began to come into focus, to take on color. She saw the pale blue wall-to-wall rug, the chintz-upholstered chairs and the grand piano in the corner.

She remembered the day, shortly before her thirteenth birthday when she'd been in this room playing a Mozart sonata with passionate intensity. Her mother had come in and walked directly over to her and brushed her hands from the keys. She had slammed the cover down. "Such beautiful music shouldn't be played by a girl with no talent for it. It's butchery. Such a deed is butchery."

She told herself that if she had lived through that day, she could certainly stand up and walk out of this room.

Martha found a lovely small apartment in the suburb of Coyoacan that she could easily afford on the dividends from her inheritance. She had never lived like this before, on her parents' money. Always, from pride and not wanting to be beholden to her mother, she had earned her own money. She had even attended City College not to have to ask them for tuition and she had worked as a waitress to pay her own expenses. Now, here she was, working through the fifty thousand her dear father had left. But it was for Taxo, she rationalized. He needed to be supported. He also needed to send money home to his children, which he did, from Martha's father's fund.

The apartment was over a garage and looked out onto a cobblestone alleyway. Taxo had the room that would have been their bedroom for his study. He left it bare, monastic, except for his work table which was lined with the books of his favorite poets—Merwin, Whitman, Neruda, Vallejo, Crane and others—his Olivetti, his reams of papers and piles of folders and a pencil holder of pressed green Coca-Cola glass. On the windowsill that overlooked the alley were four Christmas cacti, each blooming at different times of the year: Thanksgiving, Christmas, Easter, and Martha's birthday in July.

It was a tiny room and not worth making into a bedroom for them, Martha had said when she showed him the place.

"You need your own room," she'd said. "At least you can have that comfort."

He had taken her in his arms in the then empty room.

"You are so caring, Marta. You should have children. They would thrive under your care, as I am."

"No thank you," she said laughing. She went to stand at the window and looked out onto the bougainvillea below. "I can be kind to you. But with my own child I wouldn't trust myself. Like mother, like daughter, as they say."

He came and stood beside her, not touching her. "You could never write a novel, Marta. You don't understand human nature well enough." He let his hand slide over to hers on the sill. "You don't understand your own turns of nature. Your mother's harm to you bred only kindness in you, Martita. Too much kindness for your own good. It spills out of you as from a too full pitcher."

"Or too full heart?" she asked, smiling.

"Yes, or a too filled up heart."

She spent her time making the apartment a home. She bought woven cloth in rich colors, magenta to match the blooms of the cacti, lime green, and tomato orange. She gathered wooden furniture from here and there and bought glasses and dishes in the markets. She'd never fixed a home before. Though in her forties, she'd lived only alone as an adult and then in a curiously temporary way. It wasn't that she was waiting to be married. She'd never considered marriage for herself, but more as though it wasn't worth her while to do it for herself. And besides, she'd been too busy working.

Her thoughts were filled with the happiness of her new life one midmorning as she walked down the alleyway behind their house. Just as she was glorying in the light on the bougainvillea, she looked up and there Taxo was in his window, leaning over the blooming cacti.

"I'm waiting for you," he said when she came to stand under the window. "I'm waiting to see the sun on your brown hair and the fruit in the basket. Your face has become so brown, Marta. You could be from here. Maybe we belong here. Maybe we should stay here forever."

When she entered the apartment, she found that this sentimental expression covered a surging rage. He had just heard from his Mexican publisher that in Argentina they were refusing to distribute his books, old and new.

"I will be forgotten in my country." He threw the sheaf of papers that was his latest manuscript across the room.

She bent to pick it up. "You won't be forgotten, Taxo." They had been through this many times. He was obsessed with the notion of being forgotten while he was away. "People will smuggle your books into the country. You will be more famous for it." She tried to put the pages in order.

"Throw them out, damn it. They're worthless." He came at her and tried to grab them from her.

She lifted her blouse and put the pages beneath it. "Stop that. Calm yourself."

"I can't. They are killing me." He sat like a boy on his chair with his back to his table.

"No more than before," she said in a soft voice.

"But that was my body. This is my whole being. This is torture to my soul. And all because I am an artist. Because these monsters hate artists."

"God damn it, Taxo, because you are a political man. That is why they are torturing you. That is why they tortured you before." It was their usual argument. He refused to face that anything that had happened to him was because he was political. In his eyes, she was the overly political American, the do-gooder. He was the artist. Only circumstances had brought politics into his life. "If you would understand why they do this, you would feel a hundred percent better."

"Throw out the god damn manuscript. It's crap."

"It's not crap. It's yours. It's what you've written."

"Art in and of itself is subversive," he said. "That's what you don't understand. They are afraid of the freedom of words. Of uncontrollable emotions."

"Maybe they read politics into your metaphors," Marta said, still clutching the manuscript protectively. "Maybe you were making an unconscious political statement when you said, 'Beware the winds of Patagonia.'"

"You are as bad as they are, Señorita. You want to see politics in everything. I am a poet. I am not a politician. Please, if you please, don't try to pigeonhole me." He reached out his hand. "Now give me my manuscript. I have work to do. The poet would like to make some more metaphors and would rather that no one watched over his shoulder in this supposedly free state. This supposedly free home of ours."

She was shaking when she left him and went into the living room. She sat on the sofa and breathed deeply. It was one of the methods she had learned to bring herself back to herself when her mother had obliterated her with some cruelty. Though this wasn't the same. Martha had intentionally absorbed his anger, given it a focus. She knew the guilt he felt about his friends in prison—or so he hoped—friends who had disappeared, picked up from their homes never to return, while he was safe being a poet in Mexico City. Her mother carried the same guilt from living through the war and arriving safely in America. Her mother's cruelty came from the same place, though her mother's cruelty was meant to annihilate. Over the years no holds had ever been put on it, certainly not by her husband.

As she sat breathing slowly, an excitement entered Martha. She would make a special dinner tonight. She would buy sausages and steak and make a parrilla for Taxo. She would bring the good Argentina back to him. She would bring him some joy. As she planned the meal, thought of the flowers she would put on the table, how she would pull the table over to the window so they could watch the night sky, she calmed down and took hold of herself again. Her desire and energy returned. She felt elated at the thought of the earthenware plates and the bright blue napkins and the turquoise hand-blown glasses. Taxo would laugh and kiss the air, exclaiming how delicious the food was and how it reminded him of home, and how the only thing missing were the french fries of Buenos Aires.

"Wait until you have them, Martita," he said that night. "They are like the *calafate* of Patagonia, the blooming bush. They say once a person sees the *calafate* in bloom, he must always return to Argentina. Well, for me it is the french fries. I must go back to my land, if only to once again taste the french fries of Buenos Aires." He stopped and looked at her as though a sudden sad thought had come into him. "I love you, Marta. I don't know who I love more, my country or you. I don't know who inspires me more, *La Patria o ti.*"

One night after making love, they talked as they often did, lying naked side by side, bodies open and spent. It was the best time, usually.

"Marta, my dearest," he said, leaning over to kiss her forehead. She curled down and put her head on his sweaty chest. "Marta, my dearest."

"What do you mean with that, 'Marta, my dearest?'"

"Nothing."

"Not nothing. It's impossible that it's nothing with that tone of voice."

"I miss my children, you know."

She wished she hadn't asked. A hollow cylinder opened inside her.

"As you should."

"Not as I should, Marta. It has nothing to do with the subjunctive or obligation. I miss their smell. The shape of their heads. I get my photos every Christmas. I don't recognize them anymore. But I know if I could smell them, run my hand over their brows, they would come back to me, be familiar again."

She was still. She would never be that to him, nor would she ever have such a wish, such a knowledge. Her closest family was her mother. She would hate to smell her mother, or touch her brow. The cylinder in her was growing. She had nothing to barter with him over their being together. When this was over, he'd go back to them. Maybe even to Alicia, his ex-wife. She, Martha, would be of no use to him anymore.

"Why so quiet, Marta?" His hand touched her collarbone. She couldn't move, couldn't lower her cheek to the back of his hand as she usually did.

"Nothing, no reason. I'm thinking of your children, how much children must mean to a person."

"Maybe we should make you one."

"No, Taxo, never. And anyway, you need me to take care of you." She pinched his flesh around his middle. "To fatten you up. To keep you a nice full weight on me." She forced herself to laugh.

"You may be right. Alicia said the same to me. She said, 'Taxo, I love you, but you are more of a baby than my children.' You notice she said *my*. *My* children, not *ours*. How I miss them, Marta. I can taste it. It comes over me at times. I would risk everything in this moment to go back there to see them."

"I know," she whispered, thinking forbidden thoughts, wishing that the children would go away and the military would stay in forever. Wishing he would always need her.

"And I know your jealousy. I can smell it on you, just as I can smell my children on my children."

"That's not true." She tried to will herself to look at him.

"I can tell. You wish I'd never go back."

"Not because of me," she said fiercely, lying. "Only because of what your country has done to you and your friends and others."

"Oh, silliness. A country doesn't do to a person. People do to people."

"Nations can do. Nations can be evil."

"Is that what your mother said? Does she say the nation of Germany was evil, not just certain people."

"My mother never went back to Germany. She never will."

"Is your mother our guide in anything, my dear?"

"In certain things, maybe. Maybe, yes."

She knew she was on shaky ground with this one. Argentina wasn't Germany, even though there were many Germans in the country. And she had too often discredited her mother to call her up as an authority.

"But remember, you're Jewish. One of the reasons they tortured you was because you were Jewish."

"How can you say that?" He pulled himself up in bed until he was sitting. His penis that had remained full and extended, went soft now and lay to one side on his leg.

"Jacobo says that's why. Jacobo says they go for Jews before they go for anyone."

"Jacobo, Jacobo, he will use his Jewishness for whatever reason. In defense of humbleness or pride. You wait and see, Jacobo won't last two years in Israel. He can't stand being merely one Jew among many. What does Jacobo know?" He put his hand on his penis and began absently pulling it; the circumcised penis he had once told her they had ridiculed. It was the single time she had seen him cry when talking about what had been done to him. But he had immediately covered his show of feeling by touching her with seductive fingers until she had to give in to the open wetness he'd beckoned from her. He had entered her then and stayed not moving in her, large and filling, finally making her move wildly against him as she told him over and over to please help her.

Now he was saying to her, "I have told you, Marta, they went after me simply because I am a poet. They can't understand what I say, so they think I speak against them. But they are not my people, those who are in power."

"Who are they if they aren't Argentinians?" Her tone was scornful. She had never let herself talk like this before, least of all to a lover.

"They are aberrations. Don't fool yourself, my dear, you have plenty of their kind in your great democracy and given the right set of circumstances they would emerge the same. And I expect *you* don't doubt that you'll be going back to live among *them*."

Her face must have changed with the realization of what he'd said, because his face was transformed as he watched her.

"Marta, Marta, come here my love." He pulled her still betrayed body over to his. "We will be together. One place or another. We will always from this day be together until one of us dies. I promise you this."

It was after she'd been in Mexico City for two years that Martha received a call from Frank Gilbert in New York asking her to do some Amnesty work for him.

"I need a group of Friends of Prisoners down there. I desperately need the letters to be written directly in Spanish. Please, please help me, Marty old pal."

She was startled by how thrilled she was to be asked. The lists of whom she would invite to participate began forming in her mind as they talked. She got off the phone and paced around the living room. She was tempted to rush right in and tell Taxo even though she knew he would be skeptical about her doing political work. Instead she went out into the street and walked and walked.

She had tried to fill her time keeping house and occasionally attempting to draw and paint. But every time she found herself beginning to get lost in a landscape or a still life, her mother's voice would tell her it was a waste of time if one had no talent. What did the world need with another mediocre still life of mangos and bananas? So instead, she put her own work away and helped Taxo by editing his articles and reviews and increasingly she acted as his agent in his new contacts with American publishers.

But she saw now that she needed her own work, work that she knew herself to be accomplished at. Work that was hers even if Taxo didn't approve. She geared herself up for the fight with him.

To her surprise, Taxo did not object. He said he thought it would be good for her to have her independent activities, that he had been thinking that for some time. "I may be latino, Marta, but I don't enjoy a woman being at my beck and call and without her own calling."

Though, when one Sunday evening as they sat together in a plaza in Tuxtla Gutierrez, where they had traveled for a short vacation, Martha broached the possibility of Taxo writing his own letter to prisoners in Argentina, he adamantly refused. He was so angry in his refusal that she became silent. It was sunset. The sky was purple, streaked with sulfur. She watched the night hawks darting and swooping around the streetlights. The branches of the trees were as though cut by a silhouetter and something about that and about the temperature and texture of the air made her recall how, when she was a child, her parents would take her each year to the silhouetter on the boardwalk in Coney Island.

She would sit in his booth while he quietly snipped the black paper. Her parents had to stand outside the curtain while he worked so her mother couldn't tell her to sit up straighter or hold her chin up. He clipped and hummed. He took a long time. Martha wished he would take longer. She loved to be in that small space with him, with the warm light trained on her face and the soft sounds coming from him. When it was time to paste the silhouette down he called her over to his long table with another light trained on the black image as he settled it carefully on the white plaster board. He laid it down delicately with his long thin fingers. He moved it here and there by fractions of inches.

"What do you say, *bube*? A little higher? Just a little higher on the paper, no?"

Her eyelids grew almost too heavy to hold up. She let out a tiny "hmm," as noncommittal as possible, so he'd take it to mean she thought it not quite right and he'd spend more time moving it up and down and over and up with the point of the stylus. And she sat watching, letting the delicious feeling of well-being swim through her body like the dolphins through water in the aquarium. Gliding, surging, resting.

She loved the smell of the glue as he brushed it from the large glued-over bottle onto the white board. But her favorite was watching how he patiently tipped the delicate black paper that was her profile and moved it with the brush, being careful not to let any go over the sides.

"*Ja, ja, gut,*" he said. "Beautiful girl and beautiful craft."

She loved that he said she was beautiful, but his uttering it signaled the end of their session for that year.

"Good, Mr. Spiegelman. You are a very talented man indeed. You make my daughter so lovely. When we look back in the years to come, we'll forget the flaws, won't we, Martha?"

"No flaws, Mrs. Cohen. Just the marks of true beauty in this one. Imperfections that draw attention to the originality of that face." He drew his finger down her profile, lightly touching her skin as softly as a butterfly's kiss.

The memory of Mr. Speigelman's support gave her strength.

"Why do you say no to me, Taxo, with such finality? Before I can even have a discussion with you?"

"Because you already know how I feel on this matter." He turned to her, his arm on the back of the bench. The streetlight illuminated half of his face. "I don't do political work, Martita, my love. My poetry is my work. I have nothing left to give even to my country. I must preserve myself, my poetry. That is my duty."

How lucky you are, she thought. But for the first time she felt angry at his selfish arrogance. And insulted. His art was so great. Her politics was office work.

"And what if I told you they'd found Jijón Igréjas?" she said, letting the news of one of his group fall with no preparation.

His cheek contracted. The circles under his eyes seemed to grow darker.

"Where?" He spoke in a clear voice.

"He's imprisoned in Neuquen. He didn't disappear. And they don't dare kill him now because there has been a huge letter campaign started for him by Almedo, who is in Washington."

"Almedo is safe?"

"Yes."

"Oh my God." She saw tears well. His hand rose to his face and covered his eyes. The light from the lamp showed the definition of his large knuckles. Rough hands for a poet. Not like the long smooth hands of Mr. Speigelman. But gentle hands. Wonderful love-making hands.

"I don't mean to upset you," she said.

"Oh, yes you do. You wish to upset me enough to do something." He dropped his hand from his face to reveal anguish that she had never seen before on him. "You win, I will write one letter to my friend Armando Jijón. But that is it. I can do no more. You will have to do what I can't. I ask that of you. I ask that you help me in that way." He began to cry, making awful animal sounds.

She put her arms around him and brought him to her breast. "I'm sorry, Taxo, my child. I'm sorry. I shouldn't have told you."

"No, no. Marta, I am so sad. No, you had to tell me."

They sat for a long time on the bench. Long after all color had faded from the sky. Long after the nighthawks had stopped their swooping. Long after lovers had arrived and done their business and gone on their way. They sat almost through the night on their bench in the plaza in each other's embrace. Sometimes talking, sometimes not.

Then the day came when they waited by the radio to hear the news. And it arrived.

"The vote has been counted. Democracy has returned to Argentina."

Taxo put his hand on the radio and sat with his head bowed. Marta sat across the table from him, weeping with joy for him.

He looked up. His eyes were dry but shining. "We can go home, Marta." His voice cracked. "I am free to return."

When she called her mother and told her she was going to Argentina for a few weeks with Taxo, her mother said, "How can you go there? It's a fascist anti-Semitic country."

"Mother, I'm going to be with Taxo through this. He needs my help. It's difficult for him to return after six years."

"Always the helper. Martha the helper," her mother sighed.

Was there affection in that sigh? Or understanding or insight?

"Don't worry, mother, I'll be back."

"I hope so, Martha. I hope you're not planning to live among those fascists."

They arrived in Buenos Aires in the morning after a long trip from Mexico City via Rio. No one came to meet them. Taxo hadn't wanted to tell anyone he was arriving. "I need to take this step by step," he said to her. "In my own time." Going through the passport check was tense. The man in the booth who asked how long he had been out of the country was about Taxo's age.

"Six years," Taxo answered, staring straight into the man's eyes.

"Where were you living?"

"In Mexico City."

"Occupation."

"Poet." This was on his passport.

"Welcome back." The man nodded and passed the closed passport through the opening in the window.

Their baggage was thoroughly checked. Their cameras were inspected, even taken apart. They had anticipated this and re-moved the film, but they weren't body searched. "I guess they don't want to be accused of being fascists, too," Taxo said as they walked into the main waiting room.

A cab driver took them to the Hotel Rochester where Taxo had made a reservation. The cabby tried to cheat them by going the wrong way, but Taxo caught him on it. Unrepentant, when they arrived at the hotel, the cab driver asked for an exorbitant amount of money.

"I'm a *porteño*, too, my friend. A long lost port son. Don't do this to me on my first day back in six years."

"*Compadre*, forgive me," the man shrugged. "But I do my best with this inflation. You know nothing of the inflation. I have my family to feed."

"I sympathize, but I've had a bad time, too, my friend. And I'm very short on cash for the time being. I'll pay you half. If this government lasts the year, come back and I'll gladly give you a gift of the other half you try to rob me of."

"By then it will be worth nothing and I won't want to bother. Do as you wish, *compadre*. I have sympathy with your situation. I have a brother just back. It won't be easy for you."

The Rochester was a simple businessman's hotel which Taxo had chosen as the least likely place for him to be. They were treated with quiet respect at the desk.

The bellhop took them up silently in the tiny *ascensor*. He was a stocky man with light brown curly hair, in his late forties, with ruddy, lined skin. He said nothing as he led them along the carpeted halls. Once inside the room, he leaned forward to Taxo and said in a quiet voice, "I know who you are, Don Maldonado. With a full heart I welcome you back." Martha felt tears come to her eyes for Taxo. She saw that he, too, was touched by the remark. Where until now he had kept his face impassive, he smiled and clasped the hand of the man.

"Thank you, my friend. It is good to be back in my beautiful city."

The bellhop opened the curtains and windows. The roar from

the street and the smell of diesel entered the room. "You may wish to rest," he said as he turned down the blankets on the bed revealing white pressed sheets.

As Taxo was giving him a tip, the man said, "If you wish to change money, let me know, but privately. I can change dollars at a very good rate."

Taxo looked at Marta. They had planned for this.

"That will be very good, my man. What about a hundred dollars?"

The man beamed. "Give me the dollars and I'll be back in a couple of hours. I can be trusted."

"I believe you," Taxo said and handed the man the money.

Taxo and Martha stood by the window looking down onto the street. The traffic raced and people walked single file on the narrow sidewalk.

"It's like this all the time," Taxo said. "The streets of Buenos Aires are always full, from dawn to dawn. My beloved Buenos Aires!" He held his arms open. "Here I am, Taxo Maldonado, returning to you with an open heart."

Martha struggled to join his joy, but fear and sadness intruded. Where did she fit in this embrace?

"Look, Marta." Taxo pointed across the street to the roof of the next building where a group of joggers were circling on a track. "Under fascism they've taken up jogging like you Americans. I wonder if there is a connection."

Martha tightened inside. "They had to do something while they waited."

"Waited? Did these people wait, too? Maybe not, maybe they loved fascism. Maybe they are waiting for it to return."

"What is this political talk, Taxo?" she chided. "Suddenly I hear the word fascism coming from you. I didn't know that was a word you liked me to utter."

"This is difficult for me, Marta. Please understand that, my dearest."

"I do. I tried to warn you about it. I tried to help you."

"Stop it, Marta. Let me do it myself. This is my country, my city, my loss. This is my love I have come back to. What if she rejects me, harms me? What if those joggers turn me into them? A return after this many years is not an easy thing, my dear."

She was silent. She had tended to him all those years in Mexico.

She had tried to help him by getting him to talk about this and now on home turf he was turning it against her.

"I am afraid, Marta." He was crying.

She thought, your man's tears won't get to me. But she felt them slide in as they did down the lines of his face. He is spoiled, she thought. I have spoiled him. I have taken care of him. Now as soon as I step back, he calls to me. But who is going to be left? He will stay here and send me off. He will only want his children and his Alicia. Who will the American woman be to him? She wondered how many other women around the world had lovers who were now free to leave them because of the work she herself had done for Amnesty. What irony that her political work could cause this kind of anguish.

"Marta, speak to me. I need you. What if they are going to harm me when I go back? What if when I walk into my children's home, the police are there to arrest me?" He held her by the shoulders and shook her until her head bobbed back and forth.

Her mother used to do this when in a rage over some trifle.

"Stop it, Taxo. Stop it."

He looked at her in shock. "I am so sorry." He put the palm of his hand to her cheek as was his way.

She shook her head. He dropped his hand to her shoulder again and looked at her not understanding.

"No one will harm you," she said. "You've been promised. We'll call the human rights office before you go to your home to tell them that you're going, where and when, so if anything happens, they'll know. I'll stay here. If you don't call, I'll call them."

"You would do that for me?" His face was lined and old, but his affect was that of a child.

"Taxo, long ago I offered to do as much in my way. Long ago I tried to prepare you for this day. It was you who denied the help. Now we're here. I'll do what I can, you can trust that."

After he left she crawled between the sheets. They were smooth and cool. She had shut the curtains and the room was filled with an orange light. In a way she was glad she didn't have to go with him. She would be so out of place with his grown children and his ex-wife. She would be jealous of his joy at seeing them. She recalled the night, years ago, when he said how much he missed them. "I miss their smell, Marta, miss feeling the shape of their brows."

She wondered now: Had he set up the argument to keep her from accompanying him?

She pulled the sheet up to her chin and curled her legs almost to her chest. She wished she were back in their little house in Mexico City with the Christmas cacti on the sill flowering its magenta trumpets. She wished Taxo were sitting at his Olivetti by the window. She longed for his irregular tapping.

Martha woke to a sharp knocking. Her first thought was, it's the police.

"It's me, Señorita. Alonso, the bellhop." His half-whispered voice came through the door. "I have the money."

"Just a moment." She slipped her dress on and checked her hair in the mirror.

He handed the money through the half-opened door.

"If you need more, please come to me, Señorita. But be discreet, please. We are not supposed to do this. It is necessary for me, what with the inflation. Thank you, Señorita, and please, my best regards to the Señor poet. I am a great admirer of his."

Martha stayed in the room for some time. It always was difficult for her to gather the courage to go out into a new city. She had been lucky that night she'd met Taxo, to have found him on her first evening.

She finally left the hotel room by threatening herself with the shame of having to tell Taxo that she'd stayed in all day and hadn't walked around his city. She also didn't want to be completely at his mercy in the tours she knew he had planned for them.

Alonso directed her to the Calle Florida, a pedestrian mall, just a block and a half away. It was filled with people who were beginning their Christmas shopping. It was hard to believe there was a money problem, the way people looked. She had never, even in New York, seen such stylishly dressed men and women. She played with the idea of going into one of the shops, but realizing that even if she did buy something she wouldn't have anything to go with it, she decided to be content with her full skirt, blouse and huaraches. Even though every woman on the street was wearing tapered pants, straight skirts, knit tops, and high heels. Nonetheless, she held her head up and kept walking and even, she thought, got a couple of looks of interest from not so unattractive men.

She stayed out all afternoon, sat in a park, walked down major avenues, had a little something to eat in a cafe. It was moving toward dusk as she made her way back to the hotel. Taxo had said he would return around eight, enough time to wash, change and be ready to go to dinner by ten. She walked slowly down Calle Florida. Music blasted out of shops. Young hippy-style musicians were playing guitars on the street. At one corner masses of men stood in the intersection arguing politics. There were tables of literature and people with loud speakers who sounded more like religious proselytizers than the Peronistas that they declared themselves to be. Though it was exciting, there wasn't a woman among them and she felt too out of place to participate. She hoped she could talk Taxo into stopping later.

The sky was turning a rich peacock blue. The mild spring air was filled with flower smells. Directly overhead, all down the street, she noticed for the first time that thousands of electric wires crossed like a giant cat's cradle every which way from rooftop to rooftop. They looked especially beautiful against the deep, brilliant blue of the sky. As she walked, admiring this strange beauty, she imagined what it would be like if she were young, a school girl, a college student spending a year in Buenos Aires. She knew it would be overwhelmingly romantic, and that the memories of it would hold through a lifetime, coming back filled with melancholy and longing for the sweet young time when she'd been in love with herself walking down this street and with the young man who had taken her for coffee and with the charm of being a young *gringa* in this southern city. As for herself, she would have no such memories of this place, of this afternoon turning into evening. She was too old. The memories of Taxo would be heavy with sadness, with the loss that was complete, with no hope, with realistic fear that another love couldn't be found and with the adult knowledge that no love could be uncomplicated, purely delicious, but all were flawed and probably fated to failure for innumerable reasons out of one's control. She knew now, that the chance to find a love that enhanced life with cherished moments had passed her by. She knew in that moment that the extinguishing of Taxo from her life would be the passing of any hope of love. And it made her sad, not luxuriously sad, but dead sad. Despairingly so. And deeply lonely.

Back at the hotel there was no message and no sign that he had come and gone. She hung out the window for a time watching the streets fill even more, watching the throngs of people walk and jostle each other. Neon lights had been turned on and were shining red and green, yellow and turquoise, here and there around the cityscape. Lights in the office building across the way were turned off one by one. Still the phone didn't ring. Then a loud noise rose from the street, amplified speakers and the banging of drums and chanting. She couldn't see where it came from, though she recognized the rhythm of rebellion. It came closer and closer and then the demonstrators appeared at the corner. She strained to make out the words, but couldn't. She saw the signs with Malvinas printed on them, and Alfonsin's name, and "the disappeared," but she couldn't put it all together, couldn't make sense of what the exact issue was. Perhaps it wasn't one issue, perhaps it was like the wires strung chaotically across the street, making no exact pattern, but having a beauty of its own. In the case of the wires it was the beauty of organic growth as need arose. With the slogans it was the beginning of an organic growth of freedom of speech, still in a disorganized nascent stage, gradually taking form, a form that could hold, a form perhaps of loyal opposition that could keep a democratic government honest, that could keep the rigidity of dogmatism in place. Would Taxo be involved in the growth of that opposition? Or would he choose to sit in his room and write? She didn't know. She hoped she saw glimmers of change in him. She wanted to remember a man who participated, who did his part.

She began to cry. She knew it was over. He wouldn't need her anymore, and, without needing her to take care of him, he would have no need of her as a mate. But what of herself? Did she only need him when he needed her? Was that the truth about herself?

At ten when Taxo hadn't called, Martha was too frightened to wait any longer. She dialed the number he had left for her, saying it was Alicia's home.

"On the part of whom?" the woman whom Martha assumed to be Alicia asked. Behind her was loud music and laughter.

"Marta Cohen."

"Oh." There was silence, then a muffled shout. "Taxo, it's for you. Telephone." The receiver was put down loudly.

"Taxo here." She could hear his drunkenness.

"I was worried."

"Who is this?" he laughed.

"Marta." She had to hold back from crying.

"Oh, Marta, my love. I am soooo sorry. Is it time for me to be back?"

"It's all right. I was only worried."

"Oh don't worry, my sweetest. I am well. No one was here to arrest me." He laughed. "Only people who appear to love me. How are you? Have you had a good day?"

"A wonderful day, Taxo. Now I'm going to dinner."

"Dinner, dinner, dinner. I've been eating and drinking all day. I can't eat any more."

"God damn it, I'm not asking you to eat dinner. I only want to know that you're safe." She hoped her anger covered her tears.

"You are so wonderful. So understanding. I love you, Marta. Marta who always cares for me."

When she got off the phone she breathed deeply, slowly. I will survive this, she repeated. This will not seem as bad after dinner and a little wine. Even if it felt lonely, she had to go out to eat.

She easily found the restaurant he had recommended. She had seen it in the afternoon, "La Grande Papa Frita, home of the best french fries in the world!"

The restaurant was high-ceilinged. Long rows of white-clothed tables on each side of a wide aisle made it look European. There were green-stemmed rhinewine glasses on each table. The floors were shellacked to a dark brown. There were ceiling lights and fans. Pillars ran down two sides. And high on the wall a shelf encircled the entire room holding hundreds of bottles of wine.

The room was half full. Waiters in red cotton jackets rushed with plates in their hands and towels on their arms. One whizzed by her.

"Find a seat, Señorita, any table, please."

She sat halfway into the large room facing the bar at the far end. Next to her was another solitary diner. A man. He nodded to her when she took her place and then went back to his food, large round-cut fried potatoes and what appeared to be a Wiener Schnitzel.

Rhine wine and Wiener Schnitzel. How much further did the German influence go?

She drank her wine, ate the delicious salad the waiter had prepared at her table. The entire meal would cost less than ten dollars. Where were the bad times the cab driver and Alonso spoke of? Where was it hidden? She looked around the dining room. It was filled to capacity. She checked her watch. It was eleven. The crowd was well-dressed. There were couples dining together as well as groups of men, groups of women, and even, like herself, women alone. Here and there people were in deep conversation. There was laughter. There were beaming, healthy, friendly faces all around her. Where were the torturers, she wondered, buttering her bread? Where were the men who had applied the prod to Taxo's testicles and heart?

Taxo arrived the next morning while she was still asleep. She didn't wake until his naked body was in under the sheets and he was insinuating himself, his hard member between her legs from behind. Her resolve melted as his hand caressed her sleep-soft body. He touched her clitoris and played gently around. She tried to turn toward him and he said, "No, this is for you." She let herself be cared for by him, played with, let him sink his fingers into her wetness, let herself hold back, hold back, until she couldn't anymore and she arched into his body.

Only when she turned to embrace him did she smell the left-over liquor, the cigarettes, the garlic. She felt disgusted with his kisses, but only for the moment. Soon the passion rose in her again, from her vulva, up through her body, as strong as it had been moments before. He entered her. She came almost immediately. He stayed in. She didn't become overly sensitive, instead he excited her over and over, until finally he groaned, "I love you, Marta, I will always love you. I belong in you. We are the best."

The morning sun came in through the open windows and touched his shoulder. She ran her fingers along the backlit hairs, across the chest to the black polka dot scars. He kissed her so softly she could almost not feel his lips and then he turned on his back.

"I'm sorry I didn't get here last night," he yawned. "Did you have a good dinner?"

The anger rose in her again. "Of course. I had Wiener Schnitzel, red wine from Mendoza, and your legendary french fries."

"Good, good, you did well without me."

"I can get along on my own. I did fine before I met you."

"Yes, but after a few years a person can forget."

She moved her head back and forth on the pillow. "No, I think being alone is like riding a bicycle. It can't be unlearned."

"So sad, my loved one?" His hand felt for her eyes to see if she was crying.

"I'm not so sad," she said, shaking his hand away, angry with herself for revealing it. "Just stating a fact."

"This isn't the end for us, Marta. We'll find our way through this. I still need you as much as ever."

Something struck her as wrong in that. For the first time she didn't like to hear of his need.

"I need you, too," she answered.

They went out into the morning street. The busses boomed by them so close that they had to hug the walls. The diesel exhaust blasted in Marta's face, making her cough and cover her mouth and nose. This was worse than Mexico City.

Taxo led the way, then disappeared into a doorway. She followed him into a gleaming marble and brass coffee bar. He ordered for the two of them, a plate of croissant and tea sandwiches. They sat in silence at a small glass-and-wrought-iron table. The waiter in his white starched jacket worked the cappuccino machine behind the bar, breaking the silence with the whooshing of forced air through milk. A group of workmen in their blue jackets came in noisily and took a table in the rear. A bus roared by the open wall sending billows of diesel smoke over their table. She fought the impulse to cover her mouth again.

Yet the food was delicious. She felt better as she ate. When they were half through, Taxo put his hand over hers.

"Let's try to talk about this. We've always talked."

Certainly, she thought. About his difficulties as an exile, his problems with not accepting political responsibility. His problems with publishing in a new country. Always about him they'd talked. "How did it go last night with Alicia and the children?"

"It was good." he said in a sad, almost apologetic voice. "It was good to see them and some of my friends. But don't make me ashamed of my pleasure."

"But I have no pleasure to offer in return," burst from her.

"You have our pleasure together," he said, misunderstanding. "You have the goodness you give me. You have the years of helping me through those bad times."

"Thank you, Taxo, that's kind of you to say."

He cupped her cheek in his big jointed hand. She hurt to the center of her with the pleasure of his touch.

"Come," he said. "I want to show you something. Last night the others got on me the way you always do about the politics. They said if I'm to stay I must deal with certain things."

The softness and beautiful familiarity of his hand grew as he spoke. It was like the clarity that soldiers and prisoners have spoken of the world taking on before they know they are to die.

Martha and Taxo walked along the streets holding hands. As they passed under a column of blooming jacaranda trees, their purple blossoms like gauze curtains above them, she walked with her head thrown back, not to miss a moment of their excruciating beauty. Pale lavender mist against a clear blue spring sky. When she told Taxo that she wanted to spread her arms and let the breeze float her up into them, he stopped and embraced her in the middle of the lunchtime crowd. No one said a thing as they stood wrapped in each other. People skirted them and went along their way. Martha laughed. She even found it in her to say, "This is a wonderful city. I see now why you love it so."

"We have lover's luck," he said. "The jacarandas only bloom here two weeks a year."

As they crossed the large Avenida Corrientes with the noisy crowd, Taxo put his arm around her shoulder and pulled her close, holding her almost too tightly. She looked up to see his face strained with a pain she had never seen before.

They reached a spot where a small church stood alone in the center of a concrete square. Taxo continued to grip her. He led her around the church, through the dark cool shadow it cast, and then they emerged on a rise below which a street opened out in the distance to a plaza. She recognized it from photos. It was the Plaza de Mayo. The royal palms with their heads tossed by the wind. On the far side, the pink colonial building, the Casa Rosada, the government building. In the center of the plaza was a haze of white, reminding her of the purple mist of the jacarandas.

"This is where I'm bringing you, Marta." His face relaxed slightly.

At the street they had to wait again for the light. When it changed, Taxo pulled her, running across. Even so the light changed back before they got to the safety of the plaza and the cars bore down on them, honking menacingly. But as soon as they entered the plaza, passed under the palms, a silence descended. It was as though the noise of the street was sucked into the silence, was deadened by it. They walked toward the white cloud. The whiteness circled. And then she saw that the cloud wasn't one at all, but women wearing handkerchiefs on their heads. They weren't the few women that she'd somehow always imagined, the women captured in the photographs in the Amnesty office, but hundreds upon hundreds of slowly moving women with *panuelos blancos* on their heads. In black crayons, the names of their children and the dates of their disappearances were written on the handkerchiefs. She stood still, unable to move. She was filled with an unimaginable sorrow. She thought of her mother after the war, wearing her refugee sign listing members of her family. The family that was never recovered. She thought of her mother without bitterness. She thought of what she could never understand of what her mother had been through that brought her to her cruelty. She thought of these women's losses. Their children who would probably never be regained no matter how often they circled this plaza, even though Alfonsin was in power. The world shook someplace with the unspeakable sadness of this, the world had to tremble someplace for this, had to be set slightly off its course.

A woman left the circle and came toward them. She walked to Taxo and embraced him. The woman's hair was gray under the head scarf. Martha watched her face on Taxo's breast, turned in Martha's direction. The woman's expression was of grief and ecstasy. Her cheeks were flood plains.

"Come," Taxo said to Martha. "Let's join them. She wants me to join." He was weeping.

Martha was sucked into the circle just as the noise of the street had been sucked into silence, only here in the center of the circle there was no silence, instead she found the soft murmur of the women's voices as they talked of everyday matters to each other, and their exclamations of pleasure when one or another noticed Taxo among them.

As they circled, a film crew caught sight of Taxo and one of the women called to them to say who Taxo was, and the cameraman came in close and began to film, following them, following Taxo as he relaxed and kept his arm, gently now, over Martha's shoulder, and every now and then introduced her as the woman who had seen him through the worst of his exile.

How I Came To Write This Story

My fiction usually begins in fact, and when I can't remember the truth or find it unsatisfying, I veer—or fly—into fantasy. My own Associate Peace Corps Director, a brilliant storyteller himself, has his own tale of how the Peace Corps in Guatemala was saved. I originally had thought to write a piece of creative nonfiction with his story in mind, but that resolve lasted about two paragraphs. This is fiction, plain and simple. On a thematic level, I wanted to explore the idea of where our sympathies lie in the stories we hear and tell. I think often a storyteller has one hero in mind, a reader or listener, another. I submit that there are other heroes lurking in our stories, unexplored characters worthy of our attention. In fiction, as in life, these people often go ignored, condemned to live and die without fanfare or even sympathy.

—Mark Brazaitis

MARK BRAZAITIS (Guatemala, 1990-1993) was born in East Cleveland, Ohio, and grew up in Washington, DC. In Guatemala, he worked with indigenous farmers, teaching grain-storage methods and promoting the use of natural pesticides. Mark has held reporting internships with the *Richmond Times-Dispatch* and *Detroit Free Press*. He has a B.A. in History from Harvard and an M.F.A. in Creative Writing from Bowling Green State University in Ohio. He is the author of *The River of Lost Voices: Stories from Guatemala*, winner of the 1998 Iowa Short Fiction Award. His fiction has appeared in *Western Humanities Review, Hawaii Review, Beloit Fiction Journal* and other literary magazines.

THE HEROES OF OUR STORIES

by Mark Brazaitis

I was about to leave Guatemala, which meant I finally got to hear Don Jorge Morales tell the story of how he saved the Peace Corps. It was something Don Jorge, an assistant Peace Corps director, told all his favorite volunteers. Sam, a volunteer who'd left the previous year, had written to tell me I couldn't leave Guatemala without hearing Don Jorge's story, and when I'd seen Don Jorge in the Peace Corps office a month before my close-of-service date and mentioned what Sam had said, Don Jorge promised to tell me the story during his final site visit.

Don Jorge and I sat on the verandah of the Hotel Mundo, located on the highway outside Santa Cruz Verapaz, my site, awaiting our fried chicken, beans, tortillas and Coca-Colas. He asked me how I was feeling about leaving. I still felt awkward speaking Spanish with him; he'd heard me at my worst, when he came to the Peace Corps training center to meet his new group of volunteers and during our brief interview I mumbled vaguely about what I thought of Guatemala a week after my arrival: "Bonito. Muy bueno. Me gusta mucho. Bonito." Two years later, I spoke Spanish more or less fluently, yet in Don Jorge's presence I always became nervous and retreated to my original ignorance. Although he never said, Don Jorge must have been disappointed with my lack of progress with Spanish and probably wondered if I wasn't the type of volunteer who spends most of his time with other North Americans. It was entirely possible to serve two years in Guatemala and not learn Spanish; there were two hundred Peace Corps volunteers in the country, in addition to countless tourists from the States and Europe, and every weekend—which for some volunteers began on Thursday and lasted until Tuesday—someone, somewhere, had a party, and Guatemalan busses could take you anywhere quickly and cheaply, if not always safely. But I wasn't the type to seek the company of other North Americans. I enjoyed being in Santa Cruz, talking on my doorstep with whomever passed by.

So when Don Jorge asked me how I felt about leaving, I might have told him about my ambivalence. I was, on one hand, anticipating a spectacular homecoming, an event with as much pomp and joy as a ticker tape parade, featuring proud parents, a devoted sister, and, I hoped, Elizabeth, my ex-girlfriend, her arms open with the promise of love renewed. I was anxious to be swept up in the jubilation of my return and I expected the celebration to last at least as long as the two years I had spent in Guatemala.

Yet on the other hand, I felt deeply unhappy about leaving my life and the people I knew, the neighbor girls who came to my house in their newly washed *cortes* to talk to me as I did the dishes and Pablo, the 18-year-old I played basketball with as the sky turned crimson and orange over San Cristóbal, the town to the west; the two of us bragged about our respective jump shots until it was so dark the ball smacked our chests with an unexpected jolt because we couldn't see it coming. And how could I give up my work when it consisted of riding my bicycle into mountains so full of trees and birds' songs that I hardly cared, when I arrived at a village, whether the farmers even showed up or, if they did, whether they would be interested in what I had to teach them.

This was a lot to explain to Don Jorge, and although I might have been able to unburden myself to a few close friends in town, I could not even intimate the scope of my feelings to him. My reply came straight from the mouth of the me who had existed two years ago, when Spanish was a strange and intimidating babble: "Estoy triste. Un poco. Pues, mucho. Pero, me gustaría ver mi familia. Pero, me gusta la gente aquí." Finally, shrugging, I said: "Es difícil."

Fortunately, Don Jorge wasn't too concerned about my state of mind, or perhaps he was but recognized the impossibility of drawing me out in Spanish. It was one of Don Jorge's rules: volunteers could speak to him only in Spanish, although he spoke at least three languages fluently, not only Spanish and English but Russian, which he told me he'd learned because in the 1970s it was unclear which superpower was going to be running Latin America. Today he had another agenda besides my ambivalence, and I was grateful. Finally, I got to hear the story of how Don Jorge saved the Peace Corps in Guatemala.

"Quieres la versión corta o la versión larga?" he asked.

I knew that no matter what I said, I would get the long version. And of course this is the one I wanted. "Larga."

Don Jorge smiled. He interlaced his fingers and placed his palms on his giant stomach.

The waitress put plates of chicken and beans in front of us and dropped a basket of tortillas in the center of the table. "Sus aguas ya vienen," she said, and a waiter soon shuffled out with our Cokes on a platter. Don Jorge smiled again. "Había una chica, una voluntaria," he said, and then effortlessly he slipped into English. Don Jorge had earned a dual Ph.D. in philosophy and agronomy at the University of Florida when he was in his twenties. "We'll call the volunteer Ellen. She lived in this part of the country. She may even have worked in a few of the *aldeas* you work in. She liked *las montañas*."

I imagined her with long, black, curly hair and tan skin, a taller and more carefree version of my ex-girlfriend.

"She liked the children in the *aldea* of Najquitob because they were very shy. They thought she wanted to steal them. When she came to teach in their school the first time, they ran away, even when the *maestro* tried to assure them that their visitor was friendly. They ran to their houses or into the *bosque*."

I could see her. She wasn't disturbed as most volunteers would've been; she somehow expected this reaction. Or perhaps she hadn't expected it but she could deal with it. She was carefree, cool, open to the possible.

"The second time she came, all the children ran away again, except for a pair of boys who stood at the back door of the school. If something went wrong, they could, of course, leave. But they were going to be men soon, so they must have decided they couldn't run away this time, not without a reason. She didn't come too close to them—she was on the opposite side of the school-room, standing with the *maestro*—and she asked them if they wanted to play *fútbol*. She had brought a ball.

"They played, the three of them, and their laughter must have reached the *bosque* because children began to appear from the trees. Only the boys, though. They all joined the game.

"The next time, the girls stayed, and she played *fútbol* with them. They trusted her. And she was like you, well, her Spanish was *más o menos*. And she didn't speak any Pokomchi, which all the children spoke better than Spanish. But of course this didn't matter much. What mattered is she cared about the children."

Yes, she cared, but she also found the conquest satisfying, proving false the children's nightmares of wicked white women, convincing them of how wonderful she was. A soccer ball and smiles were all she needed. Oh, and she was wonderful. She was like my ex-girlfriend, only taller and cooler. Prettier, too. Smarter even. A fitting heroine.

"She grew to love the *aldea* of Najquitob very much, not just the children but their parents. Everyone. She became close to the *maestro*, a man named Alfredo."

As Don Jorge ripped a chunk out of his chicken, I tried to picture Alfredo. I imagined him tall, but this would have been unlikely. He would have been *indígena*, and therefore shorter than Ellen—short, but handsome, with a square nose and black hair he kept a little long. He had one silver tooth.

"Not too long after they met, Ellen and Alfredo became *novios*. This, of course, is fine." He paused to gaze at me. "Did you ever have a Guatemalan *novia*?"

I shook my head, although this wasn't entirely true. But how could I explain one long night at Finca de la Plata?

"Well, they don't usually work, these relationships. Too many differences. And Alfredo was *muy celoso*, like many Guatemalans. And like many gringas, Ellen didn't understand his jealousy. They would fight before school and Ellen would take long walks in the *bosque*. There are many myths about the *bosque*. Do you know the story of Mamamun and the Cannibal?"

I did: Mamamun is a king of the Pokomchis, but he allows his daughter to escape into the forest and she is eaten by the Cannibal, who is then devoured by a flock of blood-thirsty macaws.

"And there are other things in the *bosque* besides myths. Like guerrillas. And where guerrillas go, soldiers follow."

I pictured Ellen walking through the thick forest, her feet crunching the ground, the loudest sound for kilometers. There was a chirping of birds, a rustling of squirrels.

"But for a long time Ellen was lucky. She didn't meet anyone in the *bosque*. And of course she didn't walk in the *bosque* all the time. She and Alfredo had some good times together, I suspect. Some very good times." Don Jorge smiled. He'd been an assistant director for more than 20 years, and he had seen volunteers come and go, including, no doubt, many attractive female volunteers.

Gringitas chulas. I wondered how many times he'd lusted in his heart. I wondered if his lust had ever been reciprocated. Don Jorge was a plump man with white hair, but his face was square and his jaw firm.

"Eventually Ellen did not work anywhere but the village where Alfredo was the *maestro*. But this is all right. Some volunteers don't work at all, no?"

I nodded.

"Ellen was *un tipo raro*. She didn't like to come to the regional meetings. She didn't even come to her mid-service conference."

I knew what her fellow volunteers had thought of her. Snob. Thinks she's Guatemalan. But Ellen didn't care. She had her *novio*, her life in the village. She had her *bosque*. What did she need with a bunch of slack North Americans?

"One day Ellen had a fight with Alfredo, a big fight in front of all the children. She walked into the *bosque*. She walked a long way. She was furious. But on this particular day it wasn't safe to walk in the *bosque*."

I pictured a jaguar stalking her. A troop of rabid monkeys leaping on her. A snake wrapping around her ankle.

"Soldiers," Don Jorge said, and he took a sip of his Coke.

I saw Ellen in the forest, sitting on a log, already having forgiven Alfredo. She missed him and had forgotten their argument, and she knew he had as well. He was waiting for her, prepared to call off class early in order to take her back to his house—a two-room adobe hut with a dirt floor—and make love to her on his *petate* as the chickens babbled outside the window.

But soldiers, hidden behind fallen pine trees, had seen her and suspected the worst: a guerrilla. The lieutenant gave the order and they surrounded her quickly.

But then she would have showed them her passport and been released.

"The soldiers surrounded her. They thought she was a guerrilla, of course. Who else walks alone in the *bosque*? They ordered her to lie on her stomach. The group of soldiers had no official leader. Their lieutenant was sick, recovering from some venereal disease in a hospital in Cobán." Don Jorge smiled. "These lieutenants are as careless with their bodies as they are with their guns. Without their lieutenant, the soldiers were on their own. They were all young boys; the oldest was maybe eighteen. He was the leader. He asked Ellen her name, and she was trembling so much she had to repeat it three times. He asked her for identification, but she didn't have any. That's why we tell all the volunteers: always bring your passport wherever you go. They figured no ID was proof that she was a guerrilla. And they talked among themselves about what they should do."

As Don Jorge chewed on his food, I saw Ellen on the forest floor, her arms and legs spread as if in the middle of a jumping jack, her heart firing like a machine gun. She was wearing blue jeans and a white blouse. She hadn't expected the fight with Alfredo. She'd expected him to call off class early so they could retreat to his adobe hut and make love on his *petate*. She hadn't expected to be surrounded by soldiers, one wandering trigger finger away from death.

"They could have done terrible things to her. Raped her. Many soldiers would have. It's sort of expected. To be a woman guerrilla and to be caught...death would be kinder. But these soldiers were trying to do what was right, so they interrogated her. She tried to explain who she was, but her Spanish was, like I said, *más o menos*. *Pues, tal vez peor que más or menos*. And the soldiers were all *indígenas*. They had their own language and didn't speak or understand Spanish very well anyway."

As Don Jorge excused himself to use the bathroom, I saw Ellen desperately trying to communicate, her voice wild with nervousness and her accent horrible. I saw what she saw: soldiers looking at her with wide, serious, uncomprehending eyes. The soldiers had their assault rifles pointed at her as if she were a beast about to burst from a cage. I wondered if she had wet her pants. But I didn't think so. Ellen was terrified, but cool.

Like most volunteers, I'd had encounters with soldiers. They frequently stopped busses, ordering the men to step off, telling us to place our hands against the side of the bus so they could pound our pants. What were they expecting to find? Guns? Grenades? Did guerrillas even take buses? I had never been as nervous as when, a year into my Peace Corps service, I stepped off a bus and a 14-year-old soldier pointed his black assault rifle at me and grinned as if I were his enemy. Yet I had a certain sympathy for soldiers. I worked with many men who, as boys, had been recruited forcefully off their farms. Most of the men never spoke to me about their soldiering days, although about other matters we talked freely and jokingly.

On one occasion, though, Juan Valey Lopez, a *representante agrícola* who worked with me in the village of Chilocom every Friday, asked me if in the United States boys were kidnapped and impressed into the army. I told him no, and he looked at me with his head half-cocked and a low, incredulous growl escaping his lips.

"Es la verdad," I said. "En serio."

He was again disbelieving when I told him that men, and even women, actually volunteered to serve in the military. He wondered how this could be, and he told me about his own days in the army, ten years before. He said he'd been on a march in Salamá, a dry region of the country south of Santa Cruz, and his unit had been ambushed by guerrillas. The soldier in front of him was immediately gunned down.

"He wasn't wearing a helmet," Juan said, as if this detail explained why the soldier had died.

In succeeding months, Juan told me more about his experiences, and at the core of his stories—often prosaic tales of his life at the military base, or *la zona*—I always had a sense of the unrelenting terror he must have felt. He smiled only when he told me about the impromptu hunting expedition he and his fellow soldiers embarked on in the jungles of the Petén, slipping laughingly through the trees in pursuit of jaguar and deer.

Don Jorge returned. "Sigo?" he asked.

"Por favor."

"They had an interrogation. A futile interrogation." Don Jorge put a spoonful of beans in his mouth. I pictured the chief inquisitor, the eighteen-year-old soldier, a short, *indígena* man with a faint dab of a mustache, in appearance a little like Ellen's boyfriend Alfredo. And I imagined a comic inquisition:

- What are you doing here?
- Walking.
- But before?
- Before?
- Before.
- Before when?
- Before here.
- Here?
- Here.
- But before?
- Before?
- Where?

- Here.
- Before here?
- Where?
- Here.

I wondered if Ellen had found any humor in this fumbling inquisition, but even though she was cool, she couldn't have thought any of it funny. I saw her beginning to tremble, the veins on her neck and arms glowing a brilliant blue beneath her tan skin. I imagined her losing her entire Spanish vocabulary, as if it were a glass of water she had spilled, and wanting only to be home in New York City, sidestepping a homeless man. I imagined the inquisition continuing, and she being unable to remember even a single Spanish word.

"They interviewed her a long time, but they didn't discover anything. Like I said, none of them spoke Spanish well. They concluded she was a guerrilla because they didn't understand her and she was very nervous. They decided to take her to the military base in Cobán. They didn't have handcuffs, so they tied her hands with vines."

They were scared soldiers, adrift without their lieutenant, and they tied her hands tight. Her fingers turned pure white, like sticks of dry ice. She was too frightened to complain. They led her into the truck and had her sit on the floor. In frustration and fear, she pissed her pants. The soldiers felt some sympathy for her—perhaps in a gesture of goodwill they offered her sips from their canteens—but they had to do what was right. They wanted to make their lieutenant proud.

"She was put in a cell in the prison section of the military base in Cobán, and the soldiers reported to the warden of the prison and told him what had happened."

I pictured the soldiers patting each other on the back, congratulating themselves on a job well done. Perhaps they had treated themselves to beer that night, bragging in a cheap cantina. Probably, though, they preferred soda and spent the evening sipping warm Coca-Colas while sitting on wobbly wood stools in a *tienda*.

"And the warden didn't tell anyone. He heard 'guerrilla' from the soldiers, and he didn't think she was a North American. Ellen was rather dark-skinned, so it was understandable why the soldiers didn't suspect she was from the United States. And the warden never looked at the prisoners anymore. He was an old man, near retirement. So Ellen was left in the prison, and no one outside of it knew where she was."

I imagined Ellen in her cell. Had they given her clothes? Not yet. She was still in her jeans and blouse, afraid of removing her wet underwear, worried about who might be watching. She stared at the four walls around her, reading the hardly intelligible scratchings in Spanish. No, she couldn't concentrate. Her eyes scanned the walls wildly, unable to fix on any one piece of graffiti. She sat on the floor, huddled into herself, cursing and praying.

"The Peace Corps learned she was missing, and soon all the newspapers had stories about her. Front page photographs. But the photographs were from her passport, and like everyone says, no one looks like their passport photo. So even if the soldiers saw the paper, they wouldn't have recognized her. And of course they couldn't read."

The soldiers, I suspected, didn't remain in Cobán long enough to see the newspaper. Early the next morning, they were probably sent on another mission, into other mountains, to hunt real guerrillas.

"The Guatemalan military blamed the guerrillas. They said the guerrillas had kidnapped her. They even produced a witness, someone in the town she lived in, who said Ellen had been taken away by an angry *indígena* man. This was probably Alfredo, but the army didn't bother following up. The U.S. Embassy in Guatemala put all its intelligence officers on the case, but they had to work with the Guatemalan military. Besides, everyone they interviewed had a different story. It's like this with Guatemalans. If we don't know the truth, we make up a story.

"There was upheaval in the Peace Corps office. All volunteers were recalled from their sites. They were put up in a very nice hotel in the capital, El Camino, and they had a good time. They swam and played tennis.

"A week later, the Peace Corps received a call from a general in the base in Cobán. He had been doing a tour of the military prison, a coincidence, and the warden of the prison wanted to show off his prize prisoner, a woman guerrilla. It was Ellen."

I saw Ellen in prison garb, an off-white gown, but still wearing her hiking boots. Her hair was wild. She hadn't been able to take a bath. They'd only given her a bucket of cold water every other afternoon to wash herself. I saw the general stare into the cell and see Ellen's skin, the tan having receded from it during her captivity.

How pale, the general would have thought. How much like a gringa. Why, she is a gringa. She's *the* gringa.

"And so she was discovered. And of course the Embassy was furious. No, more than furious. The U.S. Ambassador, a very nice lady named Mrs. Capra, called the Guatemalan military all kinds of names and said she would pull Peace Corps out of the country unless the president of Guatemala apologized to her in person.

"This was very decisive talk from a very decisive woman. But this isn't the way to talk to a Guatemalan. You don't give ultimatums to a proud man. The president, a general named Lucas Fernández, did what he thought was necessary. He punished those who were responsible for what had happened to Ellen. But Mrs. Capra wasn't satisfied. She wanted an apology. But Presidente Fernández wasn't going to give her one. And she was going to cancel the Peace Corps. And so Presidente Fernández said, Let them go.

"But if Peace Corps was to go home, many fine and caring young men and women—the volunteers—would go home too. They didn't want to go home. They wanted to go back to their sites, where they had left their friends and their work. They liked Guatemala. And I must admit I liked my job too. If Peace Corps had left, I wouldn't have known what to do. Even then, I was an old man. My three fellow assistant directors felt the same way. They all came to me, all the volunteers and the assistant directors and even the secretaries in the Peace Corps office and even the man who cleaned the Peace Corps office three nights a week, all of these people came to me and said, 'Don Jorge, help us. Help us keep the Peace Corps.'

"I had a friend from when I played soccer years ago. His name was Reginaldo Reyes, and he was the minister of Sports and Recreation in the administration of Presidente Fernández. I called up my old friend Reginaldo and explained the situation and he said he would talk to Presidente Fernández. Well, he did talk to him and he told me, 'You know, Jorge, the presidente cannot apologize to a woman.' And I said, 'I know,' and so I believed the Peace Corps was lost. But I told my friend, 'Isn't there something we can do?' My friend said, 'I'll think about it.'

"The next day, he called me and said, 'How much does this mean to you, Jorge?' And I said, 'It means a lot to me and many other people.' And he said, 'As you know, Presidente Fernández will never apologize to this woman. He has had the offenders punished. What more does he need to do? This woman wants him to come to her and say, "I'm sorry"? No, this will never happen.' My friend paused and said, 'How bold are you, Jorge?' I didn't know how to answer, but then he said, 'Many people don't know that Presidente Fernández has an older brother who looks very much like him. And of course no gringo could tell them apart. To gringos, we are all dark-haired and dark-skinned. And anyway, I know that señora Capra has met Presidente Fernández only once.'

"I didn't know what he was trying to tell me at first, but then I said, 'The brother will stand in for Presidente Fernández?' And my friend the Minister of Sports and Recreation said, 'Only if you are very bold, Jorge, and very smart.' And he gave me the name and address of Presidente Fernández's brother and concluded our conversation by saying, '*Dios te bendiga.* I know absolutely nothing, and I will deny I ever spoke to you.'

"Presidente Fernández's brother lived in *zona cuatro*, in a *tienda* in the bus terminal. He sold backpacks. He was as tall and big-chested as Presidente Fernández, but much drunker. At least he seemed drunk. It was 10 o'clock in the morning when I saw him, and he was bare-chested, singing songs and selling his backpacks for too little. I myself couldn't resist the inexpensive prices. I bought two backpacks for my daughters, and I was considering buying one for my wife when I remembered my mission. Of course, it seemed futile. But then, what did I have to lose? If Peace Corps left the country, I would be out of a job. And many of my friends, too. And all the volunteers. No, I didn't have much to lose.

"I said, 'Señor Fernández, I have a special task for you, and I will pay you a lot of money.' This seemed to interest him, although he wore a certain expression, a cockeyed look, that indicated he didn't trust me. I said, 'It is somewhat complicated, and it will mean impersonating your brother.' Señor Fernández belched and said, 'I hate my brother. Can I make him look like a fool?'

"I told señor Fernández what I had in mind, and he agreed, although he was a little disappointed because he could not make his brother look like a fool. After my explanation, he said, 'You wouldn't want to buy another backpack?' Well, I couldn't resist— half price! I bought one for my wife and one for myself.

"Then I told him I'd be back. I went to a phone in the terminal, and I placed a call to the Embassy. I talked to security, and then for a long time to Mr. Abrams from intelligence, and then to the Ambassador herself. I told her that I'd talked to the president through one of his ministers and that he'd agreed to make the apology in person, but that there were a couple of conditions. First, he insisted that there be only three people in the room—himself, the Ambassador and me, to act as translator. The Ambassador's Spanish was atrocious—far worse than...umm, very bad I mean. Second, he asked that the Ambassador never mention his apology to anyone, never even bring it up in private when they met on other occasions. Because if she tried to reminisce about it with him, he would not just ignore her but tell her she was crazy. 'It is, señora embajadora, a difficult thing Presidente Fernández is doing, and he is doing it only because of his immense love of and respect for the Peace Corps.' The Ambassador listened to what I'd said very intently, and after a few questions to clarify what she'd heard, she said, 'I understand. I will meet you in the living room of my residence at nine p.m. tonight.'

"I returned to find Presidente Fernández's brother nipping from a bottle of orange liquid and conceding to the demand of a bulk price by a teacher who had brought her entire fifth-grade class to buy backpacks. I sat in señor Fernández's *tienda* until he'd sold his entire stock. It was about four o'clock when we left the bus terminal.

"The clothes señor Fernández was wearing were not exactly presidential, which meant we had to go shopping. Because, like his brother, señor Fernández was very tall—and we Guatemalans, as you know, tend to be very short—it was impossible to find him clothes in any of the department stores in the capital. The sales clerks would not even bother to help us; they would just shake their heads and tell us to see a tailor. Well, a tailor couldn't make a suit in five hours. I was desperate. I even thought of calling my friend, the Minister of Sports and Recreation, to ask him if there wasn't some way to steal one of Presidente Fernández's suits.

"But then I had an idea. I decided to take señor Fernández to *Ropa Americana*. There is a big distributor on *8 Avenida*—you must know it, it's near the Monja Blanca bus terminal. Yes, I know most of the used clothing sold in such stores are T-shirts and blue jeans, hardly presidential attire, but every once in a while they'll sell a Ralph Lauren polo shirt or even a Calvin Klein suit—amazing what rich people in the States give away. And so I dragged señor Fernández into *Ropa Americana*, and we stepped past the women pillaging the piles of T-shirts on the floor and walked to the rack of clothes in back. Oh, and we were lucky. There was a suit—an Arnold Palmer-designed suit. He is a golfer, this Arnold Palmer, right? But what a suit! It was a little too big even for señor Fernández, but it would do. I myself could lend señor Fernández a tie, socks, even shoes since I have very big feet. But a dress shirt was a problem, and I looked frantically in the store for a dress shirt big enough to accommodate señor Fernández. No luck. I took him to two more *Ropa Americana* stores, and we were unsuccessful. I couldn't believe it. I was going to come this close and not be able to proceed.

"Well, a desperate man won't surrender until absolutely forced to, and I was not through thinking up a solution to the shirt problem. But first I had to meet señor Fernández's demands for food, so I took him to my house and introduced him to my wife and daughters, without telling them what I planned to do. We ate dinner and afterwards, señor Fernández tried to buy the backpacks back from my daughters. I was actually hoping they would sell them back to him because when the Peace Corps left Guatemala, I wouldn't have a job and we wouldn't be able to afford backpacks or anything else.

"While señor Fernández was negotiating with my daughters, I went to my office in the back of my house to think about the shirt problem. I considered a T-shirt, but my own were far too small for señor Fernández—I was a thinner man then, and as I said, señor Fernández was very tall; my shirt wouldn't have covered his belly button. I thought for a long time, and I watched in agony as the clock ticked away. It was already eight o'clock, and the drive to the Ambassador's would take 15 minutes. I was desperate, but my mind was blank. It was 8:30, and I decided he would go without a shirt—I would simply explain to the Ambassador that like their working-class counterparts, Guatemalan presidents often went shirtless, even on formal occasions. I called señor Fernández into my office, and he brought in the two backpacks—he'd bought them back from my daughters at twice the price I'd paid him. I dressed him hurriedly in his suit, socks and shoes. I slicked back his fine black hair. He would have looked truly presidential if it weren't for his lack of a shirt. But what could I do?

"We walked to the door, waving good-bye to my daughters—they were busy counting their money, what businesswomen even then—and then said good-bye to my wife, who gave me a funny look when she saw señor Fernández in a suit without a shirt. I shrugged and we walked outside. We were walking down the path to the car when I saw a bag of limestone on the ground. My wife had been using it to fertilize some tomato plants. It was a gift from heaven! I told señor Fernández to stop a second, lifted up his tie and dusted his chest with limestone. His chest became quite white, as white as the crispest, cleanest dress shirt. We were in luck.

"I drove rapidly through the streets, not a usual tactic for most drivers in the capital, but for me a new experience. I hit 16 straight green lights before reaching a stop sign. Well, this was all señor Fernández needed. He jumped out of the car and started running. I couldn't believe it.

"I left the car in the middle of the street and chased him. He didn't go very far, only half a block to Cantina Real, where he downed two *frascos* of the same kind of orange liquid I'd seen him drinking before. It was a while before I had wind enough to curse him. He was surprised at my anger and said he simply needed a little fortification before embarking on his meeting with the Ambassador. 'No tengas pena, vos,' he said. 'It's mango juice.' He allowed me a sip from another *frasco*, and it was quite tasty, actually.

"Although it may have been mango juice, it produced in señor Fernández a reaction much like drunkenness. As we walked back to the car, he began to sing. I must admit, he had a very fine voice, but I wasn't in the mood to hear it just then. I told him to shut up and he said, 'Don't speak to your president like that' and laughed.

"We parked in the driveway of the Ambassador's residence and were escorted inside by a pair of marines. They asked us to be seated on the couch and then left. A few minutes later, the ambassador entered. We stood. The Ambassador was about 45 years old and widowed (her husband had been an oil magnate and had contributed a great deal to President Reagan's first campaign). Her hair was blond with streaks of gray. She said, 'Sit down, gentlemen,' and we did. She sat in a leather chair across from us. 'I'm glad you're here, and since we all know why we're here, this should not take too much time.' To señor Fernández, I translated this, 'Let's make this quick.'

"'I know President Fernández is aware of the serious nature of what has taken place. The United States is deeply concerned and needs confirmation that President Fernández feels this sort of thing is loathsome and abhorrent. An apology is all I ask, in the name of my country.'

"I turned to señor Fernández and said, 'OK, amigo, this is it. All you have to do is apologize. All will be forgiven. We'll stand up and walk out of here and I'll treat you to a dozen bottles of mango juice.'

"Señor Fernández looked at the Ambassador and said, 'Tus ojos son más bonitos que el mar.' I was momentarily terrified. Had the Ambassador understood? *Gracias a dios* no because she turned to me with a serious look, waiting for my translation. 'He says he is deeply sorry about what has taken place.'

"Señor Fernández continued. 'Tus labios son más ricos que un montón de cerezas.'

"Again the Ambassador looked at me, and I said, 'He assures you that this sort of incident will never happen again.'

"'Well,' the Ambassador said, standing, 'I think we're finished here, gentlemen. Thank you for your time and graciousness. Please assure the president that I will abide by the terms of our agreement.'

"I thanked the Ambassador, but señor Fernández didn't feel any special urgency to leave. He turned to me and said, 'Tell the Ambassador I would like to sing for her.' I shook my head. 'I will not leave until I sing for her,' he said. I begged him to be reasonable. I promised him a hundred bottles of mango juice, but I couldn't convince him.

"I suddenly realized the gravity of what I'd done and I imagined the worst: the Ambassador discovering my scam, contacting the real Presidente Fernández, me being thrown in jail and Peace Corps leaving Guatemala anyway. But what could I do now? Señor Fernández began warming up his voice, humming ever so softly.

"'Señora embajadora,' I said, 'it would give the president of Guatemala a great deal of pleasure to sing a song for you. I know this may strike you as a little unusual, but it is something he likes to do for people he wants to honor.'

"The Ambassador looked surprised, but then sat down again and said, 'Please tell the president I would be honored to hear him sing.'

"I turned to señor Fernández and said, 'Pick a short song.'

"Señor Fernández sang. Oh, how he sang—with a booming voice. I must admit he had some talent. By the end of his third song, even I was enjoying myself and the Ambassador was positively enthralled. By the end of his fourth song, she was sitting on the edge of her seat. By the end of the sixth, she was crying. By the end of the eighth, she was laughing and crying at the same time.

"When señor Fernández finished, the Ambassador said, 'Please ask the president if he likes to dance?' Dutifully, I translated her question and señor Fernández of course replied in the positive, and so the Ambassador went to a stereo in the corner and put on some music—an old Frank Sinatra album—and the two of them started dancing. I couldn't imagine what she thought of his shirt, or his lack of a shirt, but whatever she thought, she didn't say a thing. They danced and danced. The last time I looked at my watch it was almost two in the morning.

"The next thing I knew a maid was shaking me by the shoulder and offering me some coffee. The room was full of light. I looked at my watch: seven a.m. I panicked. I said, 'Where is señor Fernández, I mean Presidente Fernández?' The maid gave me a knowing look and winked. A few minutes later, she came out with a breakfast of eggs, French toast, waffles and strawberries. I shouldn't have been hungry, but I realized this might be my last good meal, so I ate everything. Delicious.

"It was about eight o'clock when señor Fernández strolled into the living room. He was wearing a bathrobe. I said, 'Where's the Ambassador?' and he said, 'Still sleeping, vos. It was a very long night.' And he grinned like he'd been handed a shoe box full of gold.

"I was angry and amazed at the same time, but what could I do? I wondered how long he would insist on continuing this charade. But he surprised me. He said, 'We better go now, vos, or I'll be late for work.' Grateful and relieved, I was ready to push him out the door, but he wanted me to take dictation on a good-bye note to the Ambassador. I did, adding to my translation of his flowery praises a reminder to the Ambassador that the previous night must remain entirely confidential, and must never even be mentioned between the two of them. Señor Fernández signed the note 'Fernando.'

"'Fernando?' I asked him. He blushed and said, 'This is what she called me during our love.'

"I drove him back to his *tienda*, and when I went to pay him, he said, 'Forget it, vos,' and then kissed me on the forehead like a priest.

"I waited for disaster. I even considered taking my family on a month-long holiday to Costa Rica, a wait-and-see exile. But that afternoon, word came that Peace Corps would remain in Guatemala. The Ambassador was quoted in the press release as saying, 'Thanks to the kind support of the people of Guatemala, Peace Corps will continue dedicating itself to improving the future of this vibrant and virile nation.' I couldn't help but smile over the Ambassador's word choice.

"A week later, the government of Presidente Fernández was toppled in a military coup and Presidente Fernández was forced to flee the country. A year later, the Ambassador returned to the States to help Reagan with his re-election campaign. She was given a job in the Department of Energy during Reagan's second term.

"And Peace Corps remains in Guatemala."

Don Jorge smiled. "There it is." He drank the last of his Coca-Cola.

I smiled, enthralled. As he was waving for the check, I asked, "What happened to Ellen?"

"She finished her Peace Corps service in another country, I think the Dominican Republic. The funny part about her story is that she was, in truth, helping the guerrillas. A few months after her ordeal, the army raided her boyfriend's house. They found a cache of explosives from the United States. I have no idea how they could have gotten to Guatemala, but someone had taken quite a bit of time to translate the instructions. Peace Corps compared the handwriting to Ellen's and of course it was the same. So she knew Spanish better than we ever thought! We never told the Guatemalan government. If we had, there would have been no more Peace Corps in Guatemala."

"Then the soldiers were right all along," I said. "Right about Ellen."

"Yes, they were," Don Jorge said, leaving enough money on the table to cover the bill, then standing. "Yes, they were right. But of course they were killed. Presidente Fernández had them killed. This, of course, should have been enough. But Americans always want apologies, too. Words are so meaningful to you people. I don't understand it."

How I Came To Write This Story

This story started as a chapter in a novel in which a woman and her husband arrive in Ethiopia, not as Peace Corps Volunteers, but with vague notions of "doing good." In the early drafts of "Sun", the girl who appears in the middle of the night is a stranger, but I realized the incident was meaningless unless the narrator had something at stake in terms of this girl. When she became somebody the narrator knew and cared about, the story taught me something of the complicity we all must acknowledge when we bring change to other people's lives. Every action has consequences that can't be anticipated, that ricochet at unplotted angles in other cultures: giving a small, inappropriate gift, telling a shocking personal story to a young girl, reinforcing a dream without fully understanding the context. Flannery O'Connor said that "it is the extreme situation that best reveals what we are essentially." By the end of "Sun", the narrator is caught in a twilight zone between cultures. I don't really know if she is directly responsible for Sun's death, but I couldn't avoid making clear the power of her influence.

—Kathleen Coskran

KATHLEEN COSKRAN (Ethiopia, 1965-1967) grew up in Marietta, Georgia and taught English and math in Addis Ababa and Dilla, Ethiopia. She met her husband, Chuck, on a summer vaccination project in western Ethiopia, and spent two years in Kenya where he was on Peace Corps staff. Kathleen has taught fiction writing at the University of Minnesota and Hamline University and is currently the principal of Lake Country School in Minneapolis. In 1988 her collection of short stories, *The High Price of Everything*, won a Minnesota Book Award and she has received numerous other awards including a fellowship from the National Endowment for the Arts. She is the co-editor (with C. W. Truesdale) of *Tanzania on Tuesday: Writings by American Women Abroad,* which received a Minnesota Book Award. A mother of a daughter, two sons, and two foster sons from Ethiopia, she currently lives in Minneapolis with her husband.

SUN

by Kathleen Coskran

I was there as an appendage to my husband at that time—Dr. H.
Scott Hightower. Scotty was photogenic and smart and I loved
looking at him, but the marriage pretty much ended the day we
landed in Ethiopia, although it took us another five years to admit
it. We'd been in Addis Ababa exactly twelve hours when we lost
our daughter—my version. Just a miscarriage, his version. I was
six months along. A girl. Elizabeth. You've got to get over it, Scotty
said.

I took pictures after that—which is what I do, I'm a photographer—and I collected a few phone numbers of embassy wives
and the wives of Scotty's colleagues, but I was too shy or
unsophisticated or something—too sad maybe—to make friends.
I spent my time peering through my lens, to mask my failure as a
woman, to see how other women lived.

I became involved with the Harem Sewing Circle the day I
stopped two women swathed in chiffon from ankle to chin bone
and asked if I could take their picture. The younger woman spoke
some English and extended a slim hand to introduce herself.
"Good morning, missus. This is my mother. She is Anisa. I am…"

I didn't catch her name—it was all consonants. When I tried
to say it, she laughed and repeated it, but I couldn't get it. I finally
asked her what it meant.

She inclined her head like a gazelle, smooth-eyed and elegant
in her modesty, and said, "My name is meaning sun."

I lowered my camera. "Sun. It's a wonderful name for you.
Perfect. May I call you Sun?"

She laughed and clapped her hands. "Oh, yes, I like it. Sun! I am Sun," she said, savoring the taste of the English word that named her. "I am Sun." She covered her head with her scarf and turned her luminous eyes away from her mother who was ordering off a bedraggled boy hanging on the compound gate across the road. "You are having mini for Sun?" she whispered to me.

"Mini?"

"This," she said and reached in her skirts to pull out a wadded-up magazine photo of a white girl in a miniskirt.

"No," I said. "I have nothing like that. I'm too fat for those skirts."

She took my hand and pressed it against her beautiful face. "Sun wants a mini," she said.

When I told Scotty about Sun and her mother, he said I shouldn't be taking pictures of strangers. "Especially Muslims," he said. "They believe their soul is captured in the black box of your camera. Stay away from them."

"Oh, come on. That's what I do—and besides, they liked me. They invited me for coffee. They live just across the road." I'd spent the afternoon photographing Sun, Anisa, Anisa's four sisters, and a flock of children. The women were round and small-featured in bright silks and chiffons that covered every part of their bodies except for their cameo faces and exquisite hands and feet. Only the teenaged girls like Sun let their scarves fall from their soft hair. They showed a little ankle and neck, but not much.

There were men around too, or boys at least: a couple of gangly sons played ping-pong on a plank in the front of the compound with their friends who puffed on unfiltered cigarettes and gaped at Sun and her sisters and cousins. The girls glanced furtively at the boys and once, when Sun spent too much time talking to one of her brother's friends, her mother snapped at her and Sun hurried away to perform some task.

"They remind me of Mama's quilting group—everybody eating, talking, and stitching away, kids running in and out. They're great, kind of a harem/sewing circle combo. The oldest girl, Sun, is crazy to have a miniskirt."

Scotty took a long, significant draw on his pipe and let his mouth sag into his picture-taking frown. "We didn't travel ten thousand miles to socialize with those people. You don't belong over there."

"They've invited me for every Friday. Maybe I'll get a picture of Sun swaddled in purple veils from the waist up and wearing a mini that barely reaches her thighs." I didn't mean it. I just said it to get a rise out of Scotty.

He put down the journal he was reading and parted his lips as if he were smiling. "Don't joke about things you don't understand."

"You mean that you don't understand."

He closed the journal, lined it up with the others on the coffee table, and rose slowly. He was oddly handsome, my first husband, blond and sharp-boned, but so ascetic you wanted to pinch him. "Don't get involved and we'll survive Ethiopia," he said and nodded to me as if we were distant acquaintances. "I'm going to bed."

A minute later I heard him filling a glass of water in the bathroom. Two pills and straight to sleep—his routine since the full burden of a day at Haile Selassie Hospital had descended on him. Fall into bed like a dead man. "I want to do more than survive," I shouted, but he didn't hear me. It was eight-fifteen. He'd had a hard day, lost an entire family to typhus, mother, father, baby boy, all dead, and he had two old men with rabies tied to their beds, going mad side by side. "They won't survive their treatment," he'd said at dinner. "Rabies, for God's sake."

A week later a bomb at the Empire Cinema interrupted "Zorba the Greek" and sent shrapnel into the leg and lap of the Ambassador's wife. A census of American residents in Addis was taken the next week and burglar alarms issued to everybody. Semi-official personnel like us received the scaled-down version: a pulsating siren activated by two buttons, one installed on the wall in the master bedroom and the other on an exterior wall, available to Abebe, our night watchman. The idea was that if someone came over the compound wall, Abebe would alert us by pressing the outside button; if something happened inside the house, Scotty or I would push our button.

"I do like that button over the bed," I said the day it was installed. I was at the dining room table sorting contact sheets. When Scotty didn't respond, I looked up to see if he was listening.

He was at the other end of the sitting room, hunched over his pipe and some fine-print journal.

I raised my voice. "Push that buzzer and a man comes running. It's perfect."

He peered into the bowl of his unlit pipe, then tapped it firmly on his knee as if he were trying to dislodge something. I waited. My husband wasn't one to speak and act simultaneously. "The whole thing's stupid," he said finally. "We don't need a burglar alarm."

"Yeah," I said, "I could push that button and get pregnant by and by."

He scraped the inside of the pipe bowl with the nail of his little finger, making tiny tick tick ticking sounds.

"I said, 'I could push that button...'"

"I heard what you said." He let the pipe fall to his lap and wearily raised his head. "I wish you'd just give it up, Sissy. You've failed every fertility test known to medical science."

I shrugged, as if it didn't matter, as if I hadn't actually been pregnant twice before, as if I were only making small talk, and went back to the proofs on the table. I circled a picture of Sun and me leaning against each other, giggling. The picture was slightly out of focus and we were both tilted backwards, but I liked it. It was Anisa's first try at photography and the only picture in my Harem Sewing Circle series that included me.

Abebe sounded the alarm the third day it was in operation. I was jerked out of bed by the undulating blast just past midnight and found myself crouched in an attack position in the middle of the bedroom. "God, it's that buzzer," I said.

Scotty was staggering around the other side of the bed ranting, "No...no...no...no." He was in the middle of one of his night hallucinations, induced, I thought, by his dependence on sleeping pills. He shuddered as the whine wavered through the room again.

"It's nothing," I said. "Abebe with a new toy. Go back to bed. I'll see what he's up to."

"No, I'll go," he said and stumbled past me.

I pumped our side of the buzzer to let the watchman know we were coming, threw on my bathrobe and went after Scotty. I caught up with him in the middle of the compound, shouting at Abebe. Abebe was yelling back in Amharic and inching his way towards the back wall of the compound, trying to get Scotty to follow him.

"Christ, what's he saying?"

"I don't know."

We groped behind him in the dark. The watchman stopped once or twice to shine the flashlight in our eyes and say, "Come, come."

I could hear something in the garbage pit. "Listen."

The hole was alive with rustling and squealing—some animal. A bottle hit a can somewhere below, but Abebe stopped ten feet from the dump, blinded us with his light again, then panned the sky. "Evil spirits," he whispered in Amharic. "Stay back."

Scotty raised his arm to the get the light out of his eyes. "Give me that torch," he shouted, but I got to the old man first. I took the flashlight and advanced on the writhing in the pit. As soon as the light struck the tins and orange peels, the shrieking stopped and four yellow eyes stared back. "It's just cats," I said. "Fornicating cats."

"For God's sake," Scotty said.

Abebe stared. "Yes?"

I was laughing. I didn't have the words in Amharic. "You know, whomp-uh-whomp. Make love. Sex." Scotty was already picking his way back across the gravel path. I pursed my lips for the old man. "Cat. Love. Kiss, kiss, kiss."

Abebe trembled with excitement.

"Sissy!" Scotty was barefoot and his tender soles were cut and bleeding from the sharp stones by the time I got to him.

I helped him to the porch. "You need more calluses."

He looked at me sharply. "Are you making fun of me?"

I put my hand on his back and rested my head on his shoulder for an instant, to collect myself, to be sure I said the right thing. "No, I wasn't making fun. I meant it, a physical fact. Your feet are tender as a baby's. You need calluses to be barefoot out here."

After he went in, I stood on the porch a while longer, to watch Abebe scour the compound with his light. The last sound I heard that night was the old watchman smacking his lips and giggling at the bulb in his flashlight, "Kiss, kiss."

The next week when Abebe pressed the buzzer, Scotty flopped over in bed and pulled the pillow over his head. I jumped up, skidded through the kitchen tying my robe and was met by Abebe at the back door. The old man grinned happily. "Listen," he said.

I stepped outside and heard a familiar thud and crunch against the compound wall. Ours was a corner house, down from a popular late night tedj beit. A bar girl had shown up at the gate a month earlier with a man drunk on tedj who'd fallen in a hole and broken his arm. The guy was crying and moaning, "Hakim, hakim, doctor, doctor," but Scotty wouldn't touch him. "Take him to the hospital," he'd said. "I don't do house calls."

Two or three men were bouncing off the wall just then, laughing and shouting at each other. I couldn't make out what they were saying. "What is it, Abebe? Somebody for Dr. High-tower?"

He shone his light in my eyes. "They want to fight their horses."

"Their horses?"

"Yes, madam, but do not worry. Those men have no horses."

"This is why you got me up?"

"Yes." He glowed with pleasure at the efficiency of his alarm and blinded me with the light again.

I didn't mind really. I'd expected to spend that year padding about at night, tending my baby, so I was glad of an excuse to be up. After Abebe took up his patrol of the compound again and the drunks were an echo, I lingered in the yard to taste the pungency of the night air and to savor the layers of color that weren't present during the day. I'd been doing a lot of work with black and white film, experimenting with my developer, and the veneer of deep shadow gave a grainy density to the yard that drew me into the night. The dog, Flea Trap, snorted and jerked in her doggie dreams under the back steps; the roses dying under the mimosa tree looked like bulbous flags swaying in the breeze; the fluffs of chicken sleeping along the compound fence were trembling flowers that would cluck into life with the dawn and the white clothesline webbed the yard and held it all together. I thought about trying night photography.

"I like the night," I called to Abebe as I started up the back stairs.

He quivered where he stood, as if I'd struck him in the heart. He beamed at me from the middle of the back yard, a shrunken old man swathed in white. "Yes, the night is flat and alive," he said.

After that, if I woke up to go to the bathroom, I looked for him in the yard. Sometimes he was leaning against the gate, wrapped in his long white gabi and clutching his stick, but more often he was poking in the garden, whispering to the flowers, patting the trunks of the trees. Once I saw him lying on the ground in front of the house, staring up at the sky. I came to realize that Abebe's world was defined by our corrugated tin wall, by the soft earth under his callused feet, and by the blanket of night overhead. Scotty and I never even owned keys to the gate. Everything within the compound was under Abebe's care.

I began embellishing the stories of Abebe's nocturnal buzzing and eccentric ways on my weekly visits with the Harem Sewing Circle, to keep them laughing while I took their pictures. Their house and compound were pretty much like mine with a cooker in the kitchen, sofas in the living room, table and chairs in the dining room, but Sun's father, Hamid, had constructed a traditional Harari house in the back—one large room divided into five levels. Traditionally the men occupied one level, the women another, sons across from them, unmarried daughters the fourth, the children the lowest, but those distinctions had been liberalized in the city and we lay about wherever we pleased, reclining against pillows on several layers of Persian carpets. The only item of furniture was a pink telephone.

I thought I dressed modestly enough, but Anisa insisted that I cover my legs and feet when I lounged with them on the rugs. Sometimes Sun outfitted me in her mother's filmy shifts and wrapped scarves around my wild hair. She'd whisper in my ear as she draped me in her mother's clothes: "Show me to dance," or, "Give me lipstick." Once she breathed, "cassette tape," as she passed the coffee, "blue jeans" when she handed me the pipe, and always, "Sun needs a mini."

I did ask Anisa if Sun could try on one of my shirtwaists. Sun looked at the dress hungrily, but her mother wagged a finger at me. "No, ferenj." She always called me that, foreigner.

"My mother is stupid," Sun whispered fiercely in English.

I looked at Anisa who was embroidering a pillowcase and nuzzling her youngest daughter in her lap. That woman could sew, coo at her baby, keep an eye on the servant girl preparing coffee, call to her sons scuffling in the yard, supervise her middle daughters bringing cups and bread, attend to me, to her sisters, and to the two old neighbor women who had dropped by. A flash of envy whipped through me. I had to put the camera down and take a breath—Anisa had everything I wanted. "Your mother is a lot of things," I said, "but stupid isn't one of them."

Sun fluffed my scarf impatiently and refused to speak to me or to translate for the rest of the afternoon. I felt sorry for her. She was hungry for anything I might tell her, anything but that I envied her mother and her exotic house layered with fine carpets and hung with ornate exhortations from the Koran. Sun longed for the world beyond.

One day Sun said, "My mother is asking why you don't have children."

Anisa beamed.

I blushed. How to explain. "I am a fat woman. I am not beautiful." I squeezed my round arms and made a face, trying to laugh it off.

Anisa frowned. "Your husband does not like you?" Sun translated.

"Not often enough," I said and the women collapsed against each other in giggles.

Anisa whispered something to Sun and pushed her towards me. Sun protested, but her mother snapped at her, then said something to the other woman who all urged Sun forward.

"Uh, oh," I said. "What do they want?"

"This," Sun said and pulled my blouse out of my skirt. "Show us. Take buttons out," she ordered. I started to laugh. They wanted to see my breasts. I had to keep my feet and ankles covered but now they wanted to inspect my private equipment. "Maybe there is the problem," Sun explained.

That was the way it was with the Harem Sewing Circle. Women talk. For all practical purposes, I had abdicated my female roles in Ethiopia, given up on my marriage and let my cook clean, bake, and iron Scotty's shirts. I loved taking a few pictures across the road on Fridays, laughing and nodding my head with those women even though I didn't understand a third of what they said. Or because I didn't understand. I thought I could enjoy myself without getting involved or exposed, but when Anisa gestured impatiently at my blouse, I unbuttoned it.

They laughed when they saw my big white bra. I quickly unhooked it as Anisa came over to make the inspection.

She took my right breast in both hands, assessing it like a melon. "Good. Very good, ferenj." I would make a fine mother, perfect, Anisa said. I would have too much milk. My children would grow fat. The others felt my breasts and confirmed the diagnosis. Sun was the last to touch me. "Nice, mama." Mama was a term of respect for an older woman.

"Do you really think so? I'm all right?"

"Oh, yes, yes."

I was still taking my temperature every morning and trying to seduce Scotty according to my ovulation charts. Now these fertile women said I could have my own baby. They inched closer when I started to cry, all of them surrounding me in one movement. Anisa took my hand. "Yes, of course you will be a good mother."

I held her hand to my face and blurted out everything, told them about the miscarriage, six months in the womb. "I called her Elizabeth. Was that wrong?" Scotty had said you don't name a fetus. "I wanted to bury her, but he took the child away. Hospital policy."

"No, not wrong."

"He was wrong."

I even told them about my abortion when I was sixteen, scared and guilty. I did it myself on the black and white tile floor of my mama's company bathroom. I told them the whole damn thing, half in Amharic, half Sun translating, her eyes wide and scared as I sobbed out my terrible story.

"You can speak of these things to us," Anisa said through Sun. She opened my blouse one more time and took my breast. "Is good," she said with finality and authority in her voice. "Big. Nice shape. You have good body for baby."

"My mother says you are perfect." Sun glowed with pleasure at the good news.

"I want a daughter like you," I said then and got really sloppy, laughing and crying. They held me and cooed over me, pulling me into their circle of mothers and daughters.

We dressed Sun up in her wedding dress, a voluminous red and purple affair that had been her mother's and would be her sisters' and their daughters' as well. I think they wanted to show me a little of their lives after I had spilled so much of mine.

Sun changed from her everyday clothes first, working from the inside out. She slipped off her sandals, wrapped both feet in scarves, then shimmied out of her velvet leggings, unfolded them over her feet, set them aside, pulled on a multi-colored pair of silk leggings over her covered feet, removed the scarves, and put on her sandals. She shrugged when I asked why she covered her feet to change her pants. "It is our way." I assumed some exotic taboo against having one's clothing, especially clothing that came in contact with one's private parts, touch the feet which were the only bit of public flesh. But I tended to romanticize Sun and the rituals of her life; perhaps covering her feet was a practical precaution. If you wear sandals in an unpaved world, your feet are dirty; it saves the leggings not to get them soiled every time you pull them off.

Then her aunts draped and tucked her in ten yards of red, gold and purple silk until she looked more like an apparition of beauty then a real girl. She stood before us in the wedding dress grinning like generations of Harari girls before her, with her hands clasped under the silk, and the gold pendant with the ruby in the center hanging across her smooth forehead to reflect her radiance and purity to the world.

"It's a beautiful dress," I said.

"But it's not a mini," Sun said and lifted her skirts to show a silken leg. Anisa clucked disapprovingly but I couldn't help but laugh. Sun was taunting centuries of custom and ritual. In every conceivable situation the centuries told Sun, at sixteen, exactly what to do, but she wasn't listening.

The coffee ceremony was the alleged focus of the afternoon, but the women loved the pipe best. Sun, as oldest daughter, prepared the water pipe, using charcoal from the brazier with the tobacco at the top. The hookah was a good five feet tall with a long stem that snaked across the rugs, first to Anisa, then passed woman to woman. I couldn't get the hang of it. "I never smoked in college," I explained.

Each week Anisa showed me when to suck in and how to breathe out. I filled my lungs with smoke, but the low bubbles that the others produced never gurgled forth when I smoked. I loved the process though. "This is great," I said. "Don't you feel like the caterpillar in Alice in Wonderland when you smoke this thing?"

There was a pause after Sun translated, then they laughed politely. "You don't know what I'm talking about, do you?" It didn't matter. I was Alice, putting whatever they gave me in my mouth, pushing beyond the known world. Sun was pushing too—I should tell her about Alice, I thought.

One afternoon there was a burst of whistling from the front of the compound, then Dawit, one of the servants' boys, dashed up to Anisa. She was curled back on a pillow, smoking and watching the rest of us through lowered eyelids. Her slow inhalations and exhalations resounded languorously in the burbling pipe, but she jerked up when Dawit appeared, flung the pipe stem at Sun, and grabbed the telephone, although it hadn't rung. Sun thrust the pipe at me. "You must have this. Our father is coming."

Anisa laughed into the telephone receiver.

The other women fluffed their skirts and batted their little hands in front of their mouths like kids caught with cigarettes, but by the time Hamid swung around the corner, everybody was slouched against the pillows, sewing and talking quietly, except for Anisa who whispered into the silent phone. I was slumped in the corner, with the long hookah cord snaked across me and the big mouthpiece jammed between my teeth. I sucked and wheezed, trying to make it bubble. Hamid smacked his lips disapprovingly when he saw me and raised his eyebrows.

I took a deep breath and nearly suffocated on the smoke. He stared at me a moment longer, then turned to his wife. Anisa raised her hand, said something final into the telephone, and hung up before giving him her full attention.

"What's the matter?" I whispered, but Sun hushed me with a look. I tried to inhale again and the pipe belched loudly. I fell back against the pillows, coughing and laughing, expecting the women to start up their giggling again. Their eyes flashed at me, but nobody made a sound.

Hamid's exchange with Anisa was brief and sharp, then he turned from his wife to his daughter. Sun dropped her head to her chest, her father yelped something, and then he was gone.

"What's going on? Why'd you throw me the pipe?"

"Only man is smoking," Sun whispered. "Or very old woman. Nobody cares if old woman smoke."

"Old women like me?"

Sun shook her head. "You are not old; you are ferenj. If you smoke..." She shrugged. "You are free."

"That's stupid," I said. "Women can do whatever they want these days."

Sun looked sideways at her mother, afraid that she'd heard, then she grinned. "My mother doesn't understand you," she said, giggling and falling against me to whisper in my ear. "You are right, mama. We can do everything."

Her soft hair smelled of butter and coffee. I hugged her impulsively. "I have something for you." I pulled my lipstick out of my pocket and pressed it into Sun's palm. "Persian Melon. My favorite color."

"My favorite too!" Sun exclaimed, although I'm certain she'd never heard of Persian Melon or even held a lipstick before. We both glanced at Anisa who was speaking to one of her sisters.

"Our little secret," I said.

"Yes," Sun said and snuggled against me like a small child. "Persian Melon is our little secret." We had other little secrets after that, some blush, a powder puff, a bit of mascara, a Beatles tape. My secret gifts were harmless; Sun couldn't use any of them, but she loved fondling the pretty cases and tubes they came in.

Abebe observed a three-week hiatus before pressing the buzzer again. I punched Scotty. "Your turn," I said, but he rolled away like a whale netted in soft white blankets. He'd seen his first case of small pox that day. "I should be excited," he'd said at dinner. "How many physicians of my generation will see small pox?" Then he had taken a sleeping pill and gone to bed.

Abebe met me at the back door with a pile of women's clothes in his hands. He was so excited that it took a while to get the story out of him. As best as I could make out, he'd been in the garden when he heard shouting on the street. More drunks from the tedj beit, he thought. He'd listened at the gate rather than immediately ringing for me.

But it wasn't drunks, it was Hamid Mohammed from across the street, shouting in a language Abebe didn't understand.

"Probably Arabic. He is a religious man."

"Yes," Abebe said and continued his story. Women had screamed and in the background he heard crying, then the next thing he knew, articles of clothing were flung over the gate, one by one. He showed me. A lacy bra, a pair of panty hose, some tiny black stretch pants, a brown sweater with gold flecks in it, a purple skirt. Then somebody kicked our gate, shouted some more, and then it was quiet.

"I don't get it."

"I know you want to see these things immediately."

"You are sure it was Ato Hamid?"

He was sure.

The next day I went for the regular Friday gathering of the Harem Sewing Circle. The gate was locked, which wasn't too unusual. I rattled and knocked until the small boy, Dawit, appeared. I stepped through the door when he opened it, but he waved his hand at me, no. "Nobody home," he whispered.

What I could see of the compound beyond him was empty, but I heard a woman's voice somewhere. A servant, perhaps. I left reluctantly. I'd never been turned away before.

The same thing happened the following week. I tried telephoning.

"Hello?" A woman's voice. I couldn't tell who.

"Yes, hello. This is Sissy Hightower, from across the street." I explained that I wanted to come over or they could come to my house for coffee. "I'll make cookies."

There was a long silence on the other end, then the click of the receiver. Maybe it was a servant, the woman who made coffee, or somebody who didn't know English. From the hello, I'd thought it was Sun, but Sun wouldn't hang up on me. I dialed again and let it ring and ring, but nobody picked it up. I went over and banged on the gate again. Nothing.

Abebe waited six weeks to sound the siren. Scotty didn't move when it went off. He'd taken two pills and was solid as stone. I dragged myself out of bed, padded through the living room, around the coffee table, tripped over my own shoes in the dining room. I switched on the light in the kitchen and pressed my face against the window in the back door, but I couldn't see anything. I went out.

The light from the kitchen illumined a swatch of yard, but I couldn't see the watchman. It was a dark night, misty air, low sky. I felt my way down the back steps. "Abebe?"

The door to his room was outlined with light, but I still didn't see him. A car door slammed and I stopped momentarily, holding my breath. A woman's shrill laugh rose outside the compound wall.

"Abebe? Where are you?"

A chill breeze roused the leaves of the mimosa tree, bearing a heavy perfume.

I heard muffled sobbing, but still didn't see anybody. I pulled my robe closer. "Who's there?"

"Aie! Madam?" Abebe stepped away from the house behind me. A girl cowered next to him, bent over herself, sobbing and gulping air, choking on her fist in her mouth. She wore an orange miniskirt and a yellow blouse with a chain of embroidered daisies across the scooped neck. The flowers flashed white in the dark.

"What's happened?"

"She is sick," Abebe said in Amharic.

I assumed she was a prostitute from the tedj beit, somebody wanting Scotty again. I shook my head. "I'll never get him awake."

The girl moaned.

"Let's have a look at her, Abebe. Bring her in the house."

He half-carried and dragged the girl up the stairs, pushing her legs out in front of her, making her walk like a wooden doll.

I held the kitchen door open. "Sit," I said in Amharic.

Abebe tried to bend her to a chair, but the girl shook her head and staggered to the corner next to the door and flopped on the floor with her legs twisted together. She covered her face with her thin hands and leaned into the wall. The orange skirt was streaked with blood.

"God, has somebody beaten her?" I asked. I thought of Scotty buried under the covers and wondered if there was any chance that I could get him awake enough to function. I didn't think so. "Who is she?"

Abebe said a name that echoed in my brain, but I couldn't place it. I pulled the girl's hand away from her face and turned her chin towards me.

Sun.

I hadn't seen her since her father had slung underwear over the compound wall and I'd been banned from the Harem Sewing Circle. I'd continued to knock on the gate every Friday afternoon and had smiled at the small boy who opened the gate, and had nodded as he turned me away. "Oh, Sun," I said. "I've missed you."

She curled her fingers around my wrist and used my hand to cover her face. Her smooth hot skin was damp to the touch. "I'm afraid," she breathed into my hand.

I put my arms around her sharp shoulders and held her against my chest. I felt like the mother of the prodigal child, welcoming her daughter home. I patted her awful blouse and started to laugh. "Where did you get this thing?" I said and leaned back to get a better look at her. "Oh, baby, you've got a lot to tell me. I bet your daddy had a cat when he saw you in these clothes. Did he do this to you?"

Her head shot up. "No. Nothing with him. You aren't telling him anything."

I fingered the orange skirt. "So you got your mini. Who is getting you these clothes?" She didn't look like the girl who served coffee for her mother on Friday afternoons. "And makeup. This is not my girl."

She raised her face stained with mascara and lipstick. "Persian melon," she said. Her lips cracked in a tiny smile. "If my father sees this, he will kill me."

Abebe cleared his throat. He'd been crouching in the doorway, watching.

"What?" I said.

"Lij," he whispered.

"Lij? Child?" I didn't get it.

Abebe nodded, raising his eyebrows and sucking in his breath with closed eyes. Sun sobbed as Abebe drew his bony finger across his neck and I understood with a flash of myself at sixteen, thin-armed and desperate as Sun, gulping my own spittle until my lips were crisp as hardtack, moaning on Mama's bathroom floor. "Oh, baby," I said. "I'll get my husband. He's a doctor. Hakim."

"No, mama," she moaned.

"Abebe, get ice." I slid out from under Sun. Scotty would have to get up.

I couldn't wake him. I pounded the bed. I bounced him back and forth. I put my cold hands on his face. "Scotty, goddamn it, get up. It's Sun. She's tried to throw a child."

His eyes fluttered open once or twice, but the pupils were lost in his skull. "Sun," he breathed. "Sun?"

"From across the street. Anisa's daughter. Hamid with the souk. The Harem Sewing Circle."

He flickered up for a minute and I thought I had him. "The Mohammedans?"

"Yes. She's bleeding to death all over our kitchen floor."

He raised up on one elbow and stared glassy-eyed, then fell back on the mattress. I wanted to kill him.

"It's an emergency!" I pulled at his blanket as hard as I could.

"It's always an emergency," he said, then his body went slack, and his left shoulder curved up to my face like a fist as he flopped over, pulling the blanket with him.

Sun was slumped against the wall with Abebe hovering over her with a dish of ice in his hands. I grabbed the bowl, dumped the ice in a towel and knelt next to Sun, to press the ice to her uterus. She seemed to be slipping away, going into shock. I wrapped a towel around her and asked her how she felt, but got no response.

I moved the ice lower on her abdomen and pressed as hard as I could. I leaned into her with all my strength, willing the bleeding to stop. "Live, Sun, live." I stared at the lipstick smeared across her beautiful lips. It didn't look like Persian Melon. I had an irrational impulse to wash her face, as if removing the traces of lipstick and eyebrow pencil I'd given her could save her.

Abebe stood next to me with one bare foot on top of the other, whispering something that finally penetrated my consciousness. "We must take her to the hospital," he said.

Her head fell against my chest when I picked her up with Abebe supporting her legs. We staggered down the steps and I stuffed her in the back seat of the VW as Abebe ran for the gate. He waved as I passed through the gate, but I stopped and ordered him in the car to hold onto Sun. He looked startled and refused—he'd never been in a car—but I insisted and he slowly climbed in the back.

We'd gone less than a hundred yards when Scotty suddenly appeared, bouncing alongside the passenger window in his pajamas. By the time I stopped, he had the door open and was in the car with his knees on the front seat, heaving and panting, filling the car with the odor of pipe tobacco and stale breath.

I got out to give him more room. Abebe leaned against the back window holding Sun's hand and praying over her. Her small head bent across his chest like a flower on a broken stem. Scotty stretched across the seat and pressed his fingers against her neck, then he took her narrow wrist and held it for a moment, then he put her hand back in her lap.

He got out of the car and slammed his hand on the hood. "Damn it, Sissy, don't do this to me! I knew it would be too late. I knew it! I knew it." He kicked the tire with the side of his foot, then limped away, picking his way around the sharp rocks and deep ruts, heading for our orange gate at the end of the road.

I watched him go. I couldn't look at Sun just then. Somebody was walking our way, a woman, her outline clouded by layers of scarves and soft skirts. Scotty's head went up when he passed her. They didn't speak; the woman kept coming. I felt as if I were watching a film of a woman walking, her swaying skirts, the even pace of her step. She kept coming closer, now closer, as if she had stepped off a screen. Who was she? Abebe knocked on the window of the car and held Sun's hand up for me to take the burden from him, but I couldn't move. I knew it was a woman's place to care for this girl, but the centuries had failed us both. I didn't know what to do. Maybe the woman coming would know. I waited.

How I Came To Write This Story

Perhaps to readers "Easy in the Islands" seems like a fantastic fabrication, but in fact, except for the ending, when the fellows pitch the thawing corpse of the hotelier's mother out of the plane, the story is mostly true, and in writing it I felt more in tune with my life as a non-fiction writer than with my creative self. Absurdity and surreality seem to me to be undercurrents of the Peace Corps experience, and best navigated with a sense of humor. In 1976, as a volunteer (agricultural journalist) in St. Vincent and the Grenadines, I met a young man my age, also an American, who had inherited a hotel on the island. His wandering mother, whom he hadn't seen since he was a teenager, appeared one day out of the blue, checked into her son's hotel, and in the morning was found dead in her room. The hotel's kitchen staff quit when he stored her body in the restaurant's walk-in freezer; the local police tried to accuse him of murder. For a storyteller, the circumstances were too deliciously bizarre to ignore.

—Bob Shacochis

BOB SHACOCHIS (Eastern Caribbean, 1975) is a short story writer, essayist, novelist, and educator. *Easy in the Islands* received the National Book Award for First Fiction in 1985. His second collection, *The Next New World* (1989) was awarded the Prix de Rome by the American Academy of Arts and Letters, and his novel, *Swimming in the Volcano*, was short-listed for the National Book Award in 1993. His fifth book, *The Immaculate Invasion*, a non-fiction account for the American military intervention in Haiti, will be published in 1999 by Viking. He lives in Florida and New Mexico.

EASY IN THE ISLANDS

by Bob Shacochis

The days were small, pointless epics, long windups to punches that always drifted by cartoon-fashion, as if each simple task were meaningless unless immersed in more theater and threat than bad opera.

It was only Monday noon and already Tillman had been through the wringer. He had greased the trade commissioner to allow a pallet of Campbell's consommé to come ashore, fired one steel band for their hooliganism and hired another, found a carpenter he was willing to trust to repair the bad veranda that was so spongy in spots Tillman knew it was only a matter of days before a guest's foot burst through the surface in to whatever terrors lived below in the tepid darkness, restocked on vitamins from the pharmacy, argued with the crayfish regulatory bureau about quotas. And he'd argued with the inscrutable cook, a fat countrywoman who wore a wool watch cap and smoked hand-rolled cigars, argued with both maids, muscle-bound Lemonille and the other one who wouldn't reveal her name, argued with the gardener who liked to chop everything up, argued with the customs house, argued with the bartender Jevanee. And although he had not forthrightly won any of these encounters, he had won them enough to forestall the doom that would one day descend on Rosehill Plantation.

But now the daily defeats and victories were overshadowed by a first-class doozy, a default too personal to implicate the local population. The problem was to decide what to do about his mother—Mother, who had thought life wonderful in the islands. Now she rested stiffly in the food locker, dead and coated with frost, blue as the shallow water on the reefs, protected from the fierceness of the sun she once loved without question or fear, a sun that was never really her enemy, no matter how it textured her skin, no matter what it revealed of her age.

In her room on Saturday, Mother had died mysteriously. As Lemonille had said when the two of them carried her out after the doctor had been there, *Mistah Till-Mahn, it look so you muddah shake out she heart fah no good reason. Like she tricked by some false light, ya know.*

His mother's body had been strong and brassy, her spirit itself unusually athletic for a woman only weeks away from sixty. In her quick laugh was as much vitality as a girl's, and yet she had died. In bed, early in the evening, disdainful of the bars and clubs, reading a book—Colette, rediscovered on her latest continental visit—her finger ready to turn the page. Tillman was astonished. Only after Dr. Bradley had told him that he suspected his mother had been poisoned did Tillman begin to calm down, his imperturbable self returning by degrees. Such a conclusion made no sense. The terms of life in the islands were that nothing ever made sense, unless you were a mystic or a politician, or studied both with ambition. Then every stupidity seemed an act of inspiration, every cruelty part of a divine scheme. There was no dialectic here, only the obverting of all possibilities until caprice made its selection.

Dr. Bradley couldn't be sure though. Neither he nor any of the other three sanctioned doctors on the island knew how to perform an autopsy with sufficient accuracy to assure each other or anybody else of the exact nature of death when the cause was less than obvious. Still, Bradley earned moments of miraculous credibility, as when the former Minister of Trade was brought into the hospital dead of a gunshot wound in his chest. To the government's relief, Bradley determined the cause of death as "heart failure," an organic demise, and unembarrassing.

"I will take your permission, mahn, to cut de body open ahnd look in she stomach," Dr. B. had said to Tillman as they stood over his mother's corpse in the sunny hotel room on Sunday morning, a breeze off the ocean dancing the curtains open, billowing sunlight throughout the room and then sucking it back outside. A spray of creamy rosebuds tapped against the louvered window, an eerie beckoning in the air silenced by death.

"For God's sake, why?" Tillman had said. It sounded like an ultimate obscenity, to have this fool with his meatcutter's stubby hands groping in his mother's abdomen.

"To determine what she eat aht de time of succumption."

"I told you what she was eating," Tillman said, exasperated. "She was eating a can of peaches with a spoon. Look here, there are still some left in the can." He shook the can angrily and syrup slopped onto his wrist. In disgust, Tillman wiped the sticky wetness on his pants, half nauseated, associating the liquid with some oozy by-product of dissolution. "Take the peaches if you need something to cut into, but you're not taking Mother. This isn't one of your Bottom Town cadavers."

Bradley had reacted with a shrug, and a patronizing twist to his smile. "Dis racial complexity—what a pity, mahn."

How often Tillman had heard this lie, so facile, from the lips of bad men. "One world," he said, biting down on the syllables as if they were a condemnation, or a final sorrow. "We all live in one world. What's so goddamn complex about that?"

Tillman refused to let him remove the body from Rosehill. He wrapped his mother in the mauve chenille bedspread she had been lying on, restacked several crates of frozen chicken parts, and arranged her in the walk-in freezer until he could figure out just what to do. It was easy to accept the fact that you couldn't trust a doctor in such circumstances. What was most unacceptable was that Bradley had told the police there was a possibility the old lady had been murdered. The police, of course, were excited by this news. They sent Inspector Cuffy over to Rosehill to inform Tillman that he was under suspicion.

"You're kidding," Tillman said.

He suggested the inspector should walk down to the beach bar the hotel maintained on the waterfront and have a drink courtesy of the house while he took care of two new guests who had just arrived in a taxi from the airport. "I don't believe it," the new man said in an aside to Tillman as he checked them in. "The skycaps at the airport whistled at my wife and called her a whore." His wife stood demurely by his side, looking a bit overwhelmed. He could see the dark coronas of nipples under her white muslin sundress.

"Hey, people here are more conservative than you might think," Tillman told the couple, and to the woman he added, "Unless you want little boys rubbing up against your leg, you shouldn't wear shorts or a bathing suit into town."

"But this is the tropics," the woman protested in an adolescent voice, looking at Tillman as if he were only being silly.

"Right," Tillman conceded, handing over the key. He escorted the couple to their room, helping with the luggage, and wished them well. Wished himself a dollar for every time their notion of paradise would be fouled by some rudeness, aggression, or irrelevant accusation.

He crossed back over the veranda out onto the cobbled drive, past the derelict stone tower of the windmill where every other Saturday the hotel sponsored a goat roast that was well attended by civil servants, Peace Corps volunteers and whatever tourists were around, down the glorious green lawn crazy with blossom, down, hot and sweaty, to the palm grove, the bamboo beach bar on its fringe, the lagoon dipping into the land like a blue pasture, Tillman walking with his hands in the pockets of his loose cotton pants, reciting a calypso and feeling, despite his troubles, elected, an aristocrat of the sensual latitudes, anointed to all the earthly privileges ordinary people dreamed about on their commuter trains fifty weeks a year. No matter that in a second-class Eden nothing was as unprofitable as the housing of its guests. Even loss seemed less discouraging in the daily flood of sun.

Jevanee was glaring at him from behind the bar. And the inspector sat grandly on his stool, satisfied with being the big-shot, bearing a smile that welcomed Tillman as if they were to be partners in future prosperity, as if the venture they were to embark on could only end profitably. He gave a little wink before he tipped his green bottle of imported beer and sank the neck between his lips.

"Dis a sad affair, mahn," he said, wagging his round head. Jevanee uncapped a second bottle and set it before the inspector, paying no attention to Tillman's presence. Tillman drew a stool up beside Cuffy and perched on its edge, requesting Jevanee to bring another beer, and watched with practiced patience as the bartender kicked about and finally delivered the bottle as if it were his life's savings.

"What is it with you, Jevanee? What am I doing wrong?" The bartender had come with Rosehill when he had inherited the hotel eight months ago. Somebody had trained him to be a terror.

"Mistah Trick!" Jevanee whooped. He was often too self-conscious to confront his employer head-on. Nevertheless he would not accept even the mildest reproach without an extravagant line of defense or, worse, smoldering until his tongue ignited and his hands flew threateningly, shouting in a tantrum that would go on forever with or without an audience, a man who would never be employed to his satisfaction. He turned his back on Tillman and began muttering at the whiskey bottles arrayed on the work island in the center of the oval bar.

"Mistah Trick, he say what him doin wrong, de devil. He say daht he mean, Jevanee, why you is a chupid boy ahs black as me boot cahnt count change ahnd show yah teef nice aht de white lady? He say daht he mean, Jevanee, why you cahnt work fah free like you grahnpoppy? Why you cahnt bring you sistah here ta please me?" Without ceasing his analysis of what the white man had meant, he marched out from the bar and into the bushes to take a leak. Tillman forced himself not to react any further to Jevanee's rage, which appeared to be taking on a decidedly historical sweep.

The inspector, who had not shown any interest in Jevanee's complaints, began to tap the long nail of his index finger on the surface of the bar. He made a show of becoming serious without wanting to deprive Tillman of his informality, his compassion, his essential sympathy, etcetera—all the qualities he believed he possessed and controlled to his benefit.

"Who else, Tillman, but you?" Cuffy finally concluded as if it hurt him to say this. "Undah-stahnd, is only speculation."

"Who else but me?" Tillman sputtered. "Are you crazy?" The inspector frowned and Tillman immediately regretted his choice of words. Cuffy was as willfully unpredictable as most everybody else on the island, but in a madhouse, an outsider soon learned, truth was always a prelude to disaster, the match dropped thoughtlessly onto tinder. He should have said, Look, how can you think that? or Man, what will it take to end this unfortunate business? But too late. The inspector was pinching at his rubbery nose, no longer even considering Tillman, looking out across the harbor, the anchored sailboats bobbing like a display of various possibilities, playing the image of artful calculation for his suspect.

Tillman sighed. "Why do you think I would kill my own mother? She was my *mother*. What son could harm the woman who carried him into the world?"

The inspector pursed his lips and then relaxed them. "Well, Tillmahn, perhaps you do it to have title to dis property, true?"

The absurdity was too great even for Tillman, a connoisseur of island nonsense. "To inherit this property!" Now Tillman had to laugh, regardless of the inspector's feelings. "Cuffy, nobody wants this place. In his will my father was excessively sorry for burdening me with Rosehill Plantation and advised I sell it at the first opportunity. My mother had absolutely no claim to Rosehill. He divorced her long ago."

Tillman paused. As far as he could tell, he was the only one in the world, besides the government, who wanted Rosehill Plantation. It had been on the market for years, not once receiving an honest offer. Its profits were marginal, its overhead crushing. But the hotel was his, so why not be there. What he had found through it was unexpected—the inexplicable sense that life on the island had a certain fullness, that it was, far beyond what he had ever experienced back home, authentic in the most elemental ways.

Cuffy had become petulant, studying him as if he were spoiled, an unappreciative child. Tillman was not intimidated. "Why should I tell you this anyway? It has absolutely no relevance to my mother's death."

"Um hmm, um hmm, I see," the inspector said. "So perhaps you muddah take a lovah, a dark mahn, ahnd you become vexed wit she fah behavin so. You warn her to stop but she refuse. So..." He threw out his hands as if the rest of the scene he conceived was there before him. "Is just speculation."

Tillman was tiring fast. Inspector Cuffy had no use for what was and what wasn't; his only concern was his own role in the exercise of authority. It killed boredom, boredom amid the splendor. It created heroes and villains, wealth and poverty. No other existence offered him so much.

He discovered that he was grinding his teeth and the muscles in his jaw ached. Jevanee had slipped back behind the bar, and every time Tillman glanced over there, Jevanee, now bold, tried to stare him down.

"My mother was an old lady," he told the inspector. "She was beyond love. She liked books and beaches, fruit, seafood, and rare wines. Traveling. There was no man in her life. There never was. She was even a stranger to my father."

"You just a boy," Cuffy noted in a way that made Tillman think it was a line the inspector must use frequently. "Nobody beyond love, ya know."

"So?"

"So, nobody beyond pahssion, ahnd nobody beyond crime." Tillman blinked. Damn, he thought, Cuffy's starting to make sense.

"Even ahn old womahn need a good roll to keep she happy," the inspector concluded.

"Oh, for Christ's sake," Tillman said, standing up. "I have to get back."

He couldn't get away before Jevanee butted in. Ignore Jevanee and life might possibly go on. The bartender used his mouth like a gun, the words popping spitefully while he focused on whatever spirit he had summoned to witness his oppression.

"Daht ol boney-bag he call his muddah grabbin aht every blahck boy on de beach. I see it wit me own eyes."

"Jevanee, shut up."

"Oh, yes, massa, suh. Yes, massa." He feigned excessive servitude, wiping the bar counter, the cash box, the bamboo supports with his shirt sleeve. The time would come when Tillman would have to face up to Jevanee's vindictiveness. He had been steaming ever since Tillman had told him not to hand out free drinks to his friends from the village. Jevanee insisted no one but Rosehill's tourists, who were not regular, would ever patronize the beach bar if it weren't for him. Maybe he was right. Nobody was coming around anymore except on Friday nights when the band played. More and more, Jevanee wanted Tillman to understand that he was a dangerous man, his every move a challenge to his employer. Tillman was still trying to figure out how to fire the guy without a lot of unpleasantness.

"Don't listen to Jevanee," Tillman told the inspector. "He's pissed at me these days because of a disagreement we had over a charitable instinct of his."

"I give me bruddah a drink," Jevanee said in a self-deprecating way, as though he were the victim and Cuffy would understand. Jevanee's mood would only escalate if Tillman explained that the bartender's "bruddah" was consuming a case of Scotch on his drier visits, so he refused to debate Jevanee's claim. The inspector turned on his stool with the cold expression of a man whose duty it is to make it known that he must hurt you severely, that he may cripple you or make you weep, if you disobey him.

"Look now, you," he said, taking moral pleasure in this chastisement. "Doan you make trouble fah Mistah Tillmahn. You is lucky he give you work."

"Dis white bitch doan give me a damn ting," Jevanee snarled, shaking an empty beer bottle at Tillman. "I work in dis same spot a long time when he show up. Ahnd what you doin kissin he ahss?"

"Doan talk aht me daht way, boy, or I fuck you up. Hell goin to have a new bahtendah soon if you cahnt behave."

Jevanee tried to smile, a taut earnestness that never quite made it to his mouth. Tillman arranged chairs around the warped café tables, backing away. "Okay then, Cuffy. I'm glad we had this opportunity to straighten everything out. Stay and have another beer if you want."

Cuffy looked at his gold wristwatch. "You will be around in de aftahnoon?"

"Why?"

"I wish to view de deceased."

"Uh, can't it wait till tomorrow?" Tillman asked. "I have errands to run in town. A shipment of beef is coming in from Miami."

From his shirt pocket, Cuffy had taken a note pad and was scribbling in it. He talked without raising his head. "Okay, dere's no hurry. De old womahn takin she time goin nowheres."

Tillman nodded, now in stride with the process, the havoc of it. "Cuffy, you're a thorough man. If anybody's going to get to the bottom of this mess, it's you."

The inspector accepted this flattery as his due, too certain of its validity to bother about the subtle mocking edge to Tillman's voice. His eyes were relaxed, hooded and moist. Tillman started up the footpath through the palms, kicking a coconut ahead of him, a leaden soccer ball, turning once to check what fared in his absence: and yes Cuffy and Jevanee had their heads together, the bartender animated, swinging his hands, the inspector with his arms crossed on his wide chest. Jevanee had too much energy today. Maybe his attitude would defuse if he were somewhere other than the bar for a while. He seemed to live there. Tillman shouted back down to them. "Jevanee, after the inspector leaves, lock everything up and take the rest of the day off."

The bartender ignored him.

Tillman jogged up the perfect lawn along an avenue of floral celebration—tree-sized poinsettias, arrow ginger, bougainvillea, oleander—a perfumist's tray of fragrance. On the knoll, graced with a vista of the channel, was the old plantation house, a stubborn remnant of colonial elegance, its whitewashed brick flaking in a way that benefited the charm of its archaic construction, the faded red of the gabled tin roof a human comfort against the green monotonous sheets of the mountains that were its background. Farther south, the cone shell of the windmill stood like a guard tower or last refuge. Tillman had huddled there with his guests last summer during a hurricane, the lot of them drunk and playing roundhouse bridge, the cards fluttering from the storm outside.

When he was a teenager Tillman had flown down to the island during a summer off from Exeter to help his father build the two modern wings that flanked the manor, one-level box rooms side by side, as uninspired as any lodging on any Florida roadside. Tillman's father was a decent man, completely involved in his scheming though his interest invariably flagged once a puzzle was solved, a challenge dispatched. The old man had worked for J. D. Root, one of the big ad agencies in New York, handling the Detroit accounts. His final act was an irony unappreciated—he perished in one of the cars he promoted, losing control on the Northway one rainy evening. He had gone fishing up on the St. Lawrence, convinced this time he would hook a muskellunge. Rosehill Plantation was his most daring breakaway but he never really had time for the place. Throughout his ownership, Rosehill lost money and after his death the checks from the estate in New York flowed like aid from the mother country. When a lawyer's telegram reached Tillman, asking if he wanted to pursue more aggressively the sale of the plantation, he decided to dump the Lower East Side loft where he had been sweating out the draft for two years since graduate school and make his claim on Rosehill. Nixon had just been reelected. The States no longer seemed like the right place to be.

Awash in perspiration, Tillman turned the corner around the east wing, his blood pressure a little jumpy, the skin on his face at the point of combustion, wondering if all the friction of a fast life could suddenly cause a person to burst into flame. Sometimes he felt as if it were happening. It wasn't very easy to find peace on the island unless you hiked up into the mountains. Whereas it was very easy to catch hell.

In the exterior courtyard behind the estate house, the new arrivals, husband and wife from Wilmington, Delaware, were inspecting one of Tillman's few unequivocal successes, the gazebo that housed his parrot aviary, in it seven of the last rainbow parrots on earth. The project was really the veterinarian's at the Ministry of Agriculture, a man who hated goats and cows but spent all his spare time bird-watching or digging up pre-Columbian artifacts, storing them in his living room until the far-off day a museum would be built. Together he and Tillman waged a public campaign on the island, the parrots' sole habitat, to prevent their extinction. A law was passed for appearances, its advantage being that it clearly defined for the bird smuggler *who* needed to be paid off and *who* could be bypassed with impunity.

After the crusade, Tillman decided to contact some poachers himself. They were kids, tough miniature bandits, the nest robbers. One was nine, the other eleven. Basil and Jacob, tree climbers extraordinaire, both as skinny as vanilla beans. They lived in a mountain village, a clump of wattle huts, one of the outposts before the vast roadless center of the island, all sharp peaks, palisades and jungle. When the hatching season had ended, Tillman and the boys trekked into the lush interior, camping overnight, Tillman's neck strained from looking up into the canopy, his ears confused by the wraithish shrieks and skraws— *skra-aaa-aw!*—unable to pinpoint where the sound came from in the infinite cathedral of growth. But the kids knew their business. They were fearless, scaling to the top of the highest mahogany or madrone, indifferent to the slashing beaks of the females who refused to abandon the nest, shinnying down the trunks with the chicks held gently in their mouths, polycolored cotton balls, the fierce tiny heads lolling helplessly out from between the embrace of boyish lips.

Tillman thought he would tell his guests from Delaware the story. The woman was scrutinizing the birds rather sternly. She would cluck and whistle at them, tap the chicken wire wall of the cage, but she did so without affection. When he finished talking, she turned to look at him, her eyes obscured behind oversized sunglasses, her mouth in a pout. Tillman guessed she was a bank teller, something that had made her very sure of herself without placing any demand on her intelligence.

"It's cruel," she said.

"It is not cruel. It's heroic. These islands have a way of forcing everything but the lowest common denominator into oblivion."

"Hero," she said sardonically. The husband looked skeptical. Light reflected off her glasses and sliced back at Tillman. He shrugged his shoulders. Perhaps he should bar Americans from Rosehill. Canadians made the better tourist. They allowed for a world outside themselves.

The Land Rover started painfully, a victim of mechanical arthritis. Soon it would take no more to the prosthetic miracle of wire, tin, and hardware junk. Spare parts appeared from across the ocean as often as Halley's comet.

Onto the narrow blacktop road that circumnavigated the island, Tillman drove with reckless courage and whipping flair, showing inner strength when he refused to give way to two flatbed lorries painted up like Easter eggs, one named *Sweetfish*, the other *Dr. Lick,* passengers clinging to everything but the wheel hubs, racing down the coastal hill side by side straight at him, *Dr. Lick* overtaking *Sweetfish* just as Tillman downshifted reluctantly to third and toed the brake pedal. Someday the lorries would spread carnage across this highway, Tillman thought. It would be a national event, the island equivalent of a 747 going down.

In the capital, a pastel city breathtaking from the heights above it but garbage-strewn and ramshackle once you were on its streets, Tillman honked his way through the crowds down along Front Street, inching his way to the docks. On the quay, three pallets of frozen steak destined for Rosehill were sweating pink juice onto the dirty concrete. Beef from the island was as tough and stringy as rug; if a hotel wanted to serve food worthy of the name, it had to import almost everything but fish. He located the purser in one of the rum-and-cake booths that filled every unclaimed inch of the wharves like derelict carnival booths. There was no use complaining about the shipment being off-loaded without anybody being there to receive it. That was Tillman's fault—he had been too preoccupied. He signed the shipping order and then scrambled to hire a driver and boys to break down the pallets and truck the cartons out to Rosehill's freezer before the meat thawed completely.

There were other errands, less urgent—to the marketing board in search of the rare tomato, to the post office, to the stationer for a ballpoint pen, to the pharmacist, who was disappointed when Tillman only bought aspirin. Most of his regular white customers spent small fortunes on amphetamines or Quaaludes. When Tillman had finished there, he drove over to the national hospital on the edge of town. Without a death certificate from Bradley, Mother was destined to be the morbid champion of cryogenics, the Queen of Ice in a land where water never froze in nature.

The old colonial hospital was a structure and a system bypassed by any notion of modernity. Someone yelled at him as he entered the shadowed foyer, but it wasn't apparent who or why. The rough wooden floorboards creaked under his feet. The maze of hallways seemed to be a repository for loiterers—attendants, nurses, nuns, clerks, superfluous guards, mangled patients, talking, weeping, spending the day in rigid silence. One naked little boy asleep on the floor, hugging the wall.

He found Dr. Bradley's office and went through the door without knocking. Bradley, chief surgeon, head physician of St. George's National People's Hospital, an agnostic operation if Tillman ever saw one, was reading a paperback romance, a man hovering over a fallen woman on its cover. The room smelled of sweet putrefaction and Lysol. The scent of jasmine wafted in through open screenless windows. Tillman sat down on a wooden bench against one bare wall. Flies buzzed along the ceiling. Bradley slowly broke off from his reading, dropping his feet one by one from where they were propped on the broad windowsill. His lab coat, smudged with yellow stains and laundered blood, sagged away from his middle. He recognized Tillman and smiled grudgingly.

"Mahn, I been callin you, ya know. I examine dem peaches you muddah eat. Dey was no good. I think we solve dis big mystery."

Tillman knew this was his chance to end the affair but he could not forgive Bradley his smugness, his careless manner, the suffering he had sown.

"You're sure? What'd you do, feed them to a chicken and the chicken died?"

"Mahn, Tillman, you doan have enough troubles, you must come make some wit me? Why is daht?"

"You're telling me she died of botulism?"

"It seem so, seem so."

Tillman was incited to fury. "Botulism, Doctor, causes vomiting and extreme pain. How can you not know that? My mother died a peaceful death."

Bradley turned with eyes murderous. "If it's so, de autopsy prove so. I cahnt know oddahwise."

"You're not touching her. Somebody else can do it, but not you."

"Mahn, daht's irrational."

Tillman jumped up from the bench and stood in front of the doctor's cluttered desk. "You'd be the last person on earth to touch her."

"Get out, Tillman."

Tillman was in no hurry to leave. "Remember Freddy Allen?" he asked.

"Who?" Then Bradley remembered and his face lost its arrogance.

"He was a friend of mine, a good one. He helped me out at Rosehill whenever I needed it."

"Tillmahn, consider I am only human."

"Yes, you are. So was Freddy until he came to you. You gave him bromides for acute appendicitis. The damn vet can diagnose better than you."

Bradley stood so fast, his eyes full of menace, that Tillman tensed to defend himself. "Get out," he shouted, pointing his finger at Tillman. "You muddah now a permahnent guest aht Rosehill till you come to you senses. Get out." The doctor came around from his desk to open the office door and then kicked it shut behind him.

Tillman, island hotelier, master of the business arts, student of impossibility, fond of weather that rarely oppressed, a man of contingencies and recently motherless—Tillman knew what to do. Whatever it took.

Whatever it took, Tillman told himself, back out on the streets, heedless in the late afternoon traffic. Sometimes that meant nothing at all, sometimes the gods spared you mockery, blessed you with style, and everything was easy.

At the airport he parked next to a single taxi out front, no one around to note this familiar island tune, the prolonged pitch of tires violently braked. Through the dark empty airport that always reminded him of an abandoned warehouse, Tillman searched for his friend Roland, the freelance bush pilot from Australia, a maverick and proven ace. Roland leapt around the warm world in his old Stearmann, spraying mountainsides of bananas with chemicals that prevented leaf spot and other blights. Tillman suspected the pilot was also part of the inter-island ring sponsored by the most influential businessmen to smuggle drugs, whiskey, cigarettes, stereos—whatever contraband could be crammed surreptitiously into the fuselage of a small plane. He seemed to be able to come and go as he please.

Roland's plane wasn't on the tarmac, or in the hangar. Sunset wasn't far away. Wherever Roland was, waltzing his plane through green, radical valleys, he would have to return before dark if he was coming in tonight. Tillman left a message with a mechanic in the machine shed for Roland to come find him at Rosehill.

Twilight had begun to radiate through the vegetation as he arrived back at the hotel, lifting the mélange of colors to a higher level of brilliance, as if each plant, each surface, were responding to the passage of the sun with its own interior luminosity. Inspector Cuffy was on the veranda of the west wing, laughing with Lemonille, her eyes flirtatious. They clammed up when Tillman appeared beside them.

"You haven't been waiting for me, have you?"

"Well, doan trouble yourself, mahn. I ben interviewin dis pretty young lady."

Tillman looked at Lemonille, who averted her eyes shyly. "Perhaps we cahn view de body of you muddah now." Cuffy said this without the slightest conviction. Tillman understood that, for the time being, the inspector was only interested in chasing Lemonille.

"I've had a hell of a day. Can I ask you to wait until tomorrow?"

"Daht strike me ahs reasonable," Cuffy said, allowing Tillman to experience his generosity.

"Besides, case solved, Cuffy," Tillman said, remembering the doctor, the hospital. "Bradley says something was wrong with the can of peaches my mother was eating when she died." If you want to believe such crap, Tillman added under his breath.

"I will study daht report," the inspector said. From the way he spoke, Tillman knew the investigation would drag on for days, weeks—especially if Lemonille played hard to get.

"Mistah Till-mahn?" Lemonille buried her chin, afraid to speak now that she had drawn attention to herself. More woe, thought Tillman. More hue and cry.

"What's wrong?"

"De cook say she afraid wit you dead muddah in de freezah. She say she not cookin wit a duppy so close by."

"All right, I'll go talk to her."

"She gone home."

"All right, I'll take care of it." He began to walk away.

"Mistah Till-mahn?" The woman's soft and guarded voice made him stop and turn around.

"What, Lemonille?"

"De men come wit de meat, but dey won't stock it."

Tillman inhaled nervously. "My mother again, right?"

Lemonille nodded. "Damn!" Tillman said, and scuffed the dirt.

Lemonille had one last piece of news. "Jevanee in a fuss cause you fire him."

"I didn't fire him, I told him to take the day off."

"Oh."

"Cuffy was there. He heard me." Cuffy looked into the trees and would not support of deny this allegation.

"Oh, but Jevanee tellin every bug in de sky you fire him. Daht mahn be fulla dread you goin put him out since de day you poppy die."

"Well, it's not true. Tell him that when you see him."

Tillman took these developments in stride, closing the restaurant for the evening by posting a scrawled note of apology at the entrance to the modest dining hall in the manor. For an hour he shuffled the cartons of dripping steaks from the kitchen to the freezer, stacking around the corpse of his mother as if these walls of spoiling meat were meant to be her tomb.

Event upon event—any day in the islands could keep accumulating such events until it was overrich, festering, or glorious, never to be reproduced so wonderfully. This day was really no different except that his mother had triggered some extraordinary complications that were taking him to the limit.

After showering in cold water, Tillman climbed the stairs in the main house to the sanctity of his office, his heart feeling too dry for blood to run through it, another fire hazard. What's to be done with Mother? On a hotplate he heated water for tea, sat with the steaming mug before the phone on his desk. Ministry offices would be closed at this hour and besides, the Minister of Health was no friend of his so there was no use ringing him up.

Finally he decided to call Dr. Layland. If Layland were still running the island's medical services, the day would have been much simpler, but Layland, a surgeon who had earned international respect for his papers on brain dysfunction in the tropics, had lost his job and his license to practice last winter when he refused to allow politics to interfere with the delicate removal of a bullet from an opposition member's neck. Although the case was before the Federation there was little hope of reinstatement before next year's elections.

Frankly, Layland told him, his accent bearing the vestige of an Oxford education, your position is most unenviable, my friend. A burial certificate, likewise permission to transfer the corpse back to its native soil, must be issued by both the national police and the Chief Medical Officer. The police, pending their own investigation of the cause of death, will not act without clearance from the CMO. In cases where the cause is unclear, it is unlikely that the CMO will agree to such clearance, especially for an expatriate Caucasian, until an autopsy is performed.

"But Bradley said it was the peaches, a bad can of peaches." Tillman jerked his head away from the telephone. How absurd and false those words sounded.

"Unlikely, but I see what you're getting at. Any cause is better than none, in light of your problem. But you know what sort of humbug that foolish man is. And you shan't have him on your side since you refused to have him do the autopsy."

Layland further explained that there was no alternative to removing the corpse from the walk-in freezer unless he had another freezer to put it in, or unless he committed it to the island's only morgue in the basement of the prison at Fort Albert—again, Bradley's domain. The final solution would be to bury her at Rosehill, but even this could not be accomplished without official permits. The police would come dig her up. Tillman asked if it was a mistake not to allow Bradley to cut open his mother.

"I'm afraid, Tillman, you must decide that for yourself," Layland answered. "But I think you must know that I am as disgusted by my erstwhile colleague as you are. Well, good luck."

Tillman pushed the phone away, rubbed his sore eyes, massaged the knots in his temples. He tilted back in his chair and almost went over backward, caught unaware by a flood of panic. Unclean paradise, he thought suddenly. What about Mother? Damn, she was dead and needed taking care of. Hard to believe. Lord, why did she come here anyway? She probably knew she was dying and figured the only dignified place to carry out the fact was under the roof of her only child. A mother's final strategy.

Outside on the grounds one of the stray dogs that were always about began a rabid barking. Tillman listened more closely, the sounds of squawking audible between the gaps in the dog's racket. The protest grew louder, unmistakable; Tillman was down the stairs and out on the dark lawn in no time at all, running toward the aviary.

There was some light from the few bulbs strung gaily through the branches of frangipani that overhung the parking area, enough to see what was going on, the wickedness being enacted in blue-satin shadows. In the gazebo, an angry silhouette swung a cutlass back and forth, lashing at the amorphous flutter of wings that seemed everywhere in the tall cage.

"Jevanee?" Tillman called, uncertain. The silhouette reeled violently, froze in its step and then burst through the door of the cage, yelling.

"Mahn, you cy-ahnt fir me, *I quit.*"

Tillman cringed at the vulgarity of such a dissembled non sequitur. All the bad television in the world, the stupid lyrics of false heroes, the latent rage of kung-fu and cowboy fantasies had entered into this man's head and here was the result, some new breed of imperial slave and his feeble, fatuous uprising.

"I didn't fire you. I said take the day off, cool down."

"Cy-ahnt fire *me*, you bitch."

The parrots were dead. Hatred exploded through Tillman. He wanted to kill the bartender. Fuck it. He wanted to shoot him down. He sprinted back across the lawn, up on the veranda toward the main house for the gun kept locked in the supply closet behind the check-in desk. Jevanee charged after him. A guest, the woman recently arrived from Wilmington, stepped out in front of Tillman from her room that fronted the veranda. Tillman shoulder-blocked her back through the door. She sprawled on her ass and for a second Tillman saw on her face an expression that welcomed violence as if it were an exotic game she had paid for.

"Stay in your goddamn room and bolt the door."

Tillman felt the bad TV engulfing them, the harried script-writer unbalanced with drugs and spite. Jevanee's foot plunged through the rotten boards in the veranda and lodged there. An exodus of pestilence swarmed from the splintery hole into the dim light, palmetto bugs flying blindly up through a growing crowd of smaller winged insects.

At the same time, stepping out from the darkness of a hedge of bougainvillea that ran in bushy clumps along the veranda, was Inspector Cuffy, pistol in hand. Tillman gawked at him. What was he doing around Rosehill so late? Lemonille had been encouraging him or the investigation had broadened to round-the-clock foolishness. Or, Tillman surmised, knowing it was true, Cuffy apparently knew Jevanee was coming after him and had lurked on the premises until the pot boiled over. A shot whistled by Tillman's head. Jevanee had a gun, too. Tillman pitched back off the deck and flattened out in the shrubbery.

"Stop," Cuffy shouted.

What the hell, thought Tillman. Where's Jevanee going anyway? He was near enough to smell the heavily Scotched breath of the bartender, see his eyes as dumb and frightened as the eyes of a wild horse. Another shot was fired off. Then a flurry of them as the two men emptied their pistols at each other with no effect. Silence and awkwardness as Cuffy and Jevanee confronted one another, the action gone out of them, praying thanks for the lives they still owned. Tillman crawled away toward the main house. He couldn't care less how they finished the drama, whether they killed each other with their bare hands, or retired together to a rum shop, blaming Tillman for the sour fate of the island. There was no point in getting upset about it now, once the hate had subsided, outdone by the comics.

He sat in the kitchen on the cutting table, facing the vault-like aluminum door of the refrigerated walk-in where his mother lay, preserved in ice, her silence having achieved, finally, a supreme hardness.

He wanted to talk to her, but even in death she seemed only another guest at the hotel, one with special requirements, nevertheless expecting courtesy and service, the proper distance kept safely between their lives. She had never kissed him on the lips, not once, but only brushed his cheek when an occasion required some tangible sign of motherly devotion. He had never been closer to her heart than when they cried together the first year he was in prep school, when she explained to him that she was leaving his father. She had appeared in his room late at night, having driven up from the city. She tuned the radio loud to a big band station and held him, the two of them shivering against each other on his bed. For her most recent visitation she had not written she was coming but showed up unannounced with only hand luggage—a leather grip of novels, a variety of modest bathing suits, caftans and creams. Behind her she had left Paris, where the weather had begun its decline toward winter. Whatever else she had left behind in her life was as obscure and sovereign as a foreign language. He wanted to talk to her but nothing translated.

The pilot found him there sometime in the middle of the night, Tillman forlorn, more tired than he could ever remember feeling. Roland looked worn out too, as if he had been stuck in an engine for hours, his cutoff shorts and colorless T-shirt smudged with grease, his hiking boots unlaced, and yet despite this general dishevelment his self-confidence was as apparent as the gleam of his teeth. Tillman remembered him at the beach bar late one night, yelling into the face of a man dressed in a seersucker suit, "I get things done, damn you, not like *these* bloody fools," and the sweep of his arm seemed to include the entire planet.

Tillman smiled mournfully back at him. "Roland, I need your help."

The pilot removed the mirrored sunglasses he wore at all times. "You've had a full day of it, I hear. What's on your mind, mate?"

Like an unwieldy piece of lumber, his mother's corpse banged to and fro in the short bed of the Land Rover, her wrapped feet pointing up over the tailgate. With a little effort and jockeying, they fitted her into the tube-shaped chemical tank in the fuselage of the Stearmann after Roland, Tillman standing by with a flashlight, unbolted two plates of sheet metal from the underbelly of the craft that concealed bay doors. You can't smuggle bales of grass with only a nozzle and a funnel, Roland explained.

Tillman was worried that an unscheduled flight would foul up Roland's good grace with the authorities. "Man," Roland said, "I've got more connections than the friggin' PM. And I mean of the UK, not this bloody cowpie." He thought for a second and was less flamboyant. "I've been in trouble before, of course. Nobody, Tillman, can touch this boy from down under as long as I have me bird, you see. Let us now lift upward into the splendid atmosphere and its many bright stars."

The chemical tank smelled cloyingly of poison. With his head poked in it, Tillman gagged, maneuvering the still-rigid body of his mother, the limbs clunking dully against the shiny metal, until she was positioned. Roland geared the bay doors back in place. The sound of them clicking into their locks brought relief to Tillman. They tucked themselves into the tiny cockpit. Tillman sat behind the pilot's seat, his legs flat against the floorboard, straddled as if he were riding a bobsled.

The airport shut down at dusk, the funding for runway lights never more than deadpan rhetoric during the height of the political season. Roland rested his sunglasses on the crown of his blond head as they taxied to the landward end of the strip, the mountains a cracked ridge behind them, the sea ahead down the length of pale concrete. Out there somewhere in the water, an incompatibly situated cay stuck up like a catcher's mitt for small planes whose pilots were down on their agility and nerve.

Roland switched off the lights on the instrumentation to cut all reflection in the cockpit. Transparent blackness, the gray runway stretching into nearby infinity.

Roland shouted over the roar, "She's a dumpy old bird but with no real cargo we should have some spirited moments."

Even as Roland spoke they were already jostling down the airstrip like an old hot rod on a rutted road, Tillman anticipating lift-off long before it actually happened. The slow climb against gravity seemed almost futile, the opaque hand of the cay suddenly materializing directly in front of them. Roland dropped a wing and slammed the rudder pedal. The Stearmann veered sharply away from the hazard, then leveled off and continued mounting upward. Tillman could hear his mother thump in the fuselage.

"Bit of a thrill," Roland shouted. Tillman closed his eyes and endured the languid speed and the hard grinding vibrations of the plane.

Roland put on his headset and talked to any ghost he could rouse. When Tillman opened his eyes again, the clouds out the windscreen had a tender pink sheen to their tops. The atmosphere tingled with blueness. The ocean was black below them, and Barbados, ten degrees off starboard, was blacker still, a solid puddle sprinkled with electricity. Along the horizon the new day was a thin red thread unraveling westward. The beauty of it all made Tillman melancholy.

Roland floated the plane down to earth like a fat old goose who couldn't be hurried. The airport on Barbados was modern and received plenty of international traffic so they found it awake and active at this hour. Taxiing to the small plane tarmac, Tillman experienced a moment of claustrophobia, smelling only the acrid human sweat that cut through the mechanical fumes. He hadn't noticed it while airborne but on the ground it was unbearable.

They parked and had the Stearmann serviced. In the wet, warm morning air Tillman's spirits revived. Roland walked through customs, headed for the bar to wait for him to do his business. Two hours later Tillman threw himself down in a chair next to the pilot and cradled his head on the sticky table, the surge of weariness through his back and neck almost making him pass out. He listened to Roland patiently suck his beer and commanded himself up to communicate the failure of the expedition.

"Bastards. They won't let me transfer her to a Stateside flight without the right paper."

"There was that chance," Roland admitted.

All along Tillman had believed that Barbados was the answer, people were reasonable there, that he only had to bring over the corpse of his mother, coffin her, place her on an Eastern flight to New York connecting with Boston, have a funeral home intercept her, bury her next to her ex-husband in the family plot on Beacon Hill. Send out death announcements to the few distant relatives scattered across the country, and then it would be over, back to normal. No mother, no obligations of blood. That was how she lived, anyway.

"Just how well connected are you, Roland?"

"Barbados is a bit iffy. The people are too damn sophisticated." He left to make some phone calls but returned with his hands out, the luckless palms upturned.

"Tillman, what next?"

Tillman exhaled and fought the urge to laugh, knowing it would mount to a hysterical outpouring of wretchedness. "I just don't know. Back to the island I guess. If you can see any other option, speak out. Please."

The pilot was unreadable behind the mirrors of his glasses. His young face had become loose and puffy since he had located Tillman at Rosehill. They settled their bar bill and left.

In the air again, the sound of the Stearmann rattled Tillman so thoroughly he felt as though the plane's engines were in his own skull. He tried to close his sleepless eyes against the killing brightness of the sun but could not stop the hypnotic flash that kept him staring below at the ocean. Halfway through the flight, Roland removed his headset and turned in his seat, letting the plane fly itself while he talked.

"Tillman," he shouted, "you realize I didn't bolt the plates back on the fuselage."

Tillman nodded absently and made no reply.

Roland jabbed his finger, pointing at the floor. "That handgear there by your foot opens the bay doors."

He resumed flying the plane, allowing Tillman his own thoughts. Tillman had none. He expected some inspiration or voice to break through his dizziness but it didn't happen. After several more minutes he tapped Roland on the shoulder. Roland turned again, lifting his glasses so Tillman could see his full face, his strained but resolute eyes; Tillman understood this gesture as a stripping of fear, tacit confirmation that they were two men in the world capable of making such a decision without ruining themselves with ambiguity.

"Okay, Roland, the hell with it. She never liked being in one place too long anyway."

"Right you are, then," Roland said solemnly. "Any special spot?"

"No."

"Better this way," Roland yelled as he dropped the airspeed and sank the Stearmann to one thousand feet. "The thing that bothers me about burial, you see, is caseation. Your friggin' body turns to cheese after a month in the dirt. How unspeakably nasty. I don't know if you've noticed, but I never eat cheese myself. Odd, isn't it?"

Tillman poked him on the shoulder again. "Knock it off."

"Sorry."

Tillman palmed the gear open. It was as easy as turning the faucet of a hose. When they felt her body dislodge and the tail bob inconsequentially, Roland banked the plane into a steep dive so they could view the interment. Tillman braced his hands against the windscreen and looked out, saw her cartwheeling for a moment and then stabilizing as the mauve chenille shroud came apart like a party streamer, a skydiver's Mae West. The Stearmann circled slowly around the invisible line of her descent through space.

"Too bad about your mother, mate," Roland called out finally. "My own, I don't remember much."

"I'm still young," Tillman confessed, surprising himself, the words blurting from his mouth unsolicited. Tears of gratitude slipped down his face from this unexpected report of the heart.

He looked down at the endless water, waves struggling and receding, the small carnation of foam marking his mother's entrance into the sea, saw her, through the medium of refraction, unwrapped from her shroud, naked and washed, crawling with pure, unlabored motion down the shafts of light and beyond their farthest reach, thawed into suppleness, small glass bubbles, the cold air of her last breath, expelled past her white lips, nuzzled by unnamed fish. Now she was a perfect swimmer, free of the air and the boundaries of the living, darkness passing through darkness, down, down, to kiss the silt of the ocean floor, to touch the bottom of the world with dead fingers.

They had watched her plummet with a sense of awe and wonderment, as boys would who have thrown an object off a high bridge. The pilot regained altitude and they continued westward. The realization came into Tillman, a palpable weight in his chest. I don't belong here, he said to himself, and immediately resisted the feeling, because that must have been the way she felt all her life.

Then, with the rich peaks of the island in sight, the heaviness dissipated. "It's beautiful here," he heard himself saying.

"What's that?" Roland shouted back.

"Beautiful," he repeated, and throughout Roland's clumsy landing, the jolt and thunder of the runway, "Mother, be at peace."

How I Came to Write This Story

In 1985 I went back to Togo to visit the Agbeli family, with whom I had lived as a Peace Corps volunteer in 1982 and 1983. My return followed so soon after my departure because of the way I had left: on vacation in Barcelona mid-way through my second year of service, the psychic turmoil built up during my time in Africa reached a crisis and I realized that to go back for my last six months would actually put me in danger. Instead I flew home, without having said good-bye. Letters from Togolese friends informed me that numerous people in the village assumed I had died. Though this jibed with an African idea of death as abrupt, ubiquitous, and inexplicable, it distressed me, and I went back in 1985 partly to prove that I was still alive, partly to say the unsaid good-bye and explain why I hadn't come back from Spain, and partly to let them know that I hadn't forgotten them. But no matter how one leaves, everyone who lives and works in such a place leaves with regret—for the hopes raised and then disappointed, the expectations unmet, the inequality of options, the finality of departure. I tried to convey something of this feeling in "The Water-Girl," which I wrote shortly after coming back from that 1985 trip.

—George Packer

GEORGE PACKER (Togo, 1982-1983) was born near San Francisco in 1960. After graduating from Yale he joined the Peace Corps and taught English in Togo, West Africa. Since 1984 he has lived in the Boston area, where he worked for several years as a carpenter and then as a writing teacher at Harvard, MIT, Emerson College, and the Harvard Extension School. He is the author of *The Village of Waiting*, the account of his experience in Africa, and two novels, *The Half Man* and *Central Square*, which was published last fall. *Blood of the Liberals*, a three-generational history, will appear later this year.

THE WATER-GIRL

by George Packer

Tony Mears had arrived in Ghana at a bad time. The harmattan wind was blowing—clouds of white dust, dryness in the nostrils— and on it the smells from the beach where Ghanaians relieved themselves went through the city and didn't even spare the guests of first-class hotels. Accra was swollen with young men. Expelled from Nigeria with millions of other illegal migrant workers, uneasy and unwanted here, they idled in the streets, radios blasting juju, and spoke the pidgin they'd acquired in Lagos, shamming as money lords, waylaying whites: "Change! Dollar, sterling, deutsche mark!"

Lonely on his first night at the hotel, Mears had called Sampson Omaboe from the lobby phone.

"Here so soon, *jallay*! I thought it was to be March."

"I had the IMF work it out with Finance here—a little early. I guess I wrote you about me and Jean."

"Afraid you did. So sorry. But you're among friends now, *jallay*. We'll see to it you're not gloomy." And laughter, full of promises, had hissed over the line.

The next afternoon they were drinking under the palms outside the hotel, two bottles of Black Star beer on the shellacked bamboo table between them. Every few minutes they had to move their chairs to stay in shadow. Omaboe, a tour guide, was entertaining Mears with trade stories.

"A group of Dutch comes through and the lady says, 'We want to see something of Africa, but we've only got three days.' 'Leave it to Sam' (putting on my assistant tribal chief's voice), 'he will arrange.' In three days I pack animals, Obuasi gold mine, and fetish ceremony with dancers bare-breasted. Unfortunately no time for

Ghanaians. At the end of the tour the lady says to me, 'Mr. Oombobo, in three days we feel you've shown us everything there is to see—what a remarkable guide!'"

A moist tip of tongue appeared between Omaboe's teeth. Salivary noises came up from his throat into his mouth and he laid his hands on the thick belly as if to subdue its shaking. Mears had known him for three years, but only now noticed how laughter turned the face, with its prominent ears and impish eyes, into the ape-African of old caricatures.

He said, "You've gotten cynical, Sam."

"At all! If they want to believe Africa is some place where you can eat squid for dinner and then go round the corner for Ashanti drumming, who is Sam to disappoint them?"

"Disappointment doesn't tip very well, does it."

"*Jallay*, it's you who've gotten cynical. I can see it in your eyes, like—like dried-out millet seeds! Very well, it doesn't. But why should I have to believe in it, any more than I believe in that?" He motioned across the street, where a banner suspended from the peeling facade of a government building urged popular unity with the ruling council. "The government pays me, the lady tips me. You know, we Ashanti people have a saying—'Pray over the goat, but eat it too.' You, you'd have me starve! Ha ha!"

The bargirl came by with a tray and asked if Omaboe wanted another beer. She was wearing a loose cotton shirt, and when she reached for the foam-stained bottle a tear in the armpit opened onto black dampness. In spite of the wind little drops of sweat beaded above her lip, painted cherry-red.

Mears asked, "And the Ashanti believe in—?"

Omaboe twisted around to look at the retreating figure of the girl. "Life, pleasure, what does any African? You people—" He waved, and seemed to take in the white world with it. "—you just make too many problems for yourselves where you don't need to. You, you believe in fidelity, and hard-soled shoes."

Mears nodded. "That's right. And I think you people should try to forget we ever came. Default on the debt, tear down that ridiculous ministry. Scrape the paint off the bargirl's face and clear out of Accra for the bush. Give these poor Lagos bastards some yam fields. Don't worry, we'll take the blame. Look where it's gotten us."

"*Jallay*, stop. You're talking yourself out of a job."

Mears had a private contract with the International Monetary

Fund and African governments as an economic advisor—two-week stints in a couple of countries a year negotiating loan terms. This was his fourth trip to Ghana (he thought of himself as a veteran) but his first anywhere since the split with Jean. Since Jean left him.

At 32, he was gaining a name in international finance almost as fast as he was losing interest in his life. "Don't people in Africa talk?" Jean had asked when he got back from Gambia last year. "You seem out of practice. Maybe you're going to have to choose between Africa and me." "Maybe they have nothing to talk about," he'd replied. "No Jordan Marsh, no Filene's, no condo market." She made the choice for him. After two years of living together, he was left with a dim impression of the mole on her chin, aggressive sensuality, and three dozen pairs of shoes in the closet. Suddenly alone in snowbound Boston, he didn't know what to do with himself. His tongue went dry and prickly. And whenever he thought of the African cities he'd worked in, the farmers leading goats through markets, the reviving assault of hot pepper and bright cloth, it occurred to him that this might be the thing to do: go back.

With a wink Sampson Omaboe assured Mears he would be looked after—and what did he think of the girl who was waiting on them? Or there was a woman at the bureau—.

Mears shook his head. That wasn't what he needed. But just this morning, on his first full day, something strange had happened. He had plunged into the market and, overcome by heat and human smells, sat down on a yam-seller's bench and squinted up to see a water-girl lifting her styrofoam bucket off her head. Twentyish, small, not pretty, she had wordlessly dipped her calabash in the cool murky water and brought up a drink for the foolish visitor who'd tried too much too soon. Her blue dress was "dead white man" clothing, from the Goodwill—it might have hung in a closet in suburban Boston. It was sun-bleached now and streaked with dirt around the hem. At the bottom of her bucket silver and brass coins swam and glinted. But Mears had had no change, and tried to force a 50-cedi note in her hand.

Smiling, she'd shaken her head, raised the bucket, and disappeared.

Mears said aloud, "The water-girls work one market, or go from market to market?"

Omaboe was astounded. "Water-girls, be serious, man! They

hardly have a word of English. I'm talking about someone for you, a beevie at the hotel with breasts like papaya in October! *Jallay*, you have some ideas."

"Remember, I'm not Ashanti."

Omaboe looked him up and down. "You are not Ashanti. You are blessed to be of the American male species, with hair-color like the bush in dry season and green eyes—well, a little washed-out, but close to the banana leaf. I say you could pass for an English yachtsman who's rather fond of gin. Forget about girls who never reached second form in school, *jallay*. Sam's reputation in the trade could never recover itself."

Mears smiled sourly at his friend, at the line Omaboe was walking between guide and pimp: the smile curled half his lip upward, in a way it had recently begun to set.

Having arrived, Mears didn't have the slightest interest in his work. The country was bankrupt. There were hours of meetings with Ghanaian officials who flattered him on his "success in negotiating the Gambia arrangement," but, every time a loan guideline came up, asserted, "Mr. Mears, Ghana is a sovereign state." The meetings left a residue of disgust, which he associated with the evil wind blowing from the beach, the cripple who sat in a tangle of legs and held the hotel door open for a coin, the bargirl, the gangs from Lagos.

The harmattan evenings were cool, and Accra turned spectral behind its veil of settling dust. Each evening Mears put on his jacket, left his key for the desk-clerk, and escaped the carpets and air-conditioning into streets where leather-vendors were packing away sandals and bags, market stalls had closed up under flimsy tin, heaps of rotted fruit and dirty cloth lay on the pavement from the day's commerce. "*Bruni, bruni!*"—a little boy in an oversized rugby shirt, holding his mother's hand, pointing at him in wonder. Alone, as in Boston, but no longer anonymous, he enjoyed the surprise of his skin for people who passed: in the mingled dust of Sahara winds and streets under the feet of the market crowds hurrying home, he imagined his appearance to them as something foreign and magical. With the sun down his fatigue wore off, and the city could become what he had anticipated, what he had come for. After three days, there had been no more sign of the water-girl.

"You don't remember? Monday, in the big market—"

She looked up quizzically into his face. He'd spotted her (the same light blue dress) and followed past the sports stadium, down the casket-makers' street, brushing and bumping shoulders with his eyes set 20 yards ahead on the styrofoam bucket that floated through the crowd. When he was alongside, her eyes had swiveled around and she was speechless with surprise. Sweat streamed down her cheeks.

"You gave me...I was hot from the sun...."

She must have remembered. Whites in decaying Accra were almost as rare as Ghanaians in Boston. Having lifted the bucket off the coil of cloth on her matted hair, she was going through the necessary rituals of evasion and formality.

"The big market...Ah!" She remembered: he was the one who'd gone in the sun without a hat. He should be more careful: the sun here wasn't like the one in Europe. European people weren't used to it.

"Actually, I'm American. But I'm not new here. You're from Accra?"

She shook her head. "From Volta region." She was an Ewe then. In Accra they were joked about—hicks, bush folk. It took her three tries before he understood her name was Cynthia: she said it charmingly, "Seentya." He offered the only words of Ewe he knew, picked up on another visit, meaning *Where are you going?* She screwed up her face and asked, "You say?" When she realized he was trying to speak her language she bent over and repeated the question twice in her laughter. Then, mopping her face with the coiled cloth, she answered something long in the gutturals and exclamations of Ewe.

"What does that mean?"

But she refused: she seemed to be mock-reproving him.

Mears had thought, if he happened to see her again, of asking her to meet him at the hotel bar; but there would be her shock at the chandeliered lobby, and the groups of Europeans lounging about in overstuffed chairs with pale dimpled thighs exposed by skirts and shorts. He decided on the "Jungle Bar," not far from the hotel, where young Ghanaians hung out. Sampson Omaboe had recommended it—recommended it to all his tourists who wanted some safe local color in their night life. Mears had objected to "tourist" and "local color" but had taken the suggestion.

Her lip hung open in worry, and it made him see that she was older than he'd thought, perhaps almost his age, her small breasts beginning to sag beneath the dress. It came to him in a flash that made him wince slightly at his stupidity—of course, married! She would have no ring to prove it, but at this age, a villager.... Where was her baby then? And why selling water?—an occupation for girls.

"No, I can't come," she said, two fingers over her mouth.

Mears, overcome with impatience, wondered aloud, "Do you have a husband?"

"With God."

He said he was deeply sorry. And he pressed her to come. She was widowed and alone, in a city where her language was hardly spoken, making her living off water and a styrofoam bucket. "Only a drink," he said, "to talk with each other." The moment's absurdity —in the middle of the street, among stares, a white on business from the U.S. begging a half-literate water-girl to meet him for a drink—occurred in his ear as a hissing laughter that was Sampson Omaboe's. Mears' vision was filled with something else: soft black eyes, high cheekbones, the worried lower lip. An unexpected surge of feeling was tearing through his chest, like the ripping of a muscle that's been clenched after months of slackness. In the end she agreed to meet him only when he gave his word the bar wasn't frequented by prostitutes and their white clients.

Walking toward the Finance Ministry, Mears remembered the five cedis he owed her. But he didn't run after her. He knew she would refuse it, and money would poison everything.

Dressing that evening in his hotel room, Mears went through the old and by now unfamiliar ritual of preparing to see a strange woman. The flicking back of hair, turnings from side to side in the mirror, straightening of the eyebrows with a moist fingertip. At the same time he watched himself pose. His mouth was set in its half-curl upward as a youth's nervous preenings ridiculously superimposed on a 32-year-old's unbelief. He saw himself at two, at three removes. He was aware of the fluttering against his ribs, the lightness in his fingertips; of the squalor of the whole mirrored mime-show and the pleasure it gave him; of thinking of this water-girl as the needed cleansing and knowing she wasn't; of being aware of the awarenesses.

He snapped his head away from the mirror. "You people," he said aloud, surprised by his own voice, "you make too many problems for yourselves." He finished buttoning his pink pin-stripe shirt; and he focused on the fresh clean shirtfront as a simple thing, a certainty, to hold to through the evening.

Music boomed from a tape system behind the bar, and the Africans who weren't on the floor dancing in the shower of pink and green light watched the dancers from benches and didn't talk. A girl leaned behind the bar, fist pushed against her cheek, drumming time with her fingers. The couples moved slower than the American funk and jangling Zairoise, in curt gestures, any motion a labor in the heat. But they stayed in rhythm—hands held, the man's other hand light on the woman's waist, swaying their high buttocks in quick shuffles around a single point, faces averted: a sensual arrogance on the men's, on the women's sullen compliance. In the air hung the sum smell of a hundred colognes and perfumes. As they wore off, the sharp human odor they were meant to cover permeated through and mingled with the sweetness.

Cynthia didn't like to dance. They sat side by side against the wall, he sipping beer and she Fanta. Under the noise he managed to learn that she lived with a cousin in a quarter he'd never heard of, that she had a child "by accident" back in the village with her parents, that she had come to Accra for work and "something better," that she had missed her child terribly at first but after two years didn't think about him so much.

"When I first came I am tending city gardens. After that a good job, I was maid for Nigerian family and their baby. After that stop, I start the water business."

Mears smiled: he liked the word "business" applied to her styrofoam bucket. "What happened?" he asked. "With the Nigerian family?"

"Things happen."

She was already tired of the water business, but for the moment there was nothing else. Things were bad for Ghanaians; and as if to demonstrate it, she showed him the place on her middle finger where gripping the bucket-handle had raised a hard thick callous.

That was all. The music was too loud, she was too remote—they had nothing to talk about. He didn't say a word about his work, and she didn't ask—out of reticence, or ignorance, or indifference. So they sat in a silence that embarrassed him and that she showed no sign of wanting to fill: she was a small presence in his peripheral vision, occasionally tapping one fist in the other palm. But he noted changes since that afternoon on the street: she had put on a print dress, some sort of synthetic, white and red camellias against maroon; her hair, out from under the burden of the bucket and the rolled cloth, was plaited back in thin braids that hung limp and shook when she moved her head; and a pair of garish earrings, imitation gold with shiny red plastic where the stone should have been, dangled from her ears. They annoyed him at once—they seemed a vulgar concession to him or to what an observer might have made of the situation. He wanted to tell her to take them off—she was a villager, not a tart. He would buy her real gold earrings in the market, the kind the women must wear up in villages around the gold mines.

After an hour he suggested leaving. She followed him out, weaving through the slow dancing bodies, but near the door she turned around and confronted a group of men at the bar.

"You say what?" she demanded.

One of the men had spoken. Sitting on a stool with his hands placed lightly on his spread thighs, his belly pushing out between the bottom buttons of a print shirt, he snickered and repeated something. Mears couldn't make sense of it, it was Ga, the local language around Accra.

"You are foolish," she hissed in English. "You are foolish people."

"Don't listen to him, Cynthia, let's go." Mears took her hand.

"Foolish," she repeated, dropping his hand, ignoring him. "You are rude Lagos people. You speak things of a child."

The Ghanaian looked at Mears and addressed him in Ga, as if they were in cahoots about something, man to man—at the same time mocking the white man's ignorance.

Outside, in the cooler air suddenly quiet, he took her hand again and held it insistently, turning her to face him. She came up about to his chin, and looked at him somewhere around the mouth.

"Why don't you ignore them?"

"They say foolish things—I am your *hotelito*, that I want money. They are foolish." She spoke with an angry, defensive contempt.

"Yes, they are. So you should ignore them."

"Is why I didn't like to come—because they will say such things—"

"But why do you care, since they're foolish? Why can't—"

"People hear. And others start to say things too. Accra is small city...."

But she let him hold her hand there, at the edge of the street beside a square concrete gutter with a residue of black bilge-water. Nearby a woman huddled in cloth behind a table, indifferent to them, her stacks of matchboxes and cigarettes and soaps lit orange by a paraffin wick flaming out of a tin can. Mears stroked Cynthia's fingers and searched for the place on the middle one, the place that she'd shown him inside the bar and that had shamed him, with his explanations of productivity and unemployment, his dabblings in sociopsychology: all of it amounted to this rough hard patch of yellowish skin. Stroking it, he entered what was real and alive about her, and he ached for her.

She adjusted her hand to hide the callous from his examining fingers.

"Listen, can we go to a hotel near here I know of—a friend tells me it's a good place, private—" She smiled bitterly, and looked away, at the street. "Why? Please—"

Then she looked straight at him, so abruptly it was like a challenge and he had to avoid her eyes. "I want to tell you," she said without drama. "I made a promise to my God. If I don't move with any man this year, then next first January He will answer me. That is why. Because my God will punish me! I promise Him." And she gasped with laughter, as if what she'd said surprised her as much as him.

She turned to go, and had already walked 20 feet before Mears could seize on something to bring her back. "There's an American film at the cinema tomorrow!"

She half-turned. "Tomorrow is Sunday. I pray and plait my hair."

He was with Omaboe in their usual place, at the cafe outside his hotel, in the dead hours, moving out of the sun. The beer had gone straight to his head and made him sluggish and testy. A heavy fly was circling his mug and landing on the cardboard coaster covering the rim. Once, sipping, Mears put the mug down and forgot to cover it; when he lifted it again the fly was floating in the surface froth, its bristle legs wriggling in the air. Mears watched it struggle, then reached in with a finger, dragged it up the side of the mug, and flicked it in the dust. But now the beer was no good.

When Sampson Omaboe heard the story he didn't laugh, but ran a finger over his lips in thought, and then said seriously, "I don't know, *jallay*. You're in a fine pickle now. These girls from the villages, they are too religious, you know, too religious. For God's sake, man, why can't you just pick out one of the girls at the Star or the Intercontinental and have it done with? I've told you before they won't blink for a white, and for a white man of quality like you—they would howl like, like a fox on a cold winter morning!"

Now Omaboe's laughter sputtered and shook his body, but the hot afternoon air absorbed it and he went quiet and Mears didn't respond.

"I mean, look here, why do you people have to make it so complicated? With God for a rival, *jallay*, your chances are rather slim, aren't they. And when there are so many lovely girls in Accra with less, what's the word, scruples. Instead you go and fall half crackers for this water-girl. And she's not even Ashanti or Ga!"

"So it's tribalism. And you tell tourists there's no tribal feelings in Ghana any more. You're a hired propagandist."

Omaboe shrugged at the appraisal and went on rubbing his finger over his lip, pondering the problem as if Mears had lost his traveler's checks. "And you'll be gone in—how many? Six days. What's going to come of this piece of lunacy for you?"

"Forget about the future. I'm worried about now."

Omaboe began to mutter: "But that's all shove be'ind me— long ago an' fur away, An' there ain't no buses runnin' from the Bank to Mandalay....'"

"What in hell are you talking about?"

"Kipling. My God, you Americans rule the world, and you don't know English poetry. The Africans have to teach you." And he went on reciting in a measured baritone, turning the cockney into something like a parody of slave English, relishing the drama of each word:

"'By the old Moulmein Pagoda, lookin' lazy at the sea
There's a Burma girl a-settin', and I know she thinks o' me;
For the wind is in the palm trees, and the temple-bells they say:
"Come you back, you British soldier; come you back to
Mandalay!"'"

Mears swallowed the last bit of foam in his mug.

"'Come you back, you British soldier!'" Omaboe, staring at Mears, echoed himself. "'Come you back—to Mandalay!' Ha-ha!"

"Oh spare me that—imperialist trash. It's given me a head-ache. Obviously you don't understand."

"Be careful," Omaboe said suddenly. His round impish face had fallen hard, lost its humor and turned inward and severe. His chin was near his chest, and he glared up under his eyebrows like a card player. "Be careful, *jallay*. We don't understand you people; you're right. You stay such a short time, you tourists, and we try to give you what you want, but it's difficult to know. Be careful with the girl, she may not understand too."

Banter had suddenly taken a wrong street and turned into malice. The air between them quivered with anger, and Mears was the one to flinch. He felt himself courting some danger or dis-covery in the isolation of a strange city: and he reached back for the man who had been standing there a minute ago.

"I see what you're saying, Sam. I have been careful—for example I haven't brought her here. She'd be watched: I know what people would think, whisper—oh, it's just money on her part, sex on his."

Sampson Omaboe slapped his broad hands on the bamboo tabletop. "But my God, *jallay*, what is it then?"

Mears said coldly, "I haven't given her a thing."

Omaboe opened his mouth and a faint smile materialized. It was a false lure, and Mears took it as an offer of peace and began to meet the man halfway. But then he saw. The smile was not a friend's—it encircled, mocked.

"Don't you at least owe the girl a new dress for her trouble?"

Mears couldn't identify the moment when she agreed to come. Simply, at the end of the day they'd spent together, he saw she would.

They'd walked through the market, where he amused her with his stabs at market-talk among the vendors and his skill in bargaining down the exorbitant prices quoted to whites. They'd gone out to the airport to watch Ghana and Nigeria Airways planes take off and land—she'd never seen them up close, never known anything like the scream of jet engines. Her excitement loosened him, and in the dusty breeze of the observation deck he concocted joking arguments against her promise.

"God came to me in a dream last night—He said He would allow it, He said, 'You have the poor with you always, but Mears you have not always.'"

"God hears you when you speak," she wagged a finger.

"Look at these planes, Cynthia—with Him all things are possible."

She gazed out at the jets on the runway and refused to show she was impressed. "Which plane you are leaving on?" she said.

It was Wednesday, three days before his ticket would send him home—a market day for her, and he insisted on reimbursing her for her lost income. He was astonished that it amounted to a little less than a dollar. He paid for meals, taxis, her ticket to the observation deck. He found himself silently comparing her figure with the dead white man dresses in the market, the new dresses hanging in shops. It didn't matter. He had already made the calculation: becoming one of the despised tourists, in exchange for this small joy.

They went to dinner in a European restaurant. Sitting across the table and sipping beer that had made them both slightly high, Mears was describing his country to her.

"These trains that run under the ground can take you anywhere in the city—just like that. You go under the street, and when you come up again you're on the other side of town."

"Is fast?"

"In minutes. It's wonderful. I hope you can see some day."

"If God wills...."

He hesitated, but only a second. "I'm sure He does."

Bent over her plate, she smiled at the thought; and looked up.

It was past eleven when they arrived. The hotel was on an unpaved side street, but it called itself international. The old clerk was asleep in a chair, letting out streams of snores, one hand on his groin. They roused him, he opened the crumpled guest-book, Mears signed in. The wad of dollars he laid on the desk made a passport unnecessary. The clerk didn't ask for luggage. He led them up a stairway and across a hall that smelled of dirty water and he jangled his key in the lock of number seven. Inside, he switched on the light, a single bulb screwed into the socket over the bed, and pointed vaguely at the room. "Number seven." Yawning, he went out.

Mears crossed the floor to turn on the air-conditioner under the window, a small, sooty box, which started up with a low hum. He went back to the door and switched off the light.

She undressed quickly, without ceremony, as if everything had been arranged. Before his trousers were off she was lying naked on the sheet, on her belly, her buttocks swelling up from the valley of her muscled back, her thin brown legs together, her upper body propped on elbows, hands together as if in absent-minded prayer. Around her waist were four strands of beads, the beads African girls wear from infancy to their marriage day. She had never married then, Mears thought, stripping off his socks at the side of the bed. Yet she'd said her husband was with God. The breasts bunched between her arms drooped thin and wrinkled, the one sign of her child—otherwise it was hard to believe a baby had passed through the taut belly he'd glimpsed and the narrow hips. The body of a woman who had done physical work for years but hadn't ruined it with children. Naked, he sat on the bed Indian-style, his toes touching her flank. In that position his own body, which just now struck him as hideously pale, betrayed a single fold of flesh around the belly.

Confronted with this strange brown naked form, near enough to smell, Mears went hot with shame. Cynthia waited without smiling.

She touched his knee and pulled at the blond hairs. "Is nice. For African men, no hair." She was stroking his knee lightly with her fingertips. And now she was smiling: but it was a smile Mears hadn't seen before. Heavy-lidded, heavy-lipped, it promised pleasure. It had been brought out for him.

"You don't like?"

She had felt his knee tremble and withdraw.

"I like."

But he wanted to talk. Finding something to say, he touched the earring dangling from her right lobe. "Why do you wear these?"

"I'm a girl," she said with a slight incredulous laugh. "Girls wear."

"Girls who work in bars and hotels. Gold must be cheap in Accra, no?"

"Gold! Is dear, dear." She shook her head at the idea of gold earrings. "They are lucky, the ones in bars and hotels. If I could—but...howfodo?" He knew the expression—it meant, What is one to do?

"Lucky? The men coming in to take them in exchange for tips, the way they have to paint their faces...."

"The money—is good. Hundred fifty, two hundred cedis a day. Better to sell beer than water."

"Why do you sell water? If you need help to change—"

"I sell water because last year I thought to have a husband, then I'm waiting. But...."

Her voice thinned, her hand closed. She turned to stare at the pillow.

"Husband, husband," he said. "Cynthia, Accra girls marry late, some 28, even 30. And your son is with your parents. After a husband there'll be nothing but children and chores. I see what happens to African women. Enjoy your freedom."

His knee was forgotten. Briefly, realizing the moment was ebbing, Mears panicked. He began stroking her shoulder and back—the skin was wonderfully smooth and unbroken beneath his fingers—but he could feel she had already slipped away.

"Last year I thought to have a husband," she repeated as if he wasn't listening, talking to herself. "I meet a man who work in Lagos. When he came home one time for visiting he said he will marry and support me. And he send me money every time for those months I'm waiting. When he visit, I cook for him, I move freely with this man any time. He gave me things—a watch, these—"

She touched the earring Mears had touched.

He waited a moment. "And what happened to this man?"

She went on in her privacy while he listened. "Last 9 May he have to come back to Ghana with the others from Nigeria. When I hear this I quit my work, the maid for Nigerian family, and prepare to marry. For him I quit! On 15 May I went to his house, and I saw he marry another wife in Lagos. He said her parents force him. I didn't cry, I didn't speak, but when I leave it was hard to walk across the road. When I went home to cook supper for my cousin I didn't like to eat. For two days I can't eat. And then I made my promise to my God: that He will send me a husband."

She stopped speaking, and a smile stirred her lip.

"So, my water business."

The hoarse whir of the air-conditioner had chilled the room. Mears knew the woman beside him was cold, and he wanted to cover her. She seemed small and exposed. Cynthia folded her elbows under her chest and laid her head on the pillow, turned to him but looking past.

He went to the window. Its glass louvers were shut. Eventually, with the air-conditioning off, the room would stifle them. But there wasn't a screen: and with the window open and no cold air mosquitoes would come in. An English businessman had once told him mosquitoes didn't like to bite Africans—something about the blood, evolutionary differences. Mears now wondered why he hadn't asked how malaria was contracted. He reached for the switch, then decided to leave it on and open the window. He glanced at the bed. From the pillow, over a hunched shoulder, she seemed to be staring back.

Standing half-blind in the darkness Mears steadied himself with a hand on the window-crank and said, "It's late. Let's sleep." He opened the louvers onto harmattan dust. A dry wind blew against his naked body, and he caught a glimpse of tin rooftops and an old woman grinding peppers in the adjacent yard. Just then the old woman looked up. She gasped at the sight in the window: an orange-stained hand flew to her mouth and she shrieked with laughter. In the moment before turning away Mears saw himself as she must have seen him, the comical fish-white belly, the face too full of regret to care.

How I Came to Write This Story

I wrote "The Guide" in the United States about a year after I returned from Dakar, Senegal West Africa, where I served as a Peace Corps Volunteer for two years. While in Africa I had set out alone for Timbuktu, but for some reason, when the plane arrived in Mali, I left the airport. I wandered into a brothel/hotel much like the Grand Hotel du Mali, in the fictional town, Oulaba and eventually, up into the cliffs where I spent the night in a cave and heard an animal over my head. Unlike Darren, I did not have a guide. I don't know where Jaraffe comes from. Parts of the story, including the cave filled with human skeletons, the magician, etc. come from the stories other travelers told me along the way. I felt compelled to write the story for myself, as compensation for not going to Timbuktu.
— Melanie Sumner

MELANIE SUMNER (Senegal 1988-90) was born in Middletown, Ohio, grew up in Georgia, and currently lives in New Mexico with her husband and daughter. She has been a visiting lecturer at the University of North Carolina at Chapel Hill, where she received a BA in Religious Studies. She earned an MA in Creative Writing from Boston University and won fellowships to The Fine Arts Work Center in Provincetown, MA and Yaddo, in Saratoga Springs, NY. Her first book of fiction, *Polite Society*, was published by Seymour Lawrence/Houghton Mifflin in 1995 and has won The Whiting Award and the RPCV Writers & Readers Maria Thomas Fiction Award. Her short stories have been published in *The New Yorker, Story, Seventeen*, and other magazines, and have been anthologized in various collections, including *New Stories from the South* and *Best of a Decade*. Her essays have been published in Conde Nast *Sports for Woman* and *The New York Times: Sophisticated Traveler*. Excerpts from the novel she is currently writing have been accepted for publication by *Story* and *DoubleTake*.

THE GUIDE

by Melanie Sumner

At the gate of the Grand Hotel du Mali, a brothel that served as an inn for the rare tourist in Oulaba, Darren paid her first guide. The child had only carried her pack up the short path from the road, and his dark eyes grew round as he took the one hundred C.F.A. coin into his fist. Immediately, the other boys attacked him, pawing for the money. "White lady!" one of the children shouted in French. "We all led you here. We are all your guides, and you must pay all of us!"

Darren shook her head, banged the gate shut behind her, and went down a dark corridor. Behind one of the closed doors, a whore wailed. Her voice rose and fell in a siren, now laughing, now crying, following Darren down and around the halls to the courtyard, where the sound of the television drowned it out. The black and white set perched precariously on a stack of crates, balanced by two rabbit ears. Beneath the screen, Malians sat on mats, mesmerized by a fuzzy, French-dubbed episode of Dallas. They barely turned their heads as the small, pale American wearing a man's felt hat crossed the courtyard to the bar.

"Bonsoir, Madame," she said to the stout woman leaning in the doorway. "Je m'appelle Darren." She asked for a room for the night.

The hotel keeper looked her over. She uncrossed her arms to wipe her hands on the faded pagne wrapped around her hips and reaching to her ankles. Then she folded her arms back over her chest and returned her gaze to the white woman in bed with her lover on the TV screen. The gold ring in the hotelkeeper's nose glinted in the dim light.

From a shadowy corner of the room, a boy stepped forward. "Bonsoir, Madame Darren," he said. He bowed low, like a magician on stage and said in French, "Please excuse my mother, for she doesn't speak the languages of the first world. My name is Jaraffe, and I am at your disposal." He offered a brilliant smile. "American, I presume? Americans are my favorite people. How do you find Mali? If you care to see our cliffs tomorrow, I am pleased to be your guide. You are tired. Perhaps you would like a beer? I suggest the imported beer. Normally, of course, one can't find such luxuries in Oulaba, but this is your lucky day." He lifted his thin shoulders in an elegant shrug.

She wanted to laugh at him, but she was stunned by his beauty. He was slender, with skin the color of honey and silky black curls that fell into damp ringlets at the nape of his neck. His nose was precise and delicate; his lips curved salaciously, blood red against small, even white teeth. A new T-shirt, several sizes too large, slid off one shoulder, baring the bones of his chest. As she studied him he kept his head demurely bowed, hiding his eyes beneath their lashes, but suddenly he raised his head and stared back. He had the yellow eyes of a cat.

"How old are you, Jaraffe?"

"Me? Well, I am thirteen. No, not thirteen. Did I say thirteen?" He affected a bemused chuckle and stretched himself up taller. "I am fourteen, actually. Almost fifteen."

"I'll have the imported beer," she said, sure that he would return with a flat, warm Gazelle, or something worse, and a long explanation. She sat down at a low, rusty table and rested her head in her hands. In a few moments he reappeared with an icy bottle of Heineken. She held her hand out before she caught herself.

Then she narrowed her eyes in the expression of jaded wariness that she adopted in her dealings with Africans. The expression was fake. She was alone and, more or less, lost. In a leather pouch hanging from her neck and tucked inside her khaki pants she had five hundred dollars—more money than the average African earned in a year. If she had to, she would pay an outrageous price for the cold beer, and the child knew this. "How much?" she asked.

"For you, my friend, seven hundred C.F.A."

"Six hundred."

He shrugged, handed her the bottle, and returned to his stool in the corner. After a weary sigh, he removed a crumpled cigarette from his shirt pocket and approached her again. "Do you have a light, Darren?" When she shook her head, he found some matches in his pocket, smiled apologetically, and, lighting his cigarette, sat down beside her.

The game began. Darren considered telling him that she had not invited him to sit with her, but she was too tired to get tangled in the absurd exchange that would inevitably follow such an announcement, and after all, Jaraffe was only a boy.

Three days ago she had set out from Senegal on an odyssey to Timbuktu, and since then she had not had a moment's respite from African men who considered any young white woman traveling alone to be public property. Her furious protests were as delightful to these men as if they came from the mouth of an unbranded cow wandering in their fields. In the first hour of the train ride from Dakar to Bamako, a note was pressed into her hand:

Hello my American friend. I find you is so very nice for me. So yes you please me. I love you. Now we will be together. Nice.

For the next twenty hours, no matter where she sat on the train, the man wedged himself in beside her, smiling indulgently at her rejections. He did not consider himself rude.

Now, having gained a seat at her table, Jaraffe sailed into the relationship. "Are you married, if you don't mind my asking?" Smoke curled softly out of his lips and hung in the moist air between them. He wasn't inhaling.

"Yes," she lied.

"Your husband is an oil tycoon, perhaps? Or a doctor? It's none of my business. I myself will be a surgeon. When I have saved enough money I am going to America to study medicine. Now, when I am not in school, I work as a guide. I give most of the pay to my mother, of course, but I save what I can for my journey to America. Perhaps you and your husband would like me to take you to the cliffs tomorrow? We can go and return in a single day, if you like."

"I wasn't...my husband and I weren't planning to go to the cliffs."

With a wave of his hand, he dismissed this detail. "I know the cliffs. The other boys will ask to be your guide, but, unfortunately, they are all liars and thieves."

"Thanks for the information, but we don't need a guide."

He smiled at her bad French and continued. "For you, my friend, I will only charge fifteen thousand C.F.A. a day, or fifty

American dollars if you like. You see, I must go to the cliffs tomorrow anyway, because I have a secret mission there. My father is a marabout—a magician, if you will. He can turn rocks into coins, he can make your enemies run when they see you coming down the path, and he can make it rain." He paused, watching her with his yellow eyes. "He can make the dead rise again."

Darren nodded.

"I see that you don't believe me, but that is understandable. Even in a country as great as America, you have never seen anything like this. Tomorrow my father is coming here to show his magic in the courtyard, and then you will see that Africans may be poor, but we have special powers." When she glanced over his shoulder, he said, "All right. This is a special price for you only. Thirteen thousand C.F.A. It's all settled."

A gendarme stomped into the room, pushing a drunk ahead of him. "Jaraffe!" the drunk shouted. The boy jumped up to run from the room, but the drunk lunged and punched him in the face. Then Jaraffe's mother came forward and with one smooth swing of her arm she struck the drunk in the temple. He slid down in the gendarme's arms, his head hanging to one side, his mouth open.

"Voilà!" cried the gendarme, who was also drunk. He shouted gaily in Bambara as he dragged his prisoner across the floor and propped him against the wall like a sack of millet. The woman crossed her arms over her chest again and said nothing. Again, the gendarme cried, "Voilà!" He was a handsome, barrel-chested man in a khaki uniform, with skin as black and gleaming as the pistol that hung in the holster slung around his hips. He turned his attention to Darren. "Excuse us, Madame!" he roared. "Bon-soir, Madame Américaine? Ou Madame Francaise? I hope we are not disturbing you."

"C'est Madame Américaine," she said firmly.

"Monsieur Gendarme. Enchanté." He thrust his hand forward. "Bière!" he shouted, and dropped down on the bench beside her. "Are you in Oulaba to visit our spectacular cliffs?"

"No," she said. "I was on my way to Timbuktu. I was going to fly out of Mopti, but—" She stopped, remembering that he was a gendarme. In Mopti, the police discovered that she wasn't carrying the licence de photographie they required of all foreigners with cameras. The fine for this crime was the camera itself or jail. Using the alibi that she was going back to her hotel to get the permit, she had jumped into the first available jitney, ending up in Oulaba, a town that wasn't even on her map. Now she forced a thin smile. "This boy, Jaraffe, offered to be my guide. Do you know him?"

"You want Jaraffe? I'll sell him cheap." He slammed his fist down on the table, shaking Darren's bottle, and threw his head back to laugh.

"Is he a bandit?"

"No! I can't sell bandits cheap. The bandits are expensive!" He howled at his own joke and then composed himself.

"C'est Madame Américaine, ou Mademoiselle?"

"C'est Madame."

"I like your hat, Madame," he said, peering under the brim at her face. "Give it to me."

"Tomorrow," she said.

"Ah, you know Africa too well!" He shouted for Jaraffe. The doorway to the bar remained empty. "The boy is ashamed," said the gendarme. He took a drink and turned the bottle around in his broad hand. For a moment his brow creased into deep lines. His voice became maudlin. "That's the boy's father," he said, inclining his head to the drunk on the floor.

Darren turned to look at the man slumped against the wall. His torn robe was soiled to the uniform gray of fools' rags, and the nails on his hands were twisted and yellow, like the nails of a madman. A thin line of blood dribbled from his slack mouth.

Three whores dressed in tight miniskirts and stiletto heels walked into the room. They laughed at Darren in her hat. One of them sat beside her and said, "You are my sister." She reeked of beer and cheap perfume, and her painted mouth was frightening. Darren motioned to Jaraffe's mother, who led her across the courtyard and down the corridor to a door she opened with a skeleton key. The room had a concrete floor and walls, and near the ceiling there was one tiny window with no pane, crossed with iron bars. The foam mattress on the floor was covered with a dirty pagne. "Merci, ma mère," said Darren. The woman tucked Darren's two bills in her bra. Talking rapidly in Bambara, she locked and unlocked the door several times, and Darren nodded. "Yes, I'll lock it," she said in English. "Thanks."

In the morning, in the bloody light of the rising sun, Darren saw the cliffs for the first time. They rose up and shimmered all around the dusty village like huge gold nuggets piled by the hands of giants. No matter where she turned she saw the low, golden mountains, scintillating in the sun like broken glass. They drew her toward them. Reason told her that mountains are farther away and higher than they seem, that she was an inexperienced climber and would not be safe out there alone; but, although Darren always put on a great show of being practical in front of other people, when left to her own devices she was as hapless as a child alone on the moon.

Her only concern was that Jaraffe might find her and insist on being her guide, so she shouldered her pack and hurried down the road. She stopped at the market to stock up on whatever seemed edible: dried dates, canned sardines, a strange fruit that rattled when she shook it. "Cheese?" she asked. "Bread?" But the women just shook their heads and laughed, holding out their rough palms for money. She wondered how Jaraffe had been able to get his hands on a Heineken. He was not among the pack of children who followed her to the edge of town, calling "Hey, white lady, look at me! I am your guide!"

The children escorted her to the banks of a muddy river where young women waded with their pagnes pulled up over their knees, balancing brightly colored plastic buckets on their heads. One of them knelt and drank.

They all watched curiously as Darren pulled off her Gore-Tex hiking boots and rolled her jeans up to her knees. When she waded across with the pack on her back, they shouted to each other and laughed.

"Au revoir!" the children yelled from the bank. "À bientôt!" The bravest boys smacked their lips to make loud kissing noises as she went down the narrow, sandy path and curved out of their vision.

She had to keep herself from breaking into a run. The desert opened up all around her and she gulped the fresh air until her throat was parched. Within half an hour she began to burn. The sun bore through the sunscreen on her face and arms, resting on her soft freckled skin like a warm iron. She shifted the light pack on her shoulders and marched on, imagining telling her brothers in Tennessee about this adventure. As a child, she used to stand crying in the doorway when they left the house in their oiled hiking boots, shouldering heavy packs filled with Bunsen burners, gorp, and powdered eggs. "We girls have to stay home," her mother said, and she tried to teach Darren how to knit. What was a lap of tangled yarn compared to entrance in the horizon? When the boys came home, smelling of wood smoke, sweat, and leaves, she ripped out every stitch she had painstakingly knitted in the sweater sleeve. "I'm a prisoner!" she yelled. "I'll run away! You'll see!" Her mother told her to keep her voice down, and her brothers smirked.

As the sun rose higher, the cliffs lost their golden sheen and became hot, dry rocks. Darren had no sense of measure; the mountain could have been a thousand or ten thousand feet high, but the top of it seemed rather close to the clouds. When she began to climb, some of the rocks tipped under her weight. There was no sound but the dry scrape of her breathing and the slide of her boots.

Then the silence broke. "Darren!" a thin voice called. She looked at the bare rock all around her and up at the wide, empty sky. "Madame Darren! I am here!" Two yards away, through a wide crack in the rock, Jaraffe poked out his curly head. Her heart sank.

"Quelle bonne surprise!" he exclaimed, slithering out of the rock and landing on his feet like a cat. A purple bruise shone around one eye. "Here I was, just going along on my secret mission, all alone, and I find Madame Darren, my American friend!" He grinned from ear to ear. "And you're all red and tired, but still so beautiful. Were you frightened and lonely? Dismiss all your fears—your guide has found you."

She had been warned about this. If she refused his services out here he would follow her back to town and tell everyone that he had guided her but she refused to pay him. If she did accept him now as a guide, there would be no one to witness the bargain, and he might do the same thing.

"Where are your shoes, Jaraffe?"

He glanced down at his dusty feet as if he fully expected to find shoes there, then looked up and shrugged. His hands were as small as sparrows, and when he held them out by his sides, palms up, he appeared to be the most vulnerable little boy on earth. Suddenly she was furious.

"How much do you charge for this tour?"

At the nasty tone of her voice he raised his eyebrows in a perfect arc.

He dragged one toe along the rock. "Two hundred American dollars."

She laughed, and he joined her in a child's falsetto. She raised her hand to him. "You are a child, and you will speak to me with respect!" When he ducked, she was ashamed of herself.

Out of reach, he smirked contemptuously and said, "Well of course, I am actually here on a secret mission for my father, as I explained last night, and so if you choose to follow me, well then, I assure you that you will see what no tourist ever sees. I thought you were my friend, and so I had planned to show you a sacred burial cave filled with Dogon treasure. But this obviously bores Madame, I beg her pardon."

"You lie, boy." He looked at her, and for a moment she was afraid, but she continued, raising her voice. "There is no sacred treasure, and your father is not a magician."

"You lie!" he yelled. "You don't have a husband. You lie, and also you speak French like a dog!" He stepped back from her and mocked her accent, laughing in a high whine.

"Your father isn't a magician. He's a drunk."

Blood rose to his cheeks and his eyes turned almost black. "Whore! Dog-French white-lady whore!"

"Well, you've lost your fancy manners, haven't you," she said softly in English. "You snot-nosed little brat."

For an instant he gazed at her mouth, wrinkling his smooth brow, as if the words still hung about her lips and might be grasped, but then he turned his head away. "I don't understand your language and I hope the hyenas eat you!"

"Five thousand C.F.A.," she said in French. "Fifteen American dollars. That's the price—if I see the Dogon burial cave."

He spit. Then he jumped from one rock to the next, leaping the boulders like a kid goat until he was gone.

Soon she heard his spook sounds—strange whistles and long, sad wails echoing in the caves inside the cliff. Clinging to the rock, she inched her way toward the sky. At noon, when she stopped to eat, her body trembled. Sweat stung her dry lips, salting the food as she put it in her mouth. The warm, heavily chlorinated water was delicious, and she was sorry she hadn't brought more than one canteen. She removed her hat, stretched out on the rock, and dozed.

First she sensed his presence. When he was close enough, she smelled his sweet child's sweat, already familiar.

"Six thousand C.F.A.," she said without opening her eyes. He did not answer. Instead, he touched her sunglasses and then her hair. He was leaning over her face now, so close that his breath stirred the tiny hairs in her nose. She felt the wet, exquisite curve of his lips on her ear, whispering in a strange tongue. Then he sneezed.

Abruptly, she sat up. "What is your problem?" she yelled in English. He stared at her mouth, his eyes large and dark, the purple bruise glistening. He smiled hopefully. "If this desert were hell, you'd be Satan," she said. She continued to speak in English as she busied her shaking hands with the water bottle. She gave him a drink. "Where are your shoes? Are you hungry? Here, eat." She set out the dates and the sardines. Pressed close against her legs, he began to eat with feline grace, sucking all the sugar from the fruit and all the oil from the fish, finishing everything she dropped before him.

When he had eaten his fill he said, "Seven thousand C.F.A." Without waiting for a response, he tossed her bag across his narrow back and began zigzagging up the side of the cliff. She faced the first boulder he had mounted, fingering the smooth surface for a grip. Then she jumped, catching the top of the rock with her hands, scraping her knees and elbows as she lugged herself over the edge. From a perch far above her head he looked down and said in heavily accented English, "What is your problem?"

He told her to remove the hiking boots and hang them around her neck. As they climbed, the soft pink soles of her feet became familiar with the wrinkled face of the rock, and she moved more swiftly, but no matter how quickly she climbed, Jaraffe skimmed ahead of her. His bronze legs disappeared against the rock, and his blue shirt melted into the sky. Only his black curls stood out against the horizon, and, when he turned, the flash of his smile. She did not look down.

At last, when the sun was easing down over the mountain, Jaraffe stopped to rest. She handed him her canteen and he drank half of what was left. She took two short drinks, hesitated, took a third.

"Where is this Dogon cave?"

"Here."

"Where?" There was nothing around them but rock, and, far below, the tiny squiggle of a sand path cutting through a velvet desert. When she climbed around the rock where they were resting, she saw a field cut in furrows as thin as pencil marks, dotted with Dogon farmers.

He rolled over and grabbed her ankles, whispering, "Come back, you fool. The Dogons will see you. We are on sacred ground!"

She edged herself back against the wall. "Don't grab me," she said, whispering back despite herself. "I am older than you. Respect me."

"The dead are older than you. Respect them."

"Shut up."

"Shut up," he mimicked in English.

She lowered herself into a sitting position, keeping her back to the stone. For the first time it occurred to her that they wouldn't be able to get back down the cliff before nightfall. Her hand played with the cap of the canteen, twisting it back and forth.

"I'm going into the cave," he said. "You may follow me if you so desire. In the case of catastrophe, you are not my responsibility. I'm just informing you. Americans like to know these things beforehand."

"Jaraffe, we have to spend the night up here. You told me we could make the climb in one day."

"Maybe I will find you some beautiful earrings, or some money. But if you are complaining I won't give the present to you. Then I will give it to one of my other girlfriends, or perhaps I'll keep it for myself."

She ignored the girlfriend reference. "We need water," she said.

"I am going on my secret mission." He rolled his eyes in cool mystery. "Are you coming?"

The entrance to the cave was blocked by a boulder. "Otherwise," Jaraffe explained, "the hyenas would eat the corpses." They stood on either side of it and rolled it away. Jaraffe asked for Darren's flashlight, peering over her shoulder as she dug in her pack for it. He switched it on, dropped to his hands and knees, and crawled behind a scraggly bush. A second later, Darren knelt down, too. She followed the pink soles of his feet into the tunnel, slapping her hands over the thin edge of light that moved behind him. She could smell something rancid, like rotting steak. Jaraffe began to hum. The hum reverberated in the narrow shaft, sounding in her bones as she and Jaraffe wound down into the belly of the mountain. Then they turned the last corner, and Jaraffe stood up and moved the circle of light around the room.

It was filled with human skeletons. They were stacked from the floor to the ceiling. Some of them were seated along the walls, behind urns full of beads and trinkets. The flashlight threw quivering strips of light into stark eye-holes, gaping jaws, and the thick spaces between yellow ribs. The room stank.

Jaraffe sang. It was a low, mournful tune, full of strange notes and nonsensical words. They stood beside a pile of corpses. The bottom of the heap was nothing but dust, and the human form seemed to rise out of this, a shoulder pushing up, a jaw jutting out, a broken hand digging back down into the powder. In the middle of the stack the skeletons were complete; at the top, near the ceiling, scraps of faded pagnes hung off the bones. It was as though the corpses on top had grown out of the dead beneath them. It was as though Darren and Jaraffe, panting and sweating, had rolled off the top of the heap, obscenely alive.

Jaraffe slid behind the pile, leaving her in darkness. She heard him rattling in the bones but she did not follow. Once his light shot across the room, illuminating a skeleton sitting cross-legged against the wall, holding an urn between its knees. Inside the urn, besides beads and a few C.F.A. coins, there was a rusted can opener. She felt despair. What hand was cruel enough to create a human being, a sad fool who could see his end, and then smash him to dust? The light was dimming. "Jaraffe, don't burn out the batteries," she called softly, and the sound of her voice frightened her.

"Oui, j'arrive!" He rummaged noisily in the pile of skeletons, shaking the fingers on the hands, the toes on the feet, turning the heads this way and that. His hum was high, loud, and uncertain. At last he scurried back to her. "Come! Hurry!" He dropped down on all fours and sped up the shaft. Darren followed, knocking her head against the ceiling, scraping her knees, senseless to the pain.

Outside, the sun fell in graceful surrender to the night, throwing out its last miracles as it cloaked the jagged edge of the horizon in shadow. Birds sang myriad unearthly notes, brazenly breaking the day's long silence. In the dying sun, Jaraffe's bare arms and legs turned gold. When he stood on the ledge holding the skeleton of a human hand like a scepter over the Dogon farmers in the fields below, he looked like a god. A few farmers still bent over their short, primitive hoes, but most of them had thrown the shafts over their shoulders and were walking toward the mountain. Their villages were built so cleverly into the sides of the cliffs that one could walk right by them and never see a human dwelling. Like the birds, the farmers had begun to sing out to each other.

"Forgive me for calling you a liar this morning," Darren said. "I'm glad that you're my guide." He turned his head to hide the frank pleasure on his face.

"This is the cave where we will sleep tonight," he said, motioning to an overhanging rock. "I hope it pleases you."

She crawled inside. The ceiling was so low she couldn't stand up, but the floor was large enough for the two of them to stretch out when they slept. A hollow in the back wall led to other passages that were too dark to see.

"Jaraffe," she called, stepping out onto the ledge, "I think there are too many openings; something could come—" She stopped. He had opened her pack. The camera hung around his neck and he was rubbing a stick of deodorant along his face. His nostrils flared delicately as he sniffed the scent.

She snatched the deodorant out of his hand. "Do not ever open my pack without my permission!"

He hunched his shoulders together and then lifted his chin. "I don't care. Mosquitoes don't bite Africans if they can bite white ladies."

"What?" She burst into laughter. "That's not mosquito repellent. That's deodorant; it goes under your arms. Oh, never mind." She pulled the camera off his neck and tried to take his picture, but he turned his back to her.

"You don't have anything good to eat in your pack," he grumbled. "The other Americans had chocolate, and macaroni and cheese. You don't even have a stove."

"You aren't required to eat with me." As she knelt beside him, putting the items back into the pack, she smelled the deodorant on his face and chuckled. "I'm sorry, Jaraffe. It's just that it's funny to Americans."

With her army knife, he cut a string from her roll of twine and tied the skeleton hand around his neck. "The other Americans had Kool-Aid as well. Grape." He held up the fruit she had bought in the market and looked at it with disgust before he cut off the top. "Beggars' food," he snorted, sliding two fingers inside the hard shell and popping a fleshy seed into his mouth. "Food for lepers."

"Where's the water?"

"Africans don't need water."

"Well, Americans do." She turned up the canteen he had nearly emptied.

"Americans carry extra batteries," he said. She tried to turn the flashlight on; the batteries were dead. He smiled and handed her the fruit. The sweet and sour seed puckered her lips and burned her stomach, but the juice soothed her thirst. He laughed at her grimaces.

"Are you cold?" she asked.

"Africans don't get cold."

She tossed a sweater at his head and carried her own warm clothes to the cave to change. When she looked back, he was smelling the sweater, running his fingers over the cashmere and sliding it along his cheek. Inside the cave, something rustled. Wind? She couldn't make herself crawl inside. With her back turned, she changed her clothes and returned to sit beside him.

Black curls fell across his forehead and his eyes gleamed yellow in the falling darkness. The sweater swallowed him. The cuffs flapped below his hands as he crossed his arms and commented, "Your body is very beautiful, but I find your derriere too small."

"Shut up, Jaraffe."

"I see that you are frightened to go in our cave, or perhaps you have fallen in love with me."

The muscles in her back tensed. "You? You are a child!" His face stiffened in humiliation. He began to hum.

The stars came out in rapid succession, crowding the huge black sky until they nearly touched each other. She lay on her back looking for Sirius, the great star of the Dogons.

When she gazed too long at the sky, she lost all sense of direction and had to press her hands flat against the cold rock. Behind her the gaping mouth of the cave waited, and she dreaded it. The boy seemed a stranger to her now, chanting his lonely, foreign hymns, accompanying the sole bird that remained awake. The birdcall was like nothing she had ever heard. It wasn't a screech or a caw or the notes of a song, but something chilling and abrupt, like the scream of a woman.

"Jaraffe, what is that bird?"

"There is no bird."

"Yes, listen. It screams like a woman." It screamed then, louder than before. "That one."

"That's a hyena."

"Where is the hyena?"

"It's here." The scream came again, and her heart pounded. "She smells your fear," he added reproachfully.

"Aren't you afraid?"

"I am the son of a magician, do you forget so quickly? I went into the sacred Dogon grave and took my talisman." He rattled the fingers on the skeleton hand. "The hyena is afraid of me."

"What happens if the hyena comes into the cave while we're sleeping?"

She heard him yawn. The bank of clouds rolled across the sky, and the stars blinked out, one by one, like lights going off in a house.

"You aren't earning your keep as a guide," she said.

"Ha! Ha! Ha! I am a child, remember? I am a child when Madame decides that I am to be a child. Now Madame is afraid and needs a man. Am I to be a man now?"

He reached for her breast, laughing when she knocked his hand away. "A child, then. Well, the child is going to bed. Sweet dreams, Madame."

She lay on her back looking up at the sky until the last star blinked out. Then it was terribly dark, and cold. Every sound—the rustle of weeds, the roll of gravel, the rasping of her own breath—was magnified until her nerves were taut with fear. She saw the empty stare of the skeletons. When the hyena screamed again she jumped up and ran to the mouth of the cave.

"Jaraffe?" He did not answer. She leaned down and pushed her head through the opening, blinking in the darkness. "I'm not coming in until you answer me." Suddenly, something swished behind her. With a thud, the animal landed on her back. She screamed.

"Waa!" Jaraffe cried, rolling off her back, doubled over in laughter. He leaped about her, pulling his hair, rolling his eyes, crying out in sharp female wails. "Waa!" he cried. "Oh, oh, help me! Where is my big, strong, handsome guide?"

With her heart still knocking in her chest, she swung her fist at him. He ducked it like a boxer. "Damn you!" she yelled. He shrieked—a scared, mean laugh. She lunged for him and caught hold of his skinny arm, but he slipped out of her grasp. For a moment they stood facing each other in the dark, panting, and then she hissed, "I despise you." She began to sob in broken screams that scraped her throat raw. It was a horrible, lonely sound. She covered her mouth, choking in the effort to stop the noise. She felt his presence somewhere in front of her, small and no longer fierce, and she crawled into the cave. She made a thin pallet from the rest of the clothes in her pack and lay down, first on her back, then on her stomach. Then she rolled over on her back again. Each lump in the rock made a distinct stab into her flesh. She began to wonder about Jaraffe and to want him with her, if only to slap him.

A few minutes later, he scooted into the cave. "And where is my bed?" he demanded. She remained silent. "You are angry with me." He stretched out beside her on the hard floor and pushed her arm. "Say something, Darren, my dear friend, Darren." When she rolled away from him, he patted her head like a baby. "You were crying, and I did not help you. Now I have scared you. You are so good to me, giving me food and water and this sweater. I do not even like grape Kool-Aid and macaroni and cheese and chocolate—well, maybe chocolate. I like the sweater; it keeps me warm and smells very nice." He gave a loud, appreciative sniff.

"You annoy me."

"This is true. I am annoying and rude and bad. I am ugly." He waited for her to contradict this last statement, and when she did not, he continued. "Many people share your opinion. It is all true." He let his voice become pitiful. "Surely I will burn in hell. Or Allah will find some way to punish me, so that I never forget my sins against you and am always ashamed."

Despite herself, she spoke. "When I first met you, last night, I thought, here is a boy different from all the other little bandits in Africa. Here is a serious boy. Now I see that I was mistaken. You are just like all the other scoundrels in the street."

"My remorse is more enormous than the sky."

"You are not sincere."

"This is true. I am sorry. Will you forgive me?"

She tossed him the roll of pants and shirts that had been her pillow and closed her eyes. Noisily, he made his bed beside her and continued his apology. His voice purred against the cold, black walls. He spoke nonsense. At last, he lay down against her back, throwing an arm around her neck and sticking his cold feet between her calves.

"I don't like that, Jaraffe. Stop it."

"I don't have any socks. My feet are cold."

"You can take some socks out of my pack." She listened as he rummaged through her things, mumbling to himself in various tongues, and then she felt him once again press his small hard body against her back. When his arm circled her neck, the skeleton hand, still tied around his neck, cut between her shoulder blades. "You will take me with you back to America, and I will go to medical school and become a great surgeon..." he murmured sleepily in her ear. "We will get married...and have a big house in Dallas, Texas."

She fell into a light sleep nettled with nightmares and awoke strangling in his skinny arms. His breath shot out in hard, quick pants, and his heart, racing against her own, knocked on her chest. Above them, the hyena's scream tangled with the anguished shrieking of another animal. The beasts thrashed and rolled on the roof of the cave, knocking pebbles and clumps of dirt through the cracks. Jaraffe's arms gripped her like thin iron rods. His heart was banging so hard in his chest that she thought he would explode. She hugged the clinging boy tighter against her, hiding her face in his hair, and thought, I will live. I will. For a long time they lay in their rigid embrace, listening to the hyena chew its shrieking victim. The boy's glowing yellow eyes made the only light in the cave.

When Darren awoke, Jaraffe was gone. He had taken her camera and her hat with him. The leather purse hanging around her neck was flat and empty. Even her passport was gone. "Bastard!" she screamed out over the desert. "Thief!" She threw a rock over the side of the cliff, and then another, screaming as tears ran down her cheeks. She didn't want to climb back down into the world, not ever, but Jaraffe had drunk all of her water and her tongue was swollen with thirst. She shouldered the pack and began to back slowly down the cliff.

By nightfall Darren was back at the Grand Hotel du Mali. Jaraffe's mother stood in the doorway of the bar, watching her stagger, hatless, dirty, ragged, across the courtyard. Silently, the hotelkeeper went behind the bar and handed Darren a beer. Then, without expression, she wet a towel, and leaning forward, roughly scrubbed Darren's face and hands. Darren stood still, in shock; then she sat down at the table and ate the plate of macaroni and tough, greasy meat the woman brought to her. When she pushed her plate back she saw the passport under it. "They're all cunning," she said softly, and pushed the small blue book into her bra. Then she waited for Jaraffe. While she waited, she drank beer. Each time she took a fresh bottle of Gazelle from Jaraffe's mother, she felt a new surge of power. I'll kill him, she thought.

Around ten o'clock Jaraffe sauntered into the bar, wearing a new white suit and a shirt the color of lemons. Darren's brown felt hat was tilted at a rakish angle on his head. A cigarette dangled from his lips. After a brief moment when it looked as though he might run back out the door, he flashed his best grin and said, "Darren, ma chérie, at last I find you! Oh, at last!" She waited. She let him swagger to her. As he bent down to touch his lips to her cheek in the French manner, she smelled alcohol and cheap perfume. "Why did you worry me like this? I thought you were lost forever." When he leaned forward to kiss her other cheek, she grabbed his neck. She pressed her fingers into the soft skin, digging them in between the tendons, and shook him until her hat fell off his head. His strangled cries filled the room. "Mama!" he yelled. "Help me!"

His mother came and stood silently before them. "Help!" cried Jaraffe, and the gendarme ran out from the back room, buckling his pants. Then the doorway filled with whores and men, shouting and pushing against each other to get into the room.

"He stole my money!" Darren yelled.

"I did not. This woman hired me to be her guide. I took her into the cliffs, as she asked me to, and then she paid me and told me to go. I gave the money to my mother, who needs it to take care of my poor father." The crowd pressed noisily into the room and around Darren. One of the whores pushed her painted face down close and whispered, "He's a thief, that one." Darren felt the prostitute's long nails rest briefly on her arm. Jaraffe's mother stared straight at the wall.

The gendarme looked into Darren's eyes. "I will help you," he said. He laid his broad hand on her shoulder. "Have confidence in me." His hand moved slowly upward until his fingers rested in her hair. She shook it off wearily. "You are an educated woman, eh? You know many things? Some languages? You know perhaps how to drive a car? You know how to work a computer? Many, many things live in this head." He rolled his hand over her head as if it were a coconut. "Your head is no good here, eh?" He picked the hat up off the floor and pushed it gently down over her ears, as if to stop her from thinking. Then he snapped his fingers at Jaraffe's mother.

The woman brought two beers; then, from inside her bra, she took a roll of soft bills and laid them silently before Darren. Jaraffe swaggered over and set down her camera. Darren waited a moment to see if the gendarme meant to demand her permit. The man grinned at her, then turned away and drank up, and she stuffed the camera into her bag.

In the morning she took a jitney back to Bamako, and all along the way, young boys begged to guide her.

How I Came To Write This Story

The title refers to the Buddhist concept of being trapped within an endless cycle of death and rebirth. Only by eliminating desire can one attain release from existence. I was curious about what sort of creature—or creatures—might emerge if this paradigm of "non-ego" were realized. The story is generated by the interaction between two characters, each of whom displays an atrophied sense of volition. The area rep clings to the dubious "freedom" of the foreigner. He is meant to be the quintessential ex-pat, someone who resides in a foreign culture in order to avoid commitment. Jane, the Volunteer, is a comic embodiment of the self-renouncing ideal. She is perceived only within the assumptions about her that the area rep maintains and is thus in a sense "created" by him.

—John Givens

JOHN GIVENS (Korea, 1967-1969) was born and raised in California. After the Peace Corps, he studied art and culture in Kyoto, Japan for four years, then entered the University of Iowa, Iowa Writers' Workshop where he received a Teaching/Writing Fellowship, and taught English literature and creative writing. In addition to short stories, essays and books about photography, he has published three novels: *Sons of the Pioneers, A Friend in the Police,* and *Living Alone.* Givens worked in Tokyo for eight years. He and his wife currently live in New York City. A new novel about seventeenth century Japan is in progress.

ON THE WHEEL OF WANDERING-ON

by John Givens

1.

The area rep stood gazing at the jumble of shoes in the entryway, relieved that the woman hadn't invited him inside. He wiped his palms on his trousers. The sultry afternoon sky glowed above him with a dull yellowish tinge, as if a membrane of old cellophane wrap had been stretched over the city. "It's very summer," the area rep said uncertainly. He never knew how to respond to the way Koreans lived in their homes.

The woman waited for a moment then agreed that he had identified the season correctly.

"Yes. No. What I mean is...I mean it's hot," the area rep said, "a very hot day today," and the Korean woman acknowledged the accuracy of this observation, too.

A dirty white dog with stubby legs emerged from a crawl space beneath the side of the house, wriggling out as if produced by an incomplete peristalsis. The dog shook itself then limped forward, dragging a short chain and augmented by a convoy of flies that maintained themselves in sluggish orbits, like a squalid evocation of Bohr's atomic model. The dog advanced to where it could observe the foreigner at the entryway then squatted, tongue lolling out of the side of its mouth, a beast too enervated to both watch and hold itself upright.

"Well, then," the area rep continued, "I suppose the American Volunteer Jane Joule is not here again?"

The Korean woman acknowledged promptly that once again this seemed to be the case then asked if the area rep would drink some barley tea.

"No. Thank you. I don't need tea." "Need" wasn't quite the right word, the area rep knew, but the woman seemed to understand.

"Some boiled drinking water then?"

"No. Thank you."

The Korean woman kept her eyes averted. "She goes when she wants and comes back when she wants," the woman declared, as if addressing the bundles of pepper plants that were strung from the coils of razor wire topping the wall behind the area rep. "I understand this behavior to be acceptable."

"Yes, of course it is," the area rep said. He also turned to regard the clumps of drying pepper pods that hung toward him like desiccated fingers, each scarlet pod shrinking and tightening inwardly on itself, clenching the fiery seeds at its core.

"I hope to discover what Jane Joule does on these days of absence," the area rep stated, "and where she does it and why," but the Korean woman only shrugged ambiguously. It was not for her to wonder about how a foreigner chose to spend her time.

"Yes. I see." The area rep extended a hand in greeting toward the dirty white dog. The creature yawned in response and snapped dutifully at one of its flies then returned its tongue to the heat-dissipation mode, pleased with itself.

"Maybe the dog wants to drink water," the area rep suggested.

The Korean woman also observed the dog for a moment, as if determined to be fair in all things, then said she thought not, explaining that the dog had a basin of water near its hole in the back garden.

"I see," the area rep said. "But I think the dog's chain is broken."

It was not broken.

"I mean the end is...open, the end of the chain that is not attached to the dog end, is not attached to a thing, to any thing."

The dog preferred it that way.

"Yes? But, then, why is there a chain?"

The woman again looked past the area rep and pondered this. Certain concepts needed to settle briefly within her before they could be expressed. "Because it is a dog chain," she explained sensibly.

Jane Joule was a tall, slender woman with pale white skin and closely cropped, silver-blond hair. Her face was small and wistful and vague. Her nose and mouth were particularly small and this made her eyes seem larger. Jane Joule attended agency gatherings but always arrived by herself and left the same way. She seemed neither aloof nor shy. She would find a place to stand or sit where she could watch the others without participating herself. She was detached. But this detachment was not a demonstration of exaggerated self-reliance so much as an intensified preference for being alone. Jane Joule had a kind of soft, diffident way of behaving that the area rep found puzzling and intriguing. Every action seemed preceded by a slight hesitation, an almost imperceptible offer at the instant before the doing, as if to suggest that that gesture, no matter how trivial—opening a door, picking up a cup, checking the time on one's wristwatch—would be abandoned if the other party so desired. The area rep did not admit to himself that he was in love with her.

"You have a tendency toward self-obsession," the area rep's ex-wife had once told him. "And it's odd because it's not so much narcissistic as the result of a failure to perceive the entire range of possibilities." He had been caught at the time with a forkful of food nearing his mouth, and he held it uncertainly in the air before him, watching the woman he had promised to love forever, waiting for a clarification. "You're like somebody who spends a lot of time on a driving range perfecting his golf swing." She looked down briefly at the pieces of food on her own plate then again met his gaze. "But who never actually goes out and plays golf."

The area rep pulled Jane Joule's gate shut behind him, causing the coils of razor wire to rattle briefly.

High walls the color of dried bone closed him in on both sides as he walked down the narrow alley to the boulevard where his car was waiting. He could hear the sounds of laughter and bickering coming from behind the walls as he passed, and of babies crying and children singing and fighting, and of things falling over and banging together and breaking—all the clumsy tumult of too many people living packed in too tightly together.

The area rep had failed to advance within the volunteer agency. He was over forty now, divorced and stalled, reporting to a recently appointed national director ten years his junior. The area rep lived alone, and he suspected that not having a wife limited his social acceptability, particularly at the high-profile diplomatic level national directors would occupy. But he liked his job well enough and believed in the agency and was fond of Korea and Koreans and sorry he hadn't gotten a better grip on the language. He just didn't seem to have an ear for it.

A small object came skittering weakly past the area rep's ankles, like something thrown by a child made listless by disease. He paused when he reached it. The freshly severed head of a chicken stared up at him, eyes glazed and beak cracked open, as if aghast at the suddenness of its disreputability. The thing had been tossed over the wall in the process of striking it off and so could not have been meant as a message for him. Yet the area rep stood with it, trapped by the occurrence and feeling familiar doubts as to choices he had made filled him with an equally familiar shame at his failure to resolve them, even as the delicate shell of the bird's skull disassembled beneath the sole of his shoe.

"You look at your face in the mirror the way other men watch sports on TV," his ex-wife had said once. "You're interested in the game, but it's not as good as actually being there."

The area rep got into his car before his driver had a chance to open the door for him.

The street was clogged with overloaded buses that rolled groaning past at close intervals, each more improbable than the one before, a grotesque pantomime of public transportation befouling the world with clouds of exhaust fumes and churned-up yellow dust, halting unexpectedly then lurching forward again, the whole procession like an array of preposterous creatures which had not originally been intended for mobility but were pressed into service as an afterthought, as apt conveyance for the hapless seed of a diminished god.

"Where we go now?" the area rep's driver demanded brusquely in English. "I think maybe PX?"

2.

The area rep last saw his ex-wife at her father's funeral. A hurricane had dragged itself up the Atlantic coast that day, and the air pushed ahead of it was as stale and unpromising as the inside of a refrigerator left unplugged too long. After the final ceremony at the grave site, the area rep wandered down along a row of grey-green Italian cypresses, the tall, conical trees like Chia-pet ICBMs ready to be launched into the leaden sky.

A battered yellow backhoe tractor was parked behind the trees, out of the view of the mourners. The female backhoe operator and her female assistant had positioned the articulated boom of the scoop bucket in such a way that they could sit side by side on the operator's seat, bracing their feet against the protruding safety flanges that restricted lateral movement of the bucket assembly. The women were examining a magazine together, sharing it equitably, turning a page only after each had finished.

The area rep wondered what would cause women to become backhoe operators in a cemetery. Was this another victory for feminism? Or a demonstration that the range of demeaning occupations open to women was still widening?

He didn't know. His ex-wife had complained that he became too easily distracted by trivialities; so instead of joining the women mounted on their practical machine, the area rep turned back toward the grave site.

The mourners had returned to their cars, and the first cars were departing, leaving only a trio of funeral home employees still holding temporary vigil beside the deceased. The three men stood in a polite row with their hands held together before them in the way naked men protect their genitals when frightened, a habit the funeral employees had fallen into, as if subconsciously fearing that repeated exposure to the dead in their boxes might pose risk of contamination, might split DNA strands like the damaged ends of long hair, or snap apart key chromosomes; as if the grasping dead in their dismay sought to impinge themselves upon the as yet unengendered, extracting them from their natural membranes, pinching them out the way a sushi chef pinches out fetal eels.

"You should ask yourself what you want out of life," the area rep's ex-wife had decided when it was clear they would separate. "Because you just might get it."

The area rep had wondered if that meant she herself feared she would not find personal satisfaction?

"But I didn't say anything about personal satisfaction!" his ex-wife had declared cheerfully. "What makes you think that?"

She had added later that she was fond of his idiosyncrasies and would no doubt miss them. At least for a while.

The backhoe operator and her assistant filled in the grave efficiently. They glanced at the area rep once or twice, no doubt curious as to why he was still there, but did nothing he could have interpreted as an invitation.

3.

Jane Joule dutifully attended the all-Korea summer conference in Seoul. She seemed more gawky than the area rep had remembered, and taller and thinner, with her small hands folded in her small lap and her pale blond hair now grown out long enough to tuck girlishly behind her ears.

The area rep pointed out the current state of her hair, and Jane agreed that she needed to get it cut.

"Does that seem important to you? To keep it very short?"

"Not really."

The area rep observed her thoughtfully for a moment. Then why did she do it?

"I like short hair," Jane said.

As a public expression of self-denial?

"It's easy to take care of." She lifted one hand and tentatively fingered the top button on her blouse. "But what you really want to know is where I spend my weekends," Jane Joule said softly. "You could have just asked, you know." The hand sank back to her lap.

There was an old Buddhist nunnery tucked away in an isolated stretch of the rugged coastal mountains west of Pusan, just above the main battleground where UN forces had finally stopped the enemy's advance in the summer of 1950. The area was inaccessible by car, and hiking in from the nearest village took about four hours. The nunnery had been marked with a Buddhist swastika on an old pre-war Japanese map that Jane had found in a used book store, but it did not appear on any contemporary documents. As far as she knew, no one else ever went there.

The nuns still living at the Temple of the Twice-polished Mirror of the Truth of the Law were old and frail, forgotten women with little to offer modern young Koreans, who were more interested in television and pop music. "Some of the temple buildings have collapsed. They just sink back into the earth and become low, overgrown hills. Except rectangular. That's how you know what they were."

There was no electricity, no running water, no commercial products of any kind. The old nuns grew their own food and wove their own clothing. Rice was the only thing they imported. "But they don't have any money. So they pay for it by offering sutra readings to soften the souls of those who died bitterly." Jane smiled and looked away, as if indicating a modification of what was known in order to accommodate the expectations of another. "Have I done something wrong?" she asked.

The area rep didn't answer immediately. His ex-wife had explained that she was leaving him because he was too thick, too heavy, like a weight pressing down on her, and she needed to be free, to be lighter, to live her life in the open air.

That was how he felt now—heavy and ponderous, like someone trying to run through waist-deep water. "And so you help the nuns? Is that it? Do repairs or something?"

"I don't do anything."

"So that's not why you go?" he asked, studying Jane Joule. He, too, wanted to become lighter.

"No." Some of the old nuns had been there since they were girls. But most had come after living in the world with men, taking their vows so they could die within the embrace of the lotus of the law. The oldest women knew nothing about modern Korea. They no longer remembered that there had been a war, did not remember that American soldiers had been transported to their country in huge ships and placed in oblong holes cut into the Korean earth, the holes organized in grids of evenly spaced rows, with the heads all pointing in the same direction, each soldier labeled with name and date, as if the affliction could be muted through the application of structure, as if death were vulnerable to occurrences of repeatability.

"Old women go there to die?" the area rep asked.

That seemed odd?

She didn't think so?

"The Buddha Hall is at the side of the compound, and the mountain comes very near, almost to the back edge of the garden. You can't tell where the garden ends and the forest begins. I sit by myself on the corner of the veranda that faces directly into the mountainside. For the quiet. Just the sound of the wind in the trees. And the birds. Sometimes I sit all day. The valley's steep so the sun sets early. I watch the forest get darker and darker late in the afternoon. I like the way the orange of the light climbs up to the peaks of the mountains and then just disappears into the twilight sky."

The area rep had nodded and frowned and smiled and leaned forward with his elbows braced on his knees and his hands locked together with fingers laced but index fingers upright, creating a house of worship just under his nose. Jane Joule sitting on the chair across from him seemed unfathomably smooth and simple, a creature perfected by its habitat, like the blind, translucent fish that spend their lives in subterranean grottoes. "But what do you do there?" he asked finally.

"Nothing." Just let the mind settle. "So you can see how the world is," Jane said.

And how was it?

Fine.

In the area rep's handbook was a chapter on pathological stress-response patterns with a description of the psychological profile characterizing a state of emotional breakdown known in the profession as the *rapture of the experience of the perfect freedom of the foreigner.* You weren't to startle or entrap or even argue against the destabilized volunteer. You nudged him back toward reality, tapped at him gently, like someone propelling golf balls with blows from a pencil.

"You've been thinking about this a lot," the area rep had said finally. "I can tell."

4.

Jane Joule is six today and so old enough to walk all the way to the store and back by herself. Her mother lets her wear her pink party dress. It is a nice warm Saturday afternoon in a nice town on Long Island.

Jane's long blond hair is combed straight back and a pair of matching pink barrettes hold the sides away from her face. She has a little handbag that she carries, and inside is a hankie with lace edges and a tiny coin purse equipped with a few coins.

At the toy store, Jane intends to buy a pink plastic tea set. She knows this is exactly the kind of present her parents would want her to want. The entire plastic tea set will cost slightly less than four dollars, including tax, and Jane has added this amount of money to her purse. The little girl has never possessed this much real money before, and she has indicated by her behavior that the experience makes her feel formal.

Today is Jane's birthday, and the pink plastic tea set is to be her birthday present, and the right to go alone and make the purchase by herself is also an ingredient of the pleasure it is thought by her parents she will feel at its possession.

"You just sit there on the couch," the area rep's ex-wife had told him. "You haven't moved, have you?"

He had gotten up once or twice.

"But you always come back to exactly the same spot!" His ex-wife had returned early from a party that she had not enjoyed, and the evening's failure to produce ignition had left her in a sour mood. "That's what I can't stand. One of the things. You're always just sitting there!"

So the little blond girl sets out on her three-block walk, and the lawns she passes are well-manicured and bordered by attractive flower beds and pleasantly-shaped bushes. Many of the houses behind the lawns and bushes have children living in them, and many of those children are near enough to Jane's age to function under the expectations she lives with—or, rather, she agrees to behave as if she lived with. Jane knows most of the children on her route. They all go to the same school, and several are in Jane's class. But another part of Jane's birthday present is the right not to have a birthday party and so not to have to invite any of the neighborhood children for anything. So Jane in her pink dress with her purse containing the money she has been given walks to the store alone without exchanging a word with any of the children she encounters.

The tea set is where she knew it would be. She lifts it off the shelf and places it on the counter. The funny old man who runs the toy store asks her if that will be all and Jane says yes, thank you. She holds out her four dollars. Her change is thirty-seven cents, which the man counts out in front of her, naming the coins as they are placed on the counter, as if he himself had played a small role in the minting of them. Jane has told him that the tea set is to be a birthday present so he wraps it in colorful paper with a pattern of clowns and juggling bears and attaches a bright red bow.

Does she need a birthday card?

No, she thinks not.

Her parcel wrapped, Jane makes the return walk, carrying the awkward bundle hugged to her chest in her pudgy little-girl arms.

The children who notice Jane watch silently as she passes. No one asks her what is in the package.

Jane places the packaged tea set on the dining room table for her mother to find then goes to her room and dutifully changes back into her play clothes.

"You make a dent! The shape of you sinks in! Just there, you see? You have any idea how disgusting that is to other people?"

The area rep had tried to defend himself. "There's a positive side to it," he had said as his ex-wife unzipped her dress then pulled it over her head irritably and tossed it aside, as if much had been its fault. "A lot of women appreciate consistency," he added.

"You might be right." She unhooked her bra and dropped it and thrust down her panties and stood in front of him naked, idly scratching a constellation of pink welts that had formed where an undergarment chafed her skin. "So then I guess you should go find one of them," she had concluded reasonably.

That evening of her sixth birthday, Jane Joule and her mother and father had a dinner of her special food—hot dogs and potato chips and Orange Crush. After dinner, there were ice cream sundaes with warm chocolate sauce poured all over and a squirt of whipped cream with a Maraschino cherry at the top.

Jane's mother and father wished her a happy birthday again, and Jane's father made gin-and-tonics for himself and Jane's mother while Jane settled in the family room, waiting to open her present.

"She's fine, really," Jane's mother said, and her father said, "Yes, she seems to be," and splashed in another half-inch of gin.

5.

Jane Joule sat across from the area rep with her back straight and her knees together and her hands folded meekly in her lap, trying to describe what she found at the Temple of the Twice-polished Mirror that made it so important to her. She would have recognized that she was burdening the area rep, and for Jane Joule, failing to justify her choices created a willingness to compensate those whom she inconvenienced. She would have thus permitted the area rep to copulate with her, for example, but he failed to intuit this allocation and opted instead to remind Jane Joule that although volunteers were encouraged to take on independent projects, nothing religious or political could be allowed. This prohibition was not ambiguous. And in the weeks after the conference in Seoul, as Jane Joule continued to spend more and more of her time at the Buddhist nunnery, the area rep finally had no choice but to react.

He hiked up through a rocky hillside sparsely grown with stunted pine trees, the twisted shapes and meager needle clusters revealing how difficult life was in that stony land. There were no signs to guide by, but he had been assured this was the only way. The path grew steeper and he entered a mass of towering granite cliffs, upthrust pinnacles that recalled the violence of the forming of the world, as if they had been intentionally set there as a cautionary lesson. He climbed then rested then climbed again. The surfaces of rock he touched were cold against his palms, and loose flecks of black mica came off at his touch and glittered in the cold thin light. He met no one and found no indications of human passage, neither recent nor ancient. The pine trees thinned out as he gained altitude then finally disappeared, leaving him with only the immense faces of blind rock like primordial watchers, like the Korean equivalents of the seaward gazers on Easter Island, their cheeks and chins leprous with pale grey patches of lichens. He climbed higher. Grey cumuli of granite billowed above as he hiked, and a clammy mist settled down over him, entering his clothing and wetting his skin, as cool and lonely and persistent as the unreconciled fingers of the dead.

The path led up through a cold, dark notch created where an immense stone skull had been split apart as if from a single blow. The interior was lightless and the footing icy. He heard sounds that came from no source he could identify. The path grew level and he emerged onto a broad shelf of rock beyond which he saw the emptiness above the valley that would lie far below. The area rep wondered if what he had heard was his own breathing.

He should have been able to see the ocean from here, and perhaps even some of the outlying islands off the southern coast of the peninsula. But there was nothing. Only more mist and rock and cloud, the shades of grey and the densities varying only slightly so that the rolls of mist that rose up into masses of granite became them, and the rock itself rose into the low clouds hanging above, asserting the shared nature of substance, so that all he saw seemed reconfigurations of an ultimate and unwavering consonance.

The area rep stood for a long moment, feeling his skin stroked by the fingers of mist and studying the downward path that twisted out of sight into the obscurity below. It occurred to him then, as he made his way down toward the shrouded valley, that God did not suppress what He would not have known but instead revealed the truth of things with such terrifying clarity that the viewer himself would deny the seeing of it.

6.

The area rep and Jane Joule sat together on the veranda of the Buddha Hall and talked circumspectly, like old tennis partners finding new things in common after one of them has had a leg amputated.

The abrupt granite scarps towering above them in the late afternoon light were bare of vegetation, but the narrow valley itself had never been cleared of trees, and the forest pressed in around the perimeters of the temple grounds, as if drawn by the immense statue of the Amida Buddha squatting in the gloomy interior behind the two Americans. The tissue-thin layers of gold foil that had been ritually applied to the Buddha's cheeks and nose and chin and hands by centuries of believers glinted in the gloom above the tall altar candles, but lower down where those same believers could apply their needs more urgently, the massive knees of the statue had been rubbed and rubbed and rubbed until the bare wood was exposed.

The area rep told Jane Joule he was glad she hadn't shaved her head or replaced her regular clothing with mouse-colored robes.

"But I'm not a Buddhist," Jane declared. And she wasn't going to play at being one. "I'm just the way I am."

The area rep nodded thoughtfully, as if demonstrating that whatever answer she gave would be evaluated on merit alone. "And you can be that better here?" he asked, indicating the silent mountain temple with twilight settling around them like a pale ink wash on rice paper.

"Because I'm a foreigner," Jane said. She glanced at him quickly then leaned to the side and pulled something out of the back pocket of her trousers. "See?" She was showing him her registered alien ID card.

The sun had set behind the rugged western peaks, and darkness filled the trees of the forest then gradually overcame the open space of empty ground between the forest wall and the temple veranda. Jane wore indigo trousers and a loose cotton blouse that was the dark green of sea grass, and as the light seeped away around them, the shadows of the trees settled more and more deeply over the veranda of the Buddha Hall, making Jane's bare arms and throat and face and hair seem whiter, more radiant, almost phosphorescent.

But then what did she do here? the area rep asked again, and Jane again told him that she did nothing.

But why did she have to come so far? Why couldn't she find what she wanted in Pusan?

"I'm not strong enough," Jane said. She thought for a moment. "I'm not honest enough," she amended.

Candles in handmade paper lanterns were suspended from iron hooks that protruded from the lintel beams, forming pools of light at evenly spaced intervals down the length of the veranda, like portholes on the ship of the temple as it sailed through the silence of the night sea, transporting the immense substantiation of the Buddha on its unending and perfect journey.

The area rep had brought a bottle of Cabernet he had been saving for a special occasion, and as the little tables and trays and dishes for their evening meal began appearing nearby, he opened the wine.

"Everything is from here," Jane said, "gathered or grown."

"Except the rice, right? Gifts from the dead?"

Jane looked out at the dark forest. "Yes," she said, "all the sad old dead." She turned toward the area rep. "The dead grow older too, you know," she declared, as if daring him to deny it.

After the meal, their trays were taken away, and the little nuns retired to their sleeping quarters. Jane Joule and the area rep sat together in the muted glow of the paper lanterns and finished the last of their wine. When his fingertips found the back of her hand, Jane Joule turned her face toward him slightly, her short, silver hair glistening in the candlelight, but she neither drew nearer to the area rep nor moved farther away. He touched her breasts and felt her nipples respond. She raised her arms when the blouse was lifted over her head to remove it, and she leaned back onto her elbows and lifted her hips when the equivalent operation was applied to her trousers and underpants. She remained sitting beside him, with her knees pulled up against her chest and her arms wrapped around her shins. The dark shape of an owl silently crossed the back corner of the garden and disappeared into the darkness of the forest. Neither of them spoke. Pale, improvident moths died in the candle flames with quick snaps of incandescence, dropping out of the air onto the dark planks of the veranda, their wings burned off and their tiny corpses partly charred, as if the fire had jerked them back into a negative version of their larval state.

The area rep's ex-wife had stood looking at him from the open doorway, framed by the brightness of the daylight world. She hadn't said anything. The driver from the car service placed her suitcases in the trunk of the car then slammed down the lid harder than would have seemed necessary.

Then the front door was still standing open, still showing him what lay beyond the walls of his house, but his ex-wife was no longer there. When he finally got up and closed the door, everything he saw outside was exactly as he had expected it to be.

Jane Joule presented her attention to the silent forest surrounding the temple.

"Is everything all right?" the area rep whispered anxiously and Jane said, "Yes, fine, thank you."

"I mean, we don't have to do this if you don't want to."

Jane didn't look at him. "I don't mind," she said.

The silent forest waited, breathing in the darkness, cupping them like a gigantic hand that wasn't going to squeeze all the way into a fist.

The area rep gathered Jane's pale body into his arms. He lifted her onto his lap and held her, conscious of the inverted mountain of air above them, cradled between the upright granite sheaves of the valley walls, and conscious also of the starry night sky attending above that mass of air, and also of the nothingness in its absence beyond that, the nothingness in the great soundless chasms that mathematicians describe as poised beyond those farthest stars. And the area rep sensed himself almost knowing it, knowing himself almost, his real self almost, almost knowing within his near-understanding of how exactly he was there at that moment, and that therefore all reflection upon the moment that had just passed and all speculation on the moment that was about to occur were both irrelevant. And he was almost able to grasp it, just as it was. And yet he was also snagging on Jane Joule, on the fact of her, on the fact of his desire for her, and on not knowing what to do about it, and on not knowing why he didn't know.

So he sat in the vacant air, and he almost grasped that the negation of being has no meaning. Starlight sifted down over them in a shimmering silver dust of impossibly fine granules. And yet even as the area rep recorded to himself his occasion of near-understanding, it was gone. His mind had wandered on, and he knew that he was already just remembering the instant. And that memory and anticipation—God's bifurcate malediction at His parting in dismay from what He had made—would ensure the impossibility of his ever getting as close to it again.

"What I discovered is that I don't want to help anyone," Jane Joule said softly but clearly. "It's an odd thing to learn about yourself. Particularly if you're a volunteer. Other people all work together to make things better for everyone. But I don't. And even if I try to pretend to behave like somebody who wants to do something for others, it's never very convincing."

The area rep didn't say anything. He could feel the slight movement of her body as she breathed, the air on her skin.

"And also that I don't care," Jane Joule added. "I don't care at all about other people."

The following morning, it was determined that Jane Joule would not return to Pusan or take on a new teaching assignment elsewhere in Korea, and a week later, she was on a flight back to New York. Talking about her experience would help her understand what had happened to her so Jane Joule joined a group therapy program at a mental health facility in the city near Astor Place. One of her fellow participants was a burly young lawyer whose recent recruitment by a high-profile Wall Street law firm hadn't eliminated the urge he felt to inflict physical violence on his fellow human beings, and it was as a result of this man's character flaw that Jane Joule died.

Keith White knew he had to control himself better. It wasn't just anger that impelled him. Chronic Assault Syndrome was a form of addiction. Like smoking or drinking or gambling. It was hunger Keith White experienced, a need to feed directly from the world, as if only by the act of implanting himself within others could he find temporary peace.

And Keith hadn't liked the way Jane Joule sat gazing at him. "You think you don't have any addictions?" he demanded bluntly. Then why was she there?

"Because I don't have anything at all."

What was that supposed to mean?

"I'm not sure." Jane smiled at him, backing down. She looked at the others then looked at Keith White again. She told him it was fine, it didn't matter.

Keith's eyes had settled on her face like two frozen moons orbiting a dead planet. "It matters to me," he said.

Several months later, against the advice of almost everyone who knew one or the other or both of them, they were married in a simple ceremony in a sun-washed garden in a nice part of Long Island. Keith's knuckles and fingers were swollen and broken from a fight he had gotten into the night before, and Jane's joy at the happiness she was able to provide her parents by giving herself to another person was diminished only slightly by her premonition that she would never provide them with grandchildren—an intuition realized within the year, her neck broken, her head twisted back at a grotesque angle, like a medieval rendition of one of the damned, like a malefactor punished inventively by Dante, like a doubter, a refuser of God's simple gifts, a woman condemned eternally to trying to see what she looked like from behind, as if in punishment for an excess of pride in the pleasures of abnegation.

7.

The area rep came out of the sleeping cubicle he had been assigned. Gems of dew on cobwebs in the garden trees caught the misty morning sunlight and offered as if for his approval crystalline nets of tiny suns, each perfect within itself. He sat on the veranda alone and dangled his legs off the edge.

The sky above the valley was a hard, flat blue. Summer was ending already. The sun had just risen above the mountain rim so the western wall stood out bright with sunlight while the eastern side of the valley was still lost in shadows.

No one came. The area rep didn't mind. He would sit on the veranda and be content to wait for someone to do something. Pads of grey-green moss thickened the rocks in the garden. A ceramic pot on an oblong slate held a single wild orchid, its mauve and labial organs lifted above fleshy leaves.

He tried to be aware of that only. But he couldn't. He was already just remembering it.

"You don't love me," Jane had said to the area rep on the night before she departed from Korea. It was a farewell dinner, just the two of them at the Han-il Kwan, one of Seoul's best *pulgogi* restaurants. "You look at me, and you think I'm something you should want. That's all."

The area rep had declared his feelings after a couple of flasks of *soju* rice wine. He had come up to Seoul specifically to say goodbye to her in such a way that she would know everything was fine, and now he felt ashamed of himself for screwing it up. "I remember once you told me you've never had a boyfriend," the area rep said. "So you've never felt drawn to anyone?"

Jane's eyes had scanned his face briefly, like somebody checking the fronts of unfamiliar houses at night, searching for an address. "What do you mean by 'drawn'? You mean sexually?"

"Well, yes, as a matter of fact." The area rep picked up a *soju* flask and shook it to see if still contained wine. "There's nothing wrong with that."

"I like sex," Jane said.

"But you haven't had a boyfriend, at least not here, have you?"

"Why do you keep saying that? You don't need a boyfriend to have sex."

Suddenly the area rep understood. "You mean...with women? Is that why you were with those nuns?"

"No. When I have sex, I do it with men," Jane explained. "I'm just saying you don't need all the extras attached. If you want to have sex. And there's a man there who wants to. Then you do it. That's all."

The area rep gazed down into his tiny wine cup, frowning in concentration, like somebody studying roofs on fire in the distance, wondering which way the wind was pushing the flames. "But that night in the mountains, we didn't...do anything."

Jane picked at the dish of radish kimchi, as if rearranging the display of cool, peppery cubes in order to make them more appealing. "You didn't want to," she said. "You started. And then you stopped."

"Not because I didn't want to."

Jane nodded. "Because you thought you were in love with me, or had to be in love with me, or thought I had to think you were, or something like that." Jane continued to toy with the dish of radish kimchi, positioning two cubes side by side as if in comparison then removing one and replacing it with another. "You have a tendency to sort of...settle on things," she said softly. "On ideas. But without really admitting to yourself what they are."

"I know what I want," the area rep declared.

Jane's eyes found his. And for the first time since he'd known her, she actually seemed to be observing him. He had thought she was going to challenge him, or question him about himself, but she had only held him with her calm, incurious gaze, asking nothing, offering nothing, and he finally had had to look away.

Sunlight flooded directly into the temple garden, and the dew on the cobwebs had disappeared so that the cobwebs themselves were no longer visible. The area rep realized the old abbess was watching him from where the garden blended into the edge of the forest. He stepped into his boots and scuffed over to her, laces dragging behind him.

The old Korean woman stood silently for a moment then held open a woven rice straw basket she had filled with small, grey-green fern shoots. You picked them just before dawn, she told the area rep. The taste was sweeter.

"You know why I have come?"

The old abbess made no response.

"The woman who was here, the American, she died," the area rep said in his halting Korean. "I said this yesterday. To the nun who greeted me. I worry she didn't say it to you."

The old abbess looked back at him steadily but said nothing.

"My Korean is poor," the area rep added.

"No, no, it is excellent," the old woman said.

"Perhaps I was unclear. The foreign woman who stayed here? She was killed. By her husband. Just last month. I was told about it in Seoul."

The old abbess nodded at this last piece of information. "Seoul is a very fine city," she said.

The area rep gazed into the dark forest behind the old abbess. "But did you not understand what I said?"

"About the American woman? Yes, I understood it."

"And aren't you sorry?"

The old abbess said nothing for a moment. Then she asked was he sorry?

"Yes. Of course."

The woman stared at him for another long moment. "You want to hope for something," she said more firmly. "You want to go toward some thing, some goal. It is because of this habit that you become dissatisfied."

"I am not religious," the area rep said.

"Because you doubt."

"My experience makes me doubt."

"Because you believe your experience has disappointed you," the old woman said. "But that's foolish."

"My experience is all I have," the area rep replied, but the abbess ignored this.

"Salvation from the sadness and terror of existence is offered to all who call for it. You have only to want to be saved—truly, deeply, without any reservations, want to be saved. And if you invoke the Buddha's name once truly and deeply and without reservation, then you will be freed from the wheel."

"I see," the area rep said. But he did not believe it. And even if he had, he knew that the lightness needed to call for help truly, without doubting, was beyond him. And always would be.

The last time he saw Jane Joule, the area rep had forced himself to meet her gaze again. All around them was the noisy hubbub of people eating and laughing and shouting at each other. Only Jane Joule remained serene, coolly studying his face. The area rep thought he had never seen eyes so pale blue. And her eyelashes, too, were delicate, nearly transparent filaments of silvery gold. "I want you," he had said, trying to generate all the force of sincerity he could, trying to make it be true through the sheer power of his need to convince her he believed it.

"And what would you do with me?" Jane put down her chopsticks abruptly, as if holding them had suddenly made no sense to her. "You'd get bored in a month."

"No, I wouldn't."

"But I don't do anything," Jane said. "I really don't."

"I'd never get bored with you," the area rep declared stubbornly, even though he knew she was right.

"You are already," Jane maintained. "But that's okay. I don't mind."

The area rep had looked away from her then. Young waitresses hurried from table to table delivering platters of thinly sliced meat soaked in soy sauce and minced garlic. It was true. He was ready to get back to Pusan, back to his regular life. The clatter of the noisy restaurant suddenly seemed too much, and he turned to face Jane Joule, wondering how to suggest that they finish their meal and go only to discover her already waiting behind her chair, having once again guessed correctly what he would want to do.

They had stood together in the street in front of the restaurant. Jane Joule declined his offer to walk her back to her hotel. "If you need anything," the area rep had offered, "if I can do anything for you, just ask."

Jane had nodded once in a single, abrupt gesture, like someone flipping a drop of moisture off the tip of her nose, then turned away and was absorbed into the crowded summer street.

After the old abbess had left him, the area rep returned to his usual place and resumed sitting on the veranda. The sun set. The stars appeared like the web of a basket in the dome of the sky. He slept better that night than he had the night before.

The area rep sat on the edge of the veranda and tried not to be waiting for anything. The morning sun warmed the garden as he watched it, and the wind sifted through the tops of the pine trees, combing out clusters of loose needles and transporting them onto the bushes and rocks and raked gravel of the garden.

The area rep thought he heard crows in the forest but none were visible nor could he recall having seen any signs of them on the day he hiked in. Yet the sound of crows calling was there.

The little nun who had apparently been assigned to him brought the area rep his morning bowl of roasted barley tea. The tea bowl was the color of the earth, and he lifted it in both hands and tasted the barley tea as he drank, trying to train himself to pay attention to the world as he was in it.

The old abbess occasionally watched the area rep from where the garden merged with the forest. She never seemed to have come intentionally to observe him. It was as if she simply materialized at that spot, as if she extracted sufficient molecular structure from the surrounding mountains and rocks and trees to occupy a place at a time.

"We loved each other," the area rep's ex-wife had told him when she had finished bringing her suitcases down to the front door, "and then we stopped loving each other. And that's all you can say about it."

It occurred to the area rep that what he had thought were crows could have been the creaking of boughs rubbing against each other. Or it could have been crows.

The area rep sat on the edge of the veranda in the sunlight.

The sun crossed from the east to the west and set behind the granite western wall and the air grew chilly but the area rep held his position.

The sky darkened and the basket of stars revealed itself.

Paper lanterns were provided as they had been each night, and the meal he was given was the same as the meal he had had the evening before. When his trays were taken away he sat in the muted candlelight then blew out the candles and sat in the darkness.

The area rep sat on the veranda in the morning sunlight. The afternoon was silent and windless. The wind rose. The eastern wall held the last of the sunlight. A single, elongated white cloud that had clung to the top of a distant peak broke free and sailed off into the open sky.

The sun set and the sky darkened and the stars came out.

The sun rose to the misty garden, to the bright western face of the granite walls, to the glowing tops of the trees, to the droplets of dew strung like jewels on cobwebs.

The area rep watched it all. He knew he could die.

How I Came To Write This Story

As a Peace Corps Volunteer, I'd always loved being part of the excitement and commotion of an African marketplace. When I lived in Niger as a Peace Corps staff spouse, I didn't have the freedom I'd had as a PCV and I missed being "among the people" in a bush marketplace. Except for the sassy, noisy boys who demanded to guard your car, barter a price, or carry your loads, the market that most reminded me of my Volunteer days was at Ayarou, near the Mali border. One Sunday at Ayarou a small boy followed me all through the market. He was shy and hesitant and I thought I could ditch him, but then he'd reappear in my shadow again. I finally paid him to go away. But I kept thinking about him—what his life might be like, how he perceived Westerners, and how easily Westerners become oblivious to the lives of ordinary people like him. Trying to imagine his life, I wrote "On Sunday There Might Be Americans".

—Leslie Simmonds Ekstrom

LESLIE SIMMONDS EKSTROM (Nigeria, 1963-1965) never saw the world beyond California till she traveled through India as a college sophomore. She joined the Peace Corps after graduating from UC Berkeley and served as an English (TESL) teacher in northern Nigeria. Back home, she worked as a Peace Corps trainer at UCLA and taught English in inner city Los Angeles. As a Peace Corps staff spouse, she then lived in the U.S. Virgin Islands, Niger, and Cameroon. Over that period of time, she mostly had babies on-site and wrote articles for American Embassy and Peace Corps newsletters. Settled in the Washington, DC, suburbs for the past 20 years, she works as a technical writer. Her nonfiction articles and commentary pieces have been published in numerous community publications, as well as *The Washington Post*. Her fiction has appeared in small magazines and *The Bridge*, a national publication on cross-cultural affairs.

ON SUNDAY THERE MIGHT BE AMERICANS

by Leslie Simmonds Ekstrom

Musa sat up on his mat and he knew he was done with sleep. He strained to see a sign of light beyond the door of his mother's hut. The muscles in his legs were jumping already and he had to stand. He walked to the door and pressed his eye against a crack in the straw. There above the rim of the compound wall he could see a sliver of blue. It was Sunday morning.

Each night the family began their sleep outside, the suffocating heat of day lingering long past sunset. But in the chill Sahara dawn, one by one, they dragged their mats back inside the thick mud walls of the huts, where Musa shivered now though he'd wrapped himself in his blanket. He pulled back one side of the door and looked into the compound. Only his uncle, Old Baba, still lay asleep in the middle of the compound, stretched out like a crane skirting the edge of the river, his arms spread like wings and his cracked, spindly toes almost pointed. Old Baba slept soundly whenever he closed his eyes, warmed by dreams of the cities he'd seen when there had been work on the other side of the desert.

Musa turned back to look at his mother. She lay on her mat with his baby sister, Fatouma, folded into the curve of her body. He knew his mother's dreams. Sometimes when she first awoke she called him by another name. Then she would tell him a story about one of his brothers or sisters who'd died of spots, a cough, or a mysterious fever the village doctor couldn't cure. He remembered some of their faces.

He stepped out of the hut, pretending not to notice the other wives of the compound emerging from the doors of their huts, kneeling to light fires where they would cook the morning meal. One or two had already gone to the center of the compound to pound millet, and soon the soft thunk of their heavy wood pestles joined in a rhythm that reverberated through the village. The sound of the pestles made him hungry for porridge, but today he could leave without food—it was market day. The cars would drive up from the capital city, full of Europeans looking for things to buy. There might be one who would let him follow in the market and be the go-between. Maybe an American. Americans would pay 10 or 20 times what anything was worth, and then they'd give you a tip so foolish you could buy food and a pair of sandals on the same day.

Musa slipped out through the forecourt, hoping the other wives wouldn't see him and gossip that his mother never fed him. He stood for a moment in the narrow door of the entrance hut, listening for the sound of his name; but he had not been noticed. He pulled the blanket up over his head and walked out into the village, staying close to the wall, following it around to the rear where he could face the eastern sky. The sky changed slowly, veiled by a dull brown haze. Rain had fallen only three times this year and the slightest wind stirred the arid earth into the sky, where it stayed.

Musa's compound was at the back of the village. From where he stood against the wall, he could watch people on their way to the market, treading the wide, worn path that ran through the uncleared bush. They moved almost silently in the early light. He heard the bells of a train of camels before they emerged out of the haze, bringing in salt from the desert. The gray-white slabs hung in rope slings on either side of the camels' humps, bobbing heavily with each long, loose stride. The drivers, seated high above their cargo, swayed forward and back, forward and back. As they came nearer, Musa could hear the clucks of the drivers urging the beasts on and the deep, irritable growl the animals gave in reply. The men might have been half asleep but they kept their feet pressed against the base of the camels' woolly necks, pushing hard into their flesh to keep them moving forward when they smelled the river and strained to turn toward it.

The women who scurried along the path carried large calabash bowls on their heads and babies tied against their backs. Musa knew the bowls would be laden with roasted groundnuts, dried okra, guinea corn, or locust bean cakes. His mouth watered, though even if he had money he wouldn't stop them now. They had to hurry. From his village it was only three more kilometers to town, and some of these women might have left their villages two hours before dawn, to arrive early at the market grounds, hoping to get a good place where there would be shade at midday. The Europeans could arrive at any time of day, taking shelter from the dust and heat in the machine-cooled rooms of the Hotel.

He saw a woman on the path that he recognized and ducked his head into the blanket. She had been a wife in his compound, the second of his father's younger brother, but she'd quarreled too much so he divorced her, sending her back to her village with all her belongings tied in a bundle on her head. She had been industrious, but the other wives called her greedy and they were glad when she was gone. He saw her glance up at the compound wall, her neck askew from the weight of a tray of bottles on her head. She could only roll her eyes toward the wall to take in as much of her former home as there was to see in the flat, cracked surface. When Musa's father had been prosperous, he'd had four wives. Long ago, his mother had been the favorite and Old Baba once told him she had been the most beautiful.

Musa pressed his back against the wall, let his knees bend and his buttocks slide to a seat on his heels. From here, he would watch the new sun as it rose above the horizon. When it had come between the earth and the first branch of the *gao* tree, he would check his mother's hut. If she had not awakened, he would leave without food.

"So you have not yet gone, Ugly One," his mother said, seated at a fire near the door of her hut, her eyes squinted with sleep.

"It's still early."

"Baba's goat has milk," she said. "You can have milk if you want it." She held out a small round gourd. Now the wives would say she spoiled him.

"Give mine to Fatouma." Musa squatted near the fire to feel the heat of the coals. In a few hours, the air would be as hot.

"Eat porridge at least." She handed him a bowl full of yesterday's pounded millet. It had not been heated through.

Fatouma toddled out of the hut on her fat baby's legs, hurrying to sit near him. "Moo-SA," she called. He opened his blanket to set her on his lap and wrapped her up beside him so that only their faces peeked out.

"You look like two morning flowers," his mother said with pleasure, "waiting for the sun to open your leaves." Abruptly she lowered her eyes and stirred the fire, poking it too much, fearful of what she had just said. Tempting Allah.

"But Fatouma is so ugly," he said, easing his mother's anxiety. "Allah would never want to take this ugly child." He felt his sister's body warm against him and gave her his porridge. He pulled her closer to him, looking down into her clear, dark eyes. Seeing her brother's face so near, she reached up and touched his chin, twisting up her mouth in the way she knew would always make him laugh. He laughed to please her and pressed his cheek against the soft down on top of her head.

Musa joined the stream of people on the path that led into town. A group of Bela women, grunting like beasts of burden, came up behind him, pushing past anyone in their way, eager to reach the market and unload the wood racks they balanced on top of their heads. Each rack held a half-dozen clay jars, but these women, their shoulders deep and muscular as men's, could bear the precarious weight of the load. Their dark skin, black as a cooking pot, already shone with sweat. Musa had to jump out of the path to avoid the tilting racks.

Three Fulani girls, sisters most likely, rode by on donkeys alongside the path. Each wore an identical head cloth, brilliant green and woven with golden threads; too fine for a bush market. These were girls whose father might wear a watch. They laughed and talked too much as they passed the others who traveled on foot, and one of them looked at Musa, turned her head to stare at him, speaking to him with her eyes. Uneasily, he looked away. This had begun to happen often, even with girls in his own village. He had grown tall for his age, but he was still too young to answer back.

The path ended at the river where the market grounds made up half the town. The Hotel sat on a rise above the river, surrounded by flame trees and high white walls. When he came within sight of the Hotel, his stomach contracted, as it always did, seeing that there were at least a dozen boys milling around, expectant, hovering near the Hotel gates. He saw no cars there yet. The road at the post office, by which the cars always came, was quiet and empty. The morning air still felt cool. The sun barely showed through the murky sky.

Musa walked near the group of boys, keeping his distance, cautious of their intensity. Many of these boys were his friends with whom he studied the Koran at the *malam*'s house, but no one wanted competition when the Europeans arrived from the capital city. Like a pack of hunting jackals, each was on his own. Perhaps many Europeans would come today and there would be enough for all of them. If they were lucky, there would be Americans.

A tall, green car came fast around the corner at the post office, making a dust storm, and the boys ran, frenzied, straight out in its direction. They met it head on and jumped out of its way to run wildly at its sides, back toward the Hotel. Musa joined them, shouting at the Europeans who sat cool and impassive inside the enormous car. The Hotel gate swung open and the guard leaped out from behind the wall. He came after the boys with his cattle whip, beating them away. The leather snapped against Musa's thigh and he swallowed a yelp of pain.

There were six men in the green car. Six opportunities to be the go-between. They got out and dropped money into the palm of the guard. The guard followed behind them so none of the boys could get to them before they entered the Hotel. Musa knew they would have coffee and bread before they went into the market. He tried to see beyond them, to the inside of the Hotel. He had heard stories of the wondrous tables there, covered with crisp, white cloth and spread with sugar and butter set out to be eaten at will.

A small gray truck came more hesitantly around the corner, stopped, then turned away from the Hotel and drove directly into the restless throng of animals tethered for sale at the market's outer edge. A man with pumpkin-colored hair and skin speckled as eggs stuck his head and arms out of the truck, taking photographs, one after another, of the bawling baby camels tied in clusters on the open grounds. The boys left their position at the Hotel gate, tearing toward the gray truck. Musa stayed where he was, rubbing the flesh that still stung from the snap of the guard's whip.

Now a white sedan appeared at the post office road. A Peugeot. Musa could name the car. He felt a thrill of self-importance, as though he alone possessed secret knowledge of the world outside his village. The Peugeot moved slowly into the large open space that separated the market from the Hotel.

Inside the Peugeot he could see one man, one woman, and their child, a little boy leaning out the window, whose hair seemed to shine with silver light. Musa touched his own head, pressed his fingers down into his dull black, tightly curled hair. The woman in the car held her child as he stretched out the window. "Cow," he shouted, pointing his finger at a wild-eyed bull rocking its head against ropes that tied it to a tree. Musa thought he recognized the little boy's word. Was it English? These might be Americans and the others hadn't heard.

Instead of going through the Hotel gates, this car drove up next to the wall of the Hotel compound. The swarm of boys ran back to the Peugeot and the guard came at them again with his whip, cursing their mothers because he stumbled and nearly fell. The man locked the car and walked with his wife and child toward the market, the guard hovering around them until they had gone too far from the Hotel.

Musa ran with the pack, circling the couple to offer help in the market.

"Leave us alone," the man shouted in the boys' own language. "We don't need you," he bellowed, his white man's accent falling hard on the wrong syllables. But none of the boys wanted to be the first to give up. "Get away from us!" He raised his arm threateningly. The boys moved back, more amused than afraid. Many Europeans who came up to the market were like that. They wanted to be on their own and wouldn't ask for help even if you followed them around all day.

One of the boys sent up a shout and the rest of them turned like a herd of sheep and stampeded toward the Hotel, bursting into the dust of another car. Musa watched them go and turned to look toward the market. He could already see a shimmering mirage hanging above the market stalls. The heat of day had begun. The sky had cleared and the sun was eating the air. This might not be the Sunday he had hoped for. He should have taken some porridge.

The young couple were walking into the cattle lot, moving cautiously around the nervous long-horned animals. Their little boy pointed his finger again and again, twisting in his father's arms, excited, his eyes wide. The woman stopped to watch a Tuareg paint yellow lines on the backs of his bulls, to identify them and mark them for sale. Her husband placed the boy on his shoulders, spoke a few words to her, and he left her. She was alone. Musa's legs moved before his mind had made its plan.

The woman walked briskly into the marketplace without the usual hesitation of a European. She seemed at ease in the noise and clutter of an African market.

"Gud marn-ning, Madame," Musa said, the only English he knew, phrasing the words in a lilting tone that he thought sounded friendly. He alternately galloped and tiptoed as he spoke, trying to maintain a strategic position at her side. The woman ignored his greeting, gave him a look of impatience and made her way through the crowd, heading into the center of the market.

He watched her go. She was tall, and slender as a young girl, with hair yellow and straight as millet stalks. She wore pants the same as her husband's—washed-out blue and tight as skin. The shirt she wore was no finer than those he'd seen on boys coming back from the capital city. How strange it seemed. These people would spend on one bottle of beer what a man in his village couldn't earn in a day's work, yet they spent no money on the clothes they wore, and the women dressed as plain as the men. He glanced down at her shoes. With sudden excitement he almost turned to shout at one of his friends. She was USA! The white cloth shoes she wore had a bright blue symbol on both sides, shaped like the blade of a butcher's knife, curved back at the end. Only Americans wore those shoes.

The American woman stopped at the stall of a Hausa merchant, knelt down to examine a pile of his painted glass beads. The merchant ceremoniously opened a box to show her more beads, then another, and when she didn't react, another and another, making grand movements with his arms like a storyteller, pouring out the beads on the mat where he sat on the ground. They formed little pools of color all around him. He thrust his hand under her face to show her a necklace, which seemed to irritate her, and she stood up to move on, the merchant shouting at her to come back and buy something—look at the mess he'd made for her.

Musa followed her, staying close, guarding his claim, pretending he'd been hired.

They were walking through the pottery lot, Musa noiselessly on her heels, when the woman stopped suddenly. She stepped aside, out of the path that separated the grain pots from the water jars, and stood there waiting, her back to him. Musa froze. He turned around and walked the other way. Then she stepped back into the path and continued in the direction she'd been going. He turned again to follow her. After a few more steps, she whipped around and looked him straight in the eye. Musa lowered his head and passed her, as though on his way to some purpose. She walked off in the opposite direction, disappearing into the dense, noisy crowd.

Musa maintained his ploy for only a minute, then spun on his heels and darted into the rows of fragile clay containers. He craned his neck to find her, then anxiously looked down to watch his feet, taking small, careful steps between the pots and jars, avoiding the disaster of a debt he couldn't pay.

The American woman was not far away. He saw her. No other boy had found her. But he leaped too quickly into the next narrow path and his foot hit the top of a long-necked water jar. It fell over on its side. He heard an old woman screaming at him; a shrill toothless voice that made people turn and look.

Musa stopped in the path, wishing he'd never left his mother's hut.

The old woman stood up, shaking her hands at him, imploring Allah to strike down this dangerous boy. She lifted the jar to show a gathering group of market women the damage that had been done. Miraculously, the jar came up off the ground in one perfect piece. The cackling old voice stopped in surprise. Musa lifted himself into the air and galloped down the path in search of his American.

She had stopped in a path that wove through a field of enameled tinware—dozens of bowls, pots, cups, and trays displayed on the ground, brightening the hard-baked dirt with their painted fruits and flowers. Among the tinware, a half dozen Bela girls stood in front of his American. They giggled and pressed against each other, holding their henna-dyed fingertips delicately over their mouths. The girls were all dressed the same, wrapped in indigo cloth that gave up some of its inky color on their skin. Plastic rings and beads covered the girls' heads, woven into the thin, intricate braids they wore hanging down stiffly on all sides. They smelled of honey.

One of the Bela girls wanted to sell her bracelet and a small crowd had formed to watch. The woman was interested in the bracelet, but she couldn't understand what they were saying about the price. Now she would need him.

Musa spoke up in careful French. "How much would you like to pay, Madame?"

"Five hundred francs," she answered.

Musa addressed the girls in their own language. The people of his village looked down on the Belas, whom they considered coarse and low, but one of the girls had large soft eyes, gentle as a calf's and full of words. She turned from Musa's glance and lowered her eyes to the ground. He was distracted by his need to look longer at this shy Bela girl.

"The white woman will pay five hundred," he said. The Bela girls rolled their eyes and giggled; they tilted their heads and whispered. They loved the crowd and were taking their time. "Five hundred," Musa repeated, almost inaudibly. His mouth felt full of dust and he longed for a drink of the river.

At last one of them answered him, holding her fingertips over her mouth like a little red-orange cage, feigning modesty. "Not less than seven hundred and fifty," she said firmly.

Musa looked up at the woman. "They want one thousand francs. But I'm sure I can help you. I will tell them seven hundred and fifty."

She listened to him and repeated the amount he would offer. He nodded. "All right," she said. "Good."

"She has agreed to pay seven hundred and fifty," Musa said. The girls squealed and leaned on each other in a haphazard circle. They studied Musa, flashing their eyes at him. Bold girls. He had to look away from them, but his eyes darted irresistibly back to the shy one, who was watching him, too, her head down, stealing a glance sideways.

The American woman counted out the coins, took the bracelet, and slipped it on her arm. The golden white brass lost some of its radiance against her pale skin. But she seemed pleased. As she walked away from the Bela girls, she was smiling. And he had helped her. He looked around to see if anyone noticed, staying close to her, making helpful comments. Which she seemed to ignore.

Suddenly Musa saw Aliyu. Sly Aliyu with the angel face. Who saw Musa's American.

"Bonjour, Madame," sang Aliyu, and held out both his hands, filled with rough clay beads. "My mother made these," he said in French.

The liar! "Your mother eats with hyenas," Musa muttered, his head turned away. If his American understood what he'd said, she might disapprove.

Aliyu ignored the insult and looked up appealingly at the woman. "My mother made them yesterday in our village."

"How much?" she asked. She spoke directly to Aliyu, ignoring Musa, her go-between.

"Seven hundred and fifty francs," smiled Aliyu.

The woman was furious. "Your mother eats with hyenas!" she snapped at Aliyu with the angel face, and Musa was staggering back and forth, holding his stomach, shrieking with laughter. This was *his* American.

She turned her back to Aliyu and walked away. Musa followed, suppressing his triumph for the business at hand. He could see that her shirt was wet and stuck to her back; she would be done with the market now.

If she gave him twenty-five francs, he would buy rice and sauce. If fifty, rice and sauce with meat. Today he would have meat.

She took off the heavy Bela bracelet and put it in the bag that hung over her shoulder. She looked at her watch, lifting her hand to shield her eyes from the glare of the sun. "It's too hot." She looked at him now, spoke directly to him, using words in his own language. He held his breath. "I will eat at the Hotel. Then I want to go back into the market. Can you help me buy a Tuareg ring?"

"Yes," he said, trying to appear serious and mature.

"I will be back soon." She walked away then, heading for the Hotel. She took out a cloth and wiped her face. She did not take out any money.

Musa followed her to the Hotel, taking no chances. He would wait there until she came out again. Somewhere in the shade on the other side of the wall, he could hear the guard sleeping noisily. One half of the double gate stood open and Musa looked inside, all the way to the wide glass doors of the Hotel. He watched the woman disappear behind one shining panel of glass and for a moment, he saw his own reflection—an almost beautiful, too thin boy in rumpled khaki shorts and a T-shirt that hung awry at the bottom. He thought again of the Bela girl. He imagined himself a young man coming back from the capital city, bringing her a gift the likes of which she would never see in this bush market. By then he would be living in the hut of the unmarried sons. He would wear new creased pants and a shirt as crisp and white as the Hotel table cloths.

He looked into the sky to judge the time. It was midday. The sun seemed to have risen on wings that were closing down around him, suffocating him. He felt his head grow light, as though it would separate from his body. Other boys who had followed a European in the market might already be paid by now, sitting at a food stall under a thatched roof, eating rice and sauce. Rice and sauce. He would be satisfied with stale porridge. Musa slid down into the thin shade against the wall and set his swelling head against his knees, wondering why Allah had made the world unevenly.

He woke at the sound of a car's engine. He opened his eyes to see that the sun had left the top of the sky. He had slept too long. Shadows dropped from the trees around the market grounds. He looked out behind the Hotel where the afternoon sun made a hundred thousand mirrors dance on the surface of the river. Boys his age, some of them naked, dived and rose up through the cool, sparkling water, rolling and turning on the surface like hippos. He would join them soon.

He heard the creak of dry hinges and looked over to see the guard walking the gate open. The guard saw Musa and slashed the air with his whip. Then he bowed absurdly low as the tall green car drove out through the gate. Large black letters marked the car: RANGE ROVER. Who had followed the white men in the Range Rover? Which of his friends there in the river had received more than twenty-five francs?

The sound of laughter came from behind the wall, a child's. The little boy with the silver hair ran out through the gate, turned to look behind him, bending his legs with his hands on his knees, as though to brace for a run. Musa's American came after him, let her son run a few paces, then grabbed him up in her arms. The husband walked out after her, held out his hand to the guard. Musa heard the sound of more than one coin.

The husband took the little boy and walked to the car. She followed behind, taking a cloth out of her bag and tying it around her hair. The guard bowed and smiled, leaning toward her, his brown teeth coming too close to her face, and she hurried past him.

Musa stood up.

The woman did not see him, took quick steps along the wall toward the white Peugeot. She opened the car door, got inside, and rolled down the window. She was not going back into the market.

The car moved back toward Musa, passing the guard, who doffed his dirty hat and bowed again. When the car stopped in its backward path, his American twisted her head around to take a last look at the market. "Oh," she called, seeing Musa there. "I forgot about you."

The Peugeot turned its wheels and sped away from the wall, making a long dust cloud that flared wider and higher at the post office road.

Musa looked again out behind the Hotel. A herdsman was forcing his cattle into the river, smacking their hindquarters with a strip of curled hide to get them across the shallow water. Musa's friends stopped their play to whoop at the timid cows. He decided not to join them. He could swim just as well farther down the river, near his village.

"There you are, Ugly One," his mother said. "It's late. What did you do in the market all day?"

"I helped a woman from the capital city. An American. She wanted to buy a Bela's bracelet."

"You bargained with a Bela?"

"Yes. But only for her. My American."

"And did she give you something for your work?"

"Two hundred francs."

"So much!"

"I bought you a fine new water jar. And red bracelets for Fatouma."

"Did you eat in the market?"

"I ate rice and meat. I ate so much meat I can barely move."

"But you are moving very well, I see. You can't eat a little more?"

"Maybe some porridge. A little."

His mother filled his bowl to brimming with pounded millet. It was fresh and hot. He breathed in the steam as it rose to his face, clearing his head of the market dust.

"So where is our new water jar?" she asked. "The old one is frail as Baba's bones."

"It was too big. I had to leave it in town."

"With Fatouma's bracelets?"

"Yes. I'll get them next week."

"You will try again next week?"

"Americans come every Sunday," he said, and he stretched out his legs to make a place for Fatouma.

How I Came To Write This Story

One of the easiest political charges to level against a Peace Corps Volunteer goes something like this: "You're only slumming. You're out of here whenever it gets too tough for you, whenever you feel like it. Your passport protects you, so whatever you have to offer isn't really relevant." I wanted to write a story about a volunteer who took the charge seriously and tried to find out for herself whether she could prosper in her adopted community without the official shield of the Peace Corps. At the same time the story includes a critique of some of the easy assumptions about Third-World solidarity and First-World responsibility that inform the view of the world that sees an unbridgeable chasm between North and South. Finally, I wanted to write a story in which the political was connected intimately to the personal, one in which those separate aspects required each other to make fullest sense.

—Mark Jacobs

MARK JACOBS (Paraguay, 1978-1980) is a foreign service officer with experience in Latin America, Turkey and Spain. He speaks fluent Turkish and Spanish. He has published widely in commercial and literary magazines including the *Atlantic Monthly*. A book of his short stories, *A Cast of Spaniards*, was published in 1984 by Talisman House and his novel, *Stone Cowboy*, was published by Soho Press in 1997. In 1998, Soho Press also published a collection of short stories, *The Liberation of Little Heaven*.

THE EGG QUEEN RISES

by Mark Jacobs

Cramps and the rain woke her before dawn. For a few minutes she lay on the cot feeling the small of her back sag into the hole in the bed spring. Then she moved by memory through the furred darkness out onto the back porch, lifted the flash from its up-bent nail. Across the slick mud crown of the patio, down the slope of killer weeds and high spiky grass, into the outhouse. Heaving didn't help. Rain patted the outhouse roof. She straightened up, felt her aloneness stab like a gas pain, heard the Gasport aunts' vicious whisper: knocked up! In Paraguay, no less.

In the dark of the yard all she saw were the shapes of shapes, and they were vaguely hostile. Back inside the house, the smoky orange blur of the lantern she lit entranced her eyes. From the high shelf in the kitchen she took her passport, stared critically at the innocent-faced blonde *gringuita* there. Then she poured kerosene on the passport, turned the pages in her hands to let the liquid soak in, set it on the damp bricks of the floor. The falling match flared. Poof. She was no longer what she had been. She went back to bed.

In her dreams she was queasy, and the Gasport aunts sang the chorus of her fall, but she felt better by the time Luis showed up for lunch. He stretched himself in the hammock she had hung in her living room and told her she was a phony while she fried his eggs.

"All you have to do is go back to the Peace Corps office and tell them you lost your passport and they'll give you a new one. Then..." He leaped from the hammock, made his arms into stiff wings and pantomimed her escape.

"I'm quitting the Peace Corps." She wondered why she could

not bring herself to tell him she was pregnant. She carried their lunch on enamel plates to the table. "As soon as the road dries up I'm going to Asunción to tell them."

"Then what? Back to Gasport?" He was not taking her seriously.

"I'm staying here, in Pueblo Santo."

It was the sharp edge to his laugh that made her keep her secret.

As he cut and chewed slowly with the bent-tined fork, she watched him, trying to decide what it was about him that had convinced her to go so far down the road with him. More than his Latin lover looks, that is. He was any woman's mental picture of that, only shorter. His skin was coffee, liquid and smooth. The wings of his mustache hovered over perfect, expressive lips. His shining black eyes put down whatever they took in; the obligation of intelligence. He walked light as a cat, meaning grace.

It was more than the politics, too, though what he taught her had been, coming from such lips, scary and seductive. Luis taught sixth grade, but he had studied in Santiago with people who taught him the words for the way the world worked: imperialism and dependency, oppression and liberation, all that powerful political jazz. When they kissed she came away with sweet lips.

"You won't last two months here without the protection of the Peace Corps," he predicted.

"In the United States the men usually wash the dishes," she told him.

"We're not in the United States."

They understood each other well enough by then. Underneath the words he was saying let's go to bed, and she was saying no. Understood. She studied her enemies list chalked on the back of the door: exploitation, domination, dependency, competition... The blue letters were fading. The rainy season damp could get inside and spoil anything. The fresh red underlining below some of the words was by Luis.

She hated even the idea of cockroaches, so she picked up the plates to wash them.

In three days the road dried hard enough to travel, and she rode by bus out of Pueblo Santo to Coronel Bogado, then onto the hardtop highway to Asunción. Having burned her passport, she looked with fresh curiosity at the cowboys and the cows, the hard-footed farmers drinking *maté* in ritual circles, the little lakes of

muddy dirt surrounding shacky houses of adobe bricks or mud
and poles, the cotton fields in which lay the blackened carcasses of
downed trees too big to haul away. Serves you right, someone in
Gasport carped in her ear. Eggs, she told herself. It was an inspiration.

The Peace Corps director had been a nun in Africa, where a
mysterious tragedy she refused to discuss made her an atheist. But
she was still earnest. She heard Amanda out, signed the papers that
needed signing, earnestly shook her hand goodbye. In the back
office of a money exchange house Amanda traded her ticket home
for cash, went back to Coronel Bogado on the RYSA night bus.

In Bogado she surrendered some cash for a used motorcycle, a
red Yamaha she chose because it came with a little satchel of tools.
The egg basket would be cheaper in Pueblo Santo.

"What are you trying to prove?" Luis asked her when he saw
the big wood box lashed to the back fender of the bike.

"Nothing," she lied. Odd that she liked him less now that she
was carrying his baby.

"It's genetic," he decided after watching her pack the box with
empty egg boxes. "You're a gringa. You were born to be a capitalist.
With you people it's make money or die."

"I'm going out to Potrero." She bounced a little on the bike
seat. She felt light-headed good, buzzed up. For the moment the
baby in her womb was an unfelt presence, a support. She left town
going north into cotton country. The north road was as much sand
as dirt, so the bike went with no difficulty over the packed surface.
On the unpeopled south edge of Potrero she found doña
Marciana, who liked to get involved in Amanda's extension
projects. Marciana's body had the loose, accommodated look of a
woman with twelve children. The end of the black-tobacco cigar
in her mouth was mashed; she never had a match. In the patio of
her house under waxy-leafed lemon trees, three little kids played
with a dog whose worm-swollen belly was the same shape as theirs.

"They say you quit the Peace Corps."

"I did."

"You can't do that."

"I have a way for us to make some money, doña Marciana."

"They also say that Luis the teacher goes into your house at
night, but I don't believe it."

"Don't you want to hear my idea?"

Amanda began slowly, with the women she knew. It was not

difficult to get them to sell her a few eggs. The box on the bike was sturdy, strapped steady enough that she was able to drive back to the pueblo with no breakage. In town there was always more cash, so she had no problem getting up-front money for her eggs. As soon as she did, she turned her bike around and went back to the country. Everyone ate eggs. Eggs fed the brain. Eating eggs would make children perform better in the classroom, and husbands and wives would be better in bed. It worked. No one was getting hurt, more people were getting more protein, and she was getting a little money.

After a month and a half doña Marciana, who liked the cash Amanda gave her, built a coop to keep her chickens in one place so she would be sure to find the eggs. She also bought more chickens. After a lifetime of indifference, her husband had suddenly begun to demand eggs. To keep don Edgar happy she needed a guaranteed supply. Amanda lent her money to buy stock. She was happy. The egg business satisfied her in a way that none of the extension projects had ever done, fostered a strange sensation; it was like becoming real.

On the night of the day she suspected she was showing, Amanda had a conclusive argument with Luis. They lay in bed listening to drizzle taper on the roof. His hand was being friendly with her tired body. Things were good. The worst of the morning sickness had passed. Her mind was clear and independent. She had begun to belong to Pueblo Santo, Paraguay.

"When the Berlin Wall came down," Luis whispered into her ear as though it were a sweet nothing, a box of empty candy, "things suddenly made sense to me. It was like a vision, a political vision. I saw, finally, that the real struggle, the permanent struggle, is between North and South. The Soviets and the East Bloc Europeans were only pretending. What they are is retrograde capitalists." His breath drummed, his tongue licked lightly. She felt loved and lucky. "The struggle of the twenty-first century will be between you and all of us. It will be ugly, Amanda. The North has all the bullets, all the guns. But don't forget we in the South have our weapon: we have people, and an ideal of how human society should be arranged, how people should treat one another. Your power and your luxuries have corrupted you. When you become decadent you become vulnerable."

"Is that what you're teaching your sixth graders?"

Hurt, he pulled away his licking tongue, his friendly hand. She felt abandoned. A memory vision of aunts on rockers on a big porch in Gasport overwhelmed her. There were apples in aluminum pails, Holstein cattle in fields behind fences. Cloud shadows fell on bright brown leaves that covered the cold grass, over which striped gray cats with long tails stalked like capitalists seeking advantage. Knocked up, went the windy whisper.

"When you're sufficiently weak," Luis said, generously putting away his irritation, "we'll be there. Not me, maybe not my sons, but maybe their sons, or their grandsons. We'll be there."

"Luis?"

"Say it."

But as close as she felt to him just then, she could not tell him she was pregnant. He had earned no territorial claim. "I have to tell you something," she geared up to say.

"Then say it." He was impatient, suspicious.

It came in a rush. "I won't make love with you anymore. I can't. Things are over, in that way, between us."

The argument happened because she had found no way to break it off without wounding him. She was gringo blunt, gringo cold, gringo brutal. Near dawn she heard in his voice that he had given up and there would be no more tenderness, no more friendly hands, ever. In Gasport a single pregnant woman didn't throw away her only chance to right her wrong. She wondered what Marciana would say, but her honest, observing self knew that Marciana, finally, didn't matter either.

By the time the rains ended, several of Amanda's suppliers in the villages had begun to coop their chickens as Marciana was doing. Several of her buyers in town told her they would be happy to buy only from her; she had earned their admiration by holding price and supply steady. Amanda felt fat and happy. Her dresses were loose enough, still, to be comfortable. Only on bad days did she worry how she would manage on the bike when she came closer to term.

She was not prepared for disaster. One night a flat-footed noise in the street outside woke her, but she was able to go back to sleep by putting the pillow over her face and doing relaxation exercises, limb by aching limb. In the morning, lifting the rusted padlock from the front door, she looked at her motorcycle chained to the middle pillar on the porch. The front tire was sliced flat. Tied to the handlebar by bailing wire, in a bunch like lumpy flowers, were the heads of three chickens. Their eyes were closed, their neck feathers bloody, their beaks slightly agape as though they might whisper their murderer's name. *Yánqui*, they whispered, *Go home*.

Stunned, she tossed the heads into the street for the cats, unchained the bike, wheeled it slowly toward the central plaza. People were careful not to see her. The boy she finally found to fix the tire looked guilty, as though he was afraid she would ask who had done the slicing. When he finished she rode the bike slowly back home. The heads of the chickens were gone from the street. She rolled the bike inside and lay without thinking in the hammock, in which she could no longer swing freely. The room was full of egg cartons. The Pueblo Santo market was saturated. She had been thinking of expanding into Coronel Bogado. Her face stung from the slap.

Luis' lecture helped not at all. "It's not so much the money," he explained, playing with the ends of his Latin lover mustache.

"Then what is it?" She knew that before he left her house he would try to seduce her into bed, fat and clumsy as she was. Ever since he had figured out she was with rug runt he had been pounding at her door, which surprised her, made her respect him. She had expected her bulging belly to scare him off for good. But she would make no love, nor would she admit in words the baby was his.

"You don't understand the Hispanic temperament, Amanda."

"Then explain it to me."

"You're taking money a Paraguayan should be getting."

"But nobody else wanted to go around to the villages the way I did. Now everybody has eggs. There's no losers."

"They resent you," he said bluntly.

"Fuck them," she told him in English, and when she refused to translate he went away mad.

Disguising her hurt, after siesta Amanda went to the police. Capitán Paco Raudales was a city man; the Pueblo Santo view was that he must have offended someone important to earn indefinite exile in a place as much like nowhere as theirs. Enormously overweight, he moved slowly. He shuffled, stopped, caught his raspy asthmatic breath, shuffled again. Except to cross the street he was driven in a government pickup by a bullet-headed corporal whose only job was tending the big man's bulk.

When she registered her complaint, Raudales raised his fat-pouched eyes from his desk and stared. She was being unreasonable in a way that only foreigners could be. She timed him. It took twenty seven minutes to fill out the forms, each of which was stamped with three separate stamps. She agreed with him that it would be immoderately difficult to find the person who had sliced her tire. "Wouldn't it be easier," he asked her, his lungs sawing the damp air, "if you just went home? Do you have to stay in Pueblo Santo?"

Even the Gasport aunts laughed at the preposterousness of that idea. What she had to do was go back to selling eggs.

* * * *

When Amanda was five months pregnant, Luis told her she had to marry him. They had met on the street, stopped to gossip like small-town neighbors. The heat was dragging her body down, and the mid-morning sun, white as a bandage, blinded her. She shook her head, hid the emotion she felt. "You expect me to marry a man who wants to wipe out the entire Northern hemisphere with people bombs? My family lives up there."

"It's my kid. It's my right."

"If you want to see the baby I'll let you see him."

"You need my protection, Amanda."

"*Caca de vaca.*"

"All kinds of people resent the way you're getting rich selling the eggs they should be selling."

"You're making that up just so I'll say yes and marry you."

But he wasn't. In the course of a week and a half all her buyers told her they could no longer deal with her. Some were shamed to do so, some spiteful, one or two openly hostile. Luis told her she had two choices, either marry him or go back to Gasport.

She found a third. She began to sell directly to the egg-eating public from her house, which increased her profit even after she paid a neighbor girl to mind the shop when she was out on egg runs. As a Peace Corps Volunteer she had been reluctant to paint the facade of the house; she did not want to stand out. But now she painted it a restful pale blue and hung a wooden sign that read *Amanda's Place. Fresh Eggs.*

In a month no one in Pueblo Santo bought eggs anywhere else. She had to pay a boy from town to take her surplus stock to Coronel Bogado, where she had an agreement with a man to take as many eggs as she sent. She was three payments ahead on the Yamaha.

The honey idea was doña Marciana's. Don Edgar had one time built a few hive boxes that were rotting in a cotton field. Amanda put up the cash, Marciana fixed up the boxes, and Edgar brought swarms from a cousin in the next village.

"There's money there," said doña Marciana, waving her unlit mashed cigar at the refurbished hives. They had gone to the field to look and congratulate themselves, taking a bottle of sweet purple wine. Don Edgar, a skeptic, smiled and brushed his face with the sleeve of his shirt.

"There's more," Marciana told them both. She took a match absently from her husband's shirt and lit her cigar. "Tomatoes, carrots. Things they want in the city. We can make money."

"Maybe you can forget about cotton next season," Amanda told don Edgar, but he only bent his head and scratched at the ground with his hoe automatically, his body expressing the doubt he was too polite to put into words.

Amanda herself had the idea to get into rabbits. With rabbits they would realize a quick return on their investment, and Paraguayan people needed protein. Don Edgar, not quite swept up the way Marciana was but willing to be carried a little on the current of the women's enthusiasm, built some hutches. Their lives, they all began to think, might change. Three nights in a row Amanda had rich, agricultural dreams. All the images were vegetable.

The only problem was, she could no longer safely ride the Yamaha. She disliked losing the daily personal contact with her suppliers in the villages, but the chance of hurting the baby sobered her. The same boy who took her eggs to Bogado was happy enough to collect in the *campo* for her.

The night someone defaced the street-side wall of her house, throwing red paint over her sign and writing ugly words wherever there was space, Amanda heard nothing. Mid-morning Luis, embarrassed by her stubborn stand, came by to tell her she did not understand Paraguay. She agreed. He left her waiting for customers on her porch, but it was Capitán Raudales who came by. The bullet-headed driver leaped to open the police chief's door, and Raudales came out apologizing, waving one porky hand at the paint-splattered wall, the filthy words there whose meanings she knew.

"How is the investigation coming on my motorcycle tire?" she wanted to know.

"Señorita," he told her sonorously, his dull black eyes aggrieved, "I have been informed that you no longer work for the Peace Corps."

"I quit."

"Then you have residency status..."

"I gave back my *carnet* in Asunción."

"So you are here illegally."

"That's not fair."

"Fairness does not enter in. I am happy to overlook the legal issue."

"Thank you."

"But there is a condition."

Of course.

"Give up your egg business. What you are doing represents a source of unfair competition for legitimate Paraguayan businessmen. There have been complaints."

"How am I supposed to live?"

"You Americans are rich. If you were not rich you would not have come to Paraguay."

"Please," she began, but that was a mistake and she recognized it. He gave her two days to decide. When he was gone she locked her front door and went through the daytime dark of her house to bed. The baby in her belly was lead.

In Gasport, before Amanda left, Aunt Beth had invited her to supper on the farm. Driving out, Amanda went over corn snow that fell straight down the windless sky as if dumped from a chute, and the sun went down invisibly over the naked brown woods before she came up the long drive to the house. Cold as it was, they rocked in matching maple rockers outside on the porch. Aunt Beth slept all winter long with her window open for fear of asphyxiation. "I'll tell you all you need to know about South America," the older woman volunteered. "Down there you've got half a dozen rich men per country, and all the rest of them live and die in total misery and degradation. You want to waste two years of your life figuring that out?"

Amanda knew her comeback was weak; worse, it missed the point she didn't know how to make. "Half of it at least is our fault," she said. "Look at the fruit companies, look at the Marines in Nicaragua. We're part of the problem."

"Horsefeathers. It's just your time in life to feel bad for the way things are, that's all. I know you don't want to hear this from me, but ten years from now you'll be plenty used to the things that are driving you crazy right now."

Unable to explain what she herself didn't understand, Amanda watched her aunt's old fingers go blue in the cold crocheting something for someone's baby, and then they ate pot roast.

A customer wanting eggs knocked on the door, kept knocking, but Amanda would not get out of the bed. She thought she might be close to knowing, finally, why she had come to Paraguay. It had nothing to do with what the Marines had done in Nicaragua. It had to do with... She couldn't say.

The next morning she went on foot to Potrero. In the hammering heat, going past a field of Brahma cattle munching in the shade under a giant lapacho tree, past long ragged fields of cotton, past mud-and-pole shacks around which brown kids ran naked and screaming wild, she did breathing exercises and said aloud *Why am I here?* Floating on the dense, hot air was an answer but she couldn't grab it.

Doña Marciana took the bad news badly. Amanda found her at home shelling plates of peanuts under the lemon trees. White sunlight infiltrated the patchy shade; the heat was making Amanda dizzy. "You may as well go home," said Marciana. "Back to *los estados unidos.*"

"I don't want to go, doña Marciana."

"Then make Luis marry you."

"I don't want that, either."

Marciana nodded as if that made a sense she could appreciate. Even with twelve rugless runts of his own don Edgar was known for jumping through strange bedroom windows on moonless nights. "Then you'll have to go home."

"You can do everything we were going to do together by yourself."

She shook her head. "If they won't let *you* do it they sure won't let me do it. You were my good luck, Amanda. But anyway I'm going to keep the chickens cooped, and I'm going to collect the honey, and raise the rabbits and grow the vegetables. At least we'll eat right." She gave her plate of peanuts to her oldest daughter and told her to watch the little ones. "I'll help you pack," she told Amanda, "and tomorrow I'll go as far as Bogado with you. To say goodbye."

Strange that afterward Amanda could not remember when the plan came to her. She couldn't even remember whether she had talked it over with Marciana on the bus ride back into Pueblo Santo. They worked that night by lantern light, downing a bottle of sweet wine and getting giggly. Marciana made the signs and Amanda dyed the eggs, making her own mixture of food coloring and vinegar. She tried to smoke one of Marciana's cigars but the smoke gagged her and she felt guilty because of the baby. They went to bed late.

In the morning they carried their stack of signs and tacked them up all around the pueblo.

"You're sure you want to be seen with me?" Amanda asked her friend. "If this doesn't work people will remember we did it together."

"One night I dreamed I was driving a truck, Amanda. With a truck we could make our own deliveries all the way to Encarnación."

Though the colors varied, the message on the signs was the same: *Sale! Two eggs for the price of one. Amanda's Place, 10:00 This Morning. Music and Surprises. Don't Miss it.*

The point of starting late was to build up some suspense. It worked. By ten the street in front of Amanda's house was full of pueblo people hoping to be entertained. Amanda waved to them self-consciously as she hooked up her cassette player on the porch and played an album of Paraguayan harp music while they watched her like any other audience. Then she called for customers.

"How many?" she asked a woman in broken-heeled shoes who offered a gold-toothed grin and an open basket.

"Six, please," the woman told her, looking around to see if she was being tricked somehow in a way that was not apparent. "And I pay you for three, right?"

"What color do you want your eggs?" Amanda asked her, loud enough to be heard, and the woman laughed nervously. People in the crowd also laughed.

"The color of eggs," the woman said, flustered.

"But our eggs come in blue, and they come in pink, and they come in yellow, and green. You can have some of each, or all of one color, whichever you prefer."

Her timing perfect, Marciana brought out the first bucket of dyed eggs, and the crowd oohed appreciatively. The first woman chose blue and green, and people pushed forward eagerly behind her.

It went fast. When all the eggs were gone nobody seemed anxious to leave. Amanda gave herself a minute before making her announcement. She turned down the harp music and people paid quick attention. *"Señoras y señores,"* she told them, "this is important."

She was aware, suddenly, of Capitán Raudales in the crowd. There was no pickup, no driver. He must have walked. She felt oddly honored to have drawn him thus, on foot. She felt strong, capable, lucky. "In among all the eggs you just bought are three hollow ones."

Someone hollered the Spanish equivalent of a boo.

"If you get one of the hollow ones"—she had had to ask Marciana the word for hollow—"inside it you'll find a piece of paper. On each piece of paper a different number is written. Whatever the number is on your paper is the amount of money you win from us."

She turned the volume back up on the music, and people began to check their eggs. She paid off the three winners and brought out bottles of different things to drink before people went home. Eventually, like destiny only fatter, Capitán Raudales made his laboring way to her porch.

"I admire your ingenuity," he told her.

"I like Pueblo Santo," she told him. "I want to stay here."

"You are clever. You have won yourself some supporters. A blonde North American woman who sells colored eggs and gives away money! Be assured you are unique. For the moment you have won. I have no wish to anger these people by sending you away. Nevertheless, let me point out something you may not know: in this country all victories are temporary."

"Thank you," she told him. She watched him plow his way up the street in the direction of his office on the plaza. Carrying that weight, he must have thought it was a world away. Halfway there, she noticed, he stopped to wheeze.

In the afternoon, Marciana went back to Potrero with her half of the day's profit. The wine had left Amanda with a blurry kind of headache, so she slept until Luis was there, shaking her awake. It was night. The darkness inside her little house was like water; it had seeped in and filled up the place, making it hard for her to breathe. He must have jumped the back fence.

"You made a fool of me," Luis told her.

She sat up in the bed. "No I didn't."

"Marry me."

She shook her head fiercely, but she was not angry. "I'll let you see the baby whenever you want to. You can buy his clothes if you want to."

"Please, Amanda."

"I'm sorry, I can't marry you."

The half hour of coaxing disengagement it cost her to get him out of her house wore Amanda out as much as the wine and the excitement of besting Capitán Raudales. She cruised into the front room, shoved aside some egg cartons, and heaved her heavy body into the hammock. In the liquid dark she swung listlessly. She was uncomfortable, but the pain seemed to dissipate as she realized that she finally knew why she was in Paraguay. Both Luis and Aunt Beth were wrong. It had nothing to do with making up for America's imperial sins. That political stuff didn't interest her the way she thought it should, though she had tried. What it did have to do with was eggs. She was in South America, in Paraguay, in Pueblo Santo, to sell eggs. She was there to become someone she could not be in Gasport, New York, in the company of carping aunts. She was there to have and raise a child. The naked simplicity of that insight made it seem less than a vision. But a vision it was, and its light showed her her shape: she was the egg queen, and she was rising. Elation let her be generous. If he really wanted to, she decided, Luis could name the kid.

How I Came To Write This Story

I began writing "Mad Dogs" with the doctor character in mind, to explore the expatriate as eccentric—as even somewhat mad. I liked the idea of a government physician posted off in the hinterlands as a sort of mad scientist, with his American community as guinea pigs. I liked the idea that each of these Americans could be seen as a deviant—for having chosen a transient, unpredictable lifestyle—and that all these deviants together become clannish, feeding off of and igniting each other's quirks. I wanted to explore what the backdrop of Africa would reveal about these people, and the dramatic situation of a little girl bit by a dog seemed a good catalyst. I guess I wanted to explore how crazy all we Americans there then seem to me now. I did live in a similar community in Conakry in the sixties.

—Eileen Drew

EILEEN DREW (Zaire, 1979-1981) was born in Morocco and then moved every few years according to her father's assignments in the U.S. Foreign Service. She has lived in Nigeria, Guinea, Ghana, and Korea; she taught English as a Second Language with the Peace Corps in Zaire. Her collection, *Blue Taxis: Stories About Africa*, received the Milkweed National Fiction Prize in 1989 and was a *New York Times* Notable Book; it was also included in *Five Hundred Great Books by Women: A Reader's Guide*. Her stories have appeared in *TriQuarterly, Antioch Review, The Journal of African Travel-Writing*, and other magazines, as well as in *From the Center of the Earth*. Her novel *The Ivory Crocodile* won the 1997 RPCV Writers & Readers Fiction Award. She received an MFA from the University of Arizona in 1986, and currently lives in California.

MAD DOGS

by Eileen Drew

The embassy infirmary in Conakry had received a new centrifuge, and the doctor and his wife were always looking for excuses to prick fingers for blood samples. Like charlatans, wide-eyed with the miracle of science, they would greet their visitors, "Been feeling tired at all?" Who could say no to feeling tired in Conakry? Bedraggled by the heat, dispirited by ants in the morning cereal and cockroaches in shoes, by electricity failures and anti-American speeches by the president, who didn't seek refuge in a nap?

In 1965 the kids were the only Americans having fun in Conakry. Enchanted by the sweet, green breeze, the sight of grown men climbing trees for coconuts, by the strange language lapping at the concise island of their lives, they played like mad. Taught by Guinean kids how to chase bicycle wheels with sticks, they ran down dirt roads screaming in French, "*Attention! Accident!*" as the runaway wheels startled chickens and dogs. Apparently this was much better than riding the intact bicycles shipped among the household goods from the States. Not that they went so far as to dismantle their own bikes: they saw how their Guinean neighbors fell back, hushed and covetous, each time they sailed past; they appreciated the spindly brown arms reaching out to tag a back fender, and those who were generous enough to stop and let an African climb on could not help but appreciate the marvelous white grins. Bicycles were sacred. Besides, they came in handy for transportation. U.S. housing was scattered throughout the town, and although the children were ferried in vans to and from the American school, they biked to each others' homes.

Mothers brought them in cars to the clinic when the family shots were due. "Blood spinner," was what the kids all called the doctor's new machine, and even those who bit their lips and looked away during cholera boosters would jostle to be first to have their fingers pricked. Crowding, they watched the doctor coddle each drop of blood trapped in its tiny tube, how he fit each beaker carefully inside the bowels of the device. The shiny steel contraption sat atop his clinic counter like some domestic innovation, a space-age blender or mixing bowl, and the kids craned to see inside the cylindrical cavity before the lid was closed, the switch flicked, and the engine whipped into a scream like a thousand tiny flutes. Even the adults oohed and aahed. Until then, blood samples had always been sent to Germany.

The doctor and his wife embraced Africa. While most Americans fled to Europe for their summer R&R's, Randall Buckwood packed his family off to Kenya for safari. On their return to Conakry, the children passed around photographs: knobby-kneed Paul and Marie in faded checked shirts and khaki shorts beside their sturdy father, his rifle planted like some chiefly staff into the dusty ground, muzzle pointed at a glossy sky. Behind loomed a thatch hut on stilts: their hotel on the veldt. Mrs. Buckwood would be behind the lens.

She was always fussing in the distance, unloading the swimming fins from the car, buying oranges from a street vendor's lap, pricking fingers at the clinic. She was a registered nurse and she was taller than Randall and her round, close-set eyes were always glancing at him from her ministrations as he orchestrated, his muscular little arms waving in the air, pointing, hesitating, fingers splayed. Around the house Lorraine wore flip-flops and a bathing suit beneath a nondescript shift, and now and then she disappeared into the pool and then flapped in her flip-flops up the stone steps into the house, dripping, leaving puddles to evaporate across the tile floor. The house was like one huge bathroom, anyway, she felt; during storms, water blew in everywhere. A year of this lifestyle had taught the kids not to run inside; now only visitors and the cook, Kofi, slipped.

Lorraine and Randy had met at Portland Metropolitan and she'd fallen for his high-top sneakers on their first date to the beach. He was five feet six and the idea of him playing basketball was preposterous, yet he wore the shoes defiantly. The shoes were emblematic of what he was: self-mocking, larger than life, a jolly Napoleon. She loved his stubby authority. If one could not see his head above others in a crowd, one could easily spot the space he cleared for himself with his waving arms. He swelled, taking charge. In Portland he had prospered during the ten years since they'd married, but he outgrew his hospital, his city, his continent. It was time for the kids to expand.

So Lorraine and Randy joined the Foreign Service as a team, and were assigned to Conakry. To better meet the responsibility of keeping fifty-odd families healthy at this hardship post, Randall immediately requested a centrifuge such as the one he'd learned to use in the hospital lab. Through a series of rephrased and rerouted requisitions—there was no precedent for Randall's audacity—he finally convinced the Department of State that he needed to monitor for anemia among the staff in Conakry, where fresh meat was in short supply. The beef and pork flown in frozen from Johannesburg often spoiled on the runway before reaching the commissary. Children balked at the powdered milk, especially when their cereal was full of bugs. And most of the canned corned beef hash was getting fed to dogs.

Little Solange Carter rode her heroic blue Schwinn to Marie Buckwood's house on random Saturdays, ruffled swimsuit strapped to the rack, auburn bangs skewed as she fled the dog barking in front of a Guinean compound. Sighting him in the distance, a brown and white splotch against a cluster of huts, she would steer to the far side of the road, feet spinning airily. Ribby, wry, sinister, the dog would coagulate out of his formless nap and veer to his feet as she shot past. Amidst his throaty tirade she'd glimpse his yellow teeth yawing. People blurred—women pounding yams, children cheering—she did not know this neighborhood. She had never focused on the old man rising from his chair.

She was ten, strong, and stupidly brave. To impress her brothers she shinned up palm trees till her legs burned, belly flopped till her stomach flared pink. She had touched a dead rat's tail. For their part, the two boys simply laughed, either at her cowardice if she refused a dare, or at her bravado if she took them on, but she didn't care as long as they watched. She had heard them brag of her at school. Confronted with scraped knees and torn shorts, her mother clucked, inured by now to these small emergencies. In fact, Solange seemed to be invincible, guaranteed to bounce back like a puppy's chew toy. Thus it came as a surprise when, one day in September—well over a year after the Carters had arrived in Conakry—the doctor found her blood count short.

Only slightly short, of course, the doctor noted silently as he peered into the microscope, allowing himself to rejoice. Lifting his head, he scanned the clinic for Lorraine, but she was swooping down on the boys punching each other in the corner. Rather than being subdued by their cholera vaccinations, they seemed intent on increasing each others' pain. Carter, their father, was a different sort altogether, discreet, if somewhat strategic in his bearing, as if he always knew a little more than everyone else and wasn't telling. Probably, he did; he was CIA. He had come in earlier, on his way to work, for his cholera shot.

The mother, Noelle, stood blandly before the air conditioner, wafting. Bug-eyed in sunglasses, her oblique astonishment seemed fixed on the ceiling. She was deaf, evidently, to her sons' yelps, but they'd found an audience in Lorraine, who advanced across the clinic as if to trample them quiet once and for all. Daunted, they fell silent.

The doctor straightened, clearing his throat. Tuning in, Lorraine lifted her chin, and a feeble smack sounded as one of the boys landed a last slap. Solange hovered at the doctor's elbow, intrigued, absently swinging her vaccinated arm. He always told patients to swim after shots, to keep the arm from getting stiff and sore.

"Well, Noelle," he called across the room, "it looks like Solange hasn't been eating her meat."

"Oh, meat," Noelle sighed beside the air conditioner, her polaroid gaze falling on him. There was something dissolute about this family, this mother squelched by her sons, inscrutable behind dark lenses ever since her regular glasses had been stolen at the market. The story of that scuffle was famous, of how Noelle had clung bellowing to the strap of her purse until it broke, of how, suddenly empty-handed, she'd grabbed a ripe tomato from a pile for sale and pitched it squarely into the running thief's back. Apparently she, too, could fight; perhaps she'd decided not to waste her energy on squabbling sons.

"The corned beef hash gets old, I know," Randy continued. "I'll give you some iron supplements for her to take with her morning vitamins. We're nipping this in the bud; her blood count is barely below normal now, and we'll have her back in shape in a couple of months. Nothing to worry about."

Noelle, smiling softly at Solange as if another earnest trick had just been performed, did not look worried. Behind Lorraine, the boys looked impressed. So did Lorraine, her closely set eyes black with triumph, her mouth, tightly clamped, suppressing glee. Each case of anemia was a victory that justified the extravagant machine.

"Been feeling tired at all?" Randall turned to Solange, whose arm dangled, lifeless now at her side.

She shrugged. "No."

"Oh, no," echoed Noelle, raising her hand as if she were in school. "She's terribly active."

"I bet." He winked, and Solange grinned. "Just make sure you don't go running around with any strange dogs." It seemed impossible not to hug this sweet, needy child. It seemed impossible that she was tough.

In the angry old Rambler, roaring over the potholes toward home, the three children shared the back seat, Solange in the middle, her bottle of pills cradled like a trophy in her lap. Since she'd begun to claim her turn at shotgun, the boys had deemed the front seat sissy, so now they all stubbornly endured the back. Noelle chauffeured, singing loudly to drown out the competitive whines. "Oh, home on the range," she belted out, counting heads in the rear view mirror. Her children would not behave, the muffler had fallen off in a country devoid of car parts, and she was tone deaf. They roared through the town like a slow, broken rocket.

"This is it, this is the one," Solange shouted during a lull between Noelle's songs. Ahead, Guinean children snaked down the dusty street, sticks waving as they chased a bicycle wheel. Noelle braked. Thatched roofs like overturned funnels peeked above a fence, and a few Africans loitered brilliantly in front, splashes of fabric accenting inky skin. One dingy old man seemed to be presiding in a chair, arms judicially aligned on the arm rests, head inclined slightly toward the approaching car.

"The brown and white one there, that's the dog that always barks at me."

Indeed, a spindly dog ragged with fury rocked on its feet before the compound gate, snout elevated, teeth bared, ribs racked with effort. Undeniably, the dog was barking, although its lament was hardly audible above the car's thunderous advance.

"You're not afraid of dogs, are you?" Terry, the eldest, admonished.

"Just this one. This is the only one. Look!"

Howling, it teetered. Flanking it, the local children, having commandeered their wheel, danced and saluted the Americans. The old man squinted. They all ignored the dog. As the car drew abreast, the animal made a dash for the tires. Noelle accelerated, and as they lurched ahead, the kids turned in their seats to watch its ferocious pursuit. In the mirror Noelle saw the backs of her children's heads.

"You should see me zoom past there," said Solange. "That's the only dog I don't trust."

"That old runt?" Eddy jeered.

"He only came after us 'cause Mom sped up," Terry said. "He thought we were running away. What do you expect?" Deftly, he grabbed his sister's bottle of pills.

She wailed, and Noelle began to sing. Eddy had pinned Solange's arms behind her back, and as she struggled, she spat, "How do you know it doesn't have rabies?"

"Nah. Didn't you see all those people hanging around? If it was rabid, they'd all be locked in their huts." Terry began to unscrew the bottle lid.

"They only chase if you're afraid," Eddy added. Solange struggled. "They can sense fear, and they go after it. You're supposed to pretend you don't even see a dog barking."

Extracting cotton from the bottle, Terry let it flutter in the window, puff away. Entertained, Eddy lost his grip, and Solange startled Terry with a kick. Pills, brown and bean-like, hailed into their laps. And suddenly all three were scooping and pecking with their hands, restoring the pills to the jar, united in their scramble to undo the damage before their mother's next glance in her rear view mirror. Once, having seen no children there, she'd pulled over to find all three wrestling on the floor. Livid, she threw them out and drove away, backfiring, and they'd had to tramp the mile home. Prone to impulsive punishments, she had trained her kids not to cross certain lines, and playing with medicine was definitely out of bounds.

"There," Terry hissed, finally screwing on the cap. "Take your precious pills, sissy. You'll need them to run away from that dog."

Suddenly, from the opposite direction, a mechanical commotion to rival the Rambler's filled the road. A blue *camionette*, the toy-like sort of truck roofed in back and equipped with benches for passengers, dipped and swayed, negotiating potholes with grace. "What's this?" Noelle interrupted her aria to complain. Indigenous to major thoroughfares, *camionettes* had no business on this residential street. Yet rather than passengers in back, this truck carried speakers on the roof blaring some garbage laced with static Noelle did not care to hear. "Oklahoma!" she sang, accelerating past, muffler booming. Deafened, the children pointed at the little Guinean flags drooping in the swirls of dirt above each headlight, at the governmental emblem painted on the driver's door. The three men in the cab shook their fists and opened their pink mouths wide, shouting unintelligibly as the Rambler passed, and Solange waved.

"*Á bas les Américains! Á bas les Américains!*" was the message no one in the Rambler heard. Arch, pointed, shrill, the Guinean president's speech toured the town, his ultimatum punctuated with electrical interference and taped applause, the charged echoes settling with the dust. Pedestrians lowered the cloths from their faces, adjusted the baskets on their heads, and turned the words over in their mouths. Down with the Americans. Children waved their sticks; dogs barked.

One Saturday several weeks later, the doctor and his wife were home with the kids when the old man showed up on their doorstep with Solange piggyback. Her tear-stained face bobbed beside his creased, sepia expression of concern—his rheumy eyes blinking away sweat, his mouth parted in a pant. He was wearing a streaked tee shirt that clung to his wiry shoulders where Solange had held on; his slacks had slid low on his hips from her knees at his waist. One of her legs, dangling, was wet with blood.

Randall, summoned from the poolside by his cook, opened the front door wide. Smeared with zinc oxide, his nose bulged. Red indentations from the lawn chair striped his bare stomach and thighs. His swimming trunks were orange as Tang.

Startled, the old man was backing away. "A dog bit me," Solange announced, hanging on.

"*Bicyclette, bicyclette,*" the man mimed, interrupting his retreat to brace his hands as if on bars, steering.

"*Bicyclette*," repeated Kofi helpfully, as if to translate. There was no bicycle in sight.

"Let's take a look," Randall said, closing in on Solange's leg. The old Guinean held his ground bravely, huffing, as Randall grasped Solange's sneakered foot, peering at the wound. "Can you walk?"

She nodded, lifting a hand to wipe her eyes, and he motioned to the Guinean, who inched himself into an elaborate crouch so Solange could step away.

"Bring a glass of water for this man," Randall called in French to Kofi. To Solange, he said, "It looks like a simple abrasion, but we'll have to get you cleaned up."

Dripping from the pool, Lorraine appeared in the hallway, a pair of sandals extended to her husband. Without missing a beat, she declared, "I'll bring the clinic keys." The aroma of coconut oil and chlorine flooded the hall as Marie and Paul splashed in.

"I was riding my bike over here," Solange greeted her friends as she moved inside, gingerly skirting the puddles on the floor, "and I slowed down to show the dog I wasn't scared, and it bit me in the leg."

"The one always barking at that compound?" Marie asked, hand at her mouth.

"Where's your bike?" Paul challenged, scanning the yard through the open door.

"Oh, no, I didn't ride here after that. I fell off kicking the dog and this man carried me the rest of the way, running. He knew exactly where you lived. He kept saying, '*Docteur, docteur, vite, vite.*'"

Solange limped back to the threshold to point out her savior, but he had disappeared. Kofi stood alone in the middle of the drive, neck craned, a glass of water suspended as if toward a ghost.

"Well, that's just great," Randall said, buckling his sandals. "They're never here when you need them, always hanging about when you don't. Kofi," he switched to French, "go find that man and bring him back."

Kofi took off at a jog. He was wearing an old pair of Randall's high top shoes, Lorraine's solution to Kofi's tendency to slip in her puddles on the floor.

Lorraine had returned with the keys.

"Drive over to Carters," Randall instructed her, "and tell them what's happened. Keep your eye out for the dog—but don't stop if you see it, just remember where it was. Go by Grossmans', too, and maybe Kachikians'. See who you can round up; we may need help with a search. Kids," he shifted his white-nosed gaze, "you get dressed."

Randall herded Solange then toward the clinic across the courtyard. Head down, stiff-legged, he moved as if wading through the midday heat. By October, the hottest season in Conakry was well underway, and Randall had begun to burn. His shoulders were a rusty brown, his nose raw. In the clinic he flicked on the air conditioner, then the lights. He lifted her onto the examination table and went to scrub up.

"Can you take my blood?" she asked when he returned, his doctor's smock hanging like a dress to his bare knees.

"Sure, let's see if that ferrous sulfate's done its job. Been taking one every day?"

She nodded.

"Been feeling tired?"

She shook her head, watching as he sponged her leg. When he dabbed on the disinfectant, she was brave, but the rabies shot in her arm made her cry.

Randall summoned up an avuncular frown, minimizing alarm. "You're going to have to be tough, you know." He handed her a Kleenex. "If the dog has rabies, you'll need a shot a day for three weeks. But here, let me see your finger and we'll run the centrifuge."

Solange rallied to see the blood spinner separate her cells. Bandaged, she stood beside the machine and felt the vibration of its motor in the soles of her feet. And when Randall examined the results, he, too, felt cheered. "There, you see, you're cured!" he proclaimed, wiping zinc oxide from the microscope. "You're just as strong as you should be. Just keep taking those pills, one a day, and before you know it you'll be strong as Popeye! Let's go have a Coke while we wait for your mom."

Back across the compound, Randall's Tang trunks swished. Solange blew her nose quietly. After a minute Randall shook his head, talking as if to himself. "Damn that old man," he muttered, "he could have helped us."

Solange looked at him. "He did help us. He helped me."

Then she slowed, lifting her pricked finger with its tiny Band-Aid at the tip, to point.

The bike was propped, safe and blue, against a banana palm beside the drive. Like a spooked yet loyal horse, it seemed to have found its way.

The doctor's living room was his lair, an enclave of stripes and skins and masks off-limits to wet feet. Fringes and tassels dangled from sacs and talismans, beads glistened in shells like bowls, baskets spiraled around heaps of magazines and bills. Chairs wore the woven geometry of scratchy cloth: throw rugs from the bush. Over the past year, Randy had collected and Lorraine had arranged, and the room was now a tribute to their African stint. Especially precious were Randy's trophies—the zebra skin on the floor, the elephant feet stuffed as stools, the gazelle gently gazing from the wall. Masks stared with remote amazement, and behind Randy's desk hung a Dahomian tapestry, vast and wild in red and yellow sewn against black, men slashing air, arms and legs flying, an enraged beast frozen in a roar.

Nobody much used the room, however, until after sundown, when dry underwear replaced the damp suits and the last drops of pool water had been toweled off, mopped up. Lorraine would join Randall then for drinks as they waited for Kofi to announce dinner. Sometimes the children brought in Cokes, ice tinkling formally as they perched atop the elephant cushions on the floor, avoiding the itchy upholstery. Lorraine didn't seem to notice the awkward cloth, and Randall always claimed the leather reclining chair shipped from home. Blissfully, he flipped through Esquires and Economists, the snakeskin lamp beside him lit.

Today, however, smack in the middle of the day, Solange held a place of honor in the lair. Eyes adjusting to the plush dark, she sat where the doctor had propped her on the couch, legs protruding into space, white bandage grinning above her ankle. He had arranged a nest of shaggy pillows behind her back and sent Kofi for a Coke. Hands clasped neatly in her lap, staring down the hollow features of an angry effigy, momentarily alone, she looked as if she, too, were on display.

Marie zigzagged down the hall, dodging puddles, swinging a basket brimming with Barbie heads and limbs. "We get to play in there," she called, "and Kofi's bringing Cokes. You should get bitten more often."

Landing gracefully on her knees, she turned the basket end up, dumping onto the zebra rug a tangle of dolls and sewing gear: scissors, scraps of fabric from the Conakry market, spools of unraveling thread. "Come on, you have to finish Barbie's habit."

When Solange and Marie played Barbies, rather than making up voices and sets and manipulating the dolls, they made clothes. It was as if Conakry's scarcity infused their games, inspiring them to engineer their own props: a mermaid suit for Barbie, a gypsy dress for Midge. This time Midge and Barbie were to pose as nuns, missionaries undercover for the CIA. Ken was to be KGB. They always thought of roles for him that did not require special outfits, and so he was stuck with the same sports jacket and slacks.

"*Merci,*" Solange said, lifting a glass from the tray proffered by Kofi. Despite the scratchy couch, she was enjoying her honorary perch. "Did he find the man?" she asked Marie as Kofi squeaked away in the doctor's old shoes.

"Not yet." She was wrapping black cloth around Midge's head, positioning a pin. "But he brought your bike."

"No, the bike was here when we got back from the clinic. Kofi was still gone. I don't think Kofi brought it."

"Well, I don't know, they don't tell me anything." With an exaggerated sigh, Marie caused the bangs to lift slightly from her long forehead. She had her mother's closely set eyes, which gave her face a grown-up, focused quality.

Solange sipped. "Where's Paul?"

"Watching my father load his gun."

"Load his gun! I want to see. Can we go see?"

"He told me to stay here with you. I don't think you're supposed to see. You're supposed to be upset."

"Why?"

Marie measured out an arm's length of green thread. "Because the dog might have rabies. They're going to shoot it and cut off its head."

"What?"

"Yeah, so my mom can take the brain to Munich for tests."

"Your mom's going to carry its head on the plane?"

Marie squinted, aiming thread at the needle. "My dad said she needs a vacation."

"A head like that one." Solange pointed to the mounted gazelle, its soft, expectant eyes.

"That one wasn't rabid."

"I wonder if you stuffed the dog's head, if it would look crazy in its eyes."

"He's not going to stuff it, he's just going to send it to Germany—"

"I know, for tests. Did he really kill that deer?"

"Sure. And the elephant and zebra, too."

Solange's gaze fell on the tapestry draped above the desk. "It looks like the red men and the yellow men are at war."

Marie lowered the needle she was still trying to thread. She squinted helpfully. "It's a war about money, too—see the purse flying in the air?"

"They both have guns and swords."

"Machetes."

"But only the red people are fighting the lion." Solange's toes, suspended above the rug, bounced. "The lion's killing a red man on the ground. But that other red man is pointing a rifle at the lion."

"No, it's not a lion, though. Look, it's got spots on its back, but stripes on its tail. It's some magic monster."

"So, this is what I think." Solange folded her arms carefully, babying her shot. "It's a war between white people and black people. The yellow are the white, and they have the yellow monster on their side because they're so powerful. But the red people, the Africans, are mad because the white people are rich, and they've already got the purse away, and they're about to win even though some of them will die."

"Who?"

"The red people, the Africans. They're about to shoot the monster and win."

"Just like the trouble here," Marie approved. "The Africans against the whites."

Since anti-American demonstrations at the Embassy had kept the kids home from school for a day, they'd become aware of what their exasperated parents called "the trouble." Rolling their eyes, throwing up their hands, the adults spoke of the Guinean president as if he were a child. They were tired of his shenanigans and wished on him his just desserts. But life went on as before; the African kids still waved and cheered when the Americans passed on their bikes.

Rumbling approached; a faint roar. "My mom's here."

The noise built to a crescendo as the car turned into the drive. Marie stabbed her needle into a pin cushion. Doors slammed.

Solange edged herself off the couch, following Marie. Her vaccinated arm hurt more than her leg, and she advanced cautiously. A group had assembled by the time she reached the entrance hall. Her mother, begoggled as usual, stood in a puddle of water; when she saw Solange, she put her arms out.

Her two brothers, cowed and guilty, lurked beside her father in the corner. Breaking into a painful run, she slipped, landing with a thud. Terry and Eddy did not laugh.

"Oh, honey," Noelle cooed as she scooped her damp daughter off the ground. Her father stooped forward to blink at her bandaged leg, and she was enveloped in his halo of soapy cigar smell. Doctor Buckwood appeared in a doorway, rubbing his hands.

He'd changed into a safari shirt, short-sleeved with lots of pockets, and khaki pants, and boots. Zinc oxide still anointed his nose. "She's been a perfect trooper, and it's all uphill from here, especially since her blood count's back to normal. We pricked her finger and she's already strong as an ox; the iron pills have done the trick, and I want her to keep them up. The dog bite, by the way, is nothing, just a scrape, but she'll have to have the course of twenty-one injections—unless, that is, the dog tests negative for rabies."

Solange slid to her feet, and Noelle straightened. Randall had never noticed she was tall. With her sunglasses fixed on him, she seemed oddly secure, galvanized within some private, icy oasis.

"You've been wonderful," she said coolly. "You've really gone out of your way. Len wants to stay and see about the dog, but I'm going to take Solange on home. She's had enough for one day."

Something had transformed Noelle; her voice resonated as if amplified. Giving her husband a cryptic nod, she took Solange by the hand and turned to go, her motions fluid yet succinct. Gone was the flimsy woman who had gazed so blankly into space as her skirt bulged in an air-conditioned breeze; a curt amazon commanded in her place. Randall was nonplused. Clearly, it was during emergencies that Noelle was at her best.

Len Carter stepped forward as if on cue. He was a man of few words, of which many were uttered disdainfully under his breath. He yawned behind his hand.

"Lorraine will be back with more help in a minute." Randall

looked at Terry and Eddy mistrustfully. "I suppose the boys better go on home with you, Noelle."

"Can't they see the gun?" Paul lobbied hopefully.

"No." Noelle was in one of her last straw moods. She pulled the door open, stepped through with Solange, and the boys fell in behind. "Oh," she turned, glancing back at Randall. "My glasses haven't come in, have they?"

He almost laughed. She'd been perfectly content to hide behind her sunshades for months; now, suddenly catalyzed, she seemed eager to make up for lost time, to tie up each and every loose end.

"Sorry, Noelle," he shrugged. "But I'll tell you what. Lorraine will get your prescription filled in Munich if we get this dog. She'll have to fly there with a sample for the test."

"Lucky Lorraine," said Noelle, opening the Rambler's doors to air the car. Shiny, sloping, it looked about to melt. Kofi tied the blue bike onto the back, and Solange got in up front. She did not talk to the boys. She did not see the dog.

"Everybody out," Randall boomed cheerfully, veering to a stop outside the deserted compound. No kids jeered, no dogs snarled. The old man's chair had been removed. The street gaped as if in shock, and although they had hoped to be greeted by the raving dog, Randall felt the delicious flush of an impending chase. The fun was always in the hunt.

Clapping a straw hat on his head, he got out. He'd left his nose white, anticipating a palaver in the sun; if he'd learned anything in Kenya, it was that proper protection from the elements was essential to outwitting game.

Carter, Sid Grossman, and Kofi emerged slowly. The thatch fence that veiled the pointed paillotte roofs sagged.

"Hold on," Randall commanded, ducking around to the trunk. Politely, the others hesitated. Carter yawned, hands in pockets, staring at a bicycle track in the dust. Grossman, a rookie diplomat, blinked agreeably, miming support. Actually he was amused at the spectacle of white-nosed Randall on the warpath. Carter was missing his nap. Kofi, luminously white in his uniform, hovered like a starched angel in the dirt road.

Randall swung open the trunk and plucked out the rifle. He'd proved himself handy in Kenya, and now he itched to conquer the mad dog. His fingers felt damp and thick against the cool, dark steel.

Carter jerked awake. "You're not taking that into the compound, are you?"

"There's a rabid dog loose."

"This isn't a safari, Randy. Let's just wait until we find the thing. We can't go onto private property waving a gun around. We've got a bad enough image in this country as it is."

Defied, Randall bristled, gaining girth. Carter struck him as annoyingly cautious; evidently his covert expertise went no farther than his desk. Of course, Randall had no authority over his colleagues, but he'd assumed that this was his show. This was no goodwill call to the *Ministre des Affaires Étrangères* in his air-conditioned lounge above the sea. This was a matter of dogs and disease. He was going in.

The trunk shut with a bang, and Kofi flitted back a step.

"It's a matter of safety," Randall declared, "for us as well as for the locals here. I'm not having anyone else bitten."

Carter grunted. Grossman shuffled, toeing a pale orange rind. He looked up. "That thing does look a little intimidating, Randy."

"You've got to look at it through their eyes," Carter asserted. "Rabid or not, their dog has bitten one of our children, and now we've come for recompense. If it were between Guineans, an elder would settle the dispute. Nobody would be packing guns. Besides, what are they going to think, after a steady diet of nationalist propaganda about us imperialist bullies, when you storm in like a paratrooper?"

"The gun has nothing to do with intimidation; the gun is for the dog."

"Well, there's no dog here," Grossman said brightly, wiping his glasses as if waiting for the entertainment to begin. "Not much of anything. Sure we've got the right place?"

"I've seen that dog outside here umpteen times." Barreling past, Randall corralled Kofi, briefing him in French. They approached the open gate, Kofi gliding whitely beside Randall's stubborn advance. Straw hat skewed, rifle clutched before him like a shield, guardian angel at his elbow, Randall looked poised on the brink of some vaudevillian combat.

"Preposterous," Carter mumbled. Grossman bit his lip.

At the gate—really nothing more than a broad gap in the

thatch fence—Randall stopped. The scene inside was disappointingly serene. A handful of women grouped around a cookfire craned their necks. Bluish smoke spiraled. Chickens pecked crookedly at the base of a flaming acacia shading half the courtyard. Excepting a couple of naked babies flexing across a woven mat, no children were in sight. A goat blinked where it stood tethered, grazing at what looked like dirt. The five round houses were shut tight, wood doors barred.

One woman, rising, was wiping her hands on the front of the cloth she wore wrapped as a skirt. Plump and sullen, she seemed to have all the time in the world.

"*Bonjour*," she said as if to Randall's rifle, blinking reproachfully. Her eyes met his for a moment, shifted down a hair, and he remembered the zinc oxide on his nose.

"*Bonjour*," he said grandly.

Kofi stepped forward to offer his hand. She studied Kofi's uniform, down to the basketball shoes, and seemed impressed. Sharply, they shook hands, and Kofi began to speak in dialect.

Carter and Grossman crowded up behind Randall, and then all three Americans were ushered in. Sweating, they waited in the center of the dusty compound as Kofi and the women exchanged stories, pointing and snapping fingers, slapping brows. The women shelling peanuts in the shade clucked and conjectured, eyeing Randall, the gun suspended parallel to his chest. "*Américain*," he overheard. The two infants had been scooped against their mothers' breasts.

Kofi glided back to the Americans, reporting in his rough French. "She is the daughter of the *tata* who helped the girl. She say he sleeping now, very tired."

"And what about the dog?"

"She say they never know that dog; it come from nowhere down the street. It bite the girl and go. Now all the people have gone to bring the dog down for good. She say don't worry, no problem, the dog be finished for good."

"The children went as well?"

Kofi shrugged, looking around as if to unearth a few.

"And just how do they plan to bring the dog down?"

Kofi giggled. "*Mais, monsieur*, we have guns for hunting, too."

"*Mais, c'est dangereux, ça!*"

Kofi's grin vanished; deflated, he slunk back, yellowed palms out.

Randall lowered his rifle, balancing it handle-down in the dirt, muzzle up. "I mean, this dog is dangerous, Kofi. It's very dangerous. Anyone it bites can die, if they don't get medicine right away. Tell her the dog is sick, Kofi, and that it must not be touched."

"She knows," Kofi nodded. "*Mbufimbufi.*"

"What?"

"*Mbufimbufi.* That is what we call this madness. This is not a new disease."

"Tell her that if anybody touches that dog, he should come to me."

"Nobody will touch that dog. We get him buried with sticks and cloth, nobody will touch."

Randall swallowed, glancing at the woman. She was gazing at him, mouth pursed, as if she'd had enough. So they did not want his help. He felt Carter's condescension lapping at his back, Grossman's flabby smile. The hunt had already started, and he would not be able to catch up. Lorraine would not get her free trip to Germany. Yet there must be something he could still do here.

"I have medicine!" he bellowed out in French.

Loudly, Carter exhaled. "We might as well go," he mumbled.

"You really think they know what they're doing? Dragging their kids along after a rabid dog?"

"No, no, don't you see? They've sent the kids off somewhere so we can't question them; they've been expecting us, and obviously they don't want trouble any more than we do. My guess is that the dog is not rabid in the least; it's somebody's high-strung pet and it's been carted off somewhere safe because they don't want it killed. If there were any question at all of its being rabid, they'd have killed it immediately and would have nothing to hide."

Randall considered, removing his hat to fan his face and neck. Abruptly shifting gears, he addressed the woman directly. "I have a gift for the *tata* who was so kind to our little girl. May we go express our thanks?"

"Oh, come now, we're not going to interrogate him." Carter snapped a handkerchief angrily, unfolding it to wipe his forehead.

But the woman shrugged, slouching off, leading the way. Kofi floated after, his white slacks already dingy at the hem, and Randall fell in step. Carter and Grossman trailed.

Behind the semicircle of round houses, a row of sheds hugged the back fence. Slipshod, ramshackle shelters with roofs of corrugated tin, they were not much larger than outhouses. "Tata Bufoa!" she cried, approaching a door. "Tata Bufoa!"

"*Ehi*," a gravelly voice answered peevishly from within, launching into a wheezing cough.

The usher pushed her way inside the door. Wincing, Carter was jingling coins in his pockets; Kofi strained to hear the hushed consultation inside. The minute the door was wrenched open, Randall stepped forward.

Once across the threshold, there was nowhere else to go; he couldn't see a thing. The room was cool and sour and he sensed the woman's humid presence close by. Hesitating as his eyes adjusted, he took a deep breath. A forest must feel like this, he thought—dense and still and alive. He was inhaling decomposing roots, ample oxygen. Elastic foliage unraveled around him for miles; a fur of moss cushioned the ground. He'd never actually entered an equatorial forest—Conakry was surrounded by miles of cleared farmland, and Kenyan animals were hunted on the open plains—but he imagined it must feel like this. Silent, raw.

"*M'sieur.*"

Focusing in the direction of the hoarse voice, Randall identified two tiny moons floating, staring—the old man's eyes. Randall could now make out the wiry shape of someone sitting half up in bed, frozen in black space, stunned. He could see how the trim shoulders lifted slightly and then fell with each shallow breath. He could almost hear the man's heart.

If he were hunting now, he'd shoot. He remembered his moment of triumph when he'd looked straight at his gazelle, straight into its plush, electric eyes, and known that he would shoot. The thrill hit not as your animal collapsed, but in that split second before you pulled the trigger, when you could still change your mind.

"*M'sieur,*" the *tata* began again, clearing his throat. "The little girl, is she all right?"

Suddenly, Randall felt a nauseating rush of shame. What was he doing in this poor man's hut? What was he doing with this gun? No wonder the man was terrified; warned by the government about these imperialist Americans, he'd taken his chances, rushing into enemy territory with a bleeding little girl, and here, for all his efforts, was the white-nosed warrior invading his hut.

"She's fine," Randall grunted, his sunburn on fire with embarrassment. "We came looking for the dog," he quickly explained the rifle, "but we wanted to thank you, too." Deliberately, he propped the gun against a wall, fished a wallet from his pocket, and began counting out bills.

The *tata* protested, wheezing, waving his spidery hands, sitting straight up. But Randall quickly leaned forward and lay the money on the edge of the bed as he left.

Too late, he understood the flamboyance of his affront, of reducing an old man's valor to a monetary exchange. Shrinking from the light, from Kofi's seraphic white drill, from Grossman's blinding smile, Randall felt exposed. What were any of them doing here, in this roasting compound in the sun, in Africa at all? What business had he with anemic diplomats? This was a different world entirely from the Africa enshrined by skins and furs and tamed grimaces on walls. Carter, yawning at the ground, was right. There was no safari here.

Myopically, Grossman approved the cash transaction. "That'll make his day," he nodded at the billfold in Randall's hand.

Scornfully, Randall pushed on past.

Solange received the balance of her shots courageously, day after day, swinging the injected arm so that her brothers began to call her "*Singe*"—"monkey" in French.

She did not care. She'd grown a little smarter, and did not listen to them anymore, whether or not they bragged of her at school. When they challenged her claim to have been lugged piggyback to the doctor's house, she shrugged indifferently.

"How come the bike was there, then, when we drove up?" Terry wheedled.

"Yeah, admit it, *Singe*, you rode that bike yourself."

Smiling secretly, she bit into a mango to peel it with her teeth. She had solved the mystery, but this adventure was none of their business. A few days after the dog attack, assured that the dog was gone, she'd pedaled back to Marie's. As she neared the historic spot, the Guinean children had all hushed and drawn aside, soberly waiting as if for her inspection. Nobody waved. But when Solange saw the old man perched in his chair, she pulled up.

"*Merci beaucoup*," she said.

He smiled, brown creases tightening around his rheumy eyes.

"*Et le chien, ça va?*" she asked about the dog.

"*Oui, ça va.*"

She could not say much else in French. She poked her front

wheel back out toward the street. Just then, one of the kids advanced, a boy about her size although she could not tell how old. He did not look very strong, his arms and legs stringy, his stomach pumped up like a basketball. Yet he addressed her in a stream of cheerful, pink-tongued French.

"*Je ne sais pas,*" she shook her head.

Dipping and veering, he chattered on, hands braced as if on handlebars. He pointed to the bandage on her leg, the ground, the tata, himself. "*Moi,*" he curled his thumb toward his chest. "*C'était moi.*"

"Oh," she understood, "you rode the bike! You?" she pointed to him, to the bike. "You?"

He was nodding, laughing now, teeth white as bleach.

Solange offered the handlebars to him, inviting him to ride. Climbing on, he cruised down the street, standing in the pedals. His friends all chased him, tagging the back. Carefully, majestically in his ragged shorts, he circled, and then braked to a stop beside Solange.

At Marie's, Solange explained how the bike had found its way the day she got bit, but she never bothered to inform her brothers at home. Whether due to the iron pills or to something else, she was growing quietly robust, thriving beyond the boys' reach. Even when, weeks later, a riot convinced all the parents to keep their children off the streets, to ban the bikes and all communication with Guinean kids, Solange was content to entertain herself, coaxing lizards with crumbs, watching from a distance as her brothers fought.

By December, however, the Americans in Conakry were going home. The Guinean president was deporting them in phases, group by group—Pan Am, AID, saving the diplomats for last. At school, kids would suddenly be absent, deprived of a chance to say good-bye, and Solange's mother calmly told her that they could be next.

Solange could not resist one last feat. Disobeying her quarantine, she snuck her bike into the forbidden street one afternoon and sped down the road. At the compound, she found the boy who'd gallantly returned her bike to the Buckwoods' the day she got bitten. Toothy and confused, he jabbered in words she could not understand.

"*Cadeau,*" she interrupted him. "*Je vais aux États-Unis vite.*" She had composed this sentence from her French book that afternoon, wanting him to know that she was leaving, that the bike was a gift.

"*Pourquoi?*" he wanted to know, ignoring the bike.

"*Je ne sais pas.*"

He thanked her then with dignity, putting out his hand, and they shook.

"*Taxi chéz moi,*" said Solange, gesturing to make him understand she needed a ride home.

They took off shakily, Solange on the handlebars, the boy standing in the pedals, arms locked, and as they gained momentum the bike straightened out. She felt limp and safe, glad to be a passenger. Pedaling more and more quickly, the boy huffed sweetly in her ear, and Conakry slid past. Hair flying, she wanted to wave at all the blurred Africans one last time but knew that she would lose her balance if she did, and so she simply gripped the steel bars and held her breath as the boy pedaled faster and faster, as if they were late.

How I Came To Write This Story

For a long time after we returned from our time with the Peace Corps in Kenya, I was still sorting through the meaning of my experience there, aware of its immediate mark and only beginning to suspect the enduring effect it would have on my life and the lives of the other members of our small family. I began to think, and still do, about the Kenyans I'd left behind, whose lives had also changed because of the crossing of our paths. Gone from the scene, I could no longer monitor their progress or their faltering, but I could wonder and hope that there would be other resources for them to turn to, and that they would know how to find them. My great fear was, and is, that good intentions might have unexpected and damaging consequences. This story is a fantasized expression of that fear.

—Joan Richter

JOAN RICHTER (Kenya, 1965-1967) was born and raised in New York City and served as a Peace Corps staff wife in Kenya from 1965-67, and consulted for the Peace Corps on "the role of staff wives overseas." She has worked as a stringer for *The New York Times*, written for a variety of other publications and was Director of Public Affairs at American Express for ten years. She co-authored a children's book set in Africa. Her short stories have appeared in *Ellery Queen's Mystery Magazine* and in several anthologies. She lives in Washington, DC with her husband. They have two sons who shared the Kenya experience.

THE ONES LEFT BEHIND

by Joan Richter

Tetu stared out of the window and watched the dust settle in the narrow dirt drive. That was all that was left of the Europeans, the red dust from their car. The house was empty. Beds, books, clothes, dishes, everything was gone, ready for the next family to move in. Like the others he had worked for, the new people would stay in Kenya for two years, maybe four, then leave—he would never see them again. Some families he was sad to see go, others he tried to forget, like the first ones he had worked for, but that had been before Independence, when a white man could do anything he pleased with an African.

In one of the empty bedrooms, he heard a closet door open, and for a moment his mind played a trick on him. He thought it was the *Memsab*, returned from a trip to town, but he knew it was Kamba, sweeping out the closets, the last of the chores to be done.

Everything had to be clean, so the new people would see right away that he and his helper knew how to keep a fine house, that they had worked for Europeans before. The windows had been washed, the cupboards scrubbed and all the wooden floors in the house were freshly waxed. Yesterday he had used the sheepskins that fitted over his shoes to polish the dark wood. The little boy, whose hair was the color of ripe maize, had skated beside him, a pair of old stockings covering his shoes, holding onto Tetu's hand, helping for the last time.

Tetu passed a hand over his eyes and then slowly let it fall to his side where he smoothed the trouser pocket that held the thick packet of twenty-shilling notes. A month's salary and two month's farewell bonus—that was something to be happy about. The extra money would pay for his older children's school fees, at least for this year, and he would buy himself a new shirt at one of the Indian *dukas* on Bazaar Street in Nairobi. Tonight, or tomorrow, he would go to the cinema. Sometimes the English was spoken too quickly for him to understand, but he liked to watch the fast-moving pictures of speeding cars, planes and war.

Although Tetu hadn't heard him, he knew that Kamba had come up behind him. He caught the scent of the oil that he used on his hair. It had the strong, sweet smell of a ripe mango. It told of his coming or if he had passed through a room.

Kamba was seventeen, younger than Tetu by ten years. He had no experience and no training to be a houseboy, but when the old man who worked in the garden and helped in the kitchen, left to go back home, Tetu talked to the *Memsab* about letting him train Kamba to do the job. "We are of the same village and will work well together," he had told her.

"Why do you stand at the window? It is where I left you a long time ago," Kamba called to him from across the room.

There were times when Kamba spoke with a gruffness Tetu did not like, so he ignored his question. "Have you swept all the closets?"

Kamba leaned his broom against the wall and reached into his shirt pocket and made a fan of his twenty-shilling notes. "Everything is finished. Now I am ready to go to town."

"That is a lot of money," Tetu said, knowing it was more money than Kamba had ever seen before. "It would be better if you went to the post office first and started a savings account. Then go to town."

Kamba shrugged and put the bills away. "I am ready. Let's go."

Tetu suddenly felt tired and he shook his head. "Let us wait until tomorrow to go to town. I will take lunch now and then have a small sleep."

"How can you sleep when there is money to spend?"

"Because there are other things I need to think about. You should, too. Someday you will have a wife—and children. They will need clothes. You will have to send them to school." Tetu shook his head. "That takes many shillings."

"You have been working for Europeans too long, Tetu. You sound like the *Memsab.*"

Tetu stared at Kamba. It was an insult to be compared to a woman, but he decided to set aside his anger. Kamba was young and had much to learn. He did not mean the words the way they sounded.

"I will worry about a wife and children when that time comes," Kamba said. "Now I will go in to town. And tonight I will go to the cinema and after that to Mary's."

He went to Mary's himself sometimes, but Kamba went too much. The women were not like the women of their village. Their heads were not shaved clean and their painted mouths smelled of European whiskey, not *pombe,* the good sweet African beer the women in his village made. He had tried whiskey, and gin too, but it cost too much money and the next day his head hurt.

"After Mary's you will have nothing. It will be a long time before you see this much money again." But Kamba was not listening to him, so Tetu turned away and looked out of the window again, down the long driveway where the dust had settled.

"Why do you stand there? Why do you look after them?" Kamba demanded.

"Because I am sad to see them go. They were good *wazungus.* Who knows what the next ones will be like? These were your first Europeans. They are not all so kind. I told you about the first white people I worked for, when I drank water from a glass that belonged to them. The woman threw the glass away and then took the money for it from my wages."

"You have told me that before."

Tetu nodded. "So you would know the difference. So you would not be fooled and think that they are all alike—good like the *Memsab* who has just gone."

"Why was she so good? Because she gave us money? We worked. Did we not? I do not understand you, Tetu. You think only of small things that do not matter—drinking from glasses. Have you forgotten about your wife?"

"My wife?" He said it as though "wife" was a new word to him, one he had not used in a long time. "Why do you speak of my wife?"

"Because you have been talking of the **good** *Memsab*. Have you forgotten that it is this **good** *Memsab* who is to blame for what happened?"

Tetu stared at Kamba and frowned. A strange feeling began to move over him—a dry heat, as though he had gotten too close to a fire. "What happened, Kamba?"

The younger man shrugged and reached for the broom and turned toward the door. "If you do not know, I cannot tell you. There are things even a brother cannot say to a brother."

Tetu watched him leave, wanting to call after him, but his mouth was dry and his voice would not rise from his throat. There was the click of the cupboard latch from the hall, where Kamba was putting away the broom. Soon after, the kitchen door opened and closed, and Tetu knew Kamba had left the house.

From the window he saw him along the path that led behind the high bougainvillea hedge to the servants' quarters. The cinder block building had two small rooms, a cookhouse and a *choo* with running water and a shower, but from the big house only the building's red tile roof could be seen. Tetu waited until Kamba appeared again, dressed in his black trousers and white shirt, headed for town. Then he, too, left by the kitchen door.

The heat that had swept over him earlier had eased, but it left him with an ache in his stomach and a big thirst. In the cookhouse he and Kamba shared, he made tea and warmed the *posho* left from yesterday. He rolled the cornmeal paste into balls and ate them slowly, but he was not as hungry as he thought and went to his room to lie down.

"Her name is Ruth," he had said to his father. "She is of our village and I have asked her to be my wife."

His father nodded. "Yes, she is of our village, but her name comes from the white man's god book. It would be better if you found another woman. Besides, she is small and will not bear you sons."

The time had come when a man could choose his own wife and he married Ruth and proved his father's prophecy wrong. In the first year there was a son and another afterwards until there were five. Tetu was proud, but as the years passed he became troubled. His wife was young and strong. There would be more children, which meant he would need more money for food and clothes and school fees. What of his hope to buy land? If he had his own *shamba* he would not have to go to the city to find work. But with more children there would be no such money. He would never be able to stay in his village—and he would see his wife only twice each year.

The *Memsab* often came into the kitchen to talk to him about the meals he was to cook and other things about the household. Sometimes she stayed to ask him about his village and his family. Then she would sit at the table with a dictionary of Swahili and English words in her hand. There came a time when she began using words he did not know, and he told her that already she knew more Swahili than he did. "I did not learn Swahili until I went to the mission school, and I did not stay there long. In my village we speak the language of my tribe."

She asked him why he had left his village—why he had come to the city to work?

"There is no work for me there. If I had land, it would be different. Then I would grow good cash crops, like maize and pyrethrum—and I could be with my family."

"Has your wife ever been to Nairobi? Has she ever visited you here?"

Her question took him by surprise. It was something he had never thought of, because it did not seem possible. "It is very far, a day's long journey, and the bus costs many shillings."

"Would she like to come—would you like her to visit you here? I will give you the money for her bus fare."

His heart quickened and he began to imagine what it would be like to have Ruth stay with him in his room behind the high bougainvillea hedge. He had told her many things about Nairobi, its big buildings and crowded streets, its shops and many cars—and the cinema. He had told her about the Europeans he had worked for, who lived in stone houses that had kitchens with gas cookers and fridges that made ice. He described the servants' quarters that he and Kamba shared, that there was a light in the ceiling of their rooms and running water in the cookhouse and the *choo*. But always, he told her he would rather be in his village.

He looked at the *Memsab.* "No woman in my village has been to Nairobi. I would like my wife to come here—very much."

"Then ask her to come for a visit—a week. That should not be too long for her to be away from your children. I'll give you some extra money so you can take her to the cinema and so she can buy shoes."

He bowed his head and spoke his thanks. She remembered that he had told her no one in his village had shoes—the dirt paths and the earth of the cultivated fields were soft underfoot, not like the concrete sidewalks in Nairobi.

On the day Ruth was coming, he went to the bus station in Nairobi long before her bus was to come. This was her first time to the city and she would be frightened by the big buildings, the noise and the crowds.

How proud he was when he saw her come down the high

step—her head was wrapped in the blue cloth she always wore, and she was wearing shoes. But the bus had not stopped where he thought it would and as he struggled through the crowd, he saw her eyes searching for him, growing wide with fear. He fought his way through and when he finally reached her side, she lifted her face up to his. A relieved whisper passed her lips, and over the noise around them he heard her familiar voice and saw her lips form his name. "Tetu," she said softly and stayed looking at him for a long while. Then she lowered her eyes, in a way that made him follow her glance, and only then did he see the child she held close to her breast. "This is your newest child, another son, just new-born. I could not leave him."

She looked up after a while and he saw that her lips were trembling. "Will the *Memsab* be angry that I have brought the *toto* with me?"

Although he did not know the answer to her question, he shook his head and made his voice sound strong. "She will understand. A mother cannot leave so new a child." But her worry became his and it began to grow in him and was there when he walked up to the front door of the big house to present his wife to his employers.

The little boy saw them from the window and came running outside. He threw his arms around Tetu's knees and shouted his name. The child at his wife's breast woke and began to cry. The *Bwana* and the *Memsab* came to the door.

The *Bwana* frowned when he saw the child, but the woman's blue eyes were full of welcome as she shook Ruth's hand. She touched the baby's cheek, and then bent down to lift up her own small son so that he might see Tetu's child.

How big a man he felt before his wife that week, but the time went too fast and there was still so much he wanted Ruth to see, mostly he did not want her to leave.

It took great courage for him to go to the *Memsab* and ask if his wife could stay one more week.

A frown began, but did not last. She nodded and smiled. "All right. One week, but no more. There is no room for her and the baby to stay with you here—and your other children need her. How many are there now?"

"With the new child it is six."

"Tetu, you are young to have such a large family." Her voice was troubled.

"My father had two wives and many sons. I have only one wife, but already I have many."

She nodded. "In your father's time it was the custom to have many children. But these are different times. If you have too many, you will not be able to send them to school."

"Yes, Madam. I know. I know all my children should go to school. But what can I do?"

She looked at him for a long moment and then spoke slowly. "There is a clinic at the hospital in Nairobi where you can go. They will tell you what can be done to keep from having more children."

Although her voice was gentle, her words sent a shiver of fear through him. He had never been to a hospital, but he had not forgotten the boy he had known at the mission who had gone with a bad sore on his leg and came back with his leg cut off.

He did not say this to her, but when she spoke again, he wondered if she had seen his fear.

"This clinic is not a hospital for sick people. It is a place for men and women to go to ask questions about how they can keep their families small. There are doctors and nurses who will be able to speak to you in your own language and explain things I don't know the words for. They will tell you what you can do to keep a child from beginning to grow." She smiled gently. "Go with your wife and listen to what they have to say."

And so he and Ruth went to the clinic and heard things they never imagined could be. A nurse showed them the small white curl of plastic that when put in a woman's body meant no child would grow.

He became a big man in his village, not only because his wife had been to the city and had shoes, but because after giving him six sons, she would have no more. And with no new child beginning, Ruth could work in the coffee fields and there might be money to save.

Tetu told Kamba about the clinic. "It would be good for you to know these things before you take a wife, before you have many children." But Kamba shook his head. "When I marry, I will not waste my seed."

He did not like the sound of Kamba's words and he answered angrily. "It is a waste to plant more seeds than a plot of ground can grow."

"You are a fool, Tetu. This is a *wazungu* idea, to keep Africans from having children, so there will always be more of them."

"It is you who are the fool. This is a new nation. What was good for our fathers is not good for our children. They must go to school. I don't want my son to be a houseboy, like me. What are you, Kamba? A houseboy's helper! Is that what you want for your sons?"

The look that came to Kamba's face told him that his insult had been felt and he was glad, but his heart softened and he wished his words had not been so harsh, until Kamba spoke again.

"We are not talking of the same things, Tetu. You talk of school and education. I am talking of your wife and what you had done to her. And what has happened to you because of it."

Tetu frowned. "What has happened to me?"

"You are no longer a man."

Tetu smiled and shook his head. "You do not understand. I am a bigger man now than I ever was because I am thinking of the future."

"You are a bigger fool. Now that no seed will grow inside your wife, she can lie with any man and you will never know."

Kamba's mocking laugh filled the room.

Tetu stared at him for a long moment and then turned away. He told himself that Kamba knew only the ways of the women at Mary's, and he should set his words aside, but it was not an easy thing to do. A few days later, when Kamba left to go home on leave, Tetu was glad to see him go.

As he did his work and Kamba's also, he thought of Ruth. He could hear her small laugh and see her fine, strong legs as she stretched high to pick the ripe red coffee berries. Her small face came to him, full of the brightness that shone in her eyes when they were alone together. He heard his name, a soft whisper on her lips. It was four months since he had seen her and many weeks before he was scheduled to go home. If Kamba had not been on leave he would have gone to the *Memsab* and asked for time to make a short trip home, but the rule of the house was that only one of them could be away.

When his loneliness was so deep that he could think of nothing else, the *Memsab* came into the kitchen and told him the family was going on *safari* and the house would be closed for a month—he and Kamba could have the time off, with pay.

The bus ride to his village was always long, but this time it seemed longer than ever before. He slept for a while, but when he woke the sky which had been bright before was filled with dark clouds. He prayed the rains would wait until after the bus passed the low stretch near the river, but before his prayer ended, the sky opened and the dirt road turned to mud and the bus could not go on.

Those who had far to go wrapped themselves against the night's approaching chill and stayed huddled in their seats. Others who lived nearby left the bus and set off to walk the rest of the way.

By road it was too far to walk to Tetu's village, but he thought they were not far from the mission school, and he began to wonder if the path was still there, the shortcut that crossed the valley and went up the escarpment. He had taken it many times—but that was many years ago.

An icy rain fell on him as he set out and began his search. So much had changed. The trees had grown tall and the stretch of bamboo that had been a small thicket was now a forest. He shivered as much from fear that the path was gone, as from the cold that chilled his bones.

The day's last light was about to fade when he came upon the narrow track. An old song rose in his throat, a made-up song he used to sing on his way to school, an ululating call that swept across the wide valley where the grass grew as tall as a man. It was a warrior's song that warned of his coming. In his school days, birds rose from their foraging and wheeled across the sky, and the snakes he knew were there moved out of his path.

It was the middle of the night when he reached his village. Rain had blackened all the outside fires, and the houses, each one like the other, with thatched roofs and mud and wattle walls, were dark round shapes, shrouded in the thickness of the night. At the curtained doorway of his house, his lips parted, ready to announce his coming, but he kept his silence and pushed past the drape of cowhide and stepped into the place where his children slept. The murmuring sounds of their sleep rose in a hushed chorus around him. He took in their warmth, and breathed in the scents of their bodies, mingled with the smell of corn meal and spices and *posho* left in the cooking pot. He listened to the rain falling on the thatched roof, over his head, and was glad to be home.

He hung his clothes and rubbed his body dry. Then, with his footsteps silent on the earthen floor, he felt his way past the half wall to the place where his wife slept. Even in the charcoal darkness he knew it—in the corner was a stool and next to it a wooden box where Ruth kept her clothes and the shoes she had bought for her trip to the city. A circle of colored beads decorated its lid. Two steps away was the reed mat on which she lay.

He would speak in a whisper, so she would not be frightened, soft words she would know were only his. She was not expecting him—only a few days ago Kamba had arrived and she knew they could not be away at the same time. Kamba would be happy to know he would have a whole month off from work.

He knelt down and reached out to explore the dark, seeking to find the round curve of his wife's head, looking for the feel of the scarf she always wore over her closely shaved hair. But what his fingers found made his hand withdraw. It was not the familiar feel of the woven cloth he had touched, but hair that was coarse and crisp.

He rose quickly, thinking the dark night had misled him, and that he was in someone else's house, but with his backward step his bare foot touched the corner of the box that should be there, and he stood unsure, until he passed his hand over its lid and felt the circle of beads rise under his touch. No one else in his village had a box such as this.

In the darkness he heard a stirring and the frightened, whispered voice he knew.

"I hear a noise. Go! Go quickly!"

The hurried rustle of cloth and a shifting of limbs moved the still air. Although the unlit dark offered nothing, he knew as though he saw, that a man had risen from the reed mat on which his wife lay, and was already gone.

Silence held him and he stood as still as stone, but a wild and searing pain had pierced his heart and encircled it with flames. A fire leapt and blazed inside him, and set fire to his brain. He fell upon his wife, the wife he thought was only his. He found the small pulse in her throat and felt it grow wild and faint and still. Around him the blackness swirled and outside the night's rains fell.

When he reached the river road it was almost morning, but the sky was still as dark as night. The water had risen and came past his knees. Inside the bus everyone slept.

A whole day passed before the rains stopped and another day before the road was dry enough for the bus to continue on its way. By then a fever raged in him, and his tongue was a lump of charred coal in his mouth. He could not speak or see or walk.

He dreamt that an old woman came to him and brought a cup of water to his lips. He thought she was his mother, yet he knew his mother had been dead many years. She came again and lifted his head and gave him more to drink. He tried to speak, but if words passed his lips, he did not hear them, nor her voice in answer. But he knew the old woman was Kamba's mother. He was in Kamba's house.

Time stretched before and behind him, an endless river of chilling ice and blazing fire, of dark dreams and sorrow blacker than any night. Into one of the dreams a strong, sweet smell left a trail, and when he woke he knew Kamba would be there.

"You have been sick a long time," he heard Kamba say. "It is eight days since the bus brought you. It took two men to carry you here."

He lifted his head, but it would not rise. The words he spoke were hoarse and dry. "Why am I not in my own house?"

Through eyes already closing, he saw a strange look move across Kamba's face. He did not hear his answer.

When again he woke, it was Kamba's mother who was at his side and he took her hand. "Thank you, old friend, for all you have done for me. But tell me, why am I here? Where is my wife?"

Her face darkened and she peered at him through clouded eyes. "Has not Kamba told you?"

"He has not told me."

She tried to draw her hand away. He held on fast. "Tell me, old friend."

She nodded, but was slow to begin. She looked away and then at her hands and finally raised her eyes. "Three days before you were carried home, there was a night of dark and drenching rain, like none that I have seen. Your wife went to sleep that night, but when morning came, she did not wake."

His fever returned and with it the fires and the drenching icy rains. It was a long time before he could sit up, before he could walk, longer still before he was strong enough to return to the city, to the big house where the *Memsab* greeted him with kind, sad eyes. The little boy, grown taller in the time that had passed, ran to him, and took his hand.

He did not talk about his wife, not to Kamba or to anyone, not until today—when Kamba spoke of her.

Tetu pushed aside his blanket and left his bed and went to the door of his room. Outside, the night air was cool. The moon was large and round and bright. It made the stars seem dim. It was not like the night of his dark journey home, when the big rains had fallen and he had been cold and wet and filled with longing.

He remembered the murmurs of his children, the warm smells of their sleeping that mingled with the smell of the spices and *posho* left in the cooking pot. Later there was the lingering, sweet scent of the oil that had rubbed off Ruth's body onto his.

How I Came To Write This Story

Despite, or due to, my dozen or so years overseas with the Peace Corps, I've always been intrigued by what appears to be the inverse proportion of my time spent in a place to my understanding of its people and culture—the longer I spend in a place, the less I truly know about it. For me, this comes with learning how to recognize the blank spots, and learning a bit more about the culture's subtleties; soon, the hubris I'd developed by learning some language or a few customs is chipped away, sometimes rudely.

The character in this story, an American in Africa, feels that same alienation. The more he learns, the less he understands. Finally, an incident occurs that destroys his distinctions between cultural differences and what he thought were core human values. He eventually comes to a nascent realization—I hesitate to call it a resolution—of sorts: It's good to intellectualize being a stranger in a strange land, but that's the easy way; it's better, and more honest, to know it.

—Karl Luntta

KARL LUNTTA (Botswana, 1978-1980), originally from East Hartford, Connecticut, was a mathematics instructor in Botswana. He later became a trainer and Peace Corps administrator in other parts of Africa, the South Pacific, and the Eastern Caribbean. In 1989 he returned to the States and settled in Massachusetts with his family, where he writes newspaper features and a column, and travel articles. He is the author of books on Jamaica and the Lesser Antilles, and has contributed to national travel publications such as *Caribbean Travel and Life*. His fiction has been published in *International Quarterly, Buffalo Spree, Sensations, Baltimore Review, Talking River Review*, and smaller publications.

A Virgin Twice

by Karl Luntta

In the early evening, as the jacaranda trees opened their blossoms to do battle with the stale heat of the day, a small boy appeared on Kevin's stoop. It was less than four hours since the incident with Mdongo.

"Ko ko," the boy said. "Sah, sah!"

Kevin came to the door and the boy was on one knee, his eyes averted.

"You don't have to do that," Kevin said. "It's not necessary." He realized it was foolish of him to say it, yet he always felt compelled to say it. Sometimes he did, and sometimes he didn't.

"Yes, sah," the boy said, but kept his eyes and knee to the ground. His head was powdered with fine dust and his back rose and fell rapidly.

"Yes?" Kevin said.

"I am sent by Kgosi Lesetedi. He is calling you," the boy said, breathlessly.

"Yes, of course he is," Kevin said, still feeling numb about the whole thing. "There you go."

"Go to where, sah?"

"Not you. I meant—it's an expression."

"Yes, sah."

"Okay, you can tell the kgosi that I'm coming."

"Will I wait for you?"

"No, I need to wash first. Just tell him I'm coming."

"Yes, sah," the boy said. He remained on the ground, waiting to be dismissed.

"What is your name?" Kevin asked.

"Mosimanegape, sah," the boy said.

In his mind, Kevin flipped the pages of his language manual. "What does it mean?"

"It means 'another boy,' sah."

Kevin looked down at Mosimanegape. His back was covered, in a manner, by a brown schoolboy's shirt, tattered at the collar and threadbare at the broad of the shoulders. "You're not one of my students, are you?" Kevin asked.

"No, sah. But next year I will have you for maths."

"Looking forward to it?"

"Yes, sah," the boy said.

Kevin nodded, but the boy didn't see it. "Mosimanegape, just for my information, when would a boy like you be allowed to stand and talk to an adult?"

The boy kept his eyes to the ground while he thought about it. "I have never thought about it, sah," he said, finally.

"Never? Let's say that you were sixty years old, would you look me in the eye when you talk to me?"

The boy giggled, embarrassed by the thought. "No, sah," he said.

"Why is that?"

"Because when I am sixty, you will be dead."

"Well," Kevin said. "You know your maths, at any rate."

"Yes, sah."

"Just tell him I will be there soon," Kevin said. He hesitated for a moment. "Okay, you may go."

The boy stood up and backed away, his eyes still to the ground. When he reached the main gate, he turned, waved, and sprinted off.

Kevin walked back to his tiny kitchen and picked up his yet untouched gin and tonic. He decided against it, and placed it back on the shelf next to some tin plates and cups. He took a brown paper bag and placed it over the drink, to shield it from bees.

He went into his bedroom to dress for the occasion. He was, after all, meeting with the chief of the entire village. He decided shorts would be too informal, and a T-shirt would be close to disrespectful. He settled on clean khaki trousers and an ugly African-print safari shirt, one that he'd bought early on at Patel's Haberdashery in Gaborone. He hadn't even liked the shirt when he saw it, but bought it anyway, reasoning that it was the type of shirt that would bring him closer to the people. Within days he realized he hadn't seen a single African man wearing the same type of shirt. Those who did were all whites—British expatriates, development workers. When he checked the label and saw it had been manufactured in Taiwan, he considered throwing it away. Still, he was sentimental about it, and held onto the shirt. It was a landmark shirt.

Kevin stripped down to his waist and rubbed the bruise on his shoulder where Mdongo, who was both the headmaster of the school and a madman, had bitten him. Mdongo had not, in the words of the medical manual Kevin used to treat himself, "impugned the integrity of the skin." Still, he was grateful for delivery from tetanus or God knows what. It was God knows what that could kill a person out here. The nearest hospital was half a day's ride.

He examined the scraped knuckles of his right hand, and doused them again with hydrogen peroxide. The liquid bubbled and fizzed, raising a stinging strawberry parfait on his knuckles. He vaguely recalled that a student had snatched Mdongo's tooth from the ground after it had left the headmaster's mouth and arced in slow motion, tumbling through the air before it hit dust. The student no doubt still had the tooth, and would later use it as a fetish, insurance against bad grades and capricious discipline.

Five minutes later Kevin was dressed and out of the house. The jacaranda mingled with the acrid smoke of acacia-wood cooking fires, as women prepared dinners throughout the village. As he walked, small children darted in and out of the compounds, chewing on a chicken leg here, pushing a toy truck constructed from soft-drink tins there. Some stopped and stared when they saw him, calling out, "Mistah Keveen!" But when he looked back at them, they averted their eyes and giggled.

Miss Ndlovu's compound was subdued. A few children chased goats from the plastic water basins, but most of her people would be at the kgosi's place, waiting to hear the story. Miss Ndlovu was, of course, well on her way to the hospital, if not already there.

Peter Zimunya's rondavel was also dark and quiet. Kevin was sure his friend was already sitting with Kgosi Lesetedi, exchanging pleasantries about the weather and lack of rain, or about the status of cattle diseases this year.

Kevin approached the entrance to the school and saw a small crowd gathered around the staff room. Some simply peered, awestruck, through the burglar-barred windows. Others talked excitedly and pointed at Kevin as he walked by. "Jesus," he said to himself. "What now?"

The crowd was at a distance, so he tried to wave them off. Some waved back, good-naturedly, misinterpreting his gesture. In the crowd he spotted Rose, a woman he'd been sleeping with. He would have preferred to say that he was having a relationship, even affair, with her, but she would have no part of those words. "The village is too small," she'd told him. "I cannot be seen with a lekgoa. When your contract is over, then who will I be? The woman whose white boyfriend left her."

Still, at the instant Kevin saw Rose, he felt a warm rush of energy along his spine and (this interested him) his sinuses. And as they nodded discreetly to each other, he had two simultaneous thoughts: "What am I, a caveman?" and "I need to get a bigger bed."

Kevin approached Kgosi Lesetedi's place just as darkness fell on the village. He paused at the entrance to the compound. "Ko ko."

"Dumela," came a reply from the dimly lit circle of huts. "Tsena."

Kevin crouched and walked toward a circle of older men seated around a low fire. He spotted Kgosi John Lesetedi at the far end of the circle, seated on a stool slightly higher than the others. Peter Zimunya sat next to the old man, still shaken and looking for all the world as if he were sitting on a puff adder. Kevin knew the whole scene would be harder on Peter than on him, only because, and this was the irony of his life in Botswana, it was Peter's country, not his. Because he was a foreigner, he was excluded from certain culpabilities. At the same time, he knew his mistakes and inept handling of what had turned out to be an incomprehensible language made him a great source of entertainment throughout the village.

For example: Soon after his arrival, Kevin had struck up a conversation with a woman at the water pump. She'd had a baby swaddled in blankets resting on her back. In his mind, Kevin formed the sentence, "Your baby is beautiful."

"Your baby is a rabbit," he'd said.

Kevin nodded at Peter, and crouched lower, eyes averted, approaching Kgosi Lesetedi while extending his right arm. "Dumela, kgosi," he said.

"Dumela ngwanaka, o tsogile jang?" Hello, son, how did you arise? Kgosi Lesetedi asked. They shook hands.

"Eh," Kevin replied. Fine.

"Sit, Mr. Mahoney," Kgosi Lesetedi said. His voice was like sand and his eyes rheumy. He seemed tired. Greetings were passed between Kevin and the rest of the men. No women were visible in the circle, but Kevin knew they stood in the darkness, tending to chores, listening to every word.

"I would like to speak English," Kgosi Lesetedi said.

"We can speak Setswana," Kevin said. "I'll try."

"I don't mean to insult you," Kgosi Lesetedi said, "But we have important things to discuss. We are not talking about rabbits."

The men snickered and Kevin thought, not unkindly, at least I give these people pleasure.

"Pardon me," Kgosi Lesetedi said. "The point is, I don't want you to miss anything. Besides, I enjoy English, isn't it."

Kevin looked to the other men for a reaction. Several nodded assent.

"Don't worry," Kgosi Lesetedi said. "What they don't understand, I will tell them later. English?"

"Okay," Kevin said.

"Mr. Zimunya?"

"Eh," Peter said.

"Well, then," Kgosi Lesetedi said. He leaned forward. "What do you think of the Bruins this year?"

"Sir?"

"The ice-hockey team, the Boston Bruins."

"Yes, I know them."

"You are from Boston?"

"South Boston, sir. But I don't really...I mean, I'm not sure."

"You are wondering how I know of this game, isn't it. I know of Boston. Popcorn and hot dogs, you see. And this game fascinates me. We have all seen ice, of course, but a field of ice, a lake of ice? No, never. I can't conceive it. It is a dream of mine, to see an ice-hockey field."

"Do you actually follow the team, then?" Kevin said.

"No, in point of fact, I am a fan of the New York Rangers." He paused for effect. "You may very well ask, how is that? It would be an intelligent question."

Kevin remained silent, slightly stunned. The old men, even Peter, smiled.

"Well?" Kgosi Lesetedi said.

"How is that, sir?" Kevin asked.

Kgosi Lesetedi leaned back into the darkness and hissed. A young girl appeared, and, as near as Kevin could understand, the kgosi told her to fetch something from inside. He leaned back. "Wait," he said, satisfied. Then, as a second thought, he leaned back into the darkness and shouted, "And bring tea!"

After a moment the girl emerged from the darkness with a shiny photo album. She dropped to one knee and handed the album to the kgosi, who took it slowly, and with some reverence. He took a pair of bent bifocals from his breast pocket and brought them to his grooved and stubbled face. Nevertheless, he squinted as he searched the album.

"Ah," he said. "There." He handed a photo to Kevin.

In the photo, a young man, as dark as a glass of merlot and made darker by the cap and gown he sported, made darker still by an overcast day, held a diploma out to the camera. He was alone in the photo.

"My son," Kgosi Lesetedi said. "The third-born. Columbia University of New York City."

The young man was long and elegant, and wore his cap at an angle. He smiled broadly. "What is his degree?" Kevin asked.

Kgosi Lesetedi frowned and leaned back into the darkness. "A re eng?" What did he tell us?

A woman's voice came from the darkness and filled the circle of men. "Biology," she said, "pre-med."

"Precisely," Kgosi Lesetedi said. "He is still there, in New York. He is going to be a medical doctor."

Kevin nodded. "You must be proud."

"Of course. It is expected," Kgosi Lesetedi said, softly. "And it is he who sends me news of the New York Rangers. But you know, I have always wanted to ask him something. What precisely is a hot dog?"

"Ah," Kevin said, glad he could help. "Well, it's ground meat in a tube. Sort of, I guess, like a sausage."

"And the meat? What type of meat is it?"

"Meat? To tell the truth," Kevin said, "I really don't know."

"Beef? Lamb? Is it in fact, perhaps, dog?"

"Dog? No, no," Kevin said. He thought about it for a moment. "God, no."

"Good. Then, why is it you call it that?"

"Well, I'm not exactly sure," Kevin said. "It's just English, I suppose. As a matter of fact, we call a lot of things 'dogs.' Feet, food, even people. It's a peculiarity."

"All languages have it, I suppose, isn't it," Kgosi Lesetedi said, and he smiled. He leaned back and let out a long breath. "At any rate, you have knocked some teeth out of Mr. Mdongo's head."

"Oh," Kevin said. "One tooth, actually."

This is what Kevin knew of Kgosi John Lesetedi: he was the paramount chief of Bobokong village of northern Botswana, a man clearly venerated by his people, and, by Kevin's count, his nine living wives, fourteen living children, and uncountable grandchildren and great grandchildren. He seemed to be a man used to being loved. They said he once was tall and broad, but now he stooped slightly, and had grown a flawlessly round belly. He still showed power around the eyes and mouth.

Kgosi Lesetedi was something of an eccentric. He wore several garish rings on his fingers, and had two gold teeth and a walking stick made from the mummified penis of an elephant—at least that was what he claimed. Kevin was not quite sure, he had never to his knowledge seen an elephant's penis, let alone a mummified penis, so he took the kgosi's word for it. It was long and black and had the appearance of an oversized fruit roll, and did indeed seem to be the mummified remains of something. If the kgosi was having him on, Kevin thought, so be it.

The kgosi owned a short-wave radio, and listened to the news of the world daily, from Russia, the U.K., France, and so on. This, even though he spoke only Setswana, English, and Afrikaans. He had learned English and Afrikaans in South Africa, during several years of education there. His English was proper, the queen's language. But he listened to the foreign language news nonetheless. It fascinated him, he said, to hear other languages.

Kgosi Lesetedi was a devout Roman Catholic, though that never stopped him from relentlessly marrying throughout his entire adult life. One of his daughters was, in fact, a Catholic nun. Kgosi Lesetedi had once told Kevin that he also listened to the news from Vatican City, for he had great admiration for the pope, who was, in his words, the most important man on earth, limited only in that he could not marry. Kgosi Lesetedi, however, suspected that the pope must have several children, because, even though it is true that we are all his children, how could he resist having a few who looked like him? No man could.

The overriding impression Kevin had of Kgosi Lesetedi, after having lived in the village these six months, was that the chief was a powerful and slightly sad man who did not take his duties lightly, and he was a man with dignity.

"One tooth, actually," Kevin said.

Kgosi Lesetedi nodded his head slowly.

"I didn't intend to."

Kgosi Lesetedi turned to Peter. "Mr. Zimunya?"

"Yes, I also hit him," Peter said in a tremulous voice. "I think."

"How do you think?"

"It all happened so fast."

"That is why we are here. To make it happen slowly, so we can understand. So, who would like to start?"

Kevin exchanged glances with his friend, and knew Peter would start because he was the elder of the two, by three or four years. It was custom, like children kneeling in the presence of adults. Peter cleared his throat.

"Before I begin, sir, I beg your permission. There is a problem we should soon resolve."

Kgosi Lesetedi nodded.

"It is Mr. Mdongo. He is locked in the staff room, even as we speak."

The photo-album girl arrived with tea, and placed the tray behind Kgosi Lesetedi. As Peter talked, she served each man a cup of the same formula: bush tea, a dollop of sweetened condensed milk, and two spoonfuls of sugar. As always, Kevin would nurse his cup for an hour or more.

Kgosi Lesetedi frowned. "Yes, I have heard as much. It was necessary at the time, isn't it. Has he been attended to?"

"He has water, and a bucket for toilet. I have instructed my girl to bring some palache to him later."

"What is preventing him from leaving?"

"The windows have burglar bars, and I have the key to the door in my pocket. The girl will pass the food through the windows."

"How long has he been in the room?"

Peter shrugged his shoulders, and Kevin realized he was the only one in the crowd with a watch. "About five hours," Kevin said.

"And his wounds?"

Kevin jumped in again. "I think it was only the tooth. He didn't seem to be in much pain, at least when we put him in the staff room."

Kgosi Lesetedi sighed. "Pain has a way of coming later. You will release him after our meeting, and tell him to see me tomorrow morning."

Peter and Kevin exchanged glances. "Sir," Peter said. "He is mad."

A shimmer of amusement furrowed the kgosi's forehead, then subsided. "He has not always been mad, isn't it. Now, tell your story."

Peter took a deep breath and began.

"I was in my classroom, during the afternoon study period. Mr. Mahoney was in the room next to mine, with his class. Then, suddenly, from the direction of the headmaster's office, I heard a woman's scream. It was very terrible."

Kgosi Lesetedi turned to Kevin. "Mr. Mahoney, you heard this as well?"

"Yes, sir." It was, as Peter had said, a chilling scream.

"So I poked my head out of the classroom," Peter continued, "and in the next moment Miss Ndlovu burst from the headmaster's office, followed by Mr. Mdongo. She was howling, and he had a hoe, a garden hoe, in his hands. He beat her on the head and body with the hoe as she ran from him—"

"Why is it that he had a garden hoe in his office?"

"Well," Peter said, "that is where we store our agricultural class supplies."

"Interesting," Kgosi Lesetedi said, stroking his chin like a detective. "Continue."

"Yes, sir," Peter said. "Anyway, he ran after her, the both of them screaming all the while."

"What did he say?" Kgosi Lesetedi asked.

"It was, ahh, something impolite."

"Which was?"

"He referred to Miss Ndlovu's mother's vagina."

A quiet murmur rose from the men seated around the circle, signaling that some understood what had been said. A teacup clattered to its saucer.

"Then what happened?" Kgosi Lesetedi asked.

"Then, well, it all happened very fast. There was such a clamor, I am not sure. The next thing I remember was that everyone, students and all, poured out from the classrooms, and I ran with Mr. Mahoney toward the headmaster and Miss Ndlovu."

Peter took a breath. "By the time we got to them, Miss Ndlovu had fallen to the ground and the hoe had broken. Mr. Mdongo was beating her with the stick, and kicking her while she was on the ground. I reached him first.

"I don't recall clearly, but I think I grabbed him from behind. His eyes were black and small, and he had foam on his lips, coming from the corners of his mouth. All this while the children were shouting and jeering and making a racket."

Kgosi Lesetedi shook his head from side to side and made a clucking sound. "And Mr. Mahoney," he said. "you reached Mr. Mdongo as well?"

Kevin cleared his throat. "Yes, Mr. Zimunya held Mr. Mdongo from behind. Miss Ndlovu was on the ground, bleeding, but I went to help Mr. Zimunya with Mr. Mdongo. He was screaming and kicking out with his feet." Mdongo was a small man, but Kevin remembered the strain in Peter's eyes and neck. "That's when Mr. Mdongo bit me."

"He bit you? How extraordinary. I would like to see."

Kevin unbuttoned the top of his ugly landmark shirt and pulled it down over his shoulder. The kgosi took out his bifocals again, and stood up to examine the bite, brushing it slightly with his coarse fingers. He nodded to the men, who, in turn, stood up to examine the bite mark. Even Peter stood up to have a look.

"That is when you hit him?" Kgosi Lesetedi asked, after all were settled again.

"Not exactly. I pulled his head back and pushed him away, and that is when he kicked me."

"He kicked you."

"Yes, in the...groin area."

The men raised some eyebrows, and Kgosi Lesetedi smiled. He turned to the men and, in the way of translation, pointed to his crotch. Several men winced.

"And that is when you hit him?" Kgosi Lesetedi asked.

"It was a reaction, more or less," Kevin said. "I didn't really think about it. I just punched out."

"Yes, isn't it," Kgosi Lesetedi said, to no one in particular.

"But it had the effect of stopping Mdongo," Peter interjected. "He deflated in my arms, like a baby. He wasn't unconscious, he merely gave up. But he continued to shout at Miss Ndlovu as we carried him away."

"Then we carried him to the staff room, and shut him in, and locked the door," Kevin said. "We left him pacing, cursing to himself, like—"

"Like a wild animal," Kgosi Lesetedi said.

"He was mad, sir," Peter said.

"Mmm," Kgosi Lesetedi said. He reached into his back pocket and pulled out a bandana, and wiped his forehead and bifocals. He placed the rag back in his pocket, and stared at the ground, drumming his knee with his fingers. He drummed for a full minute. Kevin timed it.

"Well," Kgosi Lesetedi finally said, still staring at the ground. "It certainly has been a wretched sort of day. Mr. Mahoney, I must apologize for my countryman. Now, do either of you have an idea why Mr. Mdongo would attack Miss Ndlovu in such a way?"

Kevin did not. Not the slightest. So much happened—he realized this with full force now—so much happened in and around his life in Botswana about which he was utterly oblivious, that he felt like a ten-year-old in the company of adults. Which was why he knew at that instant what Peter's response had to be.

"I think I know," Peter said. He hesitated until he was sure of everyone's attention. "It was love. Mdongo had been proposing love for many months to Miss Ndlovu, and she refused him."

"Ah ha," Kgosi Lesetedi said. The other men nodded in agreement, as if this explained why a man would become perfectly demented in the middle of a working day and attempt to kill a woman with a garden hoe.

"He was taken with her, then," Kgosi Lesetedi said.

"She refused him," Peter said.

"I guess he didn't get the message," Kevin said. No one responded. "Anyway, isn't he married or something?" He winced as soon as he said it.

"He has some wives in Zimbabwe," Peter said, nonchalantly. "But they are far away."

"Banna le basadi," one of the men said. Men and women. The others nodded.

Kgosi Lesetedi leaned back and sighed with some resignation, as if the incident was now in perspective. "I will hear Mr. Mdongo's side of the story tomorrow, isn't it," he said.

"But, I mean," Kevin said, "wives or no wives, he beat Miss Ndlovu severely. They took her to the hospital, she's there right now."

"I know this. It was my truck that took her there. One of my sons drove," Kgosi Lesetedi said. "Still, I will have to hear Mr. Mdongo's side."

"And Miss Ndlovu's side," Kevin said, before he could stop himself. One of the men coughed. Peter averted his eyes.

Kgosi Lesetedi squinted, as if he'd seen Kevin for the first time. "And Miss Ndlovu's side," he said slowly. "Now, I think it is time you released Mr. Mdongo. He cannot spend the night in the staff room. Tell him to meet me first thing in the morning, and since tomorrow is Saturday, you'll have no classes to worry about, isn't it."

"Eh," Peter said. "But, with respect, what if he is still mad?"

"He won't be. But if he is, Mr. Mahoney can punch him again, isn't it." Kgosi Lesetedi laughed. "The old one-two!"

Kevin forced a laugh, and the men joined in.

The meeting was over. After several minutes, Peter and Kevin excused themselves, and backed away from the circle until they reached the darkness. Peter took out his flashlight, "torch" he called it, and they walked toward the school.

"What do you make of it?" Kevin said.

"Kgosi Lesetedi will listen to Mdongo, and Miss Ndlovu later, but I think he has his mind made up already."

"Which is?"

"Which is that Mdongo is not only a man, but he is the headmaster. Ndlovu is a teacher. There is hardly a contest. Mdongo will be punished, but lightly. He will be seen as a fool, but a fool blinded by a woman. Maybe he'll pay a small fine."

"Get out of town!" Kevin said. "You—"

"Pardon?" Peter asked.

"It's an expression. What I mean is, you can't tell me that after Mdongo has beaten one of his own teachers in public, has most likely fractured her arm, he'll be allowed to return as headmaster?"

"That is exactly what I am telling you. He will probably pay a small fine, and that will be that. And what is more, Miss Ndlovu will be very happy with the judgement, I am telling you."

"How?"

"My friend, listen. Miss Ndlovu will be happy after Mdongo returns, because he will no longer bother her. She now has the power."

"Power? What power? He beat her up, not the other way around."

"Yes but he humiliated himself in public. He is a buffoon. And that is her power. She emerges with strength, and so do you and I, by the way. Any one of us could rub his face in cow dung now, and he would not retaliate."

"You're saying that Mdongo will never strike out at her again, not out of anger, not because of this humiliation. Not even because he is crazy. I mean, he is mad, you said it yourself."

"Yes, I said it. Who knows, maybe it was madness over a woman, not real madness. Then again, he may be a genuine lunatic. Who can tell?"

"Are you saying Kgosi Lesetedi can tell?"

"He is the kgosi. I know you don't get it," Peter said. "That is because you are from out of town. Don't worry, it is perfect."

They approached the staff room, and noticed a small candle-light glow from within. The crowd had disappeared, and from the distance, they heard Mdongo's voice. He was singing, lightly, to himself.

"What is that?" Kevin said.

"It is a baby's song, how do you say it?"

"A lullaby."

They reached the door. "Ko ko," Peter said.

The singing stopped. "Eh," Mdongo said.

Kevin peered inside and saw Mdongo seated, his feet up on a desk, his hands behind his neck. He was relaxed.

"Sir," Peter said through the window.

"Ah, you're here," Mdongo said, and he lowered his legs to the floor.

"Yes, sir," Peter said.

Mdongo stood up and smoothed his jacket, straightened his tie. He was a thin man, and short. He reminded Kevin of Sammy Davis, Jr. He had Sammy Davis, Jr.'s eyes as well, quick-moving and slightly skewed. There were small flecks of dirt and dust on his white collar, and Kevin saw a thin, dried trickle of blood at the corner of his mouth.

"May we come in?" Peter asked, in English.

"The real question, Mr. Zimunya, is may I come out." Incredibly, Mdongo laughed.

"Is everything fine?" Peter asked, warily.

"Fine? Mr. Zimunya," Mdongo said from behind the door, "you sound like an airline stewardess. Yes, I am fine, if you don't count being held here against my will. I have suffered no lasting wounds. And, Mr. Mahoney, the tooth seems to have come out clean, I feel no real pain."

"I'm glad to hear that," Kevin said. He debated what to say next, and went with convention. "I'm sorry."

"No, I am the one who is sorry," Mdongo said. "I believe I struck you first. And if you two are worried that I will try something, I can allay your fears. I have control. I am as calm as a sleeping baby."

Peter nodded at Kevin. Kevin shrugged.

"Mr. Zimunya?" Mdongo said.

Peter fumbled with the keys for a moment, and opened the staff room door.

Mdongo stepped out and Peter's torch displayed his smile, wide and almost silly. Mdongo clapped his hands to his chest and thumped. "Ahh!" he said. "Freedom!" He raised his arms to the night sky, as if to embrace the stars, and for one horrible moment, Kevin thought he might try to hug them both.

"Yes," Mdongo said to himself and the stars. "The jacaranda is in the air. It smells like chalk and old tea bags in there." He breathed deeply through his nose and chortled.

"I'm sorry, it was the only place we could think of." Peter's voice trailed off.

"To stash me away while I calmed down? Well, and a good thing, too. I am almost grateful you did so."

"We had no choice," Kevin said, horrified by Mdongo's composure.

"Of course not," Mdongo said, and clapped his hands together in the gesture of a person who wants to be somewhere else. He re-straightened his jacket and tie, and said, "Well, it is getting late. I think a good night's sleep will do us all well."

"Kgosi Lesetedi asks that you see him first thing in the morning," Peter said.

"All the reason for a good night's sleep," Mdongo said, not skipping a beat. He was almost jovial.

"Mr. Mdongo," Kevin said. "Miss Ndlovu is in the hospital."

"Of course, of course," Mdongo said. "I've heard. They took her there in Kgosi Lesetedi's truck."

"Her arm is fractured," Kevin said.

Mdongo stopped rubbing his hands. "Then it is good she is at the hospital, I would say."

"Mr. Mahoney," Peter said, "didn't you have some books you wanted to collect at my house?"

"That's all?" Kevin said, and he stepped forward. "That's all you can say?"

Peter stepped forward as well. "Mr. Mahoney, I think it is time we collected those books. Good night, sir."

"Well, good night, Mr. Zimunya, Mr. Mahoney," Mdongo said.

"That's all you can say?" Kevin said. He felt heat across his face, and his hands were balled into fists. "That's it? Not, 'I'm sorry about the whole thing, boys'? or 'Let's hope Miss Ndlovu is okay, boys'?" He saw that Mdongo had dropped his hands to his side.

"Come, Mr. Mahoney," Peter said, and he pulled Kevin's arm.

"Nothing else, goddammit?"

Mdongo stepped back with his eyes fixed on Kevin. They were grey and empty, like bullet heads. He quickly turned into the darkness with a wave. "I can find my way. And good night again." He walked away, rubbing his hands together. Peter and Kevin stood for a moment and listened as Mdongo's shoes crunched stone and sand.

"God Jesus," Kevin said. He felt unsteady.

"You will be forgiven," Peter said. "You see? You are using your power already."

"It wasn't power," Kevin said. He was exhausted. "So, what about you, what about your power?"

"Don't worry, I have plans," Peter said. "Now you should go home. We both should."

The two stood for a moment, and Kevin saw a shooting star arc across the southern sky and disappear into the horizon. It reminded him of Mdongo's tooth.

"Which home?" Kevin asked.

"You are making too much of this," Peter said.

They said their good-nights, and parted.

When Kevin reached his small house, he found Rose sitting in the kitchen, sipping his gin and tonic. She had lit a candle and was reading one of Kevin's books, *To Kill a Mockingbird*.

"Nice shirt," she said, and snickered.

The light glanced off Rose's high cheekbones and chin, and darkened the hollows of her eyes. Her thin fingers wrapped themselves around *Mockingbird* as if the book was a sandwich. Rose took his breath away, always, and Kevin suddenly felt vulnerable and weak. The bruise on his shoulder throbbed.

"Thanks," Kevin said. "I wore it just for you."

"Keveen," she said, "This Boo has a difficult life, would you say?"

"It gets worse," he said.

Rose cocked her head. "You look unhealthy."

"I've had a bad day."

"Come," Rose said, as she pushed away from the table. "Shall I rub your back?"

Kevin felt a need to be grounded, to regain his foundation. "Rose, what do you think about the Mdongo thing?"

Rose picked up the gin and tonic and handed it to Kevin. "I think he is a pig, and I think Miss Ndlovu was lucky that you and Zimunya were there."

"So why do I feel...unhealthy?"

Rose shook her head.

"Has he ever asked you out?" Kevin said.

"Who? Mdongo or Zimunya?" she said, and laughed, placing her hands over her mouth.

"Lovely. Is there a choice?"

"No. Anyway, Mdongo has proposed love to me and to every woman he has ever seen in his life. He has no boundaries, his god is between his pockets." She hesitated. "You are a hero now, did you know?"

"So I'm assuming you didn't accept," Kevin said. He sipped the warm gin and tonic.

"Jo jo jo," she said in a tone of disgust. "What am I, a common person?"

"It's just that you were up at the staff room earlier."

"The whole village was there," she said. "It was a pleasure to see him locked up. If I knew he wasn't going to get out, I should have spit on him."

Kevin tried one more time. "What do you think Kgosi Lesetedi will do to Mdongo?"

"What do you mean?"

"I mean, Peter thinks Kgosi Leseledi will let him off. That nothing much will happen, and even that Miss Ndlovu will be happy about it. Does that sound right? That the headmaster attempts to murder a teacher, and then he's let off with a slap on the wrist?"

"Slap on the wrist?" Rose said. "I doubt it. It is usually either a caning or a fine."

"It's an expression," Kevin said. "What I mean is that we'll all be back at school again, pretending nothing happened."

Rose sighed. "You are not at fault, why do you worry? He is nothing, and you saved her life."

"But, is it right?"

"Is it right? No, it is finished," Rose said. "You have beaten him, in front of everyone. He has been punished. Anyway, what I think is not important. Kgosi Leseledi will do the right thing."

"I don't doubt that," Kevin said. "I just don't get it."

"We have a proverb here," Rose said. "Lesilo le boela nnyo gabedi. It means 'A fool returns to a virgin twice.'"

Kevin stared at her, dumbfounded. "What could that possibly mean?" he asked.

Rose remained silent for a moment. "Who knows? People often say proverbs at these moments, they sound interesting."

Kevin circled the kitchen and sat at the table. He gulped the gin and tonic. "Does it imply that a person can't go twice to a virgin because after the first time, she'll no longer be a virgin? Or does it mean that if you go to a virgin and she refuses you, you are a fool to go again?"

"Kevin," Rose said. "I have long ago forgotten how virgins think. It is only a proverb."

"You know," Kevin said, "it's not a bad proverb."

"Has it given you new purpose?" Rose asked. "Then I am happy I said it. Otherwise, I am sorry I said it. Come, it is late."

"Not new purpose," Kevin said. "Something." There was something, something strong about it.

"Then do not look too deeply. Leave it. Proverbs are ephemeral by nature, as are virgins. You can only be disappointed in them eventually."

"'Ephemeral'?"

Rose picked up the candle. "Don't be a snot."

"Sorry," Kevin said. "It's a fine proverb." He surprised himself by taking Rose's hand and kissing it.

Her eyes widened. "Maybe we should sleep."

"In a minute." He pulled her gently by her hand, and encircled her waist with his arms. "You know, you really have to love this shirt."

Their faces were inches apart. "We have another proverb," Rose whispered. "Would you like to hear it?"

"Absolutely."

"Ke tla ja ga se ke jele. Ke jele ke yo mompeng."

"Wait," Kevin said. "Let me try. It means 'I want you in more ways than a hyena has spots.'"

"No. It means, 'I will eat' is not 'I have eaten'. 'I have eaten' is that which is in the stomach."

"I was thinking that," he said.

"It is just an expression," Rose said. She held his arm, and he followed the candle's light.

How I Came to Write this Story

I wrote "Ma Kamanda's Latrine" 16 years after I left the Peace Corps. The main character is based on a woman in the village where I was placed. When the lorry full of new volunteers dropped me off in a village I had never seen, I realized I was more or less on my own. Thank God for someone like Ma Kamanda, who provided support for me in that strange place. I believe it was through her efforts, not through Peace Corps administration, that I was finally moved to a house near the school. There was no lodging for me when I arrived. I spent my first few nights with a local family who gave me my own room. Then I moved to quarters behind the village co-op store. Customers of the co-op walked through my area to get to the one and only indoor toilet in the village. The co-op's "security guard" lived in a room off the hallway that separated the store from my room. I kept a diary during my two years in Sierra Leone. When I was ready to transform my memories into fiction, I used the diary as a resource. According to the "latrine" entries, I campaigned for one by paying a visit to the village chief. However, I can't help but believe that Ma's influence was at work.

—*Marla Kay Houghteling*

MARLA KAY HOUGHTELING (Sierra Leone, 1968-1970) lives in northern Michigan with her husband, two dogs and a cat and teaches part-time at North Central Michigan College. Her poetry, fiction and essays have appeared in a variety of publications, from *The Christian Science Monitor* to *Ellery Queen's Mystery Magazine*.

MA KAMANDA'S LATRINE

by Marla Kay Houghteling

The lorry to Kenema rocked past Ma Kamanda, spattering her with red mud. It trembled to a stop beside Punumba's rusty petrol pump in front of the general store and co-op.

Like the fishermen in Freetown with their boats, the lorry drivers took pride in the names chosen for their vehicles. On this one the words "Look Road for Elvis Press-ley" were hand painted in brilliant blue across the hood and over the cab. Yellow guitars, like quotation marks, punctuated the message.

She was familiar with all the lorries that passed on the Kenema Road: "Respect Elders and Fear the Youngs," "Save Us O God," "Sleep Know No Trouble," "Make Haste Slowly," "Terror in Tokyo." She knew the drivers, most of them by name. She knew which ones packed their lorries over the limit and then overcharged—like the rat-faced Brima Tumba. His lorry was always breaking down. Not wanting to dirty his hands, he ordered his lorry boy to open the hood to jiggle things or crawl under the vehicle to pound this part with a rock or tie that part with a bit of wire.

A taxi carrying two Lebanese tore through the quiet village. It didn't slow down as it passed the general store. The taxi driver, wearing a Stetson hat, held down the horn as Johnny Cash growled, "I Walk the Line," from the tiny turntable in the dashboard. Ju-ju, in this case a furry animal foot, dangled from the hood to protect the vehicle on its precarious route.

The lorry boy released the tailgate and three passengers climbed down. The last, an old woman, carried two subdued chickens in a yellow cloth. The lorry boy made great ceremony of placing a wooden footstool for the old ma as she stepped down from the lorry. She beamed at him with a toothless grin and said something that triggered laughter from inside the lorry.

Ma Kamanda gave a disdainful tch-tch as the driver (not

Brima Tumba, but the same sort) strutted back to collect fares. He was the type who was ruining the country—a cowboy, a swaggerer, someone with a scant secondary education who was all show with his flashy watch and many rings. To indicate he was above manual labor, he had grown the nail on his right little finger to nearly two inches. But can he read books? she asked.

Ma Kamanda threw back her shoulders and concentrated on her mission. She was on her way to the edge of the village to greet the new Peace Corps, Punumba's first Peace Corps. Ah, Punumba, her village, her home again. She strode down the road like a queen, wearing her best duca and lapa of red gara cloth. The poofed-up headtie of the same material extended her air of dignity. She wore shoes from Freetown. Her skin was smooth and shiny like the wooden carvings sold by traders outside the airport.

She had lived twenty years in Freetown while her husband worked for the railroad. After his retirement, they returned to their village and took over the general store, which had been closed for many years. Business was not good. Supplies from Freetown mildewed in their cardboard boxes. Travelers no longer stayed overnight. There were no resthouses. This place was not the same place it had been before independence.

Punumba had been more than a rusty village then—an important stop on the Kenema Road with a government resthouse, shops that sold all kinds of British goods, two petrol pumps, even its own generator. But the British left the village in 1961 when their political power ended. All the jobs their system had provided disappeared in the red dust. When the government resthouse closed and became a co-op store, there was no need for cooks, servants, watchmen. Women no longer earned money washing British clothes.

Even the Lebanese, with one exception, left Punumba. The Syrian, as he was called, lived in isolation. Once a month a taxi arrived to take him to Sefadu. He always returned within two days. No one knew why he chose to stay in Punumba, for he showed no liking for the villagers, nor they for him.

Now one had to travel to Kenema for every little civilized thing. The market here was shameful. A few stalls where pens, cigarettes, and rarely, local beef were sold. Everything was purchased in daily amounts—kerosene in a Coke bottle for one night's worth of light; two cigarettes for one night's pleasure; a handful of groundnuts. People could afford no more.

The Peace Corps house was near the school, on the edge of the village. School started in two days, so Ma Kamanda was sure the Peace Corps would need help settling in.

She passed square houses, most of them made of mud covered with plaster and topped with tin roofs. The windows had no glass, no screens, just wooden shutters which were closed at night. The only signs of prosperity were two houses made of cinder block with glass windows and teef bars. Although Punumba's small size prevented much undetected crime, the teef bars stated that these houses had things worth stealing.

"Shameful, shameful," she muttered as she approached the house. "Disgraceful," she hissed. Headmaster Bockerai should have seen to the house before the arrival. What must the Peace Corps think of this place? Elephant grass reached to the windows. The bush had moved in. She picked up a stick, swishing it in front of her as she walked the narrow path to the verandah.

A young white woman, tall and bony, was backing out of the door. Her yellow hair, thin and wet, was tied with a limp ribbon. Her cotton dress was creased, and her white tennis shoes caked with red earth. Two men from the next house stood in their yard watching her. They had just returned from their farm in the bush. Machetes dangled from their hands; their mouths were slack with curiosity.

The woman jerked her head around at Ma Kamanda's rustling approach. She croaked out a greeting in Mende.

"Quite all right, my dear. I am Mrs. Kamanda. My husband and I are proprietors of the general store. Is there some trouble?"

"I'm glad you're here. You speak English," she sighed. Her trembling white right hand gripped an umbrella. "There seems to be a snake in my house," she whispered. "I tried to scream, but I couldn't remember the word for 'snake.'"

"There, there." Ma Kamanda patted the clammy, white arm. "Things have not been attended to properly. I apologize."

Ma Kamanda commanded the two men to bring their machetes and sticks. They approached the Peace Corps house without enthusiasm and entered with their tools raised before them. From inside the house came sounds of wood cracking, glass shattering, pans clanging and soul-shaking cursing. One man ran to the doorway with his stick extended in front of him. From the end of the stick dangled a thick, black snake. He yelled and tossed the battered, but still wriggling snake into the air. Both men ran to where it landed and began to alternately club and chop it. When they were satisfied that it was dead, they scraped it into a bag and tied a hard knot.

The old woman from next door, who had been watching the action while sucking on a kola nut, offered the white woman strips of tansa bark. "You hang this from the ceiling. Snakes do not like the smell," explained Ma Kamanda. "That snake was probably taking a nap in those mats and fell through. A surprise for Mr. Snake and for you too," she said, bending from the waist with laughter.

The white woman gave a shaky grin, thanking all the people in the yard. Ma Kamanda rounded up four school boys and borrowed machetes from the nearby houses. They didn't mind the chore because it gave them a chance to get a good look at the white woman.

It was four o'clock by the time things had been put in order. Ma Kamanda and the Peace Corps were sitting on the low wall of the verandah having tea. An area of ten meters on each side of the house had been cleared to make a proper village yard—an expanse of bare dirt, unattractive to snakes and scorpions. The lush, viney jungle pressed toward the house on three sides. The Kenema road passed in front. Now was the rainy season, but during the harmattan, red dust would roll over the yard, seep into the house and cover everything with a fine, red silt.

The Peace Corps' name was Wendy. Her surname had hard-edged sounds in it that made Ma Kamanda feel chilly. Miss Wendy said she was twenty-two years of age.

"But don't you want a husband?" asked Ma Kamanda. Why would a young woman want to live alone in a strange country?

"Yes, maybe someday. I just graduated from college. A real small one in Indiana. And my hometown is not as large as Kenema. I want to live in another culture. See what it's like to live in a completely different place. If I stayed in my hometown to teach, I'm afraid I'd never get out. Trapped, you know." She smiled as she bit into a soggy biscuit.

"Your mother and your father? They let you leave home when you have no husband?"

"My mother wasn't too crazy about my coming, but they accepted my decision. I'm so anxious to start teaching. It will be like the American frontier." She smoothed her wrinkled skirt over her lap. "And you, Mrs. Kamanda, when did you get married?"

"Oh, my," chuckled Ma Kamanda, "I was seventeen and so stupid." She planted her hands on her knees and gazed across the freshly scraped yard. "My husband's nephew studied at a university, I forget its name, in the state of New York. So I know that women in America do things differently. Here a woman of your age has several children and is busy all day with preparing rice and earning any money she can by selling food in the school yard or at the lorry stop."

"Do you have children?" The Peace Corps emptied the last of the tea into their cups.

"I have had three, but two died while they were infants. My son lives in Monrovia. He has a very good job with the rubber company. My husband and I are planning to visit him next month."

When she walked away from the Peace Corps house, Ma Kamanda felt she had accomplished something important. The Peace Corps had been greeted and the yard put in order. This Miss Wendy was a woman but seemed like a child. She would have to look out for her, give her sensible advice. She must warn her to beware of Headmaster Bockerai. He was charming and pleasant on the surface, but a fat snake underneath. Ma Kamanda knew for a fact that he hoarded bags of CARE food in the cupboard in his office; that he paid for favors with food meant for children. She wouldn't tell this to Miss Wendy so soon after her arrival, but she would instruct her to be firm with him.

First there was the matter of the house. She headed for Bockerai's compound in the old part of town.

While the new section of Punumba, dependent on the Kenema Road, still bore traces of the British, the old part had been untouched by western ways. She left the main road and cut through the coffee grove where the ground was strewn with fragrant white blossoms. It was cool and peaceful here. She pretended she walked through snow, a wonder she'd seen only in books. Old town was situated between the river and the Kenema Road. The smell of evening fires and the sound of goats brought feelings of something sad, something lost.

Bockerai's wife was cooking rice for the evening meal. The other pot on the three-stone fire held potato leaf sauce. The familiar tang of the sauce with its sharpness of peppers made Ma Kamanda hungry. Although both women had been born here in Punumba, their appearance was as dissimilar as a fine motor car and a lorry. Ma Kamanda wore her best clothes and walked into the yard of the compound with purpose. Bockerai's wife wore only a lapa, no shoes and no duca. Her hair hadn't been plaited properly in some time. Her breasts, lengthened by nursing many children, hung like giant shriveled peppers. As Ma Kamanda approached the fire, the headmaster's wife smiled, revealing several gaps on the gum line.

How like Mr. Bockerai, she thought. To keep his wife backward, to leave the Peace Corps' house in disrepair. The only reason the man had this position was because of favors done for the chiefdom speaker.

Speaking of Mr. Devil himself, she thought. She found the headmaster and the speaker squatting companionably under a tree while they shared cigarettes and Star beer. A small table and several chairs stood nearby. They rose unsteadily as she strode towards them.

"Afternoon, afternoon. This is a pleasant surprise." The chiefdom speaker's words flowed as smooth as palm oil.

The headmaster offered his visitor one of the chairs. She sat up straight, head high, back not touching the chair. "I'll come right to the point. You must repair the Peace Corps' house. The ceiling is falling down, the plaster on the outside has fallen away. I myself organized some of the boys to clear the yard. And there must be a latrine. Americans are not used to going in the bush." She sat back.

She had addressed the headmaster, but he was silent. He took a greedy gulp of beer. The chiefdom speaker sucked on his cigarette and regarded her as if she were a thick-headed child. "It is my impression that these Americans come here to see how we live and to live as we do. Don't you see many of the houses in the village in a worse state than that one?"

"She is a guest of the village; in fact, a guest of the country. She was invited to teach here," insisted Ma Kamanda. "A guest is not given inadequate lodgings."

"I'm sure you know that I was not in favor of Peace Corps coming to this village. After years of British, we do not need Americans telling us how to do things." The speaker squinted at her through the smoke of his cigarette.

"That may be so. However, the district supervisor and the Minister of Education, with whom I'm acquainted, felt Punumba could benefit from having a Peace Corps. And I know for a fact that certain moneys were allocated to schools for Peace Corps lodging."

In some cases name-dropping helped matters. The speaker was a bluff-man and would be intimidated by officials from Freetown.

The headmaster had not spoken during this polite but tense exchange between the speaker and Ma Kamanda. Each had his and her own sphere of power in Punumba. Now he cleared his throat. "Of course, I was not aware that work needed to be done. But you must understand," he whined, raising his hands in pure help-lessness, "that it is not easy having work done in the rainy season. This very afternoon I will see one Tamba Gombai about repairing the house." The look on his large, shiny face changed from dismay to seriousness.

"What about the latrine?" asked Ma Kamanda. She knew there was enough money to repair the house and build a latrine.

Headmaster Bockerai sighed and belched.

"My dear woman," began the speaker, "a latrine is another matter. Such an undertaking will have to be cleared by the paramount chief. Surely, the American government does not expect us to dig up our country for the convenience of the Peace Corps."

"Then, gentlemen," she said rising, "my next visit will be with the chief."

But she didn't have the energy to continue the matter today. As she crossed the compound yard and said goodbye to Bockerai's wife, the men left the chairs to squat beneath the tree. The green mountains stood against the purple sky. The racket of the palm birds intensified as the storm approached. The latrine, which would show that the people in this village were not completely backward, would have to wait.

The next week, on a day of two fierce downpours which made the ruts in the Kenema Road even deeper, Ma Kamanda left the store and walked to the Peace Corps' house. The leaves dripped, and the earth steamed. No one answered when she knocked. Only the plaster on the front of the house had been repaired. The side walls were patterned with large brown blotches where the mud showed through the crumbling plaster. She looked down the road to the school. The yard was empty. The shutters and doors of its three buildings were closed. Everyone had gone home.

Rounding the corner on her way to the back of the house, she was shocked to see Miss Wendy emerge from an opening in the jungle and struggle up the steep path with two full buckets of water.

"But what are you doing? Where is the houseboy? Bockerai has not provided you with a boy from the school?"

The white woman lowered the buckets by the back door, then wiped her damp hair from her eyes. "Well," she said with a weak smile, "I won't have to do this much longer. My province director is bringing me a 50-gallon drum to collect rain water."

"That's a good idea, for sure, but what about the other work? You must have someone." Really, such a thick head. Were all Americans so stubborn?

"Headmaster Bockerai did mention a class five boy, but I turned down the offer. I don't believe in having servants. I'm capable of doing the work myself."

Ma Kamanda forced herself to speak slowly. "But, my dear, that's not the point. It is part of our life here. Everyone who has a house, African or European, has a houseboy. It's not proper for a young unmarried white woman to be seen carrying water buckets."

Ma Kamanda didn't go to visit for several days after the bucket incident. She was growing impatient with the Peace Corps, who was making no attempt to learn their ways and just staying in her house. Although, to be fair, Ma knew the white woman had asked to see her. She had been taking a nap while her husband was minding the store. She heard the Peace Corps' flat voice, then heard her husband calling for her, but she pretended to be sleeping.

She had heard the village gossip, some of it disapproving and some just good-natured chiding at the strange ways of the white woman. Miss Wendy had been seen paying a visit to the Lebanese man, Abdul. Before independence, this Abdul had owned a fleet of lorries and several shops. He married a Mende woman, who left him because he treated her so badly. Now without money, friends or family, the man had become an invisible presence in the village. On rare occasions when he ventured to the market, he was ignored. He lived on the second floor of a crumbling house, whose ochre walls were covered with moldy tapestries. His houseboy, the man's link with the outside world, described the Lebanese's strange life with a mixture of contempt and wonder. The Syrian was reported to keep a monkey that ate at the table with him.

The houseboy had carried the invitation to the Peace Corps' house. Tongues clicked at the white woman's acceptance. The villagers felt the Syrian deserved his bad fortune, but at the same time his loss of status affected them. He was an embarrassment, a reminder of the former glory of Punumba and its present bleak economy.

Ma came to Miss Wendy's defense. "She has only been here a short while. She doesn't know our ways. Perhaps she only visits when she receives an invitation."

The old woman who lived next door to the Peace Corps leaned over the counter, cackling gleefully as she told how the white woman now locked herself in her house to bathe after being spied on. It seemed that one evening the American was taking her bucket bath in the ramshackle bamboo enclosure that stood behind the house. Some children crept up to peek and couldn't contain their giggles. The white woman screamed and threw her bath water at them.

Ma Kamanda heard that a kerosene fridge had been delivered to the Peace Corps house. It made ice which the Peace Corps gave to the children. She thought of their fridge, pushed into the corner. It hadn't worked for years. They used it as a cupboard for bottles of warm Coke and Fanta.

Some of the more ignorant women had been amusing themselves by taking their young children to the white woman's house. Some of the women had been scaring their children with silly stories of white people stealing African babies to eat. The infants were frightened by all that white skin. They had never seen a white person before. When they screamed, the women hooted with merriment, and Miss Wendy looked hurt and confused.

However, the American's behavior was beside the point; the latrine must be built. It was a matter of pride. Ma Kamanda did not want Miss Wendy writing to other Americans that she lived in a backward village in a tumble-down house with no latrine.

The Paramount Chief was asleep in his hammock when she arrived. One of his many children yelled in his ear. When his eyes popped open, the child ran away, shrieking with glee.

The old man greeted her with great courtesy and let her speak. She could not speak to him in English, for he knew only two words: "Kennedy" and "OK".

Yes, he knew a Peace Corps had arrived. He was still waiting for the new teacher to greet him here at his compound. It was her duty to come here. Yes, he had heard about the state of her house. But it had been attended to, not so?

Yes, agreed Ma Kamanda, but there was still some outside plastering and inside ceiling mats to be taken care of. The main reason for her visit concerned a latrine.

The chief sighed deeply. Surely, she had not lived in Freetown so long she had forgotten how official duties were handled in the village. The sanitary inspector was in charge of latrines. The matter could be taken up with him, but the ultimate responsibility lay with the owner of the house.

"Oh life, oh country," she moaned as she left the chief's compound. It was true that living in Freetown had made her impatient with village ways. The sanitary inspector lived in a new house right on the Kenema Road.

"Terror in Tokyo" was loading up in front of the petrol pump. Passengers reached through side slats to buy cakes and groundnuts from the huge trays carried by women and children. A white hand reached out to exchange a five-cent piece for a handful of nuts. What was the Peace Corps doing on a lorry in the middle of the week? The white woman turned to say something to the passengers next to her. Ma Kamanda ran with jerky steps, as quickly as her lapa would allow. She tapped the white woman's back. "Where are you going? Are you ill?"

The woman turned her big white face. The forehead was wrinkled in puzzlement. Ma Kamanda saw that this woman was not her Peace Corps. Up close, Ma could see that this one didn't have light hair and was fleshier than Miss Wendy. "Excuse me. I have made a mistake."

How difficult, she thought, to live in a country where everyone else was another color. Perhaps that was why Miss Wendy spent so much time in her house.

It seemed as if the gods were against her, for when she reached the sanitary inspector's house, she was told that he had gone to Sefadu. She would have to take matters into her own hands.

On Friday afternoon the Peace Corps came into the store. Ma Kamanda was behind the counter. Her husband's leg had been troubling him, so he had been resting a lot. The days of her being able to count on his strength and constancy were over.

"Hello, my dear. A letter came for you." She handed over a thin blue envelope.

"Finally. Oh thank you! This is wonderful!" For a moment Ma thought Miss Wendy might leap over the counter and embrace her. She had never seen the Peace Corps so animated. She must be very very lonely in this village.

"How is your husband?" asked the Peace Corps in a rush of interest. "He's such a knowledgeable man. He was telling me about the railroad years ago. I'd be afraid to get on it now."

"Yes, things are not the same. I think if the leg does not improve, he will need to go to Freetown to see our doctor." She lowered her voice. "The clinics are not so good in this province. It is best to go to Freetown." She noted the large satchel. "You will be away?"

"I'm going all the way to Sefadu to visit some other volunteers for the weekend. I'll return Sunday night. Is there anything I can get for you?"

Her heart was touched by the thoughtfulness of Miss Wendy. "As a matter of fact, there is. Wait a moment, please." She disappeared behind the curtain that separated the living quarters from the store.

She returned with a folded piece of paper. With care she smoothed out a deeply creased page from a magazine on the counter. It was an ad for perfume. A white woman in a long dress was being kissed passionately by a man as he pressed her against a grand piano. "I would like a bottle of this scent. One of the Lebanese shops, perhaps the one near the cinema, should have it."

The Peace Corps gave the older woman a questioning look. "You are sure this is all you want?"

"Yes, my dear, that is all." She put the ad and a five-pound note into the pale moist hand.

As she watched Miss Wendy hoist herself onto the lorry, she thought how much easier for an African to adapt to Western ways than for an American to adjust to Africa.

Her husband's snores filled the tiny bedroom. She reached far under the bed and pulled out a biscuit tin. She had been saving for the visit to Monrovia, but this matter was more urgent.

The Peace Corps' house slept in the Saturday afternoon heat. The air shimmered around its tin roof. Ma Kamanda squinted in the glare at the empty house. It hadn't rained all day; the gods were with her. But around the green top of Monkey Mountain, the sky was growing thick and purple. The workmen, their bodies shiny with sweat, had just poured the cement pad outside the door of the new latrine when she arrived. The little building looked lovely with a tall papaya tree rising behind it. The village was quiet.

The roof and sides were corrugated tin. She stretched to lift the latch on the door and peeked in, holding her lapa from wet cement. The structure was divided in two by a partition. One side contained a wooden box with a proper hole cut in it. A fine wooden lid covered the seat. On the other side was the bathing area with a drain in the middle of the floor. Ma Kamanda squeezed her hands together under her chin in approval.

"A fine, fine job," she said, paying the men with the pound notes smelling faintly of ginger biscuits.

She searched the surrounding bush for what she needed. Alone, she knelt beside the bit of cement leading to the door. She drove the stick deep in the cement as she wrote:

A GIFT TO THE U.S. GOVERNMENT
FROM THE PEOPLE OF PUNUMBA

Then she wrote the date. She hesitated, then added in smaller letters:

Presented by Kadiatu Kamanda

Overhead, the sky rumbled in its predictable, comforting way.

How I Came To Write This Story

*When I returned to the Solomons in 1991, I was struck by how
aggressive and "less traditional" many young Solomon Islands women
had become since my Solomons stay in the late 1970s. I wrote a long
essay, started a novel, tried to figure out how best to present these
"new" Solomons. Then, I read* Bridges of Madison County, *and
marveled at its enormous success (sales, readers): a modern colonial
romance where the white man sails in, not to an island paradise, but
to Iowa, finds a willing native gal (who, in Iowa, is married and an
Italian import), has a delicious romp, then sails off. Best of all, said
romp satisfies the native gal for life. Some stud! So I put Waller's hero
in the Solomons, and introduced him to the thoroughly modern Esme.
"American Model" resulted. Esme still puzzles me—I can't understand
why she doesn't always "act like a Solomon Islander," but I know that
deep down traditional values still guide her. She, like Francesca in*
Bridges, *might succumb to the charms of a visiting prince—certainly
many Solomon Islands women do—but I doubt it. Intercultural
relations are more complicated than they seem on the surface.*
— *Terry Marshall*

TERRY MARSHALL (Philippines, 1965-1967) grew up in southern
Colorado, taught English as a Volunteer in Tacloban City, Leyte, from
1965-67; was co-director with his wife, Ann, of Peace Corps programs
in the Solomon Islands, Kiribati, and Tuvalu from 1977-80; and held
several positions with Peace Corps/Washington from 1980-82. He is the
author of *The Whole World Guide to Language Learning* (Intercultural
Press), *101 Ways to Find an Overseas Job,* and *Carlsbad.* He lives in
Carlsbad, New Mexico.

AMERICAN MODEL

by Terry Marshall

I posed as a model by accident, I swear it. I told Mother it was God's will. "Yes, it must be God's will," she sighed. She is a good Catholic, and had no other answer.

But I confess: that accident was something more also.

My cousin-sister and I were acting crazy in the window of Guadalcanal Arts and Artifacts, when the American photographer passed by on Mendana Avenue. He was the accident, that Kincaid.

Jully, my cousin-sister, manages Guadalcanal Arts. I come to stori with her, to make days not boring. I am at loose ends. At the new year I begin graduate school in Canberra. Four months! I bide my time. I read, draw, stori with Jully. I taught briefly, Pijin language to expatriates, but that program ended. Mother wishes me to marry. "Esme, you are twenty-four!" she wails. I am not ready, nor is there anyone. We have lived here in the capital city, in Honiara, long enough that Father does not insist to arrange a marriage.

Today Jully tells me, "Look, Esme, Mr. Cremmins bought this bride's headband, an antique from your mother's village." (Mr. Cremmins is Jully's bossman, a whiteman from Australia. He lives in Solomon Islands sixteen years now.)

The headband is old, a century, but flawless. It is more than four fingers high, of tiny shell monies, the rare red ones, ground by a woman's hand flat and round as collar buttons, then strung on a cord woven of coconut fiber and a virgin's hair. One hundred polished porpoise teeth dangle as even as pearls from the bottom hem. I cannot resist; I must wear it. "May I?"

"I set it aside for you," Jully says.

I model before the mirror. This bridal headband tugs me like an insistent child, Come, Esme, come! Your village calls, tradition calls! Were I to return to my ancestral village, this headband would be one sparkle in a glittering array. I would parade through the village. All would bow in praise. My wedding would spawn a week of feast-days. My uncle is chief.

In the mirror, I seem a street urchin playing dress-up. A bride's headband looks foolish with a t-shirt. Jully thinks so also. She says, "Like high heels on a market vendor, eh?"

Jully's eyes dare me, and I accept her challenge. She rushes off, returns with a bandolier of red and white shell monies draped on her arm like a flowing robe, a Lau wedding sash. She has also a betrothal apron of maku, the pounded bark-cloth made by ancient Lau people.

I was twelve when we fled Sulufou to Honiara. Village life swims into memory: plant, dig, haul sweet potato; carry water; build a pit-fire, cook; tend children; so much work—but also hours free. Pre-menses, we girls ran naked. I was a butterfly tasting each bush, drawing nectar from every blossom, a barefoot skinny girl, fast as wind. Mother wore a tattered skirt, nothing more. In Honiara, we are moderns. We laugh at village women who go bare-breasted as if today were fifty years past.

At Teachers College, I formed Kakamora, a club to revive traditional dance. We crafted our outfits to be authentic—each shell necklace, headband, bark skirt, ankle rattle. But we were city girls, we refused to dance bare-breasted, not from shame—for a woman's susus are a gift from God—but to set ourselves above village girls, uneducated girls. We wore Bali bras beneath our shell necklaces, cotton panties under native skirts. The boys cat-called and laughed. They shamed us. Now we dance as Solomon Islanders should, and proudly. Men and boys neither ogle nor jeer, but admire the beauty of antiquity. A woman can be modern without rejecting her heritage, I have learned that.

Jully's attentiveness melts to an impish grin. "I think you fear a bride's jewels, Esme. Do they scare you?"

I look straight into Jully's eyes. "Me, afraid? Ha!"

I strip off my modern t-shirt. Jully drapes the bandolier of shell monies over my head and shoulder, arranges it over my susus. I shed my cloth skirt and panties and city ways. Jully ties the maku string at my hips. We flit about like wild parrots, adding braided armlets, ankle bracelets, rows of tiny knee beads, giant bone earrings, a yellow and red Kwaio comb to my hair, all the time screeching for the joy of it.

Now I prance through the store, waggling my bare bottom. The blue maku apron covers only in front, and only a hand's width. Jully thumps a beat on the shop's largest slit-drum, and my strings of shell monies sing click-clack, clickity-clack.

She guides me into the window display. "Stand here, Miss Village Bride, so the sun may enhance your charms."

"Ah, now I am lovely. You can present me for marriage."

"Yes, I shall. But who will be the husband?"

"No matter," I shrug. "A man is a man."

She laughs. She knows I do not believe that.

She studies me, as if I were an ebony carving to be priced for sale. She says, "Yes, humm, good, but we lack something." She studies me more. "Humm...ah, yes, oil!"

True, a bride must be oiled. "But this is a gallery, not the public market. We have no coconut oil."

"I know it." She stands, discouraged, then races to the counter and gets her bag. "Here, a jar of cold cream."

"And color me white? For shame! A proper bride glistens like obsidian, not a bland and milky coconut."

"True." She pauses, then digs under the counter, "I have it— Teak Oil! It makes our carvings gleam, and preserves them."

I arch my back to point my susus. They stand tall, though draped in heavy shell monies. "I am well preserved now, sister."

"In shape only; those old susus are as dull as coconut shells."

I swing at her, but she dodges, and again we are giggling children. Jully pours Teak Oil into her cupped hand and slathers me until I truly glisten. "Now, you are a model bride."

"Oh, no, not yet! I lack the itch to submit my virginhead."

"Aeii, Esme, you embarrass me."

As usual, we chatter, laugh, tell lusty stories.

I am storying, a tale of the one-toed nasty man, when Jully motions with her eyebrows. A whiteman tourist presses against the window. He hangs mid-stride, staring back at me as if, like Lot's wife, God struck him to stone. Whitemen go crazy for naked susus, I know that from the cinema. My susus are firm, not saggy like an old village woman's. My nipples are prominent and dark as ebony. I readjust my bridal bandolier, and one susu bounds free. The whiteman comes to life. He turns, and enters the shop.

"Good afternoon, Sir. May I help you?" Jully says. She is so polite, but laughter swells her breast, I feel it.

"Nah, I'm just looking." He wanders the shop. He examines

each carving, takes a spear and pretends to be a warrior, holds a shell necklace to the light. He is down each aisle, back again, working his way toward me, even yet in the window.

He gazes at me—no, not gaze—leers! "My, this carving of a woman is remarkably life-like," he says. He touches my arm and I shrink away. "Well, well, she isn't a carving after all."

"Sir, I am a bride-to-be." My voice is cold ice.

His lips move, as if to engage a retort, but no sound comes. Finally, he says, "And a very beautiful bride-to-be!" He blurts it, like a shy boy with an unfamiliar burst of confidence.

"Actually, Sir, I am modeling an antique bride's headband."

He stares, but not at my headband. "You are an exquisite model!" he says. He wishes to say more, I feel it, but his face blushes red, as only whitemen can do. He looks away.

I ask, "You are from America, Sir?"

"Yes, Bellingham."

I do not know Bellingham, but asking about America loosens his tongue. Soon, we are talking, Jully and I with him. He is doing a "shoot," he is a photographer. He starts to tell more, but a white woman enters the shop, a New Zealander from the sound of her greeting, and Jully must attend her.

The American wants to photograph me. He says, "You're incredibly beautiful, exactly what I'm looking for."

"Oh, yes, I know that!" I say. He is like those young boys in secondary school, saying pretty things so I will favor them. But he is older than Father, my goodness, and white haired.

"No, I'm serious," he says. "Strictly business. I'm doing a shoot on Sulufou, the big artificial island off Malaita. I've studied their customs. You're exactly what I have in mind."

"Sulufou?"

"Yes, have you been there?"

I only nod, but I wonder, Does he know it is my village?

More tourists enter. Jully's shop overflows with shoppers. A cruise ship must be docked at Point Cruz. Two approach us.

"Look, I'm keeping you from your work. May I explain this over dinner? I'm at the Mendana Hotel." He gives me from his shirt pocket a small paper and says, "My card!"

That he knows of Sulufou intrigues me. I will do it, even if Mendana Hotel is for whitemen. "Yes."

"Tonight?"

"Yes, eight o'clock," I say.

He lumbers off, tall as a giraffe, arms swinging, footsteps heavy. Americans are so awkward—especially in dancing. Jully says it is so cold in America their hips freeze, that is why they are so graceless. I think so. This American is odd. At first he seemed a Peacecorps—shaggy hair, faded bluejeans, workman's boots. But he wears a khaki soldier's shirt with long sleeves. No Peacecorps would do that, they know the heat. Nor wear orange suspenders! That makes me laugh. Even though Peacecorps now sends olos, men with hair gray as his, this man seems something different. His card says, "Robert Kincaid, Writer-Photographer, National Geographic, Washington, DC," also an address and phone.

I know National Geographic. So beautiful a magazine, and friend to the world. Photography is an art, I know that, and a photographer an artist. I will talk of Sulufou with Kincaid, but I will not dance with him. I am graceful; he would embarrass me.

I am something late to Mendana Hotel, half-past eight.

The maitre d' greets me, "Ho, Esme, why are you here?" He is a classmate from Teachers College.

"Oh, Tovua! An American waits me for dinner."

Tovua's eyebrows arch, but he smiles. "Well, it must be you, then. One guest told me, 'When the most beautiful girl in Solomon Islands arrives, please show her to my table.'"

"He said that?"

"Yes."

"Aeii, he embarrasses me! But he does not know our customs. He is a photographer from America, and wishes to talk of Sulufou. He had no other time to meet. Will you chaperone us?"

"But Esme, I am on duty."

"No, not to eat with us, only to watch, and if any gossips are about, to verify that we only talked, and nothing more."

"But Esme, that is not the same, you should—"

"Jully could not come, nor other friends." Tovua is such a goody-two-shoes, young, but mired in tradition. I touch his arm lightly, and ask him in our Lau language, "Please, Tovua, this is important to Sulufou, and to me."

Tovua surrenders, "You know me, Esme. I will do it."

Kincaid jumps up when Tovua presents me. He has consumed already three Fosters, the empty cans like hollow tattletales betraying his vice. The ashtray overflows with cigarette butts. He says, "Well, Miss, you did come!" He traps my hand in his. He leans too close. He reeks of stale cigarettes and beer. I hate those stinks, both. I glide away, but greet him politely, tilting my head and saying, "Mr. Kincaid, good evening." I slide into the corner booth, and Kincaid sits again. I scoot away so we are not touching. Tovua steps back. He is watching over us.

A waiter comes. I know him also, cousin of a friend. He brings water and a menu, and Kincaid asks, "Would you like a drink?" He means liquor, but I do not. Liquor is a sin to God.

We look the menus, and order dinner, and Kincaid says, "You know, I didn't get your name."

"I am Esme Soporo, a Lau of Malaita, but I do not have a card. I read that you are Mr. Robert Kincaid, an American."

Kincaid grins. Something of him attracts me, though he is sweaty-faced, not handsome. He is rugged, like Clint Eastwood in the cinema. Or maybe it is his eyes, not only their blue color, but some intrigue, some wisdom sharpened by years of travel. He says, "Call me Bob." It makes me laugh, "Bob," a blop like an escaped fart. I call him by his real name, Robert, as is proper.

Kincaid brims over with tales of so many places. He has been everywhere, even Africa and China. He displays a folder of his photographs: a tiny island in India emerging from the mist; Machu Picchu, a dead city, also Indian, but a different tribe; a bridge in Iowa. He shows many pictures of Iowa, corns growing, taller than kunai grass on Bloody Ridge, and wooden bridges with roofs and sides. "You speak as if Iowa were Heaven," I tell him.

He laughs. "Yes, it is, I guess."

Dinner comes. Mine is a small steak, filet mignon. Also rice. Kincaid has a stir fry, but without meat. Also potato.

He says, "Bon appetit!" He begins to eat.

I gaze at him. When he looks up, I whisper, "I cannot eat. I do not know how to use the eating utensils of the whiteman." Even though I know very well, I tell him that to test how well he understands our people. How will he treat me now?

He leans toward me and whispers, "Do what I do." His lips brush my hair. He exaggerates his motions with knife and fork, but discreetly so other diners do not see. I mimic him as if I am a village girl, not of the city at all. Also I mimic that he holds his knife in his right hand, cuts, then transfers his fork from left to right, unlike we, who eat in the British style, more efficiently, with knife always in the right and fork to the left.

Oh, my, I drop a cut piece of steak.

"Don't worry. It's okay," he mouths. "Try again."

I fork another piece, and this time bring it correctly to my mouth. I smile, and he gives a wink of the eye.

"You are a good teacher, Mr. Robert Kincaid."

He only shrugs. Yet his eyes sparkle, the creases soften. Whitemen love to display their talents, and instruct others.

Dinner is a blessing, eating occupies us. When we finish, nothing camouflages our silence. He tries to make conversation: "Your gallery is interesting. How long have you worked there?"

I explain that Jully manages the shop. I go to visit.

He is silent. Then, "And what do you do? Student?"

He is surprised I am a graduate, but that news frees him to talk again. Educated men love to talk of education. And I also, I chatter on about my plans. "Probably I will study cultural anthropology. Maybe journalism or literature—I love to write. Or art—I paint, village scenes, facial sketches."

He asks, "You have so many talents. Why anthropology?"

I had not thought of why before, only that I wanted to. Now, it hits me: in anthropology my interests converge. We need an islands literature, not academic treatises. My art illustrates what words cannot convey. I tell him, "Solomons draw academics like moths to a lantern, many quite famous—but all whites, and all male. Melanesians should not be defined by Europeans...or Americans. I will write true stories of our people."

Kincaid only gnaws at his knuckles, like a daydreamer, not speaking. At last he says, "That never occurred to me, but it's true, isn't it?" He leans toward me, "Esme, you're amazing!"

"No, not amazing; only becoming educated," I say softly. It is best to be gracious. He is a visitor.

Kincaid knows how to listen, he is attentive. He asks questions. With his own vignettes, he shades in the meaning of feelings I cannot express. He recites poetry, also lines from *A Passage to India*. He loves India, also Iowa.

I tell him of Lau. We are a special people. Stone by stone, my ancestors created living islands in the sea, without machines, without slaves. They drove no pilings, mixed no mortar, merely gathered stones and piled one onto another until a mound rose from the sea, then covered it with sand and earth hauled in their canoes. From their labor, villages grew.

"Sulufou is the island of my mother," I tell Kincaid. "I was born on that island, though now we live in Honiara."

"No!" he says, as if to call me a liar.

"I swear it, as God is my witness."

Kincaid takes a long drink from his beer—his sixth. He searches my face, he tries to look inside me. "I knew it, somehow I knew it," he whispers. "It's destiny."

I only smile. He is talking nonsense, or a wornout line.

Of Sulufou, Kincaid has nothing but praise. Tomorrow, he will fly to Auki, hitchhike a truck to North Malaita, hire a canoe to Sulufou. He will do a shoot, then his article.

"Your man-made islands are a wonder, amazing as the rice terraces in the Philippines," Kincaid says. "But islands are things. Only remarkable people create monuments. My photographs will capture the strength and persistence and beauty of the Lau people. When I saw you in the window today, I knew you were the perfect model. Pose for me, Esme. I will make your face known to the world. Every time people hear the name Solomon Islands, your beauty will appear in their minds."

I am beautiful, in face and form, and I have already seven boy-friends, but only to stori with, and dance, not marriage. Women should date many men, not one, nor accept to be betrothed by their fathers as was the old custom. But beauty is a blessing of God, not of being Lau. Many Lau women are plain, and many from other islands are blessed equally as I. Thus, Kincaid honors me to represent Solomon Islands to the world.

Also, I do not tell him this: Mr. Cremmins gave Jully a small camera. She photographs me, and me, her. We sneak-look the magazines Mr. Cremmins and his wife buy from Australia and America, and paper the walls of our bedrooms with our own poses.

"Yes, I will do it," I tell Kincaid.

He says, "Great! I'll postpone my trip to Sulufou," and he becomes so talkative, full of plans, full of desires.

Next day I wear my favorite outfit to Mendana Beach, so the world will meet a modern Solomon Islander: black and red Spandex bicycling pants (sent me by Mr. Cremmins' daughter in Brisbane); a white tube top from Alice's Boutique; my new Teva sandals. I wear also my Mickey Mouse wrist watch, and a gold necklace chain with a Mini Mag-lite, gifts from Peacecorps guys. I fluff my hair like a jungle fern, and top it with a spray of red hibiscus.

Kincaid waits me at the far end of the beach, beyond the great mango tree. Cameras hang from him like leeches. He waves, and starts toward me. He halts, throws both hands to his hips, like an angry father seeing his daughter come home late. I check Mickey. Ha, I am early, not yet half-four in the afternoon.

"My God, girl, what have you done?"

My mouth only opens. I have done nothing, I swear it.

"Your outfit! Where is the marriage costume?"

"Marriage costume?"

"From the store...headdress, necklaces, blue G-string."

He makes me laugh. "You are silly. I am a modern woman."

"No, don't you see, that outfit was perfect, I—"

He stops mid-sentence, as if a crocodile snapped his voice from the air. "Of course, a modern woman. Yes, a modern woman who knows and appreciates the past." He is playing with the camera, pointing it at me. "Contrasting photos, that's perfect! I'll show you in both worlds." He squiggles his pointer finger as if writing on air, "Spanning history, today's Solomon Islands women step gracefully between present and past." I see no words, but Kincaid acts as if he has sketched a masterpiece.

He poses me, and so many pictures. "Walk toward me. Good, good! Swing your arms, lift your chin, turn to the side, other side, look here, look there, arch your back," and all the time snapping photos, changing cameras. I sit on a rock, a log, in the sand. He stands, shooting down. He plops onto the sand, shoots up. I lean against the mango and cross my arms over my susus. I smile, pout, tease with my eyes. He puts more film. I throw my hands high, lock them behind my neck, stand with one hand behind my hip, kneel in the surf, sit, splash water, stretch a leg, both legs, twist sideways and smile or say cheese and look away or imagine my boy-friends or silly things. Kincaid darts around me like a coral trout, never resting, eyes alert, hands posing me, stepping back, stepping close, changing lenses, all the time talking, talking, talking. He talks even to his camera.

Shadows lengthen. Sunset pauses. I did not see it.

"A few close-ups and we'll call it a day," he says. He moves toward me, cameras clanking. With his hands, he positions my face, directs me, "Turn, turn...a bit more. I want to get your tattoos." He says that, as if my Lau marks are a tourist site, like Sulufou village or a half-sunken World War II ship. But I am Lau, proud of my lineage, and its mark—scar circle on each cheek, three scar lines toward the temple, two lines each to nose-bridge and jaw. I nod, yes.

Strong hands touch my cheeks, tender fingers trace my scars. He oozes desire. His hands slip to my shoulders, brush my susus, rest at my hips. Within me also, heat surges from my very soul, my heart is a pounding slit-drum. He has made this day special, I am indebted that he chose me as his model. That he is old, and I young, seems as nothing, nor that he is a whiteman and I, black. Touch erases such differences. His lips press toward me. I am willing. I close my eyes and try to imagine he is Po'hoa, my boyfriend. I cannot; the stench of cigarette breath forbids me. Above the surf, a fruit bat squeals, coconut crabs scurry through the rip-rap. The spell is broken. I am body-to-body with a whiteman on a public beach, about to kiss him. In Solomon Islands, every coconut has an eye, and each a dozen busy tongues. Kincaid is a photographer, seeking to create illusions. Beyond that, I do not know him, not as I know Po'hoa of Sulufou. This Kincaid blazes into my life like a meteor in the night sky, but he offers only a moment of bliss, maybe a haunting memory, nothing of commitment. He will move on, to another India or Iowa, to another passion.

"No! We cannot!" I turn aside. I am a modern woman, but I know how to control the sexual.

His kiss brushes my cheek. His eyes snap open. His hands engulf me again, draw my face toward him.

"No! I will not kiss you!" I push away.

His body sags. His eyes plead, but I am strong. His eyes narrow and he studies me. Again, he touches my scars. "Your tattoos—the design tells a story, doesn't it?"

I nod. I explain the cutting. He winces. He whispers, "Was it terribly painful to be tattooed?" His voice falters.

I laugh, as if it were a nothing. I say, "Is it terribly painful to be circumcised as they do in America?"

He is silent, no more talk of tattoos. I do not tell him of marking my cousin-sister last year. We use a hardwood sapling, hone it beyond a razor. We rub black ash into the open wound. When scabs form, we carve the other cheek, with the same result. Her mind will teach her to block away that pain, as mine did.

Some families no longer apply tattoos, especially those who left Malaita to work on Guadalcanal. We form new customs here, mixing Malaita and Guadalcanal people with those of every island.

When I marry and bear daughters, they will wear proudly the mark of Lau, but only in their heart and minds.

Kincaid says, "I'm sorry, Esme. I got carried away." He offers his hands, palms out, as if pushing me away, "Strictly business?"

"Can you do that, Sir?"

Our eyes meet, and he looks away, then back. "Yes!"

Kincaid backs away, begins shooting again. He circles like the shark. No talking now. Suddenly, he drops his camera to his side. "OK, we've got some keepers. But I still want you as a bride. Can you borrow that outfit? Early tomorrow?"

Posing is my dream, I love it. And lust no longer burns in his eyes, only work. "Yes, I will come. Jully will lend them to me." But tomorrow, I will bring Jully. I do not tell him that.

He says, "You know, it'll work out better this way. We reverse the stereotypes: modern girl in setting sun; traditional bride in dawn's early light."

Next morning, Jully and I are at Mendana before sunlight. Kincaid also. Jully dresses me. Kincaid shoots. He prowls the beach as yesterday, checking light, checking background, cameras clicking, go here, go there. But he poses me without touching. He snaps also photos of Jully, and we two together.

We finish close-up half-past seven. Kincaid rushes off to breakfast, then to Solair to arrange his flight to Malaita. He promises to come for us when he gets back, and tell us of his shoot in Sulufou. I go with Jully to her shop.

The cruise ship has gone. Jully's shop is empty. We stori. We are famous models now, but posing is only one something. We have boys and cinema and church to engage us. Mendana Avenue is Honiara's main street. As people walk by, we imagine their thoughts by their stride and expression. Our mouths go dry from talking. "I am dying of thirst," I gasp. I collapse in the agony of a Legionnaire lost on desert sands, and Jully dashes out for a Coca-Cola to rescue me from sure death.

Jully is gone too long. A customer enters and I must wait on him. He looks, but buys nothing.

Jully rushes back in, panting.

"Aeii, Esme, you are being gossiped! With that Kincaid!"

Her news pierces me like a volley of spears: alone with a white man on Mendana beach. Kisses. Caresses. Intimate dinner. She slept with him, that Esme, she snuck from his room at dawn.

"Your Auntie says your brothers have heard these rumors. They are coming, you must hide," Jully warns.

I have dishonored Lau custom. They will thrash me for it. Girls have died from such beatings. Nor is there recourse: that I am gossiped is guilt enough. I hate it.

"I cannot. That is our tradition."

"Yes, but a tradition outdated as slavery, or cannibalism. We are modern women, not chattel. Come, I must hide you!"

"Where? They know the island. I cannot hide."

"I know a place. Come!"

Jully locks the shop, sneaks me into the alley, into Mr. Cremmins' Land Rover. "It is OK. I drive it to pick up art works," she says. She hides me; I am a copra sack on the floor.

Jully drives past the airport, past the villages, takes a sandy trail into the forest of the palm oil plantation. The road ends. Jully searches, finds a shrouded path. We hike, and come to a palm-leaf house, isolated as a leper's hut. "You will be safe here. The father is a carver; his wife is a friend," Jully says. "I will find a way to dissuade your brothers."

Comes the next night. Jully brings news: gossip ferments; my brothers rant, as well Father. Kincaid remains in Honiara—my friends at Solair have sold out every flight; all inter-island boats to Malaita are full. Sulufou is off-limits. Nor can he leave Solomons. His passport has walked away from his room.

"An embassy friend of Mr. Cremmins will help," Jully says. "He will negotiate between your father and the American."

I can only wait, and have faith in Jully. I help the family in their gardens, and haul wood. I am their instant daughter.

Another day passes.

Comes morning. Jully hails our hut from the trail. I go outside. Father stands beside her, and with an angry pose.

"Did you sleep with the whiteman, Daughter?"

"No, Father. I met him only to pose for photographs."

"Did you do anything to dishonor yourself, or us?"

"No, Father, nothing. Only posing."

"Before God you swear it?"

"Yes, Father, especially to God."

He nods. "Yes, this is as Jully tells me. And the whiteman also. He paid a proper compensation. You may come home."

Kincaid is nothing to me now, another passing whiteman, a photographer, tourist, contract worker, Peacecorps. They sniff at the boundaries of our world, do their business or foolishness, disappear. Kincaid went to Sulufou. I did not see him again.

From the negotiation, Kincaid paid my family 250 dollars American and two small pigs to quiet the gossip. Jully demanded he compensate me with a camera, for his cameras were the root of these problems. Kincaid objected, but Chief Gwali Asi of Sulufou said it must be done, or Kincaid would never see Sulufou. I have that camera with me, this Hasselblad of Kincaid's, and film also.

Compensation closed the matter. Any who gossip of Kincaid and me violate custom law. They would pay dearly at the fists of my brothers, who remain eager to protect their sister's honor.

Two years pass. A package comes from America: National Geographic, five copies. As well, a dozen photographs of me at Mendana beach, modern girl and traditional, and two of Jully. He was true to his word, that Kincaid.

As for the magazine, I, Esme, am the cover, innocent bride, "Girl of Malaita's Artificial Islands." Inside displays Sulufou to the world—our island at dawn, fishermen, grandmother's leaf house, the church, an uncle in his canoe, hauling coral rock. Also a small photo of Jully and me, arm-in-arm in modern dress, and Chief Gwali Asi in ceremonial necklace and chief's medallion.

I take my package to Guadalcanal Arts at closing. Jully and I study each photo. Tiny memories flicker from the background of Kincaid's houses and faces and sceneries.

"There, behind that tree, Po'hoa first kissed me," I say.

"And what more, what more?" Jully begs. I only wink.

Jully thumbs Kincaid's magazine. There are other peoples also, peoples of Indonesia and Canada. Whooping cranes. A dirty river. A circus troop in America, with a hunchback midget.

Jully points out a tiny picture at the back of the magazine. "Look, it is that photographer!" It is Kincaid, cameras still hanging like leeches, but also with a necklace of porpoise teeth. Jully brings Mr. Cremmins' reading glass. Kincaid wears also his silver medallion, but on the Sulufou necklace, not its chain. It is pure silver, from Spain, he said, inscribed Francesca. We saw it the morning Jully and I posed for him. It fell from his shirt when he bent to take a photograph. I challenged him, "You are married, Mr. Kincaid?" He blushed. "No, not married. Not with a legal document. Francesca is my soul-mate. I wear her name over my heart so she will always be with me." He looked away, he could not face me, and whispered, "Forgive me, Esme. I am a weak man." I only shrugged, for I was angry, and hurt. I thank God for my resolve. Love is a sacred gift, not a plaything.

Jully and I spread Kincaid's photos on the counter. They are big ones, each larger than a page in National Geographic. We study each carefully, as Jully would inspect a carver's work.

"They show us to be modern women, eh?" Jully says.

I think so, but I feel an emptiness. I only nod.

We pick them up, each one. We turn them, study them.

"We pose as they do, Esme..." Her thoughts trail off.

I am wondering also. Disappointment claws within me.

Suddenly, Jully shrieks. She dashes to the back room, to Mr. Cremmins' office. Drawers open and bang shut. She sails back into the show room, clutching an armload of magazines like squirming babies. She spreads them on the counter, opens them to the fold-out pages. "Look, it is how they wear their clothes that makes them modern girls, not only the pose."

"Yes, I see it."

We race out together, to Jully's house and mine. We go beyond Mendana beach, beyond the mangroves. No one comes here.

Jully strips off her working clothes. I anoint her with oil. She drapes herself in a length of bright cloth, its mesh open as mosquito netting. She poses in halter top, unbuttoned blouse, bikini suit, in off-shoulder dress, in lava-lava slung low at her hips. I am busy as Kincaid with my Hasselblad, posing her, circling, shooting, checking background, checking light.

Jully glistens in the setting sun. Lengthening shadows enhance her dark beauty, she is more alluring than the pale girls in those magazines. Jully does not pose like girls in *Penthouse*, nor will I. They are nasty poses, nasty girls.

"OK, we've got it," I shout. I drop the camera to my side. "You are perfect, Miss Jully."

Now I become the graceful porpoise, leaping, twisting, posing my woman's curves to my friend's discriminating eye.

America will soon know the modern Solomon Islands woman, for we soon shall be featured in *Vogue* and *Mademoiselle*.

How I Came To Write This Story

During my years as a Peace Corps Volunteer in Ethiopia, school strikes were quite common. It was the only way students could protest their grievances, but rarely did these strikes involve the military or the police. While there never was a strike at the secondary school in Diredawa, I placed the story in this beautiful town on the edge of the Ogaden Desert because I loved the town's wide shadowy streets, the old market place, and the cool breeze that came up every evening off the desert. As for what happens to the volunteer. Well, there is always plenty of opportunity for tragic comedy and plenty of cross-cultural misunderstandings whenever young Americans try to do good.
—John Coyne

JOHN COYNE (Ethiopia, 1962-64), a graduate of Saint Louis University and Western Michigan University, was with the first group of Volunteers to Ethiopia and taught English in Addis Ababa. Later he was an Associate Peace Corps Director in Ethiopia and the Regional Manager of the New York Peace Corps Office. He has published eight novels and edited, among other books, *Going Up Country: Travel Essays by Peace Corps Writers.* In 1989 he founded *RPCV Writers & Readers,* a newsletter for and about Peace Corps writers. He lives in Pelham Manor, New York.

SNOW MAN

by John Coyne

When Marc entered the classroom, "Peace Corps Go Home" had already been written on the blackboard. It was neatly done, and that eliminated all but two of the Ethiopian students.

They were watching him, but he only laughed. Stepping up to the board, he erased the words, deliberately sending a spray of dust into the room. The girls near the windows waved their arms to keep the dust away, and Kelemwork stood and opened one of the windows.

Nothing was said.

Marc arranged his books on the teacher's desk, making sure he looked busy and important before them. A few faces turned away. They were unsure of what he'd do and that made him feel better. Still, he had to take a couple of deep breaths to put a stopper on a wave of his own fear.

"You're unhappy about the quiz," he began, speaking slowly. Even though they were in the third year of secondary school, they still had a hard time understanding English. He spoke slowly, too, because it helped to calm his nerves. "All right! I'm unhappy, too! A teacher must set standards. You understand, don't you?"

He wondered how much they did understand. He crossed the front of the room, pacing slowly. No one was watching him.

"What do you want from me?" he shouted. "All hundreds? What good will that do you? Huh? How far will you get? Into fourth year? So what!" He kept shouting. He couldn't stop himself. His thin voice bounced off the concrete walls.

Still they sat unmoved. A few glanced in his direction, their brown eyes sweeping past his eyes. In the rear of the classroom Tekele raised his hand and stood.

"We want you to be fair, Mr. Marc."

"Am I not fair?"

Tekele hesitated.

"Go ahead, Tekele, speak up." Marc lowered his voice.

"You are difficult."

"Oh, I'm difficult. First I am unfair, now I am difficult."

Tekele did not respond. He looked out the window, and then sat down.

They kept silent. Marc stared at each one, letting the silence intensify. He could feel it swell up and fill his eardrums.

"All right," he told them. "We will have another test."

They stirred immediately, whispering fiercely in Amharic. Marc opened the folder on his desk and taking the mimeographed sheets began to pass them out, setting each one face-down on a desk, telling them not to start until they were told. When he came back to the front of the room he announced, "You have thirty minutes. Begin."

No one moved.

He walked slowly among the rows, down one, then the next, and when he reached the far left rear corner of the room, he said, "If you do not begin, I will fail everyone. You will all get zeros."

They did not move.

He went again to the front of the room, letting them have plenty of time.

"All right!" he said again, pausing. If just one of them would weaken, look at the quiz, he would have them. "That's all!" he announced. "You all get zeros. No credit for the quiz and I am counting it as an official test." He gathered his books into his arms and left the classroom.

As the door closed, the room ignited. Desks slammed. Students shouted. He turned from the noise and went along the second floor corridor and into the faculty room. Helen was there grading papers. She glanced at her watch when Marc entered and smiled, asking, "Did you let your class go?"

He shook his head.

"What, then?" She watched as he went to the counter and made himself a cup of tea.

"They won't take my quiz."

She waited for his explanation.

"I left them in the room."

"Marc!"

"They wrote 'Peace Corps Go Home' on the blackboard."

"My, they're out to get you." She smiled, sipping her tea and watching him over the rim of the cup. She had a small round face, much like a smile button, and short blond hair.

Marc wanted to slap her.

He heard footsteps on the stairs, voices talking in Amharic, and then silence as the class walked by the open door of the faculty room. The students were headed for the basketball court.

"What are you going to do?" Helen asked. She was trying to be nice.

"Nothing."

"Aren't you going to talk to Ato Asfaw?"

"Why should I? He said discipline was our problem."

Helen put down her cup. "Marc, you're making a mistake."

"You're the one who thinks it's so goddamn funny."

"Okay! I'm sorry I made light of your tragedy." She began again to correct her students' papers.

Marc sat with her, waiting for something to happen. The faculty room was hot. The dry, hot early morning of an African winter. Through the open windows, Marc could feel the hot winds off the Ogaden Desert. He was from Michigan and that morning he had heard on the shortwave radio that the American Midwest was having a blizzard. He tried to remember snow. Tried to remember the wet feel of it under his mittens when he was only ten and walking home from where the school bus left him on the highway.

He was still sitting staring out at the desert when the school guard came and said in Amharic that the Headmaster wanted to see him. Walking to the office, Marc glanced again at the arid lowlands and thought of snow blowing against his face. It made him feel immensely better.

"Mr. Marc," Ato Asfaw asked, "why are 3B on the playground?" The small, slight Headmaster was standing behind his desk.

"I left them in class. They refused to take my test." Marc sat down and made himself comfortable. He knew his casualness upset the Headmaster; it was an affront to the Ethiopian culture. In the two years that he had been in Ethiopia, he had learned what offended Ethiopians and he enjoyed annoying them.

"But you gave them a quiz last week." The Headmaster sat down behind his enormous desk, nearly disappearing from sight.

With his high, pronounced forehead and the finely sculptured face of an Amharia, he looked like the Emperor Haile Selassie.

"Yes, I gave them a quiz. They did poorly, so I decided to give them another one."

Asfaw nodded, hesitated a moment, then said, "3B has other complaints. They say you are not fair. They say you call them monkeys, tell them they are stupid."

"They're lying."

"They say you left the classroom, is this true?"

"They refused to take my quiz."

"Perhaps you may give them another chance."

"Why?"

"Because they are children, Mr. Marc. And you are their teacher." He spoke quickly, showing his impatience.

His desk was covered with papers typed in Amharic script. Stacks of thin sheets fastened together with small straight pins. How could he help a country that couldn't even afford paper clips, Marc wondered.

"I don't see them as children," he told the Headmaster. "Some of these 'boys' are older than I am. They know what they're doing. They wrote 'Peace Corps Go Home' on the blackboard." Marc stopped talking. He knew it sounded like a stupid complaint. Helen was right, yet he wouldn't back down in front of the Ethiopian. Americans never back down, he reminded himself.

"You have been difficult with them," the Headmaster went on, still speaking softly, as if discussing Marc's sins. "They are not American students; you are being unjust, treating them as such." He stood again, as if to gain more authority by standing.

"I am not treating them as American students or any other kind of student, except Ethiopians," Marc answered back. He crossed his legs, knowing it was another sign of disrespect.

"Mr. Marc, your classes in Peace Corps training taught you Ethiopian customs. Am I correct?"

Marc shrugged. They had all been told about culture shock, how everything in the new country would disorient them. But he had weathered "culture shock" of his own, he reminded himself, and said to the Headmaster, "This country has a history of school strikes, am I right?"

"Not a history, no. There have been some strikes. But over nothing as trivial as this! This quiz!" His voice rose as he finished the sentence.

"Well, what are you going to do?" Marc asked. He hooked his arm over the back of the chair.

Asfaw picked up a sheet of paper off his desk.

From where he sat, Marc saw the paper was full of handwritten Amharic notes.

"There are many complaints on this paper," the Headmaster said again. "The students are sending a copy to the Ministry of Education in Addis Ababa. Did I mention that?" He looked over at Marc, enjoying the moment. He had the brown saucer eyes of all Ethiopians. In the women, Marc found the eyes made them timid-looking and lovely. The same eyes made the men look weak.

"These complaints are lies. You know that!" Marc stood. "I want an apology before consenting to teach that class again." He turned and walked out of the Headmaster's office without being dismissed. It made him feel great, like the protagonist of his own life story.

The students in 3B were still on strike at the end of the week. Marc kept out of sight. He stayed in the faculty room when not teaching his other classes, spending his time reading old copies of *Time* magazine. None of the other teachers, including the other Peace Corps Volunteers, ever mentioned the strike. The Volunteers stationed at the school were the Olivers, a married couple from Florida, who lived out near the school, and Helen Valentino, who had an apartment next to his place.

The town was called Diredawa and it was built at the edge of the Ogaden. There was an old section which was all Ethiopian, mostly Somalis and Afars, and the newer quarter where the French had lived when they built the railway from Djibouti across the desert and up the escarpment to Addis Ababa in the Ethiopian highlands.

Marc never saw his students in town. He had no idea where they lived. Unlike the other Volunteers, he had never been asked to any of their homes for Injera and Wat. He thought about that when he was killing time in the faculty lounge waiting out his striking class period.

He did see the other students from his class, saw them as they passed along the open hallways, going from one class to another. They watched him with their brown eyes and said nothing, did not even take a sudden breath, as was the Ethiopian custom when making a silent note of recognition.

He thought of them as brown rabbits. Like the brown rabbits he hunted every fall back home on the farm. He liked to get close to the small animals, to see quivering brown bodies burrowing into the snow, and then he'd cock his .22 and fire quickly, catching the fleeing white-tail in mid-hop, splattering blood on the fresh whiteness.

Marc raised his hand and aimed his forefinger at his students lounging in the shade of trees beyond the makeshift basketball courts. He silently popped each one of them off with his make-believe pistol.

"Singh has had classes with 3B for the last week," Helen told him. "I just found out."

It was the second week of the strike when she came over to his apartment with the news. He was dressed in an Arab skirt and sitting on his bed chewing the Ethiopian drug chat. The chat gave him a low-grade high and a slight headache, but it was the only drug he could get at the edge of the desert.

"That bastard," Marc said.

"What are you going to do about it?" she demanded.

'   Marc shrugged. The chat had made him sleepy.

"We're all in trouble because of you," Helen told him. She was pacing the bedroom, moving in and out of the sunlight filtering through the metal shutters. The only way to keep the apartment cool was to lower the shutters during the long hot days.

"It's my class," he told her, grinning.

They had been lovers in training at UCLA, and during the first few months in Diredawa.

"Yes, but we're all Peace Corps!"

"Screw the Peace Corps."

"Marc, be serious!" She was in tears, and she was holding herself, trying to keep from crying.

"I am serious. I don't give a damn."

"I'm calling Morgan in Addis. I'm getting him down here," she shouted back.

He wanted to pull away the mosquito netting and ask her to climb into bed with him, but he didn't have the nerve.

"I don't want him here. I'll handle this," he told Helen.

"You just said you're not going to do anything. Look at you! Sitting here all day chewing chat!" she waved dismissively.

"Want some?" he asked, grinning through the thick netting.

Helen left him in his apartment. The chat had made him too listless to go running after her, to pull her back to his bed and make love to her. Besides, he knew she would call Morgan. She was always trying to run his life.

Marc went to the airport to meet the Peace Corps Director. It might have been more dramatic to let Brent Morgan find him, to track him down in one of the bars, to come in perspiring from the heat with his suit crumpled, his tie loosened. But then Helen would have had first chance at him, and Marc didn't want that.

The new airport terminal was under construction and there was nowhere to wait for the planes, so Marc parked the Peace Corps jeep in the shade of palm trees and watched the western horizon for the first glimpse of the afternoon flight from Addis.

He himself had first arrived in Diredawa on the day train. It was their second week in Ethiopia and all the Volunteers were leaving Addis Ababa for their assignments. They were the only ones traveling by train.

The long rains were over and they could see the clouds rolling away from the city, leaving a very pure blue on the horizon. It was still chilly, but not the piercing cold they had felt when they first arrived in country. No one had told them Ethiopia, or Africa, could be so cold. But they were going now, everyone said, to a beautiful climate, to warm country, to what Africa was really like.

It had been their first trip out of the city. They did not know anyone, and everything was new and strange. They sat together on metal benches and watched the plains stretch away towards the mountains as they dropped rapidly into the Great Rift Valley.

The land, after the long rains, was green and bright with yellow meskal flowers. On the hillsides were mushroom-shaped tukul huts, thick brown spots on the green hillside, in among the yellow flowers. There were few green trees and they were tall, straight eucalyptus which grew in tight bunches near the tukul compounds.

In the cold of early morning, Ethiopians were going off to church. They moved in single file across the low hills towards the Coptic church set in distant groves of eucalyptus. A few Ethiopians rode small, short-legged horses and mules, all brightly harnessed, and everyone on the soft hills wore the same white shammas dress and white jodhpurs.

Marc had never been so happy in his life.

Now, sitting in the shade, he saw the Ethiopian Airlines plane come into sight; and, spotting it, he realized his eyes were blurry and that he was crying.

Marc wondered why he was crying, but also he knew that lately he was always finding tears on his face and having no idea why he was crying.

The Peace Corps Director was the first off the plane. His coat and tie were already off and his collar was open. From the hatch of the small craft, he waved, then bounded down the ramp, swinging his thick brown briefcase from one hand to the other. He came over to where Marc sat in the front seat of the open jeep.

"*Tenastelign,*" Brent said, jumping into the front seat.

"*Iski. Indemin aderu,*" Marc answered in Amharic and spun the vehicle out of the dirt lot.

Brent grabbed the overhead frame as the small jeep swayed.

"Where do you want to go?" Marc shouted, glancing at the Peace Corps Director.

"School...?"

Marc nodded, and spun the jeep abruptly toward the secondary school.

Brent kept trying to make conversation, shouting to Marc over the roar of the engine, asking about the others, telling Marc news from Addis. Marc kept quiet.

He was being an asshole, he knew, but he couldn't help himself. He wanted Brent to have a hard time. It was crazy, but he couldn't stop.

When they reached the school, a few students were standing in the shade of the building, leaning up against the whitewashed wall and holding hands, as Ethiopian men did. Brent straightened his tie and put his coat on as they went to the Headmaster's office.

Asfaw stood when they entered the office, and he came around his desk to shake hands with them both, gesturing for them to sit. Brent began to talk at once in his quick, nervous way, telling the school director why he had come to Diredawa, explaining that the Ministry of Education, as well as the Peace Corps, was concerned about the situation with Marc's class.

Asfaw listened hard, frowned, nodded, agreeing with everything, as Marc had known he would. He nodded to Brent's vague generalizations about the Headmaster supporting the faculty, and the Ministry supporting both.

Marc wondered if Brent really believed all this bullshit.

"Of course, Mr. Marc has been very strict with his pupils," Asfaw finally said, not following up on what Brent had said.

"Well, perhaps," Brent answered, gesturing with both hands, as if he were trying to fashion some meaning of the situation from the hot desert breeze. "But that really isn't the question. I mean, in the larger sense." He pulled himself forward on the chair, straining to make himself clear. Then he stopped, saw Asfaw was not comprehending, saw a film of confusion cross the Headmaster's brown eyes, and asked, as if in defeat, "What do you think is the solution?"

"Mr. Mark is not very patient with our people. They are not used to his ways."

"There are certain universal ways of good behavior," Marc interrupted, raising his voice. "They deliberately did not take my test. That's an insult! And you! They know you're too afraid to do anything."

"All right! All right!" Brent spoke quickly, halting Marc.

Asfaw nodded, then began. "If you do not mind, Mr. Brent Morgan, I would like to say something." He looked for agreement and Brent nodded, gesturing with both hands.

"We have a strike in our school. Now this is something not unknown in our country. We have had many strikes. I have been in strikes when I was a student. I say this because I do not want Mr. Marc to feel he is being subjected to prejudice by his students. So, we must not say why do the students strike, but how can we bring them back to school.

"For Mr. Brent, you have said education is the most important for Ethiopia. We must not be so hidden by these petty problems, and look instead toward larger issues. Do you not agree? Is this not what you have said?" He glanced at both of them, his face as alert as a startled rabbit's.

"Why, yes," Brent answered hesitantly. "We can certainly agree, but let's not dismiss some basic educational principles."

"And what is this?"

"That a teacher commands a position of authority within the community, that the students respect this authority," the Peace Corps Director answered quickly.

"A teacher, I was told when I studied at Ohio University, achieved respect by proving to his students that he deserved it."

"Yes, this is very true, but it is difficult to achieve when the students know the teacher is alone in his authority," Morgan answered.

"Or when they would rather have a passing grade than an education," Marc butted in.

Asfaw smiled at Marc and said softly, like a caring parent, "To be truly honest, Mr. Marc, you, too, were probably concerned mostly with point averages, I believe the term is, when you were in school."

"Let us try," Brent began slowly, "to look at this issue again." He maintained a smile, adding, "We have been missing the main point. The strike must cease. The students must return to school. Now what avenues are open to us?"

"But I have made my decision!" Asfaw seemed surprised. He looked from face to face, his brown eyes widening.

"Certainly, but do you really think Marc should return to class without an apology from the students?"

"Oh, an apology is such a deceiving thing. Yes, perhaps in America, it is important, but you must remember this is Ethiopia. We have our own ways, don't we, Mr. Marc?" The Headmaster smiled, and then shrugged, as if it were all beyond his power.

"And in Ethiopia the mark of a clever man is the ability to outwit another person," Brent answered. "You must realize if Marc returns to his classroom without an apology, or some form of disciplinary action taken, he will be ineffective as a teacher."

The small man leaned forward, putting his elbows on the desk. "I will first lecture the class. I will tell them such demonstrations will not be tolerated. And Mr. Marc, if he wishes, can have them write an essay, which I will also see is done."

"And what will happen the next time I give a test?"

"I should think, Mr. Marc, as a clever person, you will review your teaching methods. I think that you are aware that none of the other teachers, including the Peace Corps, are having difficulty with their classes."

"I have to remain in authority in my class."

"I think Marc is correct. We must be united on this point. Take a firmer position," Brent added, making a fist with one hand.

"How might you handle it?" Asfaw asked Marc.

"Give them some manual work."

"They cannot do coolie work! They are students!"

"That's the point! They don't deserve to be students. A little taste of hard labor will prove my point. They won't mouth off again."

"It could be symbolic, I should think," Brent suggested. "You could arrange a clean-up of the compound, perhaps. It would be very instructive, actually."

"Nothing less than three days. The first day it will be a joke, but the next two they'll work up a little sweat!" Marc smiled in anticipation.

"You are asking very much." Asfaw shook his head. "It is against their culture to work with their hands."

"I'm asking only enough to let me return to that classroom with the respect given a teacher."

Brent kept glancing at Marc, who in turn, kept avoiding Morgan's eyes. He liked pushing the Headmaster up against the wall.

"If you have them do at least three days of work around the school," Marc finally said, surrendering to the pressure of the moment, "I'll forget about the apology and go back to teaching."

Brent quickly glanced at Asfaw.

The Headmaster hesitated.

He was thinking of what all that meant, Marc knew. He wasn't going to be outwitted by this *ferenji.*

"It is not completely satisfactory," the Headmaster responded slowly, "but the students are not learning. I must put away my personal feelings for the betterment of education in Ethiopia. I will call the boys together and explain the requirements." He smiled.

Brent slapped the knees of his lightweight suit and stood. He was beaming with relief even before he reached across the Head-master's desk and shook the small man's hand.

Marc drove back into town after he dropped Brent at the airport. He drove past the Ras Hotel where they went to swim, and where they ate lunch and dinner on Sundays, the cook's day off. He turned at the next block and went by the open-air theater, then slowly drove along the street which led to their apartments and the piazza.

The street was heavily shaded from trees and the houses with big compounds, built up to the sidewalks. It was one of the few towns in Ethiopia which resembled a city, with geometric streets, sidewalks, traffic signs. But the bush was present. Somalis walked their camels along the side streets, herded small flocks of sheep and goats between the cars and up to the hills. Behind the taming influences of the foreign houses was Africa. Marc felt as if it were beating against his temples.

The apartment the Peace Corps had rented was not what Marc had imagined he'd be living in. He had visions of mud huts, of seamy little villages along the Nile. But not Diredawa. It was a small town with pavement, sidewalks, warm evenings filled with the smell of bougainvillea bushes and bars with outside tables. It was a little French town in the African desert.

He parked the jeep in front of the apartment building, then walked over to Helen's apartment and, going onto the porch, knocked on the door. When she didn't answer, he walked in and went into her bedroom, whispering her name. When she still didn't answer, he walked in and sat on the edge of her bed and watched her sleep. She had taken a nap, as always, after her late afternoon classes.

She continued to sleep, breathing smoothly, her arms stretched out at her sides. He could see she was naked under a white cotton sheet, and he watched her in silence for awhile before leaning forward and kissing her softly on the cheek. She stirred and blinked her eyes.

"What time is it?" she asked, waking and pulling the sheet closer.

"After three. Morgan's gone. I took him to the afternoon plane."

"Why didn't you wake me?" She turned on her side.

"I didn't know you wanted to see him."

She shook her head, pressing her lips together.

"You want to have dinner?" he asked, not responding to her anger.

"I can't. I'm going out."

Marc watched her for a moment, and then said, "Do you want me to ask with whom?"

"I have a date with Tedesse. We're going to the movies."

"When did this start?" He kept his eyes on her.

"Nothing has started." She shifted again on the bed, sensing her own nakedness under the sheet.

"What about us?" he asked weakly, wanting her to feel his pain.

"Marc, I have no idea what our relationship is, not from one moment to the next." She was staring at him. "Sometimes, you're great. You can't do enough for me. The next day, you know, you barely say hello. What do you expect?" Her eyes glistened.

"The school's bugging me, that's all. You know that. Can't you understand, for chrissake!"

"There's nothing wrong with the school," she answered. "You've created half the problems yourself." She had pulled herself up and was wide awake.

"And you top it off by dating some Ethiopian!"

"Marc, quit all this self-pity. It's very unattractive."

"I wanted to go to the movies."

"Then go!"

"Sure, and have you there with Tedesse?"

"Do what you want." She turned her face toward the white-washed bedroom wall. "Now please leave. I want to get some sleep."

"Are you in love with him?"

"I don't want to talk about it."

"I need to know."

"Marc, don't badger me."

He slammed the apartment door, leaving, and a Somali knife on the living room wall fell down with a crash.

The students began to move rock on Monday. Marc walked out to the field behind the school and watched them work. It was malicious of him, he knew, but he enjoyed it.

He stood on the mound overlooking the work area and did not speak, but he knew they were aware of him. He saw them glancing at him, whispering to themselves.

They continued to work and after a few minutes he turned and started back toward the school. It was almost two o'clock, time for his afternoon classes.

The first stone flew over his head. Marc didn't react to it. He wasn't even sure where it came from. The second one clipped his shoulder, and the next hit him squarely in the back. He wheeled about, ducked one aimed at his head, and started back at the students.

There were no obvious attackers. He saw no upraised arms. They were working as docilely as before. He stopped and cursed them, but no one looked his way, no satisfying smirks flashed on any of their brown faces.

He stayed away from the work site for the next two days, but watched them from the second floor corridor, making sure they saw him, standing there, grinning, while they sweated under the hot sun.

On the Thursday morning the class was to return, he decided to begin teaching immediately, not to dawdle on their punishment, or the rock tossing. He planned to teach just as Mr. Singh, the Indian, did, with no class discussion, nothing but note taking. He would fill the blackboard and let them copy down the facts. No more following the question where it led. No more trying to make his classroom exciting and interesting. He didn't care if they learned anything more than what they could memorize.

He rode his bike out to school early, getting there before the students or teachers, and went upstairs to the faculty room to wait for the first bell.

A few of the teachers said hello, but when Helen arrived on her bike shortly after seven, she asked what was wrong with their students.

Marc didn't know what she was talking about. Helen went to the front windows and watched the compound.

The students were too quiet, she told him. Something was wrong.

Marc stepped onto the breezeway and looked up at the three stories of classrooms. The railings were crowded. The students stood quietly, waiting and watching. A few, mostly girls from the lower grades, were playing on the basketball court. The others in the compound were in small groups of three and four. There was a little talking, but only in whispers. Gradually they turned and noticed Marc, and watched him without expression, their soft brown eyes telling him nothing.

He stepped back into the faculty room.

The Sports Master, an Ethiopian, had just come in. He scanned the teachers until he spotted Marc and came directly to him.

He had once played football for the country's national team and had a small, well-built body. Around his neck a whistle dangled from a cord. The man was sweating.

"We're having a strike," he told Marc. "Asfaw has sent for the army."

As he spoke, two Land Rovers swung into the compound and a half-dozen soldiers tumbled out. The students' reaction was immediate. The passive, quiet assembly rose up clamoring. Those students on the three tiers of the breezeway began to beat the iron railings. Girls began the strange high shrills they usually saved for funerals. And then rocks began to fly.

The windows of the Land Rovers were broken first. The officer was caught halfway between the school and the Rovers; he hesitated, not sure whether to keep going or rejoin his men.

And then the barrage escalated. From all sides, from everywhere, came the stones and rocks. One soldier was hit hard, faltered, and grabbed his buddy. From the second floor faculty room, Marc could see the blood on the man's face. And then from everywhere in the school compound came the stones and rocks.

The officer ran back to the Land Rover and grabbed his Uzi. Spinning around, he opened fire first on the students, spraying them with a quick burst of bullets. The small bodies of boys and girls bounced backwards, smashed up against the whitewashed walls of the school.

Time magazine was sold at a barber shop near the apartment. The barber saved Marc a copy when it came in on the Friday plane and he picked it up on Saturday, the day after the shooting at school, to read in the Ras Makonnen Bar. There were soldiers in the piazza, loitering in the big square facing the bar.

Occasionally a jeep would careen through the open square, its tires squealing. There were no students in the piazza, but periodically Marc heard gunfire coming from across the gully. He wondered if it had to do with the students. Were they catching more of them, chasing them down in the dark alley of the Moslem section? He smiled, thinking that might be happening while he had a peaceful practice.

He ordered orange juice, pastry, and opened *Time*, flipping rapidly through the pages for articles about the Midwest.

There had been another ice storm in Chicago, he read, that had closed down O'Hare Airport, caused a forty-five-car pile up on I-94. Marc read the article twice, lingering over familiar names and the details of the storm.

He kept smiling, thinking of home, wishing he were there for the storm. He imagined what his Michigan town might look like, buried deep in ice and snow. He could feel the sharp pain of the wind on his cheeks, feel the biting cold. He looked up, stared through the thick, bright, lush bougainvillea bushes.

There were tears in his eyes. Cold tears on his face. He didn't know he was crying.

He wiped his face with the small, waxy paper napkin, and looked out at the bright square and the loitering soldiers, who had found shade at the base of several false banana trees. They had abandoned their rifles, left them propped up against a tree. He wondered why the soldiers weren't cold.

He thought again of the killings at the school, how the officer with the Uzi had killed eight in the first burst of gunfire.

Helen had begun to scream. She was holding her ears, trying not to hear the students' cries, but still she couldn't look away from the slaughter.

He couldn't either. Several of his students, long, lanky kids, jumped and jerked when they were hit. The bullets tossed them around, made them hop and dance, before they were slammed back against the whitewashed walls of the school where they splattered like eggs, breaking bright red yolks.

Helen wouldn't stop screaming, even after silence fell in the school yard, after the lieutenant stopped firing, after the students scattered, those who were still alive.

She was standing at the windows, screaming. Marc couldn't go to her; he couldn't figure out how to walk. Mr. Singh finally seized her, pulled her away from the window as the Headmaster began screaming in Amharic at the soldiers.

Marc walked out the door then and down the stairs. He walked straight by the soldiers as if what had happened meant nothing to him. He walked away from the school, went across the open brush land to the dry gully river, which he knew he could follow into town. From the river bed, he heard the sounds of an ambulance coming out from the French hospital.

He walked to his apartment and locked himself inside, then crawled into bed and slept through the heat of the day. Helen came to get him after dark. She had told him martial law had been proclaimed and that she and the Olivers were leaving, going up to Addis Ababa on the night train. It was no longer safe in town, she told him. But he wouldn't leave, he told her. He wouldn't let the students drive him out of Diredawa.

Marc stood and walked out of the cafe bar and into the piazza. It was empty except for the soldiers. He wondered where everyone had gone, why no one was on the streets. He was lonely, knowing he was the only Peace Corps Volunteer in Diredawa. He thought that perhaps he was the only white man left in town.

But it wasn't true. There were French doctors at the hospital, missionaries from the Sudan Interior Mission, French workers with the railway. Tourists. Yes, the desert town was full of white people.

Still he hurried, cut across the open square, going home, back to his apartment where behind locked doors he'd be safe until the Peace Corps staff came to get him. They wouldn't leave him alone, he knew. This was a mistake, he thought at the same moment, crossing the empty street. He shouldn't have left his apartment and taken a chance on the streets. There might be students around.

He broke into a run.

A rock hit him on the side of the head and bounced off like a misplayed golf shot. He stumbled forward, but knew he was okay. It had only been a rock. They couldn't kill him with rocks. He was too tough. Too much of an American. These were just people in some godawful backward Third World country, half starving to death every few years.

He pulled his hand away from the side of his face and his fingers looked bright with blood.

"Shit!" he said, thinking of the mess to his clothes. And he hated the smell of blood. He stumbled forward, finding his feet, knowing he had to keep running. They couldn't catch him in the middle of the street.

A half-dozen soldiers were still loitering by the entrance of the movie theater, less than a dozen yards from him. He waved to get their attention and shouted out in Amharic. Another rock hit him in the mouth.

He tumbled over on his back and rolled in the dirt, coughing up pieces of his teeth and gobs of blood and spit. Marc raised his hand and tried to shout at the soldiers. Why weren't they helping him?

He crawled forward, still going toward the apartment, thinking only that if he could get to the gate and behind the iron fence, he would be safe.

He coughed up more blood and in his tears and pain knew he had to run, that they might swarm out of the trees, or wherever they were hiding deep in the palm-lined street, and seize him, take him back into the Old City, where it was another tribal law that would deal with him. An eye for an eye.

He got to his feet and ran.

There were more rocks, coming from the right and left, showering him, bashing his head, knocking him over once more. He fell forward, into the gutter, and smashed his head against the concrete.

If he stopped he was dead. His only hope was to reach the iron gates. Gebra, his *zebagna*, would keep out the crowd of students.

Why weren't the soldiers helping him? They hadn't hesitated to shoot when they were pelted, why couldn't they protect him?

He burst through the metal compound gate, startling Gebra. Marc shouted at him to bolt the compound door. It was the guard's job to protect him now.

He ran up the stairs to the second floor apartment and slammed the back door, locking it behind him. Running from room to room, he pulled the wide cords that dropped the heavy old metal shutters, shutting out the sunlight and sealing the apartment in the shadowy dark.

He fell in a corner, sweating from fear and exhaustion. Then he reached up and touched his forehead, felt for the rock bruise. When he took away his hand, he couldn't see his bloody fingers in the darkened room.

His hands were shaking. And he was freezing. He crept across the floor, going toward the bed, keeping himself below the windows, afraid the students might figure out which ones were his. The shutters were metal, but he couldn't be too careful, he told himself.

His whole body was trembling. It was funny, he thought. How could he be so cold in the middle of Africa? At the edge of the desert?

He thought of when he was in school, waiting on the road for the school bus and standing in the freezing cold. He shivered, and crawled under the mosquito netting, covering himself with the sheets. He would be okay soon, once he was warm. Why didn't he have a blanket, he wondered.

He watched the slanting sunlight filter through the metal window shades. The sunlight stirred the dust off the desert. It lit the room with shafts that looked like prison bars. He felt his face and wondered why there was no blood. He waited for the rocks to begin again. He thought about waking in the warmth and comfort of his farmhouse in Michigan, where he knew everyone and everything, where he was safe, and no one was different. He shivered, freezing from the cold. He opened his eyes again and saw that it had begun to snow in Africa. The flakes falling through the sunlight filtered into the room.

He would be all right, he knew. He understood cold weather and deep snow. Ethiopians knew nothing of snow. He smiled, thinking: let them try to shovel snow! They'd need him. He knew about snow. It was his heritage. He would teach the students how to make a snow man, he thought, grinning, and realized that everything was going to be okay. He was in the Peace Corps, and he had a job to do.

How I Came To Write This Story

"Alone in Africa" represents an attempt to capture part of the spectacular disparity in North American and Southern African sexual cultures. I based it on a genre of story we heard over and over, from expatriates—volunteers and official Americans alike.

—*Norman Rush*

NORMAN RUSH (Botswana, 1978-1993) was born in San Francisco, California. He graduated from Swarthmore College, and is married to Elsa Rush and lives in New York City. He and his wife were co-directors of the Peace Corps program in Botswana. In 1991, his novel *Mating* won the National Book Award. In 1992, it received the International Fiction Prize sponsored by the *Irish Times* and Aer Lingus. His book of short stories, *Whites*, in which "Alone in Africa" appeared, was a finalist for both the Pulitzer and National Book Awards in 1986. He is at work on a new novel, *Mortals*. His short fiction has appeared in *The New Yorker*, the *Paris Review*, *Grand Street*, and other literary journals. His stories have been selected three times for *Best American Short Stories*, and have been widely anthologized elsewhere.

ALONE IN AFRICA

by Norman Rush

It seemed to Frank that he was adapting surprisingly nicely to life without a wife around the house. He wondered what it meant. By now, Ione was in Genoa or Venice or some other watering place in Italy. All her stops involved lakes or the beach. It was all there in the itinerary on the wall next to the phone. He could read it from where he was sitting and drinking, if he felt like it. He thought, Ione likes it overseas and she likes being here in Botswana, but the drought is wearing her down. The government was talking about cutting the water off from eight till dawn. It was going to be inconvenient for compulsive hand-washers, which he no longer was, but which a lot of other dental and medical people were. Ione felt parched, she said. So it was goodbye for three weeks. He toasted her again. There was a poet, an Italian, who had had Dante's works printed on rubber so he could read them sitting naked in a fountain with water running over him: that was the image of her vacation she'd said she wanted Frank to have. So it was goodbye, because he had the dental care design team due in from the AID office in Nairobi to praise his plans for Botswana's dental future, or not. There it was again, the small sound in the night he was trying to ignore. It was probably animal or vegetable. He was going to keep on ignoring it.

He'd be alone for another ten days. He was used to the separations, but normally he would be the one traveling, not the one hanging around at home—which was different. Earlier in their marriage, and only for a couple of years, they had taken separate vacations. They had given it up after deciding they preferred to vacation together, all things considered. They kept each other amused. She was good at it. She was superb at it. He was missing her, especially on the sex end. He was enjoying being alone, otherwise. He was really alone, because the maid was away for a couple of days. Dimakatso's family was rife with deaths and emergencies. Women probably disliked being alone in houses more than men did because of routine small nonspecific sounds that got them keyed up. Right now he could easily convince himself that someone was horsing around outside, scratching the flyscreens. Ione kept him busy, sexually. She was six years older than he was, but no one would guess it. She had kept her figure to a T. She was sinewy, was the word. Ione had a dirty mind. In twenty years he'd never really strayed. She was a Pandora's box of different tricks and variations. Probably that was why he's been so faithful. She was always coming up with something new. How could he feel deprived? Of course, the scene in Africa was nothing like Bergen County when it came to available women. Young things were leaving the villages and coming into the towns and making themselves available at the hotel bars for next to nothing, for packs of Peter Stuyvesant. It was pathetic. They wanted to get in with expatriates. They wanted to go to expatriate parties so they could latch on to someone who would buy trinkets for them or, if they were lucky, take them away to foggy Holland forever to get neuralgia. They went to bed and breakfast for however long they could get it. The drought was making it worse, squeezing more and more people out of the villages all the time.

One guy he was tired of was the number two at U.S. Information—Egan the blowhard and world's foremost authority on sex in Botswana and the known world. Frank was tired of professional libertines, especially if they were on the United States Government payroll. Coming overseas had been an eye-opener on the subject of official Americans like Egan, who were less than gods, from the taxpayer standpoint. Egan was the mastermind behind the new thing of morale-building stag dinners for the men of America in Botswana. Frank had been once. No matter what you'd done, Egan had done it better. Somebody had made the mistake of using the phrase "naked broad." So then Egan had informed him he didn't know the meaning of the word "naked"— meaning that there was some elite whorehouse near Athens where all the women were shaved smooth as eggs. Their heads were shaved, their pubic hair, axillary hair, eyebrows. Egan had been there, naturally. The women were depilated every day. The women were oiled all over, shining, and they were different races. Only if you'd been there could you say you'd experienced lovemaking to a naked broad, had the real experience, like Egan. Egan was close with the bishop. He was a Father of the Year type. Actually, a loudmouth was the perfect choice for information service officer. What was a grown man doing showing Audie Murphy war movies to the Botswana Defense Force? Frank detested Egan, the hypocrite. Frank toasted the martyrs of science versus the church, like Giordano Bruno. There were others.

With its big block letters, Ione's itinerary was like a poster. You couldn't escape it. Ione's handwriting was showing no sign of aging. Frank wore glasses for reading and she didn't. His signature was less of a work of art than it had been. He looked at the radio. In less than a year they'd be back home where they could follow the destruction of the world by nationalism and religion in crystal-clear broadcasts on all-news radio. In Botswana, the radio was an ordeal, partly because they had never invested in an aerial. He was tired of waltzing around the room carrying the radio, trying to find the one crux of radio waves that would allow him to pick up something intelligible. The news would be about Beirut again. Beirut was religion armed to the teeth and having fun. He was tired of Beirut. Drinking this much was a change. It was fun. He was beyond his norm. Usually they never missed trying for the eight o'clock Armed Forces Radio news. Tonight he was going to skip it. Nine-tenths of the radio band in Africa was cockney evangelists. It was a shame that the minute the Batswana got literate they were engulfed in Bibles and tracts and fundamentalism, a nightmare. But he was going to take a pass on the radio because he was listening to something much better. It had rained hard, earlier, for three minutes. Now water was ticking onto the dripstones outside, a delicious sound and not long for this world.

He liked his worst bathrobe best, which is why he had dug it up from the bottom of the hamper. It must be after eight. Tick-tock, where was their clock? Except for Ione's African arts and crafts collection, there was very little in the place that would have to go back to New Jersey with them when they left. They could have a jumble sale for everything else. Basically, they were camping. This was a government house and they were living in it like campers: they dealt with the huge furniture as just another exotic thing to be made use of, like a strange rock formation. The government procured the furniture in South Africa. Ione liked to call the Republic of South Africa a "taste-sink."

They were camping. That was partly why they had done only the bare minimum on the grounds. The other part was to get at their intolerable neighbor, Benedict Christie, or as Ione liked to call him, Imitatio Christie. They lived in Extension Six, an enclave of upper-level civil servants, Batswana and expatriate. They were at the outer edge of the extension: raw bush began outside their fence on one side. Christie wanted every expatriate yard to be a model of husbandry, like his, with row after row of cabbages to give to the poor. Christie was useful in one way, because they could tell the time by him. He went to bed at nine-thirty on the dot. In Christie's house, only one room was ever lit at a time. He was a model of parsimony not to be believed. Even where people had fixed up their yards, Ione had never found the out-of-doors in Botswana that inviting. There were more lizards in the trees than birds. It was important to be alert about snakes. Ione had never adapted. Frank decided to open up the Cape Riesling they'd been saving. He went to get it. Coming back, he went through the house pulling the curtains shut on all the windows and pausing to listen for the sounds that had been bothering him. There was nothing much. He should check on the time. He chronically took his wristwatch off when the weekend came, locking it away. Not to secure it, but because he liked the symbolism. In the government houses, everything locked: closets, the pantry, dresser drawers, the credenza with his watch in it, all the interior doors. They had pounds of keys to deal with.

He was holding the wine in his mouth for longer than usual before swallowing it, for no particular reason.

Our suffering is so trivial, he thought. His thought surprised him. He wondered what suffering he was talking about, aside from being in need sexually, thanks to Ione, a minor thing and natural under the circumstances. He was in favor of her vacation. He swallowed his Riesling. Africa was suffering, but that wasn't it. He knew that much. Because a central thing about Africans was how little they complained. Whites complained at the drop of a hat. Africans would walk around for weeks with gum abscesses before coming in for treatment, even when treatment was next to free. People were losing their cattle to the drought, and cattle were everything. But the Batswana kept voting for the ruling party and never complaining. His point eluded him. He gave up. Occasionally it hurt him to think about Susan, because in a way he had lost her to superstition, to Lutheranism. If you told anybody that, they would think you were kidding, claiming to be suffering over something trivial. They would say you were overreacting. His daughter was a deaconess, the last he'd heard. That was up to her. What was a deaconess?

He drank directly from the bottle. He liked the sound of liquid going into him. He thought, It's easy to forget how remarkable it is that every member of the male race carries a pouch hung on the front of their body full of millions of living things swimming into each other. He cupped his naked scrotum to see if he could feel movement. He thought he could. The wine reminded him of Germany. Everybody should see the Rhine. But when he'd suggested it, Ione had said she hated Germany. So did the Germans, apparently, who were ceasing to reproduce—voting with their genitals, so to speak. Germany was green and beautiful. So why were the Batswana reproducing like Trojans in their hot wasteland of a country? Fecundity was everywhere. Women began reproducing when they were still children. Everywhere there were women with babies tied to their backs and other babies walking along behind them. At thirteen or fourteen they considered themselves women. Batswana schoolgirls looked like they were getting ready for sex from menarche onward. They went around with the back zippers of their school uniforms half-undone, their shoes unlaced half the time, as if they were trying to walk out of their clothes. They were always reaching into their bodices, was another thing, feeling and adjusting themselves. They were unselfconscious. He wondered if they knew what that kind of thing looked like to *makhoa*? Batswana men didn't seem to notice it. He reminded himself not to judge. Women in general were a closed book, Ione excepted. And women in somebody else's culture added up to two closed books. What could a *lakhoa* really know about the Batswana, especially the women? A lot of things were said about them that were probably lies—for instance, that they had enlarged labia because their mothers encouraged them to stretch them as a sign of beauty. That was in the north. Probably it was no longer done. It was called macronympha.

It might be a good idea to eat. He was getting that feeling of elevation on the top of his head, from the wine. The top of his head felt like it was made of something lighter than bone, something like pumice. He went to the windows. Christie was having dinner. His kitchen light was on.

What were Christie's secrets? He was an elderly Brit, a bachelor or widower. It was no fun living next door to Christie, with only a wire fence between them and both houses on narrow plots. Frank thought of the time he and Ione had gotten into a mood, acting stupid, slamming doors on each other. One of them had slammed a door on the other by accident. Then the other had taken the next opportunity to slam a door back. It had escalated into slamming doors all over the house, a contest, and both of them laughing like crazy. So it had been slightly hysterical. It had been leading to sex. But then, naturally, the next thing they knew Christie had come out of his house to stand at the fence and stare in their direction, a gaze as blank and pitiless as the Sphinx, or as the sun, rather. Christie was left over from the days when Botswana was Bechuanaland. He was with the railways. He had applied for Botswana citizenship, which was tough to get these days. Probably Christie hated the idea of leaving the perfect medium for inflicting his religion on people to his last gasp. Christie's religion was restriction: no drinking, no smoking, no sex, no dancing. That was the real business of the Scripture Union, which Christie was upper echelon in. Christie was at home too much, was part of the problem. He even held prayer meetings at home, endless events. Christie seemed to hate Ione and vice versa. There was serious bad blood there. Christie had his work cut out for him if he thought he was going to make a dent in whoring. Whoring was poor little bush babies coming to town to work as domestics and lining up outside the Holiday Inn at night to better themselves. It was upward mobility. Visiting Boers were good customers. Ione liked to use the stereo. When he'd mentioned lately that when she played it she seemed to be keeping it very low, they'd both realized it was an unconscious adaptation to Christie, their mother.

Frank could eat or he could take aspirin and drink some more. He drifted toward the kitchen. Tomorrow was Saturday. The sound was back. There was really someone at the kitchen door. There was deliberate tapping, very soft. Sometimes Batswana came to the door selling soapstone carvings or asking for odd jobs, and their knock was so tentative you'd think it was your imagination.

Frank moved quietly through the dark kitchen. He lifted the

curtain on the window over the sink. By leaning close to the glass he should be able to make out who it was on the back stoop, once his eyes adjusted.

It was a woman, a young woman. He could see the whole outline of her skull, so she was African. She stood out against the white mass of the big cistern at the corner of the house. Her breasts were developed. She was standing close to the door in a furtive way. He reached for the outdoor-light switch, but checked himself. What was happening?

The key to the kitchen door was in a saucer in the cupboard. If he put the outdoor light on it would advertise her presence to all and sundry. She didn't want that, was his guess. This could turn out to be innocent. He was ashamed. There was no key. He calmed down. Was she still there? She must have seen his face at the window. He was feeling for the key on the wrong shelf. The keys should be kept on a hook so this would never happen again. He had the key. He set it down. He could still stop. He retied the sash of his bathrobe.

It was science the way he got the key into the lock in the dark and swung the door open silently, lifting it on its hinges. Before he could say anything, she had slipped into the kitchen, holding one hand open behind her to catch the screen door as it came shut. He closed the door. This was all so fast. He was having misgivings. They stood facing one another. He could hear that her breathing was agitated. He needed a good look at her. He pressed his hair down behind his ears. He was overheated. So was she. Somebody had to say something.

He turned the ceiling light on. For once, he was grateful that only one of the two fluorescent tubes was working. The less light and sound the better. She was beautiful. He studied her in the grayish light. She was beautiful.

She was looking down. Somebody had to talk. She was wearing a dark red wraparound skirt and a faded blue T-shirt open along one shoulder seam. She was barefoot. She would have some kind of pretext worked out. What do you want? was what he wanted to say, but he had to fight back his Spanish. He was almost saying *Que quiere?* He knew some Setswana, more than the average American expatriate. But his Spanish was welling up. She was still looking down. This was something that happened, but in bars and around bars...parking lots. How old was she? At fifteen you were a woman, or fourteen, or less. The crown of her head came about to his chin. She wasn't small. She had to be at least sixteen.

She looked at him. She was familiar. He searched his memory. He had seen her around. Every property in the extension had a back house, for servants' quarters. The back houses were meant for one family apiece, but the reality was that each house was like the Volkswagen with a thousand clowns climbing out of it...endless children, relatives, transients. He associated her with the place three houses down. She lived in quarters. He had noticed her. She was a beauty. They were a family of daughters. The mother was a hawker. There were several daughters. The girl was the eldest.

She wasn't saying anything. What was he supposed to do? He concentrated. He had to get her name. He thought, Asking a name must be *O mang?* because *O kae?* means "You are where?" and *mang* means "who." People said *O kae?* when they met, all the time. The correct reply was *ke teng,* meaning "I am here." He would try *O mang?*

"*O mang?*" he asked. His mouth was dry.

"*Dumela, rra,*" she said. He had forgotten to greet her.

"Ah sorry," he said. "*Dumela. O mang?*"

"*Ke Moitse,*" she answered, barely audibly, but clearly understanding him.

"*Ke Rra Napier,*" he said, pleased with himself. *But where was her mother?* He had overlooked something even more important than getting her name. What was the word for mother? *Rra* meant Mr. or man. Mother might be the same as the word for Mrs. or women, which was *mma.* His bathrobe was embarrassing.

He said, "*O kae mma?*"

Now she looked baffled. "*Ke teng, rra,*" she answered uncertainly.

She didn't get it. This was a mess. It was like knitting with oars. He would have to go pidgin.

He was urgent. "*Mma...is...kae?..your mma.*" He pointed at Moitse for emphasis. Still she didn't understand.

Then he remembered: he had to say *Mma Moitse* to show who he meant. That was the way it was done. People identified themselves as the father or mother of so and so, their firstborns. He had to assume Moitse was the firstborn.

"*Mma Moitse o kae?*" he asked.

She understood. "*Ehe, rra.*" He was elated. *Ehe* meant "yes," "O.K.," "now I see," and so on. She continued. "My mother is to hospital. She is coming this side Tuesday week." She was full of surprises. She knew English. She probably liked it that he had tried Setswana. So far he was being a fool. But the coast was clear. It was a relief and a plus that she could speak English.

She had perfect skin. She was looking at him with a half smile, her chin held high. She said, "It is just because the mistress is gone from you, and Dimakatso gone as well. So you must say I may cook these days." But she was making no effort to convince him that this was a genuine proposition. She was trying to look brazen. Her expression was lascivious, her smile studied. She was obviously a spy. She had watched for Ione to be away, and then Dimakatso. She had been watching the house like a little spy.

He said, "So, you want to be my cook."

"*Ehe, rra.* I can cook."

Her hair was elaborately worked in tight, ridged plaits running straight back from her brows. It struck him that he had an obligation. She might be hungry. He knew what was going on. But he was not going to be put in the category of bastards who exploited somebody's hunger. She had to be fed. He wasn't going to be a bastard. She was here about sex and they both knew it. If she still felt like it when she had a full stomach, that would be one thing. They were both afraid.

He said, "Well, so, but are you hungry, to eat now? *Dijo?* Food? Do you want to eat, *kopa dijo?*" He knew he was showing off.

She nodded. She was hungry. He motioned her to sit at the table.

He liked having a task. It would steady him. Maybe it would end the whole thing. The shepherd's pie was finished. He found a bowl of raw sugar peas in the refrigerator, waiting for somebody to do something with them other than himself. Canned soup was an idea. He found a can that looked appropriate. It felt heavy. According to the label picture, it was split pea with frankfurter slices. It should be nourishing. It was imported from West Germany. The instructions foiled him. Did he add water or not? He needed his glasses. He would add some milk. Did Moitse represent some kind of trap? He got the soup into a pot and filled a tea kettle. She could destroy him. But who would want to trap him? He had no enemies in Africa, just as he had no friends: he was passing through. He was in Africa to help. His presence would be reflected in people's teeth for years to come, assuming AID Nairobi said yea instead of nay.

He stirred milk into the soup. He would prefer to know her age. But she would only lie if he asked, so he would forget it. He could have been made a fool of, trying to get her age in Setswana. He thought, Thank God I didn't try. Numbers in Setswana were hopelessly complex. Ione made a joke about numbers in Setswana, which went How do you say ten thousand in Setswana? The answer was You say *bobedi* five thousand times. *Bobedi* meant two.

There could be some small talk about her cooking for him, while she ate. But beyond that, she had to make the first move. He had certain scruples. He hoped she realized that. Excitement was his enemy. So far, he was doing nothing wrong. He was making her something to eat because she was hungry, that was all.

The soup was swelling up. He had used a pot without a handle, something that looked like it came from a Boy Scout cooking kit. It was Dimakatso's. She used it for boiling mealie. There was no potholder in sight. He stared at the foaming soup. Moitse ran to the stove and deftly shifted the pot to a cold burner with her bare hands. Bravo, he thought. She stood close to him, smiling. She was slightly unfresh. Her nipples showed like bolt heads through the T-shirt cloth. She went back to the table. She had the usual high rump. Her hem went up in back. There were traces of mud on her ankles and a few smears of mud on the floor tiles. He was eating too much lately. He was overweight. He regretted it.

He grasped the pot through the cuff of his robe and poured most of the soup into a bowl. He brought it to her, then got out bread, silverware, margarine, and chutney. He couldn't find the marmalade, but chutney was in the same ballpark. She seemed to appreciate the need to keep the sound level down. She was taking his cues. The house was an echo chamber because they had decided to forget about getting rugs. Moitse asked for salt. He wanted his breathlessness to stop. One reason the stereo always sounded so loud was because the house was an echo chamber. Christie had called them up when they were listening to Manitas de Plata. Ione had been furious, because there was no point in playing flamenco except up high.

Moitse was catfaced. She had a small jaw, but perfect occlusion. Would she want money? He had nothing smaller than a twenty, he realized. She would be ecstatic. It didn't matter, because there was never going to be a sequel to this, never, so it wasn't going to be a precedent. Ione would be back. He wasn't seeking this out. She was oversalting. Being sought out made it different. Every human being had a right to a certain number of lacunae in his conduct. His glass was empty. He got up to refill it. Should he offer her wine? Yes and no. Not doing it was saying he was making a distinction— youth and age. It would be saying she was a child, which was far from true. On the other hand, if she was going to go through with this, it had to be out of her own free will not clouded by him. He was not going to induce anything to happen here. He sipped his wine. He brought her a glass of water. Tea was coming.

It would have been friendlier to offer her some wine. It might spoil things, that he hadn't. She was just looking at the water. She could be having second thoughts or regurgitating the Ten Commandments or her catechism, like a posthypnotic suggestion. The fastest-growing part of any denomination was always in Africa. Africans were Bible fodder, or *canon* fodder was better yet. He was going to have to remember that for Ione. It was clever. He had a dream. It was to run a gigantic work camp for preachers and priests and proselytizers who were going to be told to work for a living, in his utopia. The Catholics were going to have to run homes for surplus children forever, that was settled. There was a stupefying amount of religion going on. It was the Counter-Enlightenment. But what was he doing about it? But what could one individual do, especially in Africa?

He sat down opposite her. He liked the way she ate. She was neat about it. There was a little more soup, if she wanted it. But when that was gone they'd be in the laps of the gods. It would be the next stage.

She was a lynx, he decided, or a vixen. She started to clear up, nesting her bowl in the pot along with the silver. It was too noisy. He took over.

There was another inflaming smile out of her. She was inflaming him. He was losing his grip on the dangerous part of this, the complications, which he shouldn't. The exit signs were going dark. One thing was that she would have to wash first.

He was at the sink. She was behind him and then up against him, hugging. This was it, then. Her arms were around him. She was strong. She was brave to do this. She was holding him so hard he had difficulty turning around to face her. He put his arms around her and kissed her forehead. He was sick with fear and pleasure. He let himself stroke her breasts. The thing was to get her in the shower but to make it seem like fun, a plus, not an insulting suggestion. Asking her to brush her teeth would be too extreme.

"Moitse," he said. "Do you mind having a shower, with hot water?"

She seemed hesitant. He thought of miming what he meant. She might not know about showers.

He said, "You can wash your body, Moitse."

"*Ehe*," she said. She didn't mind.

He led her to the bathroom. At the doorway, he stood aside, pointing to the shower stall. Still dressed, she stepped into the stall and pulled the curtain shut behind her. He turned the bathroom light on. He waited. There was no sound from the stall. Was it possible that this was the first time in a shower? The back houses had showers, but cold water showers only. He should go out and turn out the kitchen light. He had to be careful about lights and curtains to keep the place from turning into a peepshow. Ione's theory was that Christie had seen her naked once or twice, before she started being hypercareful about the way she walked around, before she'd realize what Christie was. Her theory was that Christie had never gotten over the shock and never forgiven her.

Back from the kitchen, nothing was changed—except that her clothes were in a neat pile on the window ledge. He pulled the shower curtain halfway open. She was naked. She was stiffly posed, her face tilted up at the showerhead, her eyes closed, her arms folded across her breasts. She was expecting him to operate the shower for her. It was touching.

He put his hand on her shoulder, guided her to step back. He could hardly think. He turned the water on, a tepid flow and not forceful. He handed her the soap. But she wanted to stand and enjoy the water: She held her pose, letting the water break directly on her upturned face. She was so calm. He wanted to touch her again. He was shaking, naturally. He touched her hip and then patted her mons. Her pubic hair was coarse, as he'd expected. "You must wash all around here," he said.

She nodded, but handed the soap back to him. She was going too fast. She lifted one foot onto the sill of the stall and torqued her body a little, thrusting her mons at him. He shied. He said,

"No, you must do it yourself, but make everywhere clean. Stay here until I come back." He had to get away from her for a minute.

He returned to the kitchen. He was the one who was supposed to be in control. This was not the kind of thing that was going to happen to him every day of the week for the rest of his life and he wasn't going to be rushed and pulled down in the corner of the shower and say goodnight. His cuffs were wet. If this was going to happen, sobeit, but it was going to be with reasonable amenity and taking an amount of time worth the risk he was running. He diluted his wine with tap water. He washed his hands. He cooled his face.

The girl was some kind of veteran, so there was no virginity issue. The interest in virgins was pretty much a dead letter, was his impression. He was half erect. It was embarrassing. He tried deep-breathing, which helped. He heard the shower stop.

Moitse was standing in the stall, a towel wound around her head in a cowl. "We have to dry yourself," he said. He was mixing things up. He could hear he was trying to sound like someone in the media.

She came forward a little. He took a towel from the rack. Reaching into the stall, he dried her shoulders and trunk. He caressed her breasts through the towel, briefly, teasing himself. He knelt on the sill and dried her legs. He pulled lightly at her right knee, to get her to uncock her leg so it could be lifted. He had to check for danger signs—lesions, scarring, rash. But it was all standard and clean. She looked down at him from beneath the cowl. All his associations for the way she looked with the cowl were religious. He wanted to lean his cheek against her belly, but he decided against it. Her foot was as hard as wood. He got up. His penis was erect. He tried to rearrange himself. She laughed and reached into his robe, grasping his penis at the base. It was painful. She pulled herself against him. She was too rough. He was speechless. She shook the towel off her head and tightened her grip. Shock gave him strength: he caught a tuft of her pubic hair and twisted it. She was going too fast again. She released him. He fell back and stood against the wall. She liked to play rough. He wanted to do all kinds of things, then. She knew how to play. She was back in the stall, standing there like a shadow. He had to think.

He needed a condom. That was next. He thanked God Ione was a varietist who came up with fantasies that involved condoms.

How many guys with postfertile wives would have condoms lying around for an emergency like this? So now he had whatever was left of the rainbow pack. And that would be the couple of red ones, a magenta and a blood red, the ones he hadn't used because he felt they were subliminally frightening. They were in a hiding place in the linen closet, safe and sound. He needed a condom. There was no way he was going to find himself in the position of Peace Corps studs coming moping into the medical office saying they'd knocked up a local because there was no way they could resist when the women said condoms were insulting. Then there was the story he was trying to forget, about another Peace Corps character who had gone back to the U.S. leaving some village girl behind, pregnant. A child had been born. Other volunteers had heard about it and collected money for the mother. Later they'd found out part of the money went for a special ceremony by a witch doctor, with all-night chanting. And the point of the ritual had been to get the whiteness out of the baby, let it be black. He told Moitse to go into the bedroom. He went to get a condom. Red was what there was.

He had a moment of fake fear. He was afraid there were no condoms where they were supposed to be. Fake fear was a juvenile thing he indulged in now and then. He would let himself fear something he knew was fake, and then be reassured—like letting himself think the car was stolen when he couldn't find it on the first try in the parking lot of the Paramus Mall. Maybe Ione had thrown out the red condoms. There had to be condoms because he was not a Boer or a fool and he wasn't going to impregnate anyone or pick up a disease. Also he should eat something, some protein, for strength. He needed something quick. He took the magenta condom from its hiding place.

In the pantry he found a jar of *sprinkleneute*, nut fragments for use in baking, which he more nearly drank than ate. He chewed violently. Afrikaans names for things always made him laugh. In the Republic, menswear was *mansdrag*. Drinks were *drankies*. Moitse would be in the bedroom now. He was chewing his best.

The hall light would have to be adequate. He doubted that Moitse would care either way about light versus dark: she was young. Ione was a good sport about leaving the lights on during sex. He was wearing the condom.

He got a surprise. Moitse had straightened things up in the bedroom. She had picked up his shirts and hung them on a chair back. His shoes were lined up under the dresser. She had tightened the sheets on the bed and was lying there dead center, a towel under her buttocks, a pillow on either side of her head, the blanket rolled down into a cylinder across the foot of the bed. She was still naked. Her clothes were in a bundle next to the door. She was lying with her knees raised, a little apart. With one hand she was lightly gripping her left breast, forcing the nipple up between her fingers. It was erotic. She seemed to be smiling. Her left hand was flat at her side, with something in it—a pad of toilet paper. The woman was a locomotive. This was not his style, but it was effective enough.

He got onto the bed, on her right. Some pleasantries would be good, but his mind was blank. He leaned on his fist and looked at her. The idea was to introduce the idea of taking it easy and appreciating things as they happened. But she let go of her breast and drove her hand under his hip, trying to lever him up and over her. His cheek slipped off his fist. Her strength was a shock again. She was using her nails. He rolled away from her, to think. In this format they were going to skip the kissing, apparently. At the movies, the Batswana laughed at kissing scenes. The stalls laughed and the whites in the balcony were serious. The good news was that she'd seen the magenta condom and hadn't blinked.

Now it looked like she had a new idea. She was covering her breasts with her hands. She was going to make him fight for her breasts. He lay against her and kissed her shoulder and neck. She drew her shoulders in. Either she disliked what he was doing or she thought it was funny. He was going to keep on. He was burning.

They heard a voice. Both sat up. She was rigid, listening. The voice was just outside, near the bedroom window.

"*TuTuTuTuTuTu,*" came to them, thrilled softly.

"What is this?" he asked Moitse, his voice hard. It was someone imitating a bird, but why? It could be a signal of some kind. He was in danger. He could feel danger. He repeated his question, but more roughly.

Moitse put her hand over his mouth and shook her head, commanding silence, while she concentrated.

"*Ninini...ninini...ninini...*" This was a second voice, different, more piping. There were two people outside.

Then both cries were uttered in unison, followed by muffled laughter and scuffling noises. Moitse hissed.

I have to escape, he thought. He could get in the car. But that was irrelevant. He told himself to start functioning.

"I must thrash them!" Moitse said. She was glancing wildly around, looking for something, probably for a weapon. She leapt up and started pulling a belt out of a pair of his slacks. She was pissing steam, to quote Egan. He went to her, to control her. He got her by the wrists. She dropped the belt.

"It is my sisters!" she said. All this had nothing to do with him. She pulled against him, jerking her wrists downward with all her strength. "They are just teasing after me," she said.

The cries were repeated, more boldly.

"You're *naked*, what can you do?" he said. Number one, she had to dress. That seemed right. They were near the door. He let go of one wrist in order to reach for her clothes. She broke away, down the hallway to the kitchen.

"Relax," he said aloud. He felt his pocket. *The key was still in the back-door lock.* But she had to be kept in the house or Christie might see her running around naked if he was looking, if she got outside. Frank ran to the kitchen. This is why motels exist, he thought.

She was turning the key. He heard her say she was going to thrash them to hell. Then she was out in the night. He felt exhausted.

Outside, she was beating them. He could hear it. He turned out the kitchen light and waited. He stood in the open doorway, listening. He could lock her out, but he couldn't, because he would never see her again, and also had her clothes. He wondered what Egan would do.

Someone small burst past him, knocking against his leg. He turned a stove burner on for light. There was a child under the kitchen table. She was badly frightened, judging by her breathing. She had to be gotten out, pronto. He crouched down to look at the huddled child. She was about six. She was shaking. She had bits of cloth in her pigtails. He stood up and patted the tabletop. "Relax," he said, as a second child burst into the kitchen. Her sister under the table called to her. He tried to catch her, but now both children were under the table. The new one was a little older. They were more ragged than Moitse, even. Moitse strode in, closing the door victoriously. The air was full of furious breathing. He wished he could laugh. The house was full of company.

Moitse was hissing in Setswana at her sisters. Something was making him weak, other than being a little tight. He wished she would stop or continue indefinitely, because there was something about the moment. It was hellish and the best at the same time, with the light from the burner the only light and shining on her naked skin, her back, the cusps of her spine, as she bent down cursing her sisters. What was the name of the bone like a beak at the base of the spine? The sacrum. He was having a certain kind of moment. It was a little like being alone in the woods when a log or rock looks like a living thing for a second.

Now she was using English. "If you go from under this table *moonmen* shall find you and eat you to dust and spit you down from their jaws." She was terrifying them. He wasn't certain, but she seemed to be spitting at them to make her point.

He could probably dress her by brute force if he had to. He was a realist. She had to dress. The adventure was over. Moitse stood up.

He had learned one thing tonight: he should lock the door and hang onto the key. He did it. He put the key in his pocket.

He confronted her. She touched his chest. The gesture enraged him. He backed away. He turned the stove burner off and the overhead light on. He had to get some normality going.

She said, "They are bad. They are punishing me." Her eyes were moist.

"You have to get dressed *right now,*" he said. "You must be dressed, fast. And then you must take your sisters home. Listen to what I say." He was speaking distinctly, he realized, like the Peace Corps schoolteachers he had met.

She pouted. She was going to be obstinate. The vamping look she'd used before was coming back. He couldn't believe it. She was going to argue.

"This is insane," he said.

"We can just go for that bed, *rra,*" she said. "They shall stay this side, as a promise. Because I shall thrash them." She was pleading and defiant. She crossed her arms. She pushed her belly forward. That was seductive, he gathered.

He was desperate. He said, "You must dress very fast or I'll hit you. Do you understand me?" She was still being inappropriate. Her expression meant that she doubted him.

He looked around the kitchen for something to threaten her with, so that she would believe he would hit her. There was nothing except a wooden ladle. A wooden ruler was what he wanted. They were used to rulers from being punished in school, probably. There was one in the living room. Ione had used a ruler to make her itinerary poster. He went to look for it.

He drew the curtains on one window to let in a little starlight. He found the ruler. As he was reclosing the curtain, something alarmed him. Christie's yard light was on. That was unusual. There was also a light bobbing along the fence. It was Christie's flashlight. Frank was paralyzed.

He struck himself across the palm with the ruler, to make himself think. Christie might stop. He might stand around and see nothing and go back in. Or Christie might be on some errand that had nothing to do with him at all. He followed the light as it went out Christie's front gate and then out of sight, as it would if Christie were coming around from the street side.

What would Christie do if Frank sat tight and didn't answer? Christie was capable of standing outside the house until daybreak, when he could see Moitse and know everything. He was like a bulldog. There was no time. Or Christie was capable of calling the police, saying he was afraid something had happened if there was no answer. Or he could pound on the door, waking up the neighborhood. Frank was going to have to face Christie down and get rid of him.

He ran back to the kitchen. He took Moitse by the shoulders and told her there was to be silence, no talking, because someone was coming there. He shook her. Again he told her to dress. He told her he was ordering her to dress. It was hard not to shout. There was nothing else he could do. He had to get back to the living room and normalize.

He could weep at what he had gotten into. He was facing humiliation beyond belief. The living room looked acceptable. Something had to rescue him. Christie had to stop. Frank would be willing to do anything. He could lose Ione. He could lose everything. He was willing to pray, if Christie could be stopped. Christie could think twice and decide to go home. Agnostics could pray. God wanted belief in Himself, was the main thing—He wanted that more than vows to give up certain vices. If he could defeat Christie, he would be willing to say it was God's help that did it. Just the act of praying in itself implied belief. That should be enough for anyone. He thought, God, please save me, amen, this will never happen again.

He was a little calmer. There was no sign of Christie's flashlight. And then there was.

Delay would look bad. Christie was there, knocking politely but steadily. Frank opened the door.

Christie was no threat, physically. He was small, gray-haired, with a heavy, seamed face. He had pronounced lips. His dentures were primitive. Insects were swarming around the stoop light. Christie stood placidly in the storm of insects. Christie had a good baritone voice, an actorly voice. Frank felt a stab: He could have given Moitse the key and told her to get everyone out the back while he kept Christie busy at the front door. But instead the key was sitting in his pocket, reminding him of his stupidity. Christie was wearing black slacks, a dress shirt buttoned to the throat, and a gray foreman's coat. The effect was clerical. He was wearing sandals and white socks.

Christie spoke. "Good evening, sir. Might I step inside?" His tone was friendly.

"What's up?" Frank asked.

"Won't you permit me in, Mr. Napier? There are matters."

"You have a complaint?"

"Possibly so, yes."

"Then what is it? Just tell me."

"We'd best sit down over it, I think." Christie was being mild. Frank felt his self-confidence pick up. Christie was coming closer, like someone hard of hearing. Frank was encouraged. It was his house. But he needed a good reason for saying no to Christie, who was coming across like a member of the family.

"What do you say to tomorrow, Mr. Christie? I'm pretty tired tonight. In fact, I was dozing...?"

What was Christie doing? *He was walking in, almost.* He had his foot on the stoop and was inside the screen door, which had never had a lock. Where should Frank draw the line? Christie had his hand on the door and was pressing it, and Frank, slowly back— but smiling apologetically, it seemed to Frank, the whole time. Frank set his foot against the door, but the waxed floor betrayed him. Frank was divided. He was furious. But he was afraid that showing his fury would kill his last chance to manage Christie. He felt sick. The thing was to convert his resistance into the opposite. He opened the door to Christie. Christie was inside.

They stood facing one another in the dim coral light of the breezeway. Christie was upset too. This was costing him something. That meant there was hope. He was going to get out of this, thanks to God. He had to choose his words. He had to get Christie contained in one place, sitting down in one place in the living room. He wanted to batter Christie. But if he could get Christie sitting down, he could go to the kitchen for tea or Fanta or anything and get the key into the right hands and get his little friends out the back door. He had to let Christie see he was astonished at him but that he was honoring Christie's emotions, whatever they were.

"This is my house," Frank said. "So won't you come and sit down, since you're here." He was pleased with the way it sounded. He would usher Christie into the living room in the same spirit. He would disarm him.

But Christie was different now, all of a sudden. He was ignoring Frank. Christie was already in the living room, staring around, sweeping the room with the beam of his flashlight. Christie had to sit down: it was all Frank asked.

"Excuse me," Frank called out. "Would you mind sitting down for a second? You said you wanted to." Frank switched the ceiling light on.

What was Christie doing? Frank felt he was always two steps behind Christie. God alone could control Christie. Frank would do more for God. Anytime the church came up, any church or sect, the stupidest, he would be silent. He'd go into radio silence until the conversation got around to something else. Christie was religion with the bit between its teeth, pushing into his house. Christie was Beirut.

He thanked God there was nothing for Christie to see in the living room. Christie was not sitting down. "I'll go get some tea," Frank said. There was desperation in his voice.

Christie reminded him of a lizard. He was quick. He seemed to be looking at something in the far corner of the room and then he was running for the hallway to the back of the house. He dodged past Frank. Frank felt betrayed. He reached for Christie, too late, stumbling. Frank was outraged. Christie would do anything. He would look under beds. Frank got to his feet and followed after Christie, his mind full of wordless pleading.

Christie was in the kitchen. Frank got there in terror. The scene amazed him.

It was brilliant.

Moitse, fully dressed, was sitting on a stool by the sink. She had a towel across her knees and the bowl of sugar peas in her lap. On the floor, sitting facing her with their legs straight out, were her sisters. They were watching her face fixedly. She was showing them how to string peas. Each of the younger sisters was clutching a handful of peas. There were little piles of string on the floor. Christie was silent.

Moitse was speaking distinctly to her sisters. "You must just go this ways. I showed you about it. You must pinch this one that is thick, and pull around the top. The pea has a top, a back, like as if it is a man lain down on his face. So you must pull the thick one along the man's back. Then you must pull the small one along the man's stomach, where it is round." She demonstrated.

Frank was weak with relief. She was brilliant. He was coming to life again. Strong vasomotor reactions swept over him. Christie was beaten. Frank could think. It was all over.

"Now you must clean," Moitse said to her sisters, who began sweeping up strings with their hands. "They are little, and we must go for home," she said directly to Christie, a little sadly.

"It's homecraft," Frank said. He was giddy. "She's teaching them homecraft. I said she could. It's nice for them. Why not? It's a nice thing. They don't have access to a real kitchen like this. So why not? Time to go, though, children."

Christie looked around at him, his face mottled, his expression intense but unreadable. He turned back to the girls, addressing then in Setswana. His first questions were in a gentle tone. Christie knew how to use his voice. Then he was impatient, and spoke sharply. He addressed questions to the younger two, but Moitse answered for them, angering him. She was hard. Frank could tell she wasn't giving anything away. She was hard as nails. He was in good hands with her. It was over. She was being sharp back to Christie. She was in charge. Frank unlocked the back door. One child's name was Gopolang. He wanted to talk to everybody, his relief was so great. That was dangerous. He was elated. He was feeling expansive. He could say too much.

"Remember to take the milk when you go," Frank said. He was improvising. He wanted to give everything in the house away, he felt so good.

"You must always listen to your sister," he said to the small girls.

He felt like talking to Christie. "You can always learn something, am I right? These peas. I always mangle them when I string them, you know? I learned something."

"It's past time they were home in bed," Christie said grimly, over his shoulder.

Frank said, "For sure. Time to get going. Better hurry. They get interested and they lose track of time. My fault, because I dozed off in the living room." The two younger sisters went out, one carrying the milk.

Christie retreated to the kitchen doorway. Frank said, "If you want to talk about anything, we can. Maybe you'd like to apologize for charging in the way you did." Christie was self-absorbed. Would he say anything before he left? Frank let himself feel slightly sorry for Christie. He could patronize Christie. He wanted to hurt Christie, but he could afford to be understanding.

Frank wanted Moitse out fast. He was avoiding looking directly at her. She might reveal something. She was still a child, smart as she was. She was enjoying her victory. He motioned her to go. Christie could turn around and revert to his animal self, the way he'd been in the living room when he thought he had the scent. Moitse left. Frank locked up. He needed two hands to do it.

Now Christie was leaving. He was hurrying. Frank caught up with him in the breezeway. Christie had the door open already.

"You owe me an apology," Frank said. He was playing. He was toying with Christie. He couldn't let Christie go easily.

Christie looked at him. "God is not mocked," Christie said, pronouncing God as "gaud," and using his most penetrating tone. "God led me here tonight. I go where He leads me. I'm His servant. I have no apology to make. My pride to me is dust and rags. I am God's man. Good evening to you."

The house was filling up with insects. Frank shrugged. He said, "Goodnight, then."

Everything was too much. He watched Christie go. He wanted to see him back where he belonged.

A draft stirred Frank's bathrobe: out of the folds the condom dropped, like a fallen blossom. It could have happened at any time in the last ten minutes. He stepped on the thing. He felt numb.

Frank went through the house and tested the locks on the doors and windows. It was a way of decelerating. He had to decelerate.

He went into the living room to watch Christie's house go dark again.

He went into the bathroom, where he took off his bathrobe and reburied it in the hamper. It was a rag and it smelled. He was ashamed. He would lie down and get up later for a shower.

He lay down on the bed. He felt his pulse slowing. Tears came to his eyes for a while. He was near sleep.

There was a scraping sound at the window above him, the sound of nails on the flyscreen. He recognized it. He sat straight up. She was back.

She was back.

CURBSTONE PRESS, INC.

is a non-profit publishing house dedicated to literature that reflects a commitment to social change, with an emphasis on contemporary writing from Latino, Latin American and Vietnamese cultures. Curbstone presents writers who give voice to the unheard in a language that goes beyond denunciation to celebrate, honor and teach. Curbstone builds bridges between its writers and the public – from inner-city to rural areas, colleges to community centers, children to adults. Curbstone seeks out the highest aesthetic expression of the dedication to human rights and intercultural understanding: poetry, testimonies, novels, stories, and children's books.

This mission requires more than just producing books. It requires ensuring that as many people as possible know about these books and read them. To achieve this, a large portion of Curbstone's schedule is dedicated to arranging tours and programs for its authors, working with public school and university teachers to enrich curricula, reaching out to underserved audiences by donating books and conducting readings and community programs, and promoting discussion in the media. It is only through these combined efforts that literature can truly make a difference.

Curbstone Press, like all non-profit presses, depends on the support of individuals, foundations, and government agencies to bring you, the reader, works of literary merit and social significance which might not find a place in profit-driven publishing channels, and to bring the authors and their books into communities across the country. Our sincere thanks to the many individuals who support this endeavor and to the following organizations, foundations and government agencies: Adaptec, Josef and Anni Albers Foundation, Connecticut Commission on the Arts, Connecticut Arts Endowment Fund, Connecticut Humanities Council, J.M. Kaplan Fund, Lannan Foundation, Lawson Valentine Foundation, National Endowment for the Arts, Open Society Institute, Puffin Foundation, and the Edward C. & Ann T. Roberts Foundation.

Please support Curbstone's efforts to present the diverse voices and views that make our culture richer. Tax-deductible donations can be made by check or credit card to:
Curbstone Press, 321 Jackson Street, Willimantic, CT 06226
phone: (860) 423-5110   fax: (860) 423-9242
www.curbstone.org